P9-DDY-398

DISCARD

ALSO BY MARILYNNE ROBINSON

HOME

HOME

Marilynne Robinson

Farrar, Straus and Giroux

New York

Farrar, Straus and Giroux
18 West 18th Street, New York 10011

Grateful acknowledgment is made for permission to reprint the following material:
"Smoke Gets in Your Eyes" by Jerome Kern and Otto Harbach, copyright ©
1933 Universal-PolyGram Int. Publ. Inc. (BMI). Copyright renewed. Used by permission. All rights reserved.
"I'll Be Seeing You" by Sammy Fain and Irving Kahal, copyright © 1938 The
New Irving Kahal Music and Fain Music Company. Copyright renewed. All rights
for The New Irving Kahal Music in the U.S. controlled and administered by Bug
Music Inc. Used by permission. All rights reserved.
"A Sunday Kind of Love" by Louis Prima, Anita Nye, Stan Rhodes, and Bar-
bara Belle, copyright © 1946 Universal Music Corp. (ASCAP), LGL Music Inc.,
and Larry Spier Music LLC. Copyright renewed. All rights for LGL Music Inc. in
the U.S. controlled and administered by EMI April Music Inc. Used by permission.
All rights reserved.

Library of Congress Cataloging-in-Publication Data
Robinson, Marilynne.
    Home / Marilynne Robinson.—1st ed.
        p.   cm.
    ISBN-13: 978-0-374-29910-1 (hardcover : alk. paper)
    ISBN-10: 0-374-29910-2 (hardcover : alk. paper)
    1. Fathers and daughters—Fiction. 2. Conflict of generations—Fiction.
3. Reminiscing—Fiction. 4. Children of clergy—Fiction. 5. Clergy—Fiction.
6. Iowa—Fiction.   I. Title.

PS3568.O3125 H58 2008
813'.54—dc22
                                                                    2008018301

Designed by Jonathan D. Lippincott

www.fsgbooks.com

1   3   5   7   9   10   8   6   4   2

For Noah and Elise

and for Beatrice

HOME

"Home to stay, Glory! Yes!" her father said, and her heart sank. He attempted a twinkle of joy at this thought, but his eyes were damp with commiseration. "To stay for a while this time!" he amended, and took her bag from her, first shifting his cane to his weaker hand. Dear God, she thought, dear God in heaven. So began and ended all her prayers these days, which were really cries of amazement. How could her father be so frail? And how could he be so recklessly intent on satisfying his notions of gentlemanliness, hanging his cane on the railing of the stairs so he could, dear God, carry her bag up to her room? But he did it, and then he stood by the door, collecting himself.

"This is the nicest room. According to Mrs. Blank." He indicated the windows. "Cross ventilation. I don't know. They all seem nice to me." He laughed. "Well, it's a good house." The house embodied for him the general blessedness of his life, which was manifest, really indisputable. And which he never failed to acknowledge, especially when it stood over against particular sorrow. Even more frequently after their mother died he spoke of the house as if it were an old wife, beautiful for every comfort it had offered, every grace, through all the long years. It was a beauty that would not be apparent to every eye. It was too tall for the neighborhood, with a flat face and a flattened roof and peaked brows over the windows. "Italianate," her father said, but that was a guess, or a rationalization. In any case, it managed to look both austere and pretentious despite the porch her father had had built on the front of it to accommodate the local taste for socializing in the hot summer evenings, and which had become overgrown by an immense bramble of trumpet vines. It was a good house, her father said, meaning that it had a gracious heart however awkward its appearance. And now the gardens and the shrubbery were disheveled, as he must have known, though he rarely ventured beyond the porch.

Not that they had been especially presentable even while the house was in its prime. Hide-and-seek had seen to that, and croquet and badminton and baseball. "Such times you had!" her father said, as if the present slight desolation were confetti and candy wrappers left after the passing of some glorious parade. And there was the oak tree in front of the house, much older than the neighborhood or the town, which made rubble of the pavement at its foot and flung its imponderable branches out over the road and across the yard, branches whose girths were greater than the trunk of any ordinary tree. There was a torsion in its body that made it look like a giant dervish to them. Their father said if they could see as God can, in geological time, they would see it leap out of the ground and turn in the sun and spread its arms and bask in the joys of being an oak tree in Iowa. There had once been four swings suspended from those branches, announcing to the world the fruitfulness of their household. The oak tree flourished still, and of course there had been and there were the apple and cherry and apricot trees, the lilacs and trumpet vines and the day lilies. A few of her mother's irises managed to bloom. At Easter she and her sisters could still bring in armfuls of flowers, and their father's eyes would glitter with tears and he would say, "Ah yes, yes," as if they had brought some memento, these flowers only a pleasant reminder of flowers.

Why should this staunch and upright house seem to her so abandoned? So heartbroken? The eye of the beholder, she thought. Still, seven of her father's children came home as often as they could manage to, and telephoned, and sent notes and gifts and crates of grapefruit. Their own children, from the time they could grasp a crayon and scrawl, were taught to remember Grandpa, then Great-grandpa. Parishioners and their children and grandchildren looked in on her father with a faithfulness that would have taxed his strength if the new minister had not hinted at the problem. And there was Ames, her father's alter ego, in whom he had confided so long and so utterly that he was a second father to them all, not least in the fact of knowing more about them than was entirely consistent with their comfort. Sometimes they made their father promise not to tell anyone, by which he knew they meant Reverend Ames, since he was far too discreet to repeat any confidence, except in the confessional of Ames's stark bachelor kitchen, where, they suspected, such considerations were forgotten. And what was their father not to tell? How they informed on Jack, telling him what Jack had said, what Jack had done or seemed inclined to do.

"I have to know," their father said. "For his sake." So they told on their poor scoundrel brother, who knew it, and was irritated and darkly amused, and who kept them informed or misinformed and inspired urgent suspicions among them which they felt they had to pass on, whatever their misgivings, to spare their father having to deal with the sheriff again. They were not the kind of children to carry tales. They observed a strict code against it among themselves, in fact, and they made an exception of Jack only because they were afraid to do otherwise. "Will they put him in jail?" they asked one another miserably when the mayor's son found his hunting rifle in their barn. If they had only known, they could have returned it and spared their father surprise and humiliation. At least with a little warning he could have composed himself, persuaded himself to feel something less provocative than pure alarm.

But no, they did not put him in jail. Jack, standing beside his father, made yet another apology and agreed to sweep the steps of the city hall every morning for a week. And he did leave the house early every morning. Leaves and maple wings accumulated at city hall until the week was over and the mayor swept them up. No. His father would always intercede for him. The fact that his father was his father usually made intercession unnecessary. And that boy could apologize as fluently as any of the rest of the Boughtons could say the Apostles' Creed.

A decade of betrayals, minor and major, was made worse by awareness on every side that they were all constantly alert to transgression and its near occasion, and made worse still by the fact that Jack never repaid them in kind, though this may only have been because their own mischief was too minor to interest him. To say they shared a bad conscience about Jack to this day would be to overstate the matter a little. No doubt he had his own reasons for staying away all these years, refusing all contact with them. Assuming, please God, he was alive. It was easy to imagine in retrospect that Jack might have tired of it all, even though they knew he made a somber game of it. Sometimes he had seemed to wish he could simply trust a brother, a sister. They remembered that from time to time he had been almost candid, had spoken almost earnestly. Then he would laugh, but that might have been embarrassment.

They were attentive to their father all those years later, in part because they were mindful of his sorrow. And they were very kind to one another, and jovial, and fond of recalling good times and looking through old photographs so that their father would laugh and say, "Yes, yes, you were quite a handful." All this might have been truer because of bad conscience, or, if not that, of a grief that felt like guilt. Her good, kind, and jovial siblings were good, kind, and jovial consciously and visibly. Even as children they had been good in fact, but also in order to be seen as good. There was something disturbingly like hypocrisy about it all, though it was meant only to compensate for Jack, who was so conspicuously not good as to cast a shadow over their household. They were as happy as their father could wish, even happier. Such gaiety! And their father laughed at it all, danced with them to the Victrola, sang with them around the piano. Such a wonderful family they were! And Jack, if he was there at all, looked on and smiled and took no part in any of it.

Now, as adults, they were so careful to gather for holidays that Glory had not seen the house empty and quiet in years, since she was a girl. Even when the others had all gone off to school her mother was there, and her father was still vigorous enough to make a little noise in the house with coming and going, singing, grumbling. "I don't know why he has to slam that door!" her mother would say, when he was off to tend to some pastoral business or to play checkers with Ames. He almost skipped down the steps. The matter of Jack and the girl and her baby stunned him, winded him, but he was still fairly robust, full of purpose. Then, after his frailty finally overwhelmed him, and after their mother died, there was still the throng of family, the bantering and bickering child cousins who distracted and disrupted adult conversation often enough to ward off inquiry into the specifics of her own situation. Still teaching, still engaged to be married, yes, long engagements are best. Twice the fiancé had actually come home with her, had shaken hands all around and smiled under their tactful scrutiny. He had been in their house. He could stay only briefly, but he had met her father, who claimed to like him well enough, and this had eased suspicions a little. Theirs and hers. Now here she was alone with poor old Papa, sad old Papa, upon whose shoulder much of Presbyterian Gilead above the age of twenty had at some time wept. No need to say anything, and no hope of concealing anything either.

The town seemed different to her, now that she had returned there to live. She was thoroughly used to Gilead as the subject and scene of nostalgic memory. How all the brothers and sisters except Jack had loved to come home, and how ready they always were to leave again. How dear the old place and the old stories were to them, and how far abroad they had scattered. The past was a very fine thing, in its place. But her returning now, to stay, as her father said, had turned memory portentous. To have it overrun its bounds this way and become present and possibly future, too—they all knew this was a thing to be regretted. She rankled at the thought of their commiseration.

Most families had long since torn down their outbuildings and sold off their pastures. Smaller houses in later styles had sprung up between them in sufficient numbers to make the old houses look increasingly out of place. The houses of Gilead had once stood on small farmsteads with garden patches and berry patches and henhouses, with woodsheds, rabbit hutches, and barns for the cow or two, the horse or two. These were simply the things life required. It was the automobile that changed that, her father said. People didn't have to provide for themselves the way they once did. It was a loss—there was nothing like chicken droppings to make flowers thrive.

Boughtons, who kept everything, had kept their land, their empty barn, their useless woodshed, their unpruned orchard and horseless pasture. There on the immutable terrain of their childhood her brothers and sisters could and did remember those years in great detail, their own memories, but more often the pooled memory they saw no special need to portion out among them. They looked at photographs and went over the old times and laughed, and their father was well pleased.

Boughton property lay behind the house in a broad strip that spanned two blocks, now that the town had grown and spread enough to have blocks. For years a neighbor—they still called him Mr. Trotsky because Luke, home from college, had called him that—planted alfalfa on half of it, and her father sometimes tried to find words for his irritation about this. "If he would just ask me," he said. She was too young at the time to understand the alfalfa putsch, and she was in college when she began to see what the old stories meant, that they were really the stirring and smoldering of old fires that had burned furiously elsewhere. It pleased her to think that Gilead was part of the world she read about, and she wished she had known Mr. Trotsky and his wife, but old as they were, they had abandoned Gilead to its folly in a fit of indignation about which no one knew the particulars, just at the end of her sophomore year.

The land that was the battlefield would have been unused if the neighbor had not farmed it, and alfalfa was good for the soil, and the joke and perhaps the fact was that the neighbor, who seemed otherwise unemployed and who railed against the cash nexus, donated his crop to a rural cousin, who in exchange donated to him a certain amount of money. In any case, her father could never finally persuade himself that objection was called for. The neighbor was also an agnostic and probably spoiling for an ethical argument. Her father seemed to feel he could not risk losing another one of those, after the embarrassing episode when he tried to prevent the town from putting a road through his land, on no better grounds than that his father would have opposed it, and his grandfather. He had realized this during a long night when his belief in the rightness of his position dissipated like mist, under no real scrutiny. There was simply the moment, a little after 10:00 p.m., when the realization came, and then the seven hours until dawn. His case looked no better by daylight, so he wrote a letter to the mayor, simple and dignified, making no allusion to the phrase "grasping hypocrite," which he had thought he heard the mayor mutter after him as he walked away from a conversation he had considered pleasant enough. He told all of them about this at the dinner table and used it more than once as a sermon illustration, since he did devoutly believe that when the Lord gave him moral instruction it was not for his use only.

Each spring the agnostic neighbor sat his borrowed tractor with the straight back and high shoulders of a man ready to be challenged. Unsociable as he was, he called out heartily to passersby like a man with nothing to hide, intending, perhaps, to make the

Reverend Boughton know, and know the town at large knew, too, that he was engaged in trespass. This is the very act against which Christians leveraged the fate of their own souls, since they were, if they listened to their own prayers, obliged to forgive those who trespassed against them.

Her father lived in a visible state of irritation until the crop was in, but he was willing to concede the point. He knew the neighbor was holding him up to public embarrassment year after year, seed time and harvest, not only to keep fresh the memory of his ill-considered opposition to the road, but also to be avenged in some small degree for the whole, in his agnostic view unbroken, history of religious hypocrisy.

Once, five of the six younger Boughtons—Jack was elsewhere—played a joyless and determined game of fox and geese in the tender crop of alfalfa, the beautiful alfalfa, so green it was almost blue, so succulent that a mist stood on its tiny leaves even in the middle of the day. They were not conscious of the craving for retaliation until Dan ran out into the field to retrieve a baseball, and Teddy ran after him, and Hope and Gracie and Glory after them. Somebody shouted fox and geese, and they all ran around to make the great circle, and then to make the diameters, breathless, the clover breaking so sweetly under their feet that they repented of the harm they were doing even as they persisted in it. They slid and fell in the vegetable mire and stained their knees and their hands, until the satisfactions of revenge were outweighed in their hearts by the knowledge that they were deeply in trouble. They played on until they were called to supper. When they trooped into the kitchen in a reek of child sweat and bruised alfalfa, their mother made a sharp sound in her throat and called, "Robert, look what we have here."

The slight satisfaction in their father's face confirmed what they dreaded, that he saw the opportunity to demonstrate Christian humility in such an unambiguous form that the neighbor could feel it only as rebuke.

He said, "Of course you will have to apologize." He looked almost stern, only a little amused, only a little gratified. "You had better get it over with," he said. As they knew, an apology freely offered would have much more effect than one that might seem coerced by the offended party, and since the neighbor was a short-tempered man, the balance of relative righteousness could easily tip against them. So the five of them walked by way of the roads to the other side of the block. Somewhere along the way Jack caught up and walked along with them, as if penance must always include him.

They knocked at the door of the small brown house and the wife opened it. She seemed happy enough to see them, and not at all surprised. She asked them in, mentioning with a kind of regret the smell of cooking cabbage. The house was sparsely furnished and crowded with books, magazines, and pamphlets, the arrangements having a provisional feeling though the couple had lived there for years. There were pictures pinned to the walls of bearded, unsmiling men and women with rumpled hair and rimless glasses.

Teddy said, "We're here to apologize."

She nodded. "You trampled the field. I know that. He knows, too. I'll tell him you have come." She spoke up the stairs, perhaps in a foreign language, listened for a minute to nothing audible, and came back to them. "To destroy is a great shame," she said. "To destroy for no reason."

Teddy said, "That is our field. I mean, my father does own it."

"Poor child!" she said. "You know no better than this, to speak of owning land when no use is made of it. Owning land just to keep it from others. That is all you learn from your father the priest! Mine, mine, mine! While he earns his money from the ignorance of the people!" She waved a slender arm and a small fist. "Telling his foolish lies again and again while everywhere the poor suffer!"

They had never heard anyone speak this way before, certainly not to them or about them. She stared at them to drive her point home. There was convincing rage and righteousness in her eyes, watery blue as they were, and Jack laughed.

"Oh yes," she said, "I know who you are. The boy thief, the boy drunkard! While your father tells the people how to live! He deserves you!" Then, "Why so quiet? You have never heard the truth before?"

Daniel, the oldest of them, said, "You shouldn't talk that way. If you were a man, I'd probably have to hit you."

"Hah! Yes, you good Christians, you come into my house to threaten violence! I will report you to the sheriff. There is a little justice, even in America!" She waved her fist again.

Jack laughed. He said, "It's all right. Let's go home."

And she said, "Yes, listen to your brother. He knows about the sheriff!"

So they trooped out the door, which was slammed after them, and filed home in the evening light absorbing what they had heard. They agreed that the woman was crazy and her husband, too. Still, vengefulness stirred in them, and there was talk of breaking windows, letting air out of tires. Digging a pit so large and well concealed that the neighbor and his tractor would both fall in. And there would be spiders at the bottom, and snakes. And when he yelled for help they would lower a ladder with the rungs sawed through so that they would break under his weight. Ah, the terrible glee among the younger ones, while the older ones absorbed the fact that they had heard their family insulted and had done nothing about it.

They walked into their own kitchen, and there were their mother and father, waiting to hear their report. They told them that they didn't speak to the man, but the woman had yelled at them and had called their father a priest.

"Well," their mother said, "I hope you were polite."

They shrugged and looked at each other. Gracie said, "We just sort of stood there."

Jack said, "She was really mean. She even said you deserved me."

Her father's eyes stung. He said, "Did she say that? Well now, that was kind of her. I will be sure to thank her. I hope I do deserve you, Jack. All of you, of course." That tireless tenderness of his, and Jack's unreadable quiet in the face of it.

Mr. Trotsky planted potatoes and squash the next year, corn the year after that. A nephew of the rural cousin came to help him with his crop, and in time was given the use of the field and built a small house on one corner of it and brought a wife there, and they had children. More beds of marigolds, another flapping clothesline, another roof pitched under heaven to shelter human hope and frailty. The Boughtons tacitly ceded all claim.

WITHIN WEEKS OF HER RETURN GLORY AND HER FATHER had settled into a tolerable life of its kind. The housekeeper, Mrs. Blank, who was a number of years older than her father, was happy to retire, now that she knew she was leaving the Reverend in good hands. Customary attentions to her father by neighbors and parishioners were bated, stealthy when they happened at all. Glory could feel how miraculous and temporary the cessation was. It was as if some signal had been given, as if a sea had parted and the waters were standing back like walls. Once when they were children her sister Grace, pondering at the dinner table, said she did not know how such a thing could have happened, that water could simply stand still like that, and Glory, who had turned this question over in her mind, said it would have been like aspic. She had not meant to explain the miracle, only to describe its effect. But everyone at the table laughed at her. Jack, too. She had sometimes felt he took more pity on her youth than the others did. So she noticed and remembered that he laughed. All the same, it had seemed to her, laugh as they might, that sticking a finger into a wall of stopped water could not differ essentially from sticking it into a molded salad—which she had occasion to do, being a minister's daughter, any number of times. She was caught at it more than once. But she thought it was inevitable that out of all those multitudes one Israelite or Egyptian must have made the same experiment, and that touching a fish in those circumstances could not differ greatly from touching a slice of banana. What a strange thing to remember. It came with being home.

Every day she swept and straightened—light work, since the house was virtually uninhabited. She did what little her father required to make him comfortable. He sat at the window, he sat in the porch, he ate crackers and drank milk and studied the newspaper and *The Saturday Evening Post.* She read them, too, and whatever else she could find. Sometimes she listened to the radio, if there was an opera or a drama, or if she just wanted to hear a human voice. The big old radio grew warm and gave off an odor like rancid hair tonic. It reminded her of a nervous salesman. And it made a sullen hiss and sputter if she moved away from it. It was the kind of bad companion loneliness makes welcome. A lesson in the success of clumsy courtship, the tenacity of bad marriage. She blamed and forgave it for its obsession with "The Flight of the Bumblebee" and Ravel's "Boléro." To appease the radio she sat beside it while she read. She even thought of taking up needlework. She might try knitting again, bigger, simpler things. Her first attempts were a baby sweater and bonnet. Nothing had come of that. It had alarmed her mother, though. She said, "Glory, you take things too much to heart." That was what they always said about her. Hope was serene, Luke was generous, Teddy was brilliant, Jack was Jack, Grace was musical, and Glory took everything to heart. She wished they had told her how to do otherwise, what else she should have done.

She wept easily. This did not mean that she felt things more deeply than others did. It certainly did not mean that she was fragile or sentimental or ready to bring that sodden leverage to bear on the slights that came with being the baby of the family.

When she was four she had wept for three days over the death of a dog in a radio play. Every time she teared up a little, her brothers and sisters remembered how she had sobbed over Heidi and Bambi and the Babes in the Woods. Which they read to her dozens of times. As if there were any other point to those stories after all but to elicit childish grief. It really was irritating, and there was nothing to be done about it. She had learned to compose her face, so that from a distance she would not necessarily seem to be weeping, and then they made a little game of catching her at it—tears, they would say. Ah, tears. She thought how considerate it would have been of nature to allow the venting of feeling through the palm of a hand or even the sole of a foot.

When she was small she had confused, in fact fused, the words "secret" and "sacred." In church you must not even whisper. There are words you must never say. There are things that will be explained to you when you are old enough to understand. She had whispered compulsively, in church and out. Her big sisters would say, This is a secret. You must never ever tell, promise you'll never tell. Cross your heart. Then they would murmur in her ear something meaningless or obvious or entirely untrue and watch her suffer with the burden of it for ten or fifteen minutes. The joke was that she could not keep a secret, that she would whisper behind a cupped hand into the first obliging ear whatever remained of the nonsense confided to her. But "hope to die" and "if I die before I wake" also became linked in her mind, aware as she was that she broke her vows constantly. Once, when she was still too young for school and Jack ought to have been in school but was not, she saw him out in the orchard, and she went to him, weeping with what had become an unbearable fear. He looked at her and smiled and said, "Damnit, kid, grow up." Then he said, "Are you going to tell on me? Are you going to get me in trouble?" She did not. That was the first secret she kept. It seemed to her she had learned honor then, perhaps simply because she was of an age and predisposed. Perhaps in the whole of her life she had never really distinguished the secret from the sacred, and loved tact and discretion better than she should. Well, in all this she may only have been a Boughton, after all.

But at thirty-eight she was still wary of country songs and human interest stories. She was wary indeed of certain thoughts, certain memories, because her father could not bear her unhappiness. His face fell when he saw any sign of it. So she did not permit herself to brood, strong as the urge was sometimes. It would make him miserable.

Her parents had watched her and worried over her in the days of what were, insofar as they might ever know, Jack's crowning disgrace, and they considered her feelings with a seriousness that interested her. Her feelings were largely untried then. She was about to enter her sixteenth year of gentle life in a quiet place, which meant only that her passions and convictions were uncomplicated and potent, that they strove together like figures in allegory. Truth must be stalwart, Loyalty absolute, Generosity unstinting, while Appearance and Convention were children of the giant Hypocrisy and must be put to flight. She had not had time or occasion to think far into the implications of loyalty or generosity. She really had no idea what she was thinking about, sheltered as she was. How it had happened that Jack had a child, for example. It seemed to her to be a fairly delightful thing, though this was an opinion she kept to herself. She knew from books and also from fragments of rumors on the same general subject that she was wrong to take so simple a view of the matter. Her parents really were the last people on earth to weep and whisper over the birth of a grandchild, and she knew she needed to find some way to take their sorrow into account. So much had never been explained to her. They were that kind of family. Things necessary to know were passed along brother to brother, sister to sister, and this was sufficient for most purposes, despite inevitable error and sensationalism. But the chain of transmission was broken when Grace left to live with Hope in Minneapolis, and her parents had forgotten the problem, having so long depended on their children to startle one another with this information.

Her parents were, in their way, fully as innocent as she was, having put aside their innocence on practical grounds, not in the belief that it had been discredited, but because they accepted the terms of life in this world as a treaty to be preferred to conflict, though by no means ideal in itself. Experience had taught them that truth had sharp edges and hard corners, and could be seriously at odds with kindness. They had learned that excessive devotion to even the highest things seemed and probably was sanctimonious, and that the one sufficient measure of excess was that look of annoyance, confirmed in themselves by a twinge of embarrassment, that meant the line had been crossed. They recognized grace in the readiness of the darkest sinner to take a little joke, a few self-effacing words, as an apology. This was something her father in particular, who was morally strenuous but sociable, too, had learned to appreciate cordially. Truly there were perils on every side in the pastoral life, and her father was wary of them all. With the dreadful rigor of an upright child Glory had noted and pondered his accommodations, however minor or defensible. This was in part an effect of her finding herself in a suddenly quiet house with only her parents to think about.

Still, Glory's view of things had an authority for them precisely because it was naïve. A baby is a splendid gift of God, after all. Her father had never christened one without saying those words. And if Jack had behaved disgracefully toward its mother—"She is so young, so young!" her father whispered—this did not alter the basic fact that the infant was a child of the family, deserving of welcome and embrace. Glory had really not understood why misery was any important part of her parents' response to the situation. The girl could not have been much younger than Glory herself, and she was fairly sure she would not have minded having a baby. Imbecile as she was then with loneliness and youth, and far as she was from understanding why her father should feel that arrogance had a part in it all, or cruelty. Or why he whispered those words with such bitter emphasis. Every Sunday when the boys were home her father would stand at the front of the church, waiting for the pews to fill. Her brothers would file in, three of them, and her father would wait a moment more, watching the doorway, glancing up at the balcony. Then his head would fall to one side, regret and forgiveness in one gesture. Sometimes, rarely, he would nod to himself and smile, and then they knew that Jack was there, and that the sermon would be about joy and the goodness of God no matter what the text was. She had never heard her father say such hard words—the cruelty of it! the arrogance!—and she had never seen him brood and mutter for days at a time, as if he were absorbing the fact that some transgressions are beyond a mere mortal's capacity to forgive. How often those same hard, necessary words had come to her mind.

But in those days their lives were lived so publicly, it had seemed to her they might as well just acknowledge what everyone would have known in any case. She had never had any reason to think her parents had other intentions, but she might have helped them, she thought, by giving them herself to worry about. They both believed firmly in the power of example. This would be a great act of moral instruction. They must act consistently with their faith. They must consider all its applications in the present circumstance. Yes! She watched as her father mustered his courage. "The Lord has been very good to me!" he said, reminding himself that his obligations were correspondingly great, in fact limitless. This was a thought he always found exhilarating. Jack had left his car keys on the piano and taken the train back to college. She was almost old enough to drive, and she was fairly sure she knew how it was done. So she took her father out into the country to see that baby. It was disturbing to remember how happy she had been then, in the very middle of his deepest grief.

It was being home that made her remember, being alone in all that silence, or sitting beside the irksome radio trying to read the book she had chosen as possibly least unreadable among the hundreds of old books in the scores of shelves and bookcases that narrowed the overfurnished rooms. "Saber Dance," of course. "The 1812 Overture." This is Gabriel Heatter with the news. Her father would rouse himself from time to time for a game of checkers or Monopoly. This was for her sake. In her childhood, when she was kept home in bed by chicken pox, measles, and mumps, or by the flu, her father came up to her room with a bag of mints and a bottle of ginger ale and the Monopoly set, and played a brief and hilarious game with her, pulling get-out-of-jail cards from his sleeves, losing his token in the bedspread and finding it behind her ear. Now from time to time he cheated for her benefit. He would slyly stop just short of landing on Boardwalk, when he had plenty of money to buy it and already owned Park Place. It made her sad. On the same grounds he was not to be trusted with the bank.

When he sat on the porch in the afternoons she worked in the garden. Those hours passed pleasantly. She cleared out patches she could break up well enough to plant with peas and lettuce.

But oh, the evenings were long. I am thirty-eight years old, she would say to herself, as she tidied up after supper. I have a master's degree. I taught high school English for thirteen years. I was a good teacher. What have I done with my life? What has become of it? It is as if I had a dream of adult life and woke up from it, still here in my parents' house. Of course plain, respectable dresses hung in her closet, suitable for the classroom. There were the cardigans and low-heeled shoes of that other life. No reason not to wear them.

She dreamed sometimes that she was back in school. She was a child pretending to teach, or a teacher who realized to her embarrassment that she was turning into a child. In both dreams she had no idea what she was talking about and invented desperately. She sensed smirking and resentment in the room, murmurs and odd looks. The students would all walk out, ignoring her, and there was nothing to say to them to make them stay. Such humiliation! She would shout over the laughter and the clash of locker doors and wake herself up in crickety, black Gilead. Better in its way than waking up in Des Moines, knowing she would be in her classroom again when morning came. Her dreams reminded her that she did not altogether love teaching, though by daylight she thought she did. That stab in the heart she felt when she woke, and the panicky doubt that her life was in her grasp, not fraud or failure, not entirely—that was a brief misery and one she could set aside by putting the light on and reading for a while. She used to ask herself, What more could I wish? But she always distrusted that question, because she knew there were limits to her experience that precluded her knowing what there was to be wished.

If she had been a man she might have chosen the ministry. That would have pleased her father. Luke had followed him, but only after it became clear that Dan would not. Jack was by then Jack, and Teddy was too young to shoulder anyone's hopes, however willingly he might have made the attempt. She seemed always to have known that, to their father's mind, the world's great work was the business of men, of gentle, serious men well versed in Scripture and eloquent at prayer, or, in any case, ordained in some reasonably respectable denomination. They were the stewards of ultimate things. Women were creatures of a second rank, however pious, however beloved, however honored. This was not a thing her father would ever have said to her. It was Hope who told her that clergy were only and always men, excepting Aimee Semple McPherson, who proved the rule. But she knew how things were before she was told. No bright child could fail to know. None of this had mattered much through all the years of her studies and her teaching, but now, in the middle of any night, it was part of the loneliness she felt, as if the sense that everything could have been otherwise were a palpable darkness. Darkness visible. That was Milton.

Those grown children had, almost all of them, bent their heads over whatever work she gave them, even though their bodies were awkward and restless with the onset of adulthood, fate creeping through their veins and glands and follicles like a subtle poison, making them images of their parents and strangers to themselves. There was humor in it of a kind that might raise questions about the humorist.

Why do we have to read poetry? Why "Il Penseroso"? Read it and you'll know why. If you still don't know, read it again. And again. Some of them took the things she said to heart, as she had done once when they were said to her. She was helping them assume their humanity. People have always made poetry, she told them. Trust that it will matter to you. The pompous clatter of "The Charge of the Light Brigade" moved some of them to tears, and then she had talked to them about bad poetry. Who gets to say what's good and what's bad? I do, she said. For the moment. You don't have to agree, but listen. Some of them did listen. This seemed to her to be perfectly miraculous. No wonder she dreamed at night that she had lost any claim to their attention. What claim did she have? Could it be that certain of them lifted their faces to her so credulously because what she told them was true, that they were human beings, keepers of lore, makers of it? That it was really they who made demands of her? Her father taught his children, never doubting, that there was a single path from antiquity to eternity. Learn the psalms and ponder the ways of the early church. Know what must be known. Ancient fathers taught their ancient children, who taught their ancient children, these very things. Puritan Milton with his pagan muses. It is like a voice heard from another room, singing for the pleasure of the song, and then you know it, too, and through you it moves by accident and necessity down generations. Then, why singing? Why pleasure in it? And why the blessing of the moment when another voice is heard, dreaming to itself? That was her father humming "Old Hundred" while he shaved. It was John Keats in Cheapside, traveling his realms of gold. No need to be a minister. To be a teacher was an excellent thing. Those vacant looks might be inwardness. The young might have been restless around any primal fire where an elder was saying, Know this. Certainly they would have been restless. Their bodies were consumed with the business of lengthening limbs, sprouting hair, fitting themselves for procreation. Even so, sometimes she felt a silence in the room deeper than ordinary silence. How could she have abandoned that life? For what had she abandoned it?

Her supposed former fiancé of so many years had told her in a letter that he knew to the penny how much he owed her. He had kept some sort of ledger. He must have kept it from the very beginning, from the time he took her to dinner and then realized he had forgotten his wallet. She blushed when she thought of it. He said he would pay it all back to the last penny, as soon as his situation began to improve. He said, "It will take some time to repay you in full, since the total is quite large." What horrible, vindictive little streak of honesty had moved him to keep a record of these "debts"? She had not kept anything like an account, had never thought of such a thing, had never even felt she was giving anything away. None of it mattered now. To have been such a fool mattered. In that letter he had said, "I am sorry if I seem to have misled you." She could not let herself remember the lonely pleasures she found in living so simply, actually enjoying the renunciations and the economies that would some time make possible—what?—ordinary happiness. The kind of happiness she saw in the luncheonette, passed in the street.

She knew there had to be Shakespeare and Dickens around the house, Mark Twain had to be somewhere. Kipling was on the dresser in Luke and Teddy's room, as he always was, but she hated Kipling. Finally she asked her father what had become of the books she liked to read; he made a phone call, and within two weeks six boxes arrived from six addresses, full of the good old books and with some sober and respectable new novels included, too, *Andersonville*, *The High and the Mighty*, *Something of Value*. She put ten of them in a stack beside the radio. At this time she could decide nothing about her life. She did not want to think about her life. She opened *Andersonville*. Her father told her, "The fellow that wrote that is from Iowa. I forget what town. He's famous now. I forget his name." She knew about MacKinley Kantor of Webster City. *Andersonville* was long and notoriously sad. It had broken the heart of greater Des Moines. She decided she would read it to the end. She could weep without upsetting her father.

Then one day the mail came, a bill or two, a note to her from Hope, and a letter addressed to her father, who had come into the kitchen for a glass of water. "This letter is from Jack," he said. "I know his hand. This is his hand." He sat down and placed the letter on the table in front of him. "Quite a surprise," he said softly, gruffly. Then he was so still she was afraid he might be having a spell of some kind, a stroke. But he was only praying. He put out his hand and touched a corner of the envelope. "I believe I'll be needing a handkerchief, Glory, if you don't mind. They're in that top right-hand drawer." And there they were, in a neat stack, large and substantial. He had always carried a beautiful handkerchief, since in his line of work he never knew when it might be needed. She brought him one, and he wiped his face with it. "So we know he's alive. That's really something."

She thought, Dear God, what if he's wrong? What if this is a mistake brought on by yearning and old age?

She said, "Do you mind if I look at it?"

"Well, it's a letter from your brother! Of course you'll want to look at it! Thoughtless of me!"

She took it up. It was slight, no more than a slip of paper, in an envelope with a St. Louis return address and postmark. Reverend Robert Boughton in a small, distinct, graceful hand. "Should I open it?"

"Oh no, my dear, I'm sorry, but I'd better do that myself, in case there's anything confidential in it. He might appreciate, you know, consideration for his privacy. I don't know. At least he's alive." He wiped his eyes.

She put the envelope down on the table, and the old man laid his hand beside it. From time to time he tipped it up to look at the writing on it, and the postmark. "Yes, it's from Jack, all right. A letter from Jack."

She thought he might be waiting for her to leave the room, and yet she was afraid to leave. He might be disappointed, or the note might really be from Jack, but upsetting somehow, written from a ward for the chronically vexatious, the terminally remiss. From jail, for heaven's sake. He had better have a good reason for rousing these overwhelming emotions in his father. He had better have a good excuse for exposing the old man to the possibility of inexpressible disappointment. Even if he was dead.

"Glory, I think you will have to help me. I was waiting till I got a little steadier, but I guess that's not going to happen. You'll want to use a penknife. We don't want to damage that return address."

She found a paring knife and sliced the envelope, removed a folded slip of paper, and handed it to him. He cleared his throat. "Yes," he said. He found the handkerchief in his lap and set it on the table. "Let's just see what he has to say." And he opened the note and read it. "Well. He says he's coming home. He says here, 'Dear Father, I will be coming to Gilead in a week or two. I will stay for a while if that is not inconvenient. Respectfully, Jack.' Inconvenient! What an idea! We'll have to write to him. I'll do it myself, but I have to rest a little first. I don't think I could hold a pen right now." He laughed. "This is quite a day!" he said. "I wasn't always sure I'd live to see a day like this." She helped him into his chair in the bedroom, slipped off his shoes, and covered him with a quilt. She kissed his forehead. He kept the letter in his hand. He said, "Ames will want to know."

So while he napped, prayed, composed himself, set aside grievances and doubts, suffered the pangs of anticipation, sought footing in the general blessedness of his life for a posture of heroic and fatherly grace, and perhaps skirted dangerously near rupture of some part of the sensorium given over to grand emotion—her father's silences were never merely silences—she walked over to Ames's house.

The place looked exactly as it always had, but swept, polished. It was built in the style of any modest farmhouse in that region, with nothing in the way of ornament about it except the spindle shape of the porch pillars and bannisters. For all the years of her childhood old Ames had seemed to live in his study on the second floor. At night she always saw light in that window, and in the daytime when she was sent with a note or a book for him she stood in the kitchen and waited until he heard her voice, finished a paragraph he was writing or reading and came down the stairs. The kitchen had smelled of cleanliness, never of use, as though an essence emerged from the linoleum to fill a vacuum left by the idle stove and the empty pantry.

Now there were geraniums in the kitchen window and there was something like glee in the whiteness and crispness of the kitchen curtains. New gardens had been planted along the walk. The Boughtons had all come home for Ames's wedding, except for Jack, of course. It was the last wedding at which her father would ever officiate, he said, and the most joyful of them all. He relented a few times, married six or seven other couples he felt a special affection for. He had expected to marry Glory, but she had sent a letter explaining that, on impulse, just to get things settled, they had gone to a justice of the peace. Her father performed a few more baptisms besides those of his own grandchildren. Still, he called the Ameses' marriage the culmination of his pastorate. Lila, the improbable bride, in her yellow satin suit and pillbox hat, had stood smiling with gentle embarrassment, tolerating their photographs, humoring them. Her arms were full of roses she had grown and gathered herself. Her roses were her particular pride. They still teased her because she had refused to toss her bouquet. Like his parsonage, old Ames seemed to have been transformed without being changed. Now he was not only fatherly but a father, not only courteous but squire to a wife who seemed to be always aware of his courtesies to her and to be wryly touched by them.

He was sitting on the porch swing reading a book, but when he saw Glory coming he eased himself up and stood waiting for her with the gallant deference he showed to anyone over the age of twelve, and by which she had always felt flattered. Now she sensed a kind of condolence in it, though she tried not to. She tried not to wonder what he knew.

"Splendid afternoon," he said. "How are you? How is your father? Would you like to sit down?"

She said, "We're fine, I think. I can only stay for a minute, though. This morning Papa got a letter from Jack. He wanted me to tell you. I mean from Johnny."

"Oh yes. A letter from Jack."

"He says he's coming home."

"Hm. Does he. How is your father taking this?"

"It's hard for him, I think. To know what to expect. Jack has never been the most reliable person in the world."

Silence again. "Did he say when he was coming? Did he say why?"

"He said he would come in the next week or two. That's about all."

"Well, that's wonderful." He said this without a trace of conviction. "Would your father feel up to a visit this afternoon?"

"I think he would."

As he followed her down the walk to open the gate for her, he said, "It might be best if he doesn't get his hopes too high." Then they laughed. He said, "Well, there's not much we can do about that." But Glory had her own hopes, which were also too high— that this visit would happen at all, that it would be interesting, and that Jack would not remember her as the least tolerable, the most officious, the least to be trusted of his brothers and sisters. She thought and hoped he might hardly remember her.

WHEN SHE CAME HOME SHE FOUND THAT HER FATHER had written his letter, addressed it, and sealed it. "Yes, I put a little check in there just to be sure. Travel is expensive these days. I hope it won't offend him, but I thought it was a way to emphasize how eager we are to see him. I thought it was a good idea on balance. I'll take it out if you think I ought to—"

"He won't be offended, Papa. You've always sent little checks."

"Well, I just worry he might not remember, you know, my eccentricities. I should have waited so you could take a look at what I wrote. I just thought we'd want to get it in the mail. He'll be waiting to hear. If it is 'not inconvenient.' Imagine! We certainly don't want him to worry about that!"

"I'm sure he was just being polite."

"Very polite. Yes. He might have been writing to a stranger. But here I am finding fault."

She kissed his cheek. "I'll take this to the post office."

"I believe it is quite legible. The address is clear enough, I think." He said, "I worried about that, the way my hands were trembling there for a while. I should have let you look it over. I hope he'll be able to read it."

"It will be just fine," she said. But she knew he did not want any wholly sufficient, entirely persuasive assurance. If he was disappointed and Jack did not come home, he could tell himself that the fault was his own, taking the bitterness of it all on himself and sparing his miscreant son. He'd have done the same for any of them, had done it for her, she knew. But it was for Jack he had always devised and deployed his greatest strategies of—what to call it—rescue. He used to say, "That boy has really kept me on my knees!" He seemed to have persuaded himself that this was yet another blessing.

Ames arrived and the two of them put their heads together

over the checkerboard. There were so many jokes between them. Once when they were boys in seminary they were walking across a bridge, arguing about some point of doctrine. A wind had blown her father's hat into the water, and he had rolled up his pant legs and walked in the river after it, not gaining on it at all, still disputing, as it sailed along in the current. "I was winning that argument!" her father said.

"Well, I was laughing too hard to keep up my side of it." The hat finally caught on a snag, and that was the whole story, but it always made them laugh. The joke seemed to be that once they were very young and now they were very old, and that they had been the same day after day and were somehow at the end of it all so utterly changed. In a calm, affectionate way they studied each other.

Ames said, "I understand that boy of yours is coming home."

"So he tells me. He sent a letter."

"Will the brothers and sisters be coming, too?"

Her father shook his head. "I've made some phone calls." There it was, the parting of the sea. "They agree it would be best for them to wait until he wants to see them. He was never much at ease with them. I believe I was at fault in that. Of course, it's good that Glory is here to help," he said, remembering she was in the room. So she went into the parlor, sat beside the muttering radio, and worked a crossword puzzle. She thought, Is it good that I am here? That might be true. I will have to remember not to be angry. She reminded herself of this because Jack would probably still be insufferable and she had spent all her patience elsewhere.

WHAT FOLLOWED WERE WEEKS OF TROUBLE AND DISRUPtion, dealing with the old man's anticipation and anxiety and then his disappointment, every one of which made him restless and sleepless and cross. She spent the days coaxing her father to eat. The refrigerator and the pantry were stocked with everything he thought he remembered Jack's having a liking for, and he suspected Glory of wanting to give up too soon and eat it all on the pretext of avoiding waste. So he would accept nothing but a bowl of oatmeal or a poached egg, while skin thickened on cream pies and lettuce went limp. She had worried about what to do with it all if Jack never came. The thought of sitting down to a stale, humiliated feast with her heartbroken father was intolerable, but she had thought it anyway, to remind herself how angry she was, and with what justification. She had in fact planned to smuggle food out of the house by night in amounts the neighbor's dogs could eat, since it would be too old to offer to the neighbors themselves, and they would no doubt feed it to the dogs anyway, tainted as it was with bitterness and grief.

Glory had rehearsed angry outbursts in anticipation of his arrival. Who do you think you are! and How can you be so inconsiderate! which became, as the days passed, How can you be so mean, cruel, vicious, and so on. She began to hope he would come so she could tell him exactly what she thought. Well, of course she was angry, with those loaves of banana bread ripening noisomely in the pantry. What right do you have! she stormed inwardly, knowing as she did that her father's only prayers were that Jack would come, and that Jack would stay.

"He says here 'for a while'! A while can be a significant amount of time!" They had Jack's address after the Great Letter came, the one that made her father weep and tremble. Her father sent another note and a little check, in case the first had gone astray. And they waited. Jack's letter lay open on the breakfast table and the supper table and the lamp table and the arm of the Morris chair. He had folded it away once, when Reverend Ames came for checkers, presumably because he did not want a doubtful glance to fall on it.

"Yes, he will definitely be coming," he would conclude, as if uncertainty on that point had to do with the language of the letter. Two weeks passed, then three days. Then came the Telephone Call, and her father actually spoke with Jack, actually heard his voice. "He says he will be here day after tomorrow!" Her father's anxiety turned to misery without ever losing the quality of patience. "I believe it could only be trouble of a serious kind that would account for this delay!" he said, comforting himself by terrifying himself. Another week, then the Second Telephone Call, again with the information that he would arrive in two days. Then four days passed, and there he was, standing in the back porch, a thin man in a brown suit, tapping his hat against his pant leg as if he could not make up his mind whether to knock on the glass or turn the knob or simply to leave again. He was watching her, as if suddenly reminded of an irritant or an obstacle, watching her with the kind of directness that forgets to conceal itself. She was a problem he had not taken into account. He did not expect to find me here, she thought. He is not happy to see me.

She opened the door. "Jack," she said, "I was about to give up on you. Come in." She wondered if she would have recognized him if she had passed him on the street. He was pale and unshaven, and there was a nick of scar under his eye.

"Well, here I am." He shrugged. "Should I come in?" He seemed to be asking her advice as well as her permission.

"Yes, of course. You can't imagine how much he has worried."

"Is he here?"

Where else would he be? "He's here. He's sleeping."

"I'm sorry I'm late. I tried to make a phone call and the bus left without me."

"You should have called Papa."

He looked at her. "The phone was in a bar," he said. He was quiet, matter-of-fact. "I would have cleaned up a little, but I lost the bag that had my razor in it." He touched the stubble on his jaw with a kind of concern, as if it were an abrasion. He had always been fastidious about such things.

"No matter. You can use Papa's razor. Sit down. I'll get you some coffee."

"Thank you," he said. "I don't want to put you to any trouble." She didn't say it was late for him to start worrying about that. He was distant and respectful and tentative. In this, at least, he was so much like the brother of her memory that she knew one hard look from her might send him away, defeating all her prayers, not to mention her father's prayers, which were unceasing. If he came and left again while her father was sleeping, would she ever tell the old man he had come and gone? Would she tell him it was her anger that had driven him away, this thin, weary, unkempt man who had been reluctant even to step through the door? And he had come to the kitchen door, a custom of the family from their childhood, because their mother was almost always in the warm kitchen, waiting for them. He must have done it unreflectingly, obedient to old habit. Like a ghost, she thought.

"It's no trouble," she said. "I'm just glad you're here."

"Thank you. Glory. That's good to know."

He hesitated over her name, maybe because he was not absolutely certain which sister he was dealing with, maybe because he did not wish to seem too familiar. Maybe because familiarity required an effort. She started putting water in the percolator. But he said, "I'm sorry about this—could I lie down for a little while?" He put his hand to his face. That gesture, she thought. "This shouldn't have happened. I've been all right for a long time."

"Sure, you go rest. I'll get the aspirin." She said, "It seems like old times, sneaking you upstairs with a bottle of aspirin." She had meant this as a joke of sorts, but he gave her a startled look, and she was sorry she had said it.

Then they heard bedsprings and their father calling, "Do we have company, Glory! I believe we do! Yes!" And then the slippered feet and the cane.

Jack stood up and brushed his hair off his brow and shook down his cuffs and waited, and then the old man appeared in the door. "Ah, here you are! I knew you would come, yes!"

She could see her father's surprise and regret. His eyes brimmed. Twenty years is a very long time. Jack offered his hand

31

and said, "Sir," and his father said, "Yes, shaking hands is very good. But I'll put down this cane— There," he said, when he had hooked it on the table's edge. "Now," he said, and he embraced his son. "Here you are!" He put the flat of his hand on Jack's lapel, caressingly. "We have worried so much, so much. And here you are."

Jack put his arms around his father's shoulders carefully, as if he were frightened by the old man's smallness and frailty, or embarrassed by it.

His father stepped back and looked at him again. He wiped his eyes. "Isn't it something!" he said. "Here I've been wearing a necktie for days, waking and sleeping as Glory will tell you, and you've caught me in my nightshirt! And what is it? Almost noon! Ah!" he said, and laid his head against Jack's lapel for a moment. Then he said, "Glory will help me out a little. I'll get my shoes on and comb my hair, and pretty soon I'll be something you can recognize! But I knew I heard your voice and I couldn't wait to get a look at you! Yes!" he said, and took his cane and started toward the hallway. "Glory, if you could help me a little. After you put the coffee on." And he set off toward his room.

Jack said, "After all these years I guess he still knows when I'm hungover."

"Well, the coffee will help. He's excited now, but he'll rest after lunch and you'll be able to get some sleep."

Jack said, "Lunch."

Twenty years was long enough to make a stranger of someone she had known far better than this brother of hers, and here he was in her kitchen, pale and ill at ease and in no state to receive the kindness prepared for him, awaiting him, even then wilting and congealing into the worst he could have meant by the word "lunch." And what an ugly word that was anyway.

"I'll help Papa shave, and then I'll bring you the razor. The cups are where they always were, and the spoons. So help yourself when the coffee is done."

"Thanks," he said. "I will." He was still standing, still hat in hand. That's how he was, all respectfulness and good manners when he knew he ought to have been in trouble. Butter wouldn't melt in his mouth. She had heard someone say that about him once, a woman at church. He cleared his throat. "Has any mail come here for me?"

"No, nothing." She went off to help her father put his socks on and shave and get his shirt buttoned, and she thought, as she often did, At least I know what is required of me now, and that is something to be grateful for. She helped him on with his tie and his jacket and parted his hair and combed it straight to one side, which is how he had always combed it himself. Well, no matter, there wasn't much left of it anyway.

When she was done, her father said, "Now I'll just look at the newspaper for a little while. I know Jack will want to get cleaned up, too."

She could smell that the coffee had gone a little past ready, and the thought struck her that he might have left, but there he was, washing up at the kitchen sink with a bar of laundry soap. The house had always been redolent of lavender and lye. She wondered if he remembered. He had hung his jacket and tie over the back of a chair and loosened his collar and was scrubbing his face and his neck with a tea towel, one of those on which their grandmother in her old age had embroidered the days of the week. No matter.

He wrung out the towel and began drying himself down with it. And then he realized she was in the room and turned around and looked at her, embarrassed that she should see him so undefended, she thought, since he rolled down his sleeves and buttoned them and pushed his hair off his brow.

"That's a little better," he said. Then he shook out the tea towel and hung it on the bar above the sink. It said Tuesday.

"You should drink this coffee if you're going to."

"Yes. I forgot the coffee, didn't I." He put his jacket back on and slipped the tie into his pocket.

They sipped bad coffee together while their father sat by the window in his Morris chair reading about the world situation. There were five years between them, and Teddy and Grace, and he had never shown much interest in her beyond tousling her hair now and then. It wasn't her fault that she was the one to have been at home when everything happened. He seemed embarrassed, this man who began to remind her more of her brother as she looked at him. It was hard for her to look away from him, though she knew he would have liked her to. He held his cup in both hands, but it trembled anyway. He spilled coffee down his sleeve and winced with irritation, and she thought how kind her father was to give him time to recover himself. She said, "You couldn't be more welcome here, Jack. You can't know what it means to him to have you here."

He said, "It's good of you to say that, Glory."

"It's just the truth."

There now. Her thought was that she might be able to worry a little less if an edge crept into her voice or if she lost patience for a minute.

He said, "Thanks for the coffee. I'll go shave."

HE HAD TAKEN HIS BAG UPSTAIRS, AND HE CAME BACK down with his jaw polished and his hair combed and smelling of her father's Old Spice. He was still buttoning his cuffs. He nodded at the towel. "Is it Tuesday?"

"No," she said, "that towel is a little fast. It's still Monday."

He reddened, but he laughed. And from the other room the newspaper crumpled and then they heard the cane and the hard, formal shoes that took a good shine and would not wear out in this world. Their father appeared, a roguish look in his eye, as there always was when he felt at the top of his form.

"Yes, children, lunchtime, I believe. Glory has been so busy getting things ready. She said you hated cream pie, but I was certain I remembered you had a special fondness for it, and she made it on my say-so, despite her reservations."

"It's pretty leathery by now," she said.

"You see, she's trying to prejudice you against it! You'd think we'd made a wager of some kind!"

Jack said, "I like cream pie." He glanced at her.

"It's for supper, in any case," she said, and she thought he looked relieved. "Jack's probably too tired to be hungry. He spent last night on the bus. We should give him a sandwich and let him go rest."

"I'm fine," he said.

His father looked at him. "You're pale. Yes, I see that."

"I'm all right. I'm always pale."

"Well, you ought to sit down anyway. Glory won't mind waiting on us this one time, will you, dear."

She said, "This one time, no."

"She works me half to death around here. I don't know what she'd do without me."

Jack smiled obligingly, and rested his brow on his hand when his father settled into the grace. "There is so much to be grateful for, words are poor things"—and the old man fell into what might have been a kind of slumber. Then he said, "Amen," and mustered himself, roguish again, and patted Jack's hand. "Yes," he said, "yes."

GLORY TOOK JACK UPSTAIRS TO THE ROOM SHE HAD PRE-pared for him, Luke and Teddy's room they still called it. He said, "That was kind of you," when she told him she had not put him in the room he had had growing up. It was the same kindness her father had showed her. When, half an hour later, she came upstairs with some towels for him, Jack had already hung up his clothes and set a half dozen books on the dresser between the Abraham Lincoln bookends, having stacked the ten volumes of

35

Kipling they had supported for two generations in the corner of the closet. He had taken a little picture out of his old room, a framed photograph of a river and trees, and set it on the dresser beside his books. Insofar as he was capable of such a thing, he appeared to have moved in.

The room was empty, the door standing open, so she stepped into the room just to put the towels on the dresser, and she did pause, noticing things, it was true. And when she turned he was there watching her from the hallway, smiling at her. If he had said anything, it would have been "What are you looking for?" No, it might have been "Looking for something?" because he thought he had caught her prying.

"I brought you some towels."

"Thank you very much. You're very kind."

"I hope you're comfortable," she said.

"I am. Thank you."

His voice was soft as it had always been. He never did raise his voice. When they were children he would slip away, leave the game of tag, leave the house, and not be missed because he was so quiet. Then someone would say his name, the first to notice his absence, and the game would dissolve. There was no point calling him. He came back when he came back. But they would look for him, as if the game now were to find him at mischief. Even their father tried, walking street to street, looking behind hedges and fences and up trees. But the mischief was done and he was at home again before they had given up searching. One time, when his absence had ended an evening game of croquet that she was for once on the point of winning, she was overcome with rage and exasperation. And when she knew he was home she had stamped into his room and shouted, "What right do you have to be so strange!"

He smiled at her, pushed his hair off his brow, said nothing. But she knew she had jarred him, even hurt him. She must have been nine or ten, still the little sister he teased or ignored. Her question sounded adult to her, perhaps to him. It sounded un-harmless, and that had startled them both. From then on his wariness included her, too—a slight change, inevitable no doubt.

And now here she was, embarrassed to have been found putting towels in a long-empty room she had been at some pains to make ready for him, as if a few shirts, a few books, were an inviolable claim on the place and her crossing the threshold an infraction. There was no use being angry. What could he have thought she was looking for? Of course, alcohol. How insulting to think that of her. But then, how insulting to him if she had actually been searching his room. The thought would not have crossed her mind, but he would not know that. Now she found that she almost assumed there was a bottle concealed somewhere, under the bed or behind the stack of Kipling. She promised herself she would never set foot in that room again.

Did she choose to be there, in that house, in Gilead? No, she certainly did not. Her father needed looking after, and she had to be somewhere, like every other human being on earth. What an embarrassment that was, being somewhere because there was nowhere else for you to be. All those years of work and nothing to show for it. But you make the best of things. People respect that. It is a blessing to know what is being asked of you. And how can this man drift in from nowhere, take a room in the house and a place at the table, and make her feel she was there on sufferance? Though in fact there was no presumption, only deference and reluctance, in his manner. Clearly he, too, did not choose to be there. She found it a little annoying how obvious that was. Of course there was nothing remarkable in the fact of a grown man wanting one room to call his own, especially since he was almost a stranger in the house. Since he was also a member of the family. She went out to the garden. The sun on her shoulders calmed her. The squash were coming up. She would check the rhubarb patch. She stooped to pull a weed or two, and then she got the hoe and began clearing out the plot she would plant in tomatoes. She had always liked the strong smell of the plants in the sun, the beaky little blossoms. The garden gave her a perfectly good reason not to be anywhere else, not to do anything else. And it always needed more time than she could give it.

She came into the house and found Jack washing his shirt at the kitchen sink. He glanced up at her, that look of wariness and mild embarrassment, as if they were strangers sharing too close quarters, seeing behind the shifts meant to maintain appearances. "I'm about finished," he said. "I'll get out of your way."

"You aren't in my way. But if you want to, you can just put your things in the wash. It won't make any difference to me. I'll show you how to use the machine, if you like."

"Thank you," he said, and rinsed and wrung out the shirt, careful and practiced. Then he took it outside, shook it out, and pinned it to the clothesline, and sat down on the back porch steps to smoke. Well, let him have his cigarette, out there in his undershirt, blinking in the sunlight, abiding by his boardinghouse notions of privacy. When he came inside he said no thank you to a piece of cake, thank you to a cup of coffee. He took the cup and the newspaper she offered him to his room.

In the town where she used to live she had sometimes seen a man on the street and thought, No, that isn't Jack. What is it about him that made me think of Jack? The stir of something like recognition lingered after she had thought, It is only his stride, only the tilt of his head. She had sometimes crossed streets to look into strangers' faces for the satisfactions of resemblance, and met a cool stare or a guarded glance, not so unlike his, a little amused, like his. She always knew how many years it was since she had last seen him, and she corrected against her memory of him because he was so young then. It was as if she had spent the years preparing herself to know him when she saw him, and here he was, tense and wary, reminding her less of himself than of those nameless strangers.

STARTING ALL OVER AGAIN, SHE MADE A DINNER TO WEL-
come him home. The dining room table was set for three, lace
tablecloth, good china, silver candlesticks. The table had in fact
been set for days. When she put the vase of flowers in place, she
noticed dust on the plates and glasses and wiped them with her
apron. Yellow tulips and white lilacs. It was a little past the season
for both of them, but they would do. She had the grocery store deliver a beef roast, two pounds of new potatoes, and a quart of ice
cream. She made biscuits and brownies. She went out to the garden and picked young spinach, enough to fill the colander, pressed
down and flowing over, as her father would say. And Jack slept.
And her father slept. And the day passed quietly, with those
sweet savors rising.

When she walked in from the garden, the house had already
begun to smell like Sunday. It brought tears to her eyes. That old
orderliness, aloof from all disruption. Sabbath and Sabbath and
Sabbath. The children restless in their church clothes, the dresses
and jackets and shoes that child after child stepped into, out
of, put on, took off, as his or her turn came. Too large and then
too small, but never ever comfortable. Eight of them, or seven,
crowded at that table, three on the piano bench, one on the
kitchen stool, practicing their manners—keeping their elbows to
themselves, not swinging their legs, for an hour not going on with
the teasing and arguing that were endless among them. Waiting
for the blessing, waiting for the guests to be served —always ancient men with some ecclesiastical dignity attached to them which
entailed special prohibitions against childish behavior. Waiting to
speak until they were spoken to, until the meal was finished, out
of respect to talk of creeds and synods. Waiting even to begin until their mother lifted her fork, which she would not do until
every major sign of impatience among them was suppressed. And
Jack so quiet, if he was there at all.

The dining room was immutable, like the rest of the house. But it was oppressive in ways that could easily have been changed. If she could have taken down the plum-colored drapes that hung over the lace curtains that covered the window shades, she'd have done it in a minute. If she could have taken up the plum-colored carpet with lavender fins or fans or fronds in a border around it. She'd have cleared the sideboard of the clutter of knickknacks, gifts displayed as a courtesy to their givers, most of whom by now would have gone to their reward. Porcelain cats and dogs and birds, milk-glass compote dishes. But in this place of solemn and perpetual evening, every family joy had been given its occasion, and here they would celebrate Jack's homecoming, if he woke up in time. When her father had been up and dressed for half an hour, he said, "You might just go knock at his door," and then they heard him on the stairs.

He stepped through the doorway and paused there. He was wearing his jacket and tie. He looked tentative, as if he were afraid he might presume, and as if he would be happier somewhere else. He looked like the old Jack. Her father must have thought so, too, because he was clearly moved to see him. A moment passed before he said, "Come in, son. Sit down, sit down."

Glory said, "You can light the candles, Jack." She went into the kitchen for the roast and came back to find the two of them silent in the candlelight, her father lost in thought, Jack toying with a matchbook. Twenty years before, they had had a quiet conversation in that room. She should have thought of that. She should have served dinner in the kitchen.

When the biscuits were on the table and she had taken her place, the old man rose from his chair to address the Lord. "Dearest Father," he said, "Father whose love, and whose strength, are unchanging, in whose eyes we too are unchanging, still your beloved children, however our fleshly garment may soil and wear—"

Jack smiled to himself, and touched the scar beneath his eye.

"Holy Father," the old man said. "I have rehearsed this prayer in my mind a thousand times, this prayer of gratitude and rejoicing, as I waited for an evening like this one. Because I always knew the time would come. And now I find that words fail me. They do. Because while I was waiting I got old. I don't remember those prayers now, but I remember the joy they gave me at the time, which was the confidence that someday I would say one or another of them here at this table. If I lived. I thought my good wife might be here, too. We do miss her. Well, I thank you for that joy, which helped through hard times. It helped very much." He paused.

"But when I think what it is that brings us to our Father, it might be grief or sickness—trouble of some sort. Weariness. And then there we are, and it's a good thing at such times to know we have a Father, whose joy it is to welcome us home. It really is. Still, humanly speaking, there is that trouble, that sorrow, and a Father has to be aware of it. He can't help it. So there is a sadness even in great blessing, which can be a hard thing to understand." He seemed to ponder.

"Lord, put the veil of time and sorrow aside for us. Restore us to those we love. And restore the ones we love to us. We do long for them—"

Jack said softly, "Amen." His father looked up at him, so he shrugged and smiled and said, as if by way of explanation, "Amen."

"Yes, well, I was finished, really. I'm sorry I went on."

"No, sir. I'm sorry—I didn't—" He put his hand to his face and laughed.

His father said, "No need to apologize, Jack! Here you've only been home a few hours and I have you apologizing to me! No! We can't have that, can we now!" He put his hand very gently on Jack's shoulder. "And here I am letting our dinner get cold! Do you want to carve, Jack?"

"Maybe Glory wouldn't mind?"

"Not at all," she said, and she cut the roast, and gave the first piece to her father, the second to herself, and the third to Jack. "There's still a little pink to that one," she said.

And he said, "It looks wonderful. Thank you."

Her father strove manfully to generate conversation at a level of undamaging abstraction. "I believe the threat of atomic war is very real!" he said. "This is a point on which Ames and I do not agree! He has never made a proper estimate of the force of sheer folly in the affairs of nations! He pretends to be mulling it over, but I know he will vote Republican again. Because his grandfather was a Republican! That's what it comes down to for people around here. Whose grandfather was not a Republican? But there is no way to reason with him about it. Not that I've stopped trying."

"I'm a Stevenson man, myself," Jack said.

"Yes. That's excellent."

She ought to have closed her eyes during that prayer, or lowered them, at least. But there was Jack, just across the table from her, studying his hands, then glancing up at the oddnesses of the room, the overbearing drapes and the frippery glass droplets on the light fixture, as if the sound of the old man's words were awakening him to the place. When he met her eyes he smiled and looked away, uneasy. Why did it seem like an elegance in him, that evasiveness? How would he look to her, seem to her, if he had not been, for so many years, the weight on the family's heart, the unnamed absence, like the hero in a melancholy tale? It seemed to her as if he ought to have been beautiful, and he was not. He had the lank face that was to be looked for in a Boughton, and weary eyes, and the coarsened skin of middle age. He put his hand to his brow as if to shield himself from her attention, then he dropped it to his lap, perhaps because it trembled. She was glad when he said "Amen," grateful. When her father spoke to the Lord he spoke in earnest—out of the depths, as he said sometimes. Out of a grief so generous it embraced them all.

When dinner was over, Jack helped her clear away the dishes, and he washed them, too, while she was helping her father to bed.

She came into the kitchen and found him almost done, the kitchen almost in order. "Amazing," she said. "This would have taken me an hour."

He said, "I have had considerable professional experience, madam. I share the Boughton preference for the soft-handed vocations." She laughed, and he laughed, and their father called out to them, "God bless you, children! Yes!"

GLORY HAD OFTEN REFLECTED ON THE FACT THAT Boughtons looked very much like one another. Hope was the acknowledged beauty of the family, which is to say the Boughton nose and the Boughton brow were less pronounced in her case. All the rest of them, male and female, were, their mother said, handsome. They all passed from cherubic infancy to unremarkable childhood to gangling youth to that adult state of Boughtonhood their mother soothed or praised with talk of character and distinction, Hope being the one exception. So adolescence was a matter of watching unremarkable features drift off axis very slightly, of watching the nose knuckle just a little and the jaw go just a bit out of square. So Glory's face had transformed itself in its inevitable turn. She remembered her alarm.

And then the brow. Their grandfather had once happened upon a phrenologist who found, in the weighty pediment of brow resting upon the tottered pillar of his nose, so much to praise that over the next few months he had dabbled in metaphysics and even considered running for public office. Fortunately, he was the sort of man who noticed the absence of encouragement and drew conclusions from it. But he did have his photograph taken, three times, in fact, twice in profile and once full face. This sepia triptych hung in the parlor in a gold frame with laurel wreaths in the corners, like a certificate of merit, and also like a textbook illustration. From the full-face portrait the sepia eyes still burned with a gleeful and furious certainty—he in his own prudent person bequeathing a higher solvency to his descendants, a remarkable soundness of spirit and of intellect. One might suspect that there was also visible a joy in the fact of discovering that the features he presented to the world were not simply heavy and irregular, whatever the uninformed observer might have thought of them. It was many years before he had even one heir, their father, the only child of a marriage approached with a caution and deliberation on both sides that was the clearest proof the parties to it ever gave of being suited to each other, or so the story went. In any case, genius might well make its abode in so spacious a cranium, though in his case as in theirs, the tenant had so far been competence, shrewd in one case, conscience-racked in another, highly refined in another, but always competence. He might have found his hopes dwindling in the moderated forms his visage took in the course of generations. His offspring were all grateful to be spared, to the degree they felt they had been spared, what was sometimes called his slight resemblance to Beethoven, though they did find comfort when needed in the thought that it might be a predisposition to genius that had put its mark on them all. Phrenologically speaking, physiognomically speaking, Jack was as plausible a claimant to character and distinction as any of the rest of them, as he must have known. Perhaps that is why he seemed mildly sardonic when he looked at her, knowing with what interest she looked at him. Yes, he seemed to say, here it is, the face we all joked about and lamented over and carried off as well as we could, the handsome face. Does its estrangement disturb you? Are you surprised to see how it can scar and weary?

AFTER TWO DAYS IT WAS CLEAR THAT JACK WOULD STAY IN his room until his father woke up, and then he would come down, presentable, respectfully affable, and attend on the old man. He said no more to her than courtesy required. He must have listened for his father's voice, or the sound of the slippers and the cane, because it was never more than a few minutes before he appeared. The thought that he listened, that he remained upstairs while his father was asleep, while it was only she who came and went and swept and dusted, played the radio—softly, of course—in short, the thought that he avoided her, was more than an irritation. He makes me feel like a stranger in my own house. But this isn't my house. He has the same right to be here I have. So she decided to take him the newspaper as soon as her father had finished with it. His interest in the news surprised her a little. *Time* and *Life* and the *Post* had drifted up the stairs and gathered in a stack by his bed, and he came down in the evening to listen to Fulton Lewis, Jr. So she would take him the newspaper and a cup of coffee. With a cookie on the saucer. She thought, I'll give him these things and go away, and he'll see it as a simple kindness, and that will be a beginning. There is a saying that to understand is to forgive, but that is an error, so Papa used to say. You must forgive in order to understand. Until you forgive, you defend yourself against the possibility of understanding. Her father had said this more than once, in sermons, with appropriate texts, but the real text was Jack, and those to whom he spoke were himself and the row of Boughtons in the front pew, which usually did not include Jack, and then, of course, the congregation. If you forgive, he would say, you may indeed still not understand, but you will be ready to understand, and that is the posture of grace.

Everyone was fairly interested in these sermons, though they recurred, in substance at least, more frequently over time, and though they told them all not to expect the grand exertion of paternal control that people always take to be possible and effective in other households than their own, and especially in parsonages. Seven paragons of childhood, more or less, all learners of times tables, all diligent at the piano, their greatest transgression the good-natured turbulence their father seemed to enjoy. And Jack. When did he begin to insist on that name?

His door stood open. The bed was made, and the sash of the

window was up so the curtains stirred in the morning air. He was neatly dressed, in his stocking feet, propped against the pillows, reading one of his books.

"Don't get up," she said. "I don't mean to bother you. I just thought you might want the newspaper."

"Thank you," he said. She wondered what it was that made him stand when she or her father came into a room. It looked like deference, but it also seemed to mean, You will never see me at ease, you will never see me unguarded. And that thank-you of his. It was so unfailing as to be impersonal, or at least to have no reference to any particular kindness, as if he had trained himself to note the mere fact of kindness, however slight any instance of it might be. And of course there was nothing wrong with that. Certainly not in his case.

She said, "You're welcome." And then she said, "Papa would like us to talk."

"Ah," he said, as if the motive behind her coming into his room were suddenly clear. He brushed back his hair. "What would he like us to talk about?"

"Anything. It doesn't matter. He just worries that we don't talk. He hates a silent house."

Jack nodded. "Yes. I see. Sure. I can do that."

A minute passed. "So—" she said.

"There actually is something I wanted to talk to you about." He went to the dresser and took up a bill that had been lying there and handed it to her. Ten dollars.

"Why are you giving me money?"

"I don't suppose the Reverend has much to get by on. I thought that might help with the groceries."

"It will help, of course. But he's all right. He gets some income from the farm. Mrs. Blank retired when I came, so he doesn't have to pay a housekeeper. And the others look after him. And the church."

"The church." He said, "And the church knows I'm here."

"Well, yesterday there were those two pies on the porch, and today there was a casserole and six eggs."

"So the word is out, then."

"Yes."

"They won't come by, though."

"Not unless they're invited."

"Good," he said. "That's good." He looked at her. "You won't invite them."

"No."

"Good. Thank you." Then, as if by way of explanation, "I need a little while to get used to this place. To try to."

It had occurred to her more than once that his thank you had the effect of ending conversation. He might not intend it that way. And just now, when the conversation had gone reasonably well, she decided not to take it that way. So she said, "What are you reading?"

Jack glanced at the worn little book he had left lying on the bed. "Something a friend gave me." He said, "It's pretty interesting." And he smiled.

"That's fine," she said, and turned and went down to the kitchen. She did not care what he was reading. She had only tried to make conversation. Her father had not said in so many words that he noticed the silence between them and that he worried about it, but she knew it must be true, and she felt no real regret about mentioning it to Jack, even though it surprised her a little when she did. Papa was asleep so much of the time. It would be good to have someone to talk to. It was rude of him to shun her. Even if his memories of her were irritating to him. There is so much more to courtesy than Thank you, That's kind of you! This was among those thoughts she hoped she would never hear herself speak out loud. She went back up the stairs.

He was still standing there, with the book in his hand. "W.E.B. DuBois," he said. "Have you heard of him?"

"Well, yes, I've heard of him. I thought he was a Communist."

He laughed. "Isn't everybody? I mean, if you believe the newspapers?" He said, "Now I suppose you'll think I'm up here reading propaganda."

"I don't care what you're reading. All I really care about is whether we can live in this house like civilized people." They heard the creak of bedsprings, and they heard the clack of a cane falling to the floor. "Coming, Papa!"

Jack said, "It's hard, Glory. I know what you think of me."

"Well, that's more than I know."

"Are you serious?"

"I'm completely serious."

They heard a clatter. She shouted, "I'm coming!" and ran down to the kitchen, and there was her father standing beside a chair that had fallen on its back. He was wearing his robe and one slipper and his hair was awry. He regarded them with anxiety that was in some part irritation. He was holding the Monopoly set. "I thought we might amuse ourselves with this. A game or two. I'd better sit down now." She helped him into a chair. "You know how it is when you jump up from a sound sleep. I thought something bad had happened—" and he fell into that doze of his that might have been prayer.

Jack took out the board, the money, and the dice. "I'm the top hat," he said.

Their father said, "Well, I'm something. I don't know quite what I am." He closed his eyes. "I guess I'm going to finish that nap anyway, so I might as well get comfortable." Jack helped him to his armchair. Then he came back to the kitchen.

Glory said, "I'm the shoe."

"The shoe?"

"I know. But it's lucky for me."

He laughed. "You play a lot of Monopoly?"

"About a thousand times more than I ever thought I would."

After four turns she had bought two utilities.

"Well," Jack said, "that looks pretty insurmountable. I see what you mean about the shoe."

"You're ready to concede?"

"More than ready."

Jack put the game away, squaring up the deeds and the money as if it mattered.

Glory said, "How do you know I'm not a Communist?"

He laughed. "You're too nice a girl." Then he said, "Not that that means anything. I'm not a Communist either."

"I'm thinking of reading up on it. Marxism."

"DuBois isn't a Communist. Not really."

"I wasn't hinting," she said. But she was. She thought if she read his book they might have something to talk about. "I'd go down to the library to see if they have anything, but the MacManus sisters work there and I can't face talking to either one of them."

"You go to church."

"Last in, first out. I have to do that. It matters to Papa."

THE CHURCH OF THEIR CHILDHOOD WAS GONE, THE WHITE clapboard church with the steeply pitched roof and the abbreviated spire. It had been replaced by a much costlier building, monumental in style though modest in scale, with a crenellated Norman bell tower at one corner and a rose window above the massy entrance. Someone whose historical notions were sufficiently addled might imagine that centuries of plunder and dilapidation had left this last sturdy remnant of grandeur, that the bell tower might have sunk a dozen feet into the ground as ages passed. The building was reconsidered once or twice as money ran out, but the basic effect answered their hopes, more or less. "Anglicanism!" her father had said, when he saw the plans. "Utter capitulation!" His objections startled the elders, but did not interest them particularly, so they drew discreet conclusions about his mental state. Nothing is more glaringly obvious than discretion of that kind, since it assumes impaired sensitivity in the one whose feelings it would spare. "As if I were a child!" her father said more than once, when the decorous turmoil of his soul happened to erupt at the dinner table.

This was a grief his children had never anticipated. Nor had they imagined that their father's body could become a burden to him, and an embarrassment, too. He was sure his feebleness inspired condescensions of every kind, and he was alert for them, eager to show that nothing got past him, furious on slight pretexts. The seven of them telephoned back and forth daily for months. He was in graver pain than he was accustomed to, and his dear old wife was failing. He was not himself. Ames sat with him for hours and hours, though even he was not above suspicion. They pooled strategies for softening the inevitable blow of his retirement, which would have been a mercy if it had come about under other circumstances. Ah well. He came back to himself, finally, reconciled to loss and sorrow and waiting on the Lord.

Now Glory was the family emissary. At holidays they went as a delegation, there to signal reconciliation not quite so complete as to induce her father to struggle up those stone steps. The no longer new pastor was youngish, plump, smiling. His admiration for Reinhold Niebuhr brought him to the brink of plagiarism now and then, but he meant well. She was always the object of his special cordiality, which irritated her.

For her, church was an airy white room with tall windows looking out on God's good world, with God's good sunlight pouring in through those windows and falling across the pulpit where her father stood, straight and strong, parsing the broken heart of humankind and praising the loving heart of Christ. That was church.

SHE PUT JACK'S TEN-DOLLAR BILL IN THE DRAWER WHERE they had always kept cash for household expenses. Every week someone from the bank came by with an envelope. She noticed that the amount it contained had gone from fifty dollars to seventy-five. Another telephone call. Even fifty dollars was never needed. When the week was over, she put whatever remained in the piano bench, for no particular reason except that her father's arrangements were no business of hers, and the cash drawer would overflow if she didn't put the excess somewhere else. She put Jack's ten dollars in an envelope of its own. That he had had it ready must have meant that he had decided how much he could spare. That he had given it to her—well, he always did act as though the house was not quite his, nor the family, for that matter. There was a gravity in the gesture, in the fact that he had intended it for hours or days before he had made it, and that he must have known the amount could not have mattered to anyone but him and yet pride had required him to give it to her. There was an innocence about it all. She felt she should be careful not to spend that bill as if it were simply ordinary money.

Every day Jack waited for the mail. However else he might while away his time, he was always somewhere near the mailbox when it came, the first to look through it, though it seemed none of it was ever for him, except once, three days after he arrived. It was his birthday, which she had forgotten. There were six cards for him, from the brothers and sisters. He opened one and glanced at it and left it with the others, which he did not open, on the table in the hallway. "Teddy," he said. "He's glad I'm here. He's looking forward to Christmas."

"Teddy's glad I'm here, too," she said. "They all are."

He laughed. Then he asked, "Is it so bad for you, being here?"

"Let's just say it isn't what I had in mind."

"Well," he said, "poor kid."

That was brotherly, she thought, pleasing in a way, though it came at the cost of allusion to her own situation, which she always preferred to avoid. What did he know about it? Papa must have told him something. She resented the condescension in "poor kid." But brothers condescend to their sisters. It is a sign of affection.

The next day there was one more card. It was addressed in

print so crude it might have been a child's. She saw it because the mailman came early, before Jack would have expected him. She took the card up to his room and handed it to him. He glanced at it and his color rose, but he slipped it unopened into the book he was reading, and said nothing to her except, "Thank you, Glory. Thank you."

AFTER A FEW DAYS SHE MIGHT FIND HIM SITTING IN THE PORCH, reading a magazine. And sometimes, if she was busy in the kitchen, he would bring his magazine to the kitchen table and read it there. A stray, she thought, learning the terms of domestication. Testing the comforts, weighing the costs. So she was tactful, careful to seem unsurprised. Once when she opened a cookbook on the table he said, "I hope you'll tell me if I'm in the way."

"Not at all. I appreciate the company." She had been waiting for the chance to tell him that.

"Thanks," he said. "I don't really want to keep to myself so much. It's just a habit."

IT WAS IN FACT A RELIEF TO HAVE SOMEONE ELSE IN THE HOUSE. And it was interesting to watch how this man, gone so long, noticed one thing and another, as if mildly startled, even a little affronted, by all the utter sameness. She saw him put his hand on the shoulder of their mother's chair, touch the fringe on a lampshade, as if to confirm for himself that the uncanny persistence of half-forgotten objects, all in their old places, was not some trick of the mind. Nothing about that house ever did change, except to fade or scar or wear. Miracles of thrift in their grandparents' generation had meant that the words "free and clear" could be spoken over the house and all it contained by the time it came into the young hands of their father. Those words blessed the stodginess and the shabbiness. All that big, crowding furniture and all that prim and doubtful taste commemorated heroic discipline and foresight, which could be, and must never be, undone by bringing other standards to bear than respectability and serviceability. Their parents often told them how fortunate they were to have all their needs supplied, while their neighbors fitted out their lives as best they could on layaway and the installment plan. The Boughtons bought outright the big wooden radio and the upright piano and the electric refrigerator and stove, because the grandparents in their remarkable providence had left them a number of debt-free acres ten miles out of town which they rented to a farmer for a mutually agreeable sum. So even the things they acquired were in effect gifts from beyond the grave, since, having no needs, they could enjoy certain pleasures and conveniences free and clear. No sooner than their neighbors did, of course. Thrift that was second nature to them in any case was reinforced by care not to seem as prosperous as they were, and was pleasantly coincident with a fondness for familiar things. Why should a pastor's family run the risk of ostentation? Why should a family with eight rambunctious children bother owning anything that could be damaged? They sat on the arms of their mother's overstuffed chair while she read to them, and they hung over the back of it, and they pinched and plucked at its plushy hide. If the nib of a feather poked through, they would pull it out and play with it, a dry little plume of down, sometimes unbroken. As they listened to the story they would turn and turn the painted vellum lampshade till the rim of it was soiled and the stems of the four nosegays on its four sides were nearly worn away. No matter that there were paths in the rugs, no matter that the big plate spoons were out at elbow with use and polishing.

She learned the word "waft" sitting in her mother's chair, breathing on a feather. Jack had come into the room, and the stir of air had floated it out of her hand. In those days the boys called her Glory B. or Glory Be or Glory Bee or Glory Hallelujah or Runt or Pigtails. Sometimes instead of Grace and Glory they had called their little sisters Justification and Sanctification, which came near irritating their father. But in general her brothers had ignored her,

Jack not so completely as the others. He had stood in the doorway that evening and watched the feather circle against the ceiling in the air he brought in with him, and then he had reached up and caught it lightly in his hand and given it back to her. "It just wafted away," he said. She might have been seven, so he would have been twelve. He was himself already then, solitary when he could be, gentle when the mood was upon him, a worry to them all as often as he was out of sight. Then there were those other years, after even Grace was gone, those tense years only she and her mother and father had lived through together in that house, when they lost the habit of mentioning Jack by name. She thought more often now, with Jack in the house, of that freckled girl sitting at the kitchen table, shy and bold at once, ignoring what was said to her, impatient to go home. That girl and her baby.

A MONTH BEFORE JACK AND TEDDY LEFT FOR SCHOOL, Grace had gone to live with Hope in Minneapolis so that she could study piano with a real teacher. They had all been instructed by Mrs. Sweet, a soft-bodied woman with a petulant smirk who was very deft at smacking hands without actually interrupting the performance of a scale or an etude. She sat on the bench beside them, reeking of lily-of-the-valley, and turned an injured look on the keyboard. Alert as a toad, Hope said, and quick as a toad, too. Whack! when a note offended, and then the return to sullen watchfulness, then again Whack! Six of them soldiered through, played their recitals, and emerged at the end of high school modestly competent and relieved to have one more tedious initiation into adulthood behind them. Sometimes Jack went along to lessons with Teddy, to laugh with him afterward about the horrible Mrs. Sweet. But Grace actually liked piano. She practiced more than she needed to and learned more than was exacted of her. Once she told her parents, weeping, that the hand smacking distracted her, so their mother went to speak to

Mrs. Sweet, who asked, indignant, "How else will she improve?" But from then on she restrained herself, barely, when Grace played and vented her pedagogical method on Glory.

Hope, who was newly married, brought her sister-in-law on a visit to Gilead. That lady heard Gracie playing and was charmed, and mentioned the benefits for such a gifted child of life in Minneapolis. Glory still remembered the day and hour that thought settled itself in the minds of her family. All of them looked at Grace as if some ring or amulet had been discovered that identified the foundling as a royal child. It would be wonderful, Hope said, and their mother relented, and bags were packed, and Glory sat in her room, absorbing the fact that there was no argument to be offered, no appeal to be made. It was Jack who noticed her. He said, "Poor Pigtails will be all alone." When he saw he had brought tears to her eyes, he said, "Sorry," and smiled, and tousled her hair.

It might have been those words that allowed her to believe for years that a special bond existed between them, that she understood him as others could not. They were the unexceptional children, she thought—slighted, overlooked. There was no truth in this notion. Jack was exceptional in every way he could be, including, of course, truancy and misfeasance, and yet he managed to get by on the cleverness teachers always praised by saying "if only he would put it to some good use." As for herself, she was so conscientious that none of her A's and A-pluses had to be accounted for otherwise than as the reward of diligence. She was good in the fullest and narrowest sense of the word as it is applied to female children. And she had blossomed into exactly the sort of adult her childhood predicted. Ah well.

Still, when she was thirteen and miserable and Jack was away at school, she could imagine whatever she liked and find comfort and satisfaction in it, a mistake she could never really regret. When she believed better of him than he deserved, she was also defending him, and she could not regret that either. Years later she had heard her father say, in the depths of his grief, "Some things are indefensible." And it was as if he thought a great gulf had opened, Jack on the far side of it, beyond rescue or comfort. She felt she could not allow that to be true, especially since it was her father who seemed to be in hell. He had come to the last inch of his power to forgive, and there was Jack, still far beyond his reach. So he stood at the verge of despair, despite whatever her mother might say to talk him away from it and despite every prayer and text old Ames could muster.

Her mother said to her once, "I believe that boy was born to break his father's heart." And once she said, "I have never seen Robert so afflicted. It frightens me"—speaking to her as to an adult. That evening Glory wrote the first of her letters to Jack, having no clear sense of what she should ask of him, except that he call or make a visit home for their father's sake.

Already she had driven her father out across the river into the country, tense with responsibility because she had only begun to drive, and excited and protective because suddenly her parents seemed to depend on her. She had waited in the car with her father outside the gate until a woman appeared in the door of the disheveled little house and called the dogs in. Her father got out of the car and waited beside it, hat in hand. Then a man walked out to the gate and stood with his hands on his hips eyeing the car. It was Jack's convertible, after all. He said to her father, "Who are you? What do you mean, coming around here?"

Her father said, "I am Robert Boughton. I understand that my family has some responsibility toward your daughter and her child. I have come to let you know we are aware of our obligation and ready to assume it—" And he offered an envelope, apologetically, almost diffidently, but the man spat on the ground and said, "What's that? Money? Well, you can keep your damn money." But the woman appeared in the doorway again, this time holding the baby, and when the man had walked off toward the barn she came out to the gate and said, "You can just leave it on the post there." Then she folded back the blanket that had concealed the infant's face.

A moment passed. Her father said, "Yes. I am Robert Boughton. This is my daughter." The woman nodded, turned away from them, and walked back to the house. A girl in a blue nightgown came out on the stoop and took the baby into her arms. She nuzzled its cheek, watching them until they drove away.

JACK DID COME HOME TO SPEAK WITH HER FATHER. GLORY thought this might have been an effect of her letter because when after half an hour of quiet talk behind a closed door he left the dining room and saw her in the parlor, sitting in their mother's chair, he had said, "Do you have another sermon for me?" He might have meant that his father had just preached to him, but he might also have meant he had felt the weight and seriousness of her letter, which did indeed draw upon every resource her sixteen-year indoctrination in moral sincerity had conferred on her, and upon all the certainty of her youth. She had spoken mainly of her father's grief, since all the rest of it was too delicate and complicated. But she had settled on the solution to it all. She had arrived at one great hope.

So she asked him, "Are you going to marry her?"

He was very pale. He smiled—that strange, hard shame of his—and said, "You've seen her."

She said, "Well, what is Papa going to do—"

"Do to me? Nothing. I mean, he's going to forgive me." He laughed. "And now I have a train to catch."

"You won't even stay for supper?"

He said, "Poor Pigtails," and smiled at her and walked out the door.

And twenty years passed. There was no way of knowing that day that anything absolute had happened. Her mother had been so upset she stayed in her room, no doubt waiting for him to come to her seeking reconciliation. She would never see him again in this life. When evening fell no lights were put on, and suppertime came and went unremarked. Her father stepped out of the dining room and saw her in the dark parlor. He said, "Yes, Glory," as if reminding himself of something, and went upstairs. She toasted two pieces of bread and ate them dry because she dreaded the sound she might make spreading butter on them. Then she went up to her room. Never had it entered her mind that their household could contain so desolate a silence.

Now she was home again, Jack was home again. The furniture and the damage done to it in the course of the old robust domestic life were all still there. And the old books. Their grandfather had sent a significant check to Edinburgh, asking a cousin to assemble the library needed for instruction in the true and uncorrupted faith. He had received in response a trunk full of large books, bound in black leather, in which they all assumed the true faith did abide. Sometimes they pondered the titles and wondered about them together. *On Predestination, an Answer to an Anabaptist*; *On Affliction*; *The First Blast of the Trumpet Against the Monstrous Regiment of Women*; *Booke of the Universall Kirk of Scotland*; *De Vocatione, a Treatise of God's Effectual Calling*; *The Hind Unloos'd*; *Christ Dying and Drawing Sinners to Himselfe. Or A Survey of our Saviour in his soule-suffering, his lovelynesse in his death, and the efficacie thereof*. They were respectfully proud to have these books in the house, as if they had been given the Ark of the Covenant for safekeeping and knew better than to touch it, except, of course, for Jack, who took down a volume from time to time and read or seemed to read a page or two, perhaps only to worry his father, who was as respectful of the Edinburgh books as they all were, and as little inclined to open them, and who clearly dreaded the thought that they might be damaged. "Are you finding anything of interest there, Jack?" he would say, and Jack would answer, "No, sir, not yet," and seem to read on, and then, after a few minutes, set the book on its shelf again. Whether he had found occasion to mar a page no one would know. There were tens of thousands of pages. And their father would not have wanted to know, since, even more than the other inexplicable and irremediable damage her brother left behind him, this might exasperate him beyond patience. Everything the rest of them treated with tacit reverence Jack found his way to. Poor old Ames. For many years he bore the brunt of it, uncomplainingly. Many things must have passed between him and the boy that Ames never spoke of, and this was a gentleness toward their father, a wordless, palpable, patient regret very much like their father's own. Those became the good days in retrospect, the days of their father's happiness.

IN THE AFTERNOON SHE WENT OUT TO WORK IN THE GARden. She had planted peas and pole beans and tomatoes and squash and spinach. Rabbits were a problem, and groundhogs. Still, the futility of it all was not yet absolute. She would have had to ask someone to put up some sort of fence, and that would involve talking to someone, which she preferred not to do.

And after a few minutes there was Jack, standing in the sunlight at the edge of the garden, smoking a cigarette. He said, "I thought maybe you could put me to work out here."

"Sure. I mean, you can put yourself to work. There's so much that needs to be done. Well, you can see that. Mama had iris beds right up the hill—"

"I know," he said. "I used to live here."

"I just meant that might be a place to start. They're so overgrown. Of course you used to live here."

"—Strange as it seems—" He said it as if he were completing her thought, or sharing it.

They heard voices from the street, and a look of alarm or irritation passed over his face. Then he saw that it was a young man and a child passing by, taking no notice of them.

She said, "That's Donny McIntire's son. And his grandson. You might remember him. He was Luke's age."

"And good old Reverend Ames has a boy of his own, I understand."

"Yes, he does. And a wife. Marriage seems to agree with him."

He said, "What did people think of all that?"

"I guess there was some talk. But who could begrudge him. Papa has felt a little neglected. He and Ames used to spend so much time together."

Jack dropped the butt of his cigarette and stepped on it. "I'd better make myself useful," he said, and went off to stand among the irises in his urban shoes and a fairly respectable white shirt with the creases of folding in it and light another cigarette. Their father came out to his chair on the porch, a project for him, a painful business. Now, with Jack there, he avoided help when he could, toiling dangerously up the stairs to shave himself with an unsteady hand. There was nothing to be done except to listen for the sounds of emergency and pray, and ignore the scruff of hair at the back of his head where his comb didn't reach. From his chair in the porch he could look out on the garden.

Jack stooped to pull a clump of weeds and tossed it aside, and pulled another one and tossed it. Then he went to the shed behind the house to find a spade. When he came back, he said, "That DeSoto in the barn isn't yours. It's been there too long."

"No, one of the boys left it for Papa. But he never really did start driving. I guess he had a license for a while. Years ago."

"It looks like a decent car."

"I tried to start it once."

"You left the keys in the ignition."

She nodded. "No safer place in the world for them."

"Well," he said, "a little gas in the tank might change that. A little water in the radiator. Some air in the tires. I wiped off the windshield to make the thing look less—humiliated. I thought I might roll it out into daylight for a couple of hours so I could get a better look under the hood. If that's all right."

"I can't imagine why anyone would object."

He nodded. "I wanted to be sure." When he was done with his cigarette he began breaking up the ground.

He used to live here, and he knew how things were done. It had somehow never seemed to her that the place had his attention, or it seemed he was attentive to strategies of evasion and places of concealment, never to the skills of the ordinary, dutiful choring that made up most of every life, and was so much the worth and the pride of that life, by local reckoning. But he spaded between the rows of irises and he was businesslike about it, too. He had rolled up his sleeves.

SHE HEARD HER FATHER CALL OUT, "SUPPER, JACK!" WHICH WAS an opinion he had formed on his own, since it was 4:15 and she had not begun to prepare anything. But Jack stood the spade in the ground and paused for a minute, looking at his hand. He walked to the porch, looking at it, and she heard her father say, "Let's see! Oh yes, yes! Glory will take care of that! Glory? He has a splinter here. From that old spade handle! I don't know how long we've had that spade! I should have said something! Glory?"

Jack said, "If I can borrow a needle, I can take care of it, I think."

"No, no. That's pretty deep, Jack!"

Her father's face was animated with concern. He held to the wrist of Jack's upturned hand and almost hurried along beside him. "We'll put some iodine on that!"

Glory said, "You can wash up and I'll disinfect a needle."

"I'll get the iodine!" the old man said, and launched a determined assault on the staircase.

Jack looked at her. "It's just a splinter."

She said, "Not much happens around here," and he laughed.

She had made him laugh twice. She took a certain satisfaction in the joke about the towel, but in order to laugh at this little remark he must be feeling pretty kindly toward her, she thought. He was never one to laugh when you hoped he would, when other people would. In those old days, that is. He was a restless, distant, difficult boy, then twenty years passed with hardly a word from him, and now here he was in her kitchen, offering her his wounded hand, still damp with washing, smelling like lavender and lye. They sat at the table and she took his hand to steady it. A slender hand, still unsteady, with a few blisters rising on it from the work he had done that morning. Cigarette stains.

He noticed her scrutiny. "Do you read palms?" he asked.

"No. But if I did, I would say that you have a splinter through your lifeline."

He laughed. "I believe you may have found your calling."

She put the needle down. "I'm afraid to do this. It might actually hurt. And your hand is trembling."

"Well, if that one is, so is the other one. I could do myself harm if I tried it, I suppose."

"All right. Stay as still as you can." She thought, If he really were a stranger, this would not seem so odd to me. She could hear his breathing. She could see the blue traces of blood under the white skin of his wrist. "Just a second—there." She extracted the splinter easily enough.

"Thank you," he said.

The cane and the creaky railing and the hard, slippery shoes, and their father hurried into the kitchen with a bottle of iodine and a spool of gauze.

"Yes, you'll want to wash it and dry it again," he said. Then he daubed iodine here and there, finally where it should have been.

Jack said, "Ow," for old times' sake, by the sound of it.

"Yes, but it is very effective!" Her father was afire with solicitude. He went to the refrigerator and opened the door and stood there, purposive. "Supper!" he said. "I believe the pies are missing!"

Glory said, "They were so old I put them over the fence for the Dahlbergs' dogs."

"You did? The way things go around here, it might be time to invest in a dog of our own!"

Jack laughed, and his father smiled at him and patted his arm and said, "Well, that's wonderful! That's what I like to hear!"

Someone had left sliced ham and a macaroni salad in the porch the day before, one of those kindly reminders that nothing passed in their household unnoticed. The grace was exuberant— "Our hearts are much too full!" the old man said, and sank into that reverie prayer had become for him.

Through supper Jack was patiently restless, hearing out his father's attempts at conversation—"Yes, this was a very different town at one time, when we were still on the main road! There were people passing through. You wouldn't remember the old hotel. We thought it was very fine. It had a big veranda and a ballroom—" He grew ruefully excited, pondering the Gilead that was, and Jack watched him with the expression of mild impassivity he wore now that the embarrassments of his arrival were more or less behind him. She felt sorry for her father, happy as he was. It was hard work talking to Jack. So little in his childhood and youth could be mentioned without discomfort, his twenty-year silence was his to speak about if he chose to, but they were prepared to appreciate his discretion if any account of it might have caused more discomfort still. Then there was the question "Why are you here?" which they would never ask. Glory thought, Why am I here? How cruel it would be to ask me that.

When his father began to weary with the effort of talk—"Yes, yes," he said, "yes"—Jack cleared away the dishes and then he said, "Sir," and took his father's arm and helped him up from the table, a thing the old man never let Glory do, and he took him to the chair in his room where he napped. He helped him out of his jacket and opened his collar and loosened his tie. Then he knelt and removed his shoes. "That old quilt—" his father said, and Jack took it from the foot of the bed and spread it over him. The manner of his doing all these things, things she had done every day for months, suggested courtesy rather than kindness, as if it were a tribute to his father's age rather than a concession to it.

63

And she could see how her father was soothed by these attentions, as if pain were an appetite for comforting of just this kind.

She did her best.

THE BOYS CALLED THEIR FATHER SIR, BUT THE GIRLS never did. Behind his back the boys called him the Reverend, or the Old Gent, but the girls always said Papa. Jack, can you tell me why you have done whatever you did, acted however you did? No, sir. You can't explain it, Jack? No, sir. That courtesy was his shield and concealment. It was his courage. His father would never raise a hand against it, would seldom raise his voice. You do understand that what you did was wrong. Yes, sir, I understand that. Will you pray for a better conscience, better judgment, Jack? No, sir, I doubt that I will. Well, I'll pray *for* you then. Thank you, sir.

When Jack helped his father from his chair, it was with that same courtesy, and she could see that his father's pleasure was partly in the surprise of recognition, as of an old promise kept, an old debt remembered. Mama had said, "That boy has you wrapped around his finger!" And her father had said, "I just don't want us to lose him." That was before her parents realized she listened and, after a fashion, understood. Hearing words like these between her parents had nerved her to say to him, "What right do you have—" and had given her that glimpse of fear she still remembered. He must have thought he knew where she had learned that question, that inflection. She remembered standing there feet planted, arms akimbo. Poor, stupid child. Because she was the youngest, they forgot she was too old to be allowed to overhear. Then whenever he was gone she knew they might have lost him. "Go away, Glory," he would say if she tried to tag after him. "Please just go away."

While Jack settled his father for his nap, Glory stood in the hall, watching. It was beautiful to see, the old man making not one sound of discomfort, soothed by the gracefulness of Jack's attention, tucked in like a weary child.

At dusk Jack came downstairs in his suit and tie. "Back in a bit," he said. He paused on the steps to put his hat on and adjust it, and then he walked down the road toward town. Her father stirred when he heard the door closing. He called, "Did Jack go out?"

"He said he'd be right back." After an hour Glory went up to his room, just to see if by some means he had gathered his few effects and slipped them out of the house, but they were there where he had put them, shirts in the closet, books on the dresser. Of course she did not turn on the light, since he might see it from the road. And of course she heard the front door open as she stood there. She crept down the hall to the bathroom and turned on the water. He came up the stairs and paused in the hallway. Then she heard him flip on the light in his room. The door had been standing ajar, she remembered. And had she left it open? Did he look for signs that someone had come into his room? He did that when they were children. Someone! Who could it be but me, she thought.

All those years ago her father had said, "I'm afraid we might lose him." And here he is again, leaving the house for an hour, and by the end of it the old man is too anxious to sit still and she is prowling in his room, intruding on his privacy—when if there was one thing on earth she was eager to concede to him or to anyone it was privacy! It was amazing. Her whole life long that house was either where Jack might not be or where he was not. Why did he leave? Where had he gone? Those questions had hung in the air for twenty years while everyone tried to ignore them, had tried to act as if their own lives were of sufficient interest to distract them from the fact that few letters came, that at Christmas there was again no phone call, that their father seemed bent under the weight of an anxiety time only increased. They were so afraid they would lose him, and then they had lost him, and that was the story of their family, no matter how warm and fruitful and robust it might have appeared to the outside world.

What had she thought? That he had dropped his suitcase out the window, absconding like someone trying to cheat the landlord? Why would he do that? But why did he do anything—come home, for example? She heard him go downstairs again, and she heard her father say, "Yes, yes, we were beginning to miss you, Jack! Glory's around here somewhere—" So she went down to the kitchen and there he was, studying the wound in his hand.

"How is it?" she asked.

"Mending nicely, thanks." His glance was mild, unreadable. "I was out looking the place over. What do people do for work around here?"

"Well, that's a good question," she said. "Aside from farming, there's the grocery store and the dry-goods store and the barbershop and the gas station and the bank."

"Teachers are always needed!" the old man shouted from his chair, and Jack said, "I guess I'd better bring him in here, hadn't I."

His father was already halfway down the hall, but he let Jack take his arm. He even handed him his cane, as if all caution and struggle ended when he had Jack to lean on. "Yes!" he said. "I have never known it to be true that an educated man could not find work as a schoolteacher! There are more children every day! I notice them everywhere!" Jack helped him into his place at the table. "They pass by in the street!" he said, as if he thought he might have weakened his case by overstating it.

Jack gave him a glass of water. "I don't really think I'm cut out to be a schoolteacher," he said.

"Well, I hope you'll give it some thought!"

"Yes, sir, I will. Is this today's newspaper?"

His father said, "Yesterday's, I believe. Not that it makes much difference. I put it aside because I didn't quite finish the crossword puzzle."

"Good. I'll read my horoscope. I've sort of forgotten what I did yesterday. Here. It says new enterprises are favored. I guess I missed my chance."

"That's the only thing it ever says! That's probably what mine says!"

"Yes, sir, it is. We have the same sign. And here's yours, Glory. 'Curiosity is not always welcome. Consider self-restraint.'" He smiled at her, folded the paper, and tucked it under his arm.

She felt herself blush hotly and, she knew, visibly. But he looked away from her quickly enough, almost, to make her believe he had not meant to embarrass her. Maybe the horoscope was real after all. She decided it was better to assume it was real, because if she took offense she would be confessing, and seeming to confess to worse by far than she had done, not that there was anything wrong with what she had done. And if she found out it was not real, that he was taunting her, everything would only be harder. That was the decision of the moment, and when she considered it afterward, she was grateful to herself for having made it. Consider self-restraint indeed, when she bit her tongue twenty times a day. All she had wanted when she stepped into his room was to know whether she had to begin hinting to her poor old father that Jack was gone again. It was not her fault that so ridiculous a fear was justified. And she did not intend to notice now that nothing suggested he had been drinking.

"I believe I'll go out for a little walk," she said. It was late enough to have made her father worry, if he had been paying attention. But he was consulting with Jack about the crossword puzzle.

She was afraid to be angry, and that made her angry. What right did he have to take over the house this way? Granting he had as much claim to it as she did, the only difference being that she had spent some months caring for the house and her father before he arrived. Now he seemed inclined to help with the old man, too, and he did it well, and as if something were communicated in it that made it more a gracious ceremony than the acting out of duty or obligation. A tacit agreement had formed between the two men that Jack would help his father with the bathing and changing that had been the uneasiest part of her caring for him, and that was a great relief, since he had been reluctant to accept the attention he needed. The fact was that she had taken comfort from the thought that her duty was plain and that a sense of obligation was becoming in anyone and so on. But things were better with Jack in the house.

"Insinuating" is an ugly word, snakey. She'd have thought of a better one if she could. He had resumed his place in his father's heart, that was clear. She believed that in twenty years there might have been four letters, because when she was newly returned to her father's house she went to the big Bible with the altogether blameless intention of soothing her mind with a psalm or two, and the Bible opened on four letters, tucked between the Testaments. The envelopes were worn enough to make her think the letters might have some family interest, but when she saw the return addresses, she put them back unread. Whatever had passed between father and son, their father had not seen fit to tell any of the rest of them, at least as far as she knew. Jack had ceased to be spoken of, almost. Now here he was, without a word of explanation, crowding her out of that big, empty house, or so it seemed to her sometimes. I should leave, she told herself once or twice, to savor the thought of their surprise, their regret. What a childish idea. Then Jack would leave, no doubt, so that she would come back, as she would have to do, and her father would be plunged in sorrow of which she was directly the cause, and which would not end in this life.

She was less inclined to pray than she had been once. In her childhood, when her father, a tall man then and graceful, had stepped into the pulpit and bowed his head, silence came over the people. He prayed before the commencement of prayer. May the meditations of our hearts be acceptable. It seemed to her that her own prayers never attained to that level of seriousness. They had been desperate from time to time, which was a different thing altogether. Her father told his children to pray for patience, for courage, for kindness, for clarity, for trust, for gratitude. Those prayers will be answered, he said. Others may not be. The Lord knows your needs. So she prayed, Lord, give me patience. She knew that was not an honest prayer, and she did not linger over it. The right prayer would have been, Lord, my brother treats me like a hostile stranger, my father seems to have put me aside, I feel I have no place here in what I thought would be my refuge, I am miserable and bitter at heart, and old fears are rising up in me so that everything I do makes everything worse. But it cost her tears to think her situation might actually be that desolate, so she prayed again for patience, for tact, for understanding—for every virtue that might keep her safe from conflicts that would be sure to leave her wounded, every virtue that might at least help her preserve an appearance of dignity, for heaven's sake. She did wonder what the neighbors thought, if anyone saw her in the street at that hour. Something fairly near the mark, no doubt.

As she considered the prayer she was not yet disconsolate enough to put into words, the unwelcome realization came to her that she loved Jack and yearned for his approval. This was no doubt inevitable, since it was assumed to be true of the whole family, separately and together, excluding in-laws, who might never have met him or even heard his name, and who could only be a little amazed by the potency of this collective sentiment if by some means they became aware of it. He was the black sheep, the ne'er-do-well, unremarkable in photographs. None of the very few stories that mentioned him suggested the loss of him could have been wholly regrettable. It was the sad privilege of blood relations to love him despite all. Glory was thirteen when he left for college, having been by that time ignored by him for years. And here she was in middle age feeling the fact of his touchy indifference a judgment on her, so it seemed to her, though he had been so grievously at fault, and her intrusions all those years ago, her excesses, whatever he might have called them, were no such thing—she had defended them in her mind a thousand times and would defend them to his face if the occasion ever arose, which God forbid, God forbid.

The thought had occurred to her more than once, even before the gradual catastrophe of her own venture into the world had come to an end, that "despite all" was a dangerous formula, and that the romance of absence was a distraction from more sustaining joys. Those years of her late childhood, when she felt so necessary, when she was so sure things would come right if only enough effort was given to making them come right—those years stayed with her as if they had been the whole of her life. The others hadn't even known—not Faith, not Teddy. Her father said it was Jack's choice to tell them or to be silent, since he might feel still less at ease with them if they knew, and not seek them out if the need arose. He might not come home when they came home, at Christmas and Thanksgiving. Her father told her with tears in his eyes that the three of them could alleviate Jack's guilt and also his shame by making the very best of the situation. So she took up knitting. It was a deep secret. They were at work on a great rescue. Her parents talked freely to her or in her hearing about it all, trusted her, and she never breathed a word except to old Ames, whose discretion was perfect. It embarrassed her to remember how happy she had been, those three bitter, urgent years until it all ended. Her brother would never know the thousand things she had done to make life tolerable for him.

Brothers. When she was a child, attention from any of her brothers was wonderful to her. It was rare, and it was wry, odd, not at all parental. Even Grace, who was older than she was by less than two years, tried sometimes to mother her, and Faith and Hope—such names!—were irksomely mature and responsible. But when any of the brothers noticed her, it was to swing her around by her hands or to carry her on his back or to show her a card trick or the husk of a cicada. When the boys had all gotten their growth, they were within an inch of one another in height, lanky young fellows with angular faces and unruly hair. Luke had left for school when she was four, Dan when she was seven. Jack and Teddy left the same year, the year she was thirteen, since Teddy was so good in school that he had skipped two grades. So when they were at home together, in the summer and at holidays, they took a conscious pleasure in it, and this was truer as the younger boys were recruited into the ranks of the fully grown. They joked and sparred and took off together in Luke's old Ford, sometimes even to Des Moines, Jack with them if he could be cajoled. They were vain of their freedom and their manhood, of their cleverness and their long legs, but gentlemanly all the same, and vain of that, too. Their mother called them the princes of the church, and they did look fine, strolling into the sanctuary together in their jackets and ties, Bibles in hand, the three of them, and then sometimes the fourth. They said things like *volo, nolo*, and *de gustibus* and "Let me not to the marriage of true minds," and she was in awe of them. Seeing Jack reminded her of those days. She knew the others now, after the manner of adult friendship. And fond as she was of them, it was hard to remember that they had ever seemed marvelous to her. But Jack was as remote from her as he ever had been, and she found herself waiting again for notice and approval, to her own considerable irritation.

After a little while she went back to the house, thinking her father might be waiting up. But Jack had gotten him to bed and had gone upstairs to his room. The porch light was left on for her.

THE NEXT MORNING SHE ROSE EARLY, EARLY ENOUGH THAT she could assume Jack was still sleeping, and she went downstairs to the kitchen, measured out coffee and made pancake batter, and then waited to hear her father stir, as he always did well before dawn, though it was his custom to wait to rouse himself until she came downstairs an hour or two later. Mornings were worst for him, and the tedium of lying awake wore on him, she knew. This morning and from now on she would do better by him. He loved pancakes. She would make them often.

So when she heard him stirring, she started the coffeepot and the griddle, then she went into his room and helped him up, held his arm while he stepped into his slippers, bundled him into his robe. She brought a washcloth for his face and hands, and combed his hair.

"Ready to greet the day, more or less," he said.

She said, "Pancakes."

"Yes, that's wonderful. I heard you out there and I thought it was part of a dream I was having. I don't remember the dream, but it had footsteps in it."

It had not occurred to her to look at the clock, assuming that, since she awoke feeling purposeful, with a highly formed intention in her mind, it must be the dark of the morning. The clock on her father's dresser said 3:10. He saw her look at it.

"Pancakes are always welcome!" he said, mustering himself.

"I can let you sleep for a couple more hours, Papa."

"Not at all! The smell of coffee," he said, "has put all thought of sleep behind me! Yes!" and he moved with halting resolution toward the kitchen, and took his chair, and sat looking alertly at nothing in particular. So she gave him a plate and a knife and fork.

"I'm afraid you children might not be getting along," he said. This remark was so apt and abrupt it brought tears to her eyes. She turned to the business of making pancakes and said, when she could trust her voice, "It is hard, you know, after so many years—I was young when he left for school, and we were never close—" and she put a pancake on his plate. He took up his fork. She poured another pancake. "And I do think he feels uneasy with me. I'm not at ease with him, that's a fact, and I might as well be honest about it—"

She set the second pancake on the first, and her father said, "If you'll put my foot on the stove there," and something else, and she realized he was asleep. He was asleep with his fork in his hand and a sociable expression on his face. She couldn't find it in her heart to wake him again, so she turned off the coffee and the griddle and the ceiling light and sat down at the table, too. And when she found she couldn't hold up her head, she rested it on her arms, and wept a little, and drowsed a little. And then she heard Jack on the stairs.

It was still long before dawn, so he switched on the light and as quickly switched it off again. He whispered, "What's wrong?"

She said, "Nothing, really."

"You're crying."

"That's true."

"Is he all right?"

"He's sound asleep. You can turn the light on."

The light came on, and Jack stood in the doorway taking in the situation. "I did smell coffee," he said.

His father stirred in his chair, and Jack slipped the fork out of his hand. "It'd be a shame to waste those pancakes," he said.

"They're cold."

"They're still pancakes. Do you mind?"

"I don't mind. And there's the cold coffee, too."

"Excellent," he said. "Thank you." He took his father's plate and cup, filled the cup with coffee, and sat down to the pancakes. "This is nice in its way. But it's a little strange. I don't mean that as criticism." Then he said, "You're really not going to explain this, are you."

"No, it doesn't matter. I don't feel like it."

"Okay." He laughed. "I'm always willing to play by the house rules." Then he said, "When we finish our breakfast, can we go back to bed?"

"No."

"I suppose I should have guessed that."

"He almost never sleeps this soundly. I'm not going to disturb him. But I don't want him to be confused when he wakes up. I'll stay here. You can go back to bed."

Jack watched his father for a moment. Then he stood up, put one arm under his knees and the other around his shoulders, and lifted him out of his chair. The old man murmured, and he said, "You're fine, sir. It's Jack." A hand floated up to touch his face, his cheek and ear. Jack carried him into his room and tucked him into his bed. Then he came back to the kitchen.

"Now you can get some more sleep," he said.

Glory said, "Thank you, I will." And she went upstairs and lay on her bed and hated her life until morning.

WHEN MORNING CAME, SHE WENT DOWN TO THE KITCHEN and made coffee and pancakes, as if for the first time. Jack's expression was opaque. Her father was drowsy, or he was pensive. Finally he said, "I have something on my mind. 'Last night I saw the new moon with the old moon in his arm.' What is that? I've been trying to think."

She said, "'The Ballad of Sir Patrick Spens.'"

Jack said, "Good for you, college girl."

"No," the old man said. "She was an English teacher. In high school. A very fine teacher of English, for a number of years. Then she got married, so she had to resign. They made them do that. 'The new moon with the old moon in his arm.' That is a very sad song. A number of times I heard my grandmother sing it, and it was very sad. 'Oh forty miles off Aberdour 'tis fifty fathoms deep, and there lies good Sir Patrick Spens with the Scots lairds at his feet.' She said the life was very difficult in Scotland, but she was always homesick. She said she would die of the homesickness, and maybe she did, but she took her time about it. She was ninety-eight when she died." He laughed. "'We that are young will never see so much nor live so long.'" He said, "You just picked me up and carried me, didn't you, Jack. Well, that's all right. I'm not the father you remember, I know that."

Jack put his hand to his brow. "Of course you are. I didn't— I'm sorry—"

"No matter. Never mind. I shouldn't have mentioned it."

The color left Jack's face. After a moment he pushed back his chair. "Well," he said. "There's work to be done." He went out to the garden and stood in the path he had made along the iris beds and lighted a cigarette. Glory watched him from the porch. She said, "I should probably help him."

The old man said, "Yes, dear, that would be good of you." So she settled her father in the Morris chair with the newspaper, and then she went out to the garden. She touched Jack's arm and he looked at her.

"What is it?" he said.

"I just wanted to say that there was nothing wrong with what you did. He hates being feeble. And he's had to put up with it for a long time."

He drew on his cigarette. "Thank you," he said.

"No, really. I thought it was gallant. A beau geste. A demonstration of your fabled charm."

"Too bad. I've found that people weary of my fabled charm."

"Well, I guess I haven't had much chance to weary of it."

He laughed. "The day is young." Then he said, "I didn't intend anything when I said college girl. I don't know what was offensive about it."

"It wasn't offensive. He just wants to make sure you think well of me. He's afraid we don't get along."

He looked at her, studied her. "He said that?"

"Yes, he mentioned it."

"Last night."

"Yes—"

"And what did you say?"

"Well, I said that you and I never did really know each other very well."

"That's all?"

"He was too sleepy to talk much."

"So he's worried about it."

"He worries about everything. It'll be fine. You've always known how to please him."

He shook his head. "No. I could always count on him to be

pleased with me. From time to time. Often enough. I never understood it myself." He shrugged and laughed. "What the hell," he said, "I don't believe I've ever understood much of anything." He threw down his cigarette and glanced at her, and there was a kind of irritation in his look, as if she had drawn him into a confidence he already regretted. "I'm not making excuses," he said.

"I know that. I want to get a bandage for your hand. I'll be right back."

The old man had moved to the porch. She called to him and waved as she passed. She brought the gauze and the tape, and there where they knew he could watch them, she tended to Jack's wound. "That should be all right."

"Very kind. Thank you," he said. And with his bandaged hand, gravely and tentatively, he mussed her hair.

SHE HAD LET HIM BELIEVE THAT THEIR FATHER WAS UP IN the night worrying. That was wrong, but it wasn't really intentional. She had wanted to tell him how beautiful it was to have taken up his father in his arms that way. She had thought it at the time, and had felt bitterly how helpless she was to be so gentle, so sufficient. To own up to this unwelcome feeling of admiration, aloud, to Jack himself, had given her a sense of freedom and strength, those rewards of self-overcoming her father had always promised. She had felt this briefly. Then she saw that wary look of his, caution with no certainty of the nature of the threat, and with no notion at all of possible refuge. He realized he did not please his father, did not know how to please his father. He would probably have liked to believe he had done something wrong so that he could at least orient himself a little, but she had told him a terrible thing, that he had done nothing to offend, that his father had found fault with him anyway, only because he was old and sad now, not the father he thought he had come home to.

They worked quietly in the sunshine, heaving up irises and separating them. Jack was very earnest about the work, and very preoccupied, reflective. Glory replanted the best of the corms, setting a few aside for Lila. "You're a friend of hers?" Jack asked.

"We get along. She's a nice woman. You haven't stopped by the Ameses' yet, have you."

"Too busy," he said, and laughed. "I'll do it tomorrow."

"She keeps a big garden herself, and she's offered to help me with this one, but I don't want to take her away from her husband. Time's wingèd chariot and so on."

"How is old Ames?"

"Papa's worried about him. He really does worry about everything. But he says, 'Ames just isn't quite right!' He says, 'I've known him all my life, and I can tell there's something the matter!'" She looked toward the porch and whispered, "He's supposed to be deaf, but he seems to hear whatever I'd rather he didn't. I'd better be careful."

Jack said, "I'd have thought Ames would come by. No wonder the old fellow misses him. I didn't know forty-eight hours could pass without a quarrel, or at least a checker game."

"I suppose he's giving Papa time to enjoy having you here."

"Ah yes. Who better than Reverend Ames to understand that special joy I bring with me wherever I go— "

"No, seriously. You don't realize what this has meant."

"What it meant until I actually showed up." He said, "The hangover was a mistake, that's for sure." He took the cigarettes from his shirt pocket and lighted one.

"Children!" the old man shouted. "I think that's enough for one day!"

She said, "Ames has mellowed a little. At least he's not as abstracted as he used to be. So much of that was loneliness, I think. And it would please Papa if you paid a call on him."

Jack looked at her. "I know. Of course. I intend to." They were walking back to the house. He flicked his cigarette away and pushed the hair off his brow, and he held the door for her. Then he stood there just inside the door, like a stranger unsure of his welcome.

THEIR FATHER HAD PUT THE CHECKERBOARD ON THE kitchen table. He said, "Jack, I like a good game of checkers. But Glory lets me win."

"No, I don't."

"She does. And I know it's kindly meant."

"I don't let you win."

"She doesn't really enjoy the game, so half the time she more or less concedes by the third move. It's frustrating. I can't hone my skills!"

Glory said, "I win about as often as you do."

Her father said, "That is my point! Half the time she is just letting me win!" And he laughed roguishly and winked at Jack, who smiled. He opened the box. "Black is my preference. Glory, you sit down here and watch. You might want to pick up some pointers. This fellow may have acquired strategies unheard of in Gilead!"

"No, sir, " Jack said. "Not where checkers are concerned." He came to the table and took a seat. He placed the red checkers on their squares.

Glory said, "I'll make popcorn."

"Yes, like the old times—" Her father made a move.

She thought, Yes, a little like the old times. Graying children, ancient father. If they could have looked forward from those old times, when even a game of checkers around that table was so rambunctious it would have driven her father off to parse his Hebrew in the stricken quiet of Ames's house—if they could now look in the door of the kitchen at the three of them there, would they believe what they saw? No matter—her father was hunched over his side of the board, mock-intent, and Jack was reclined, legs crossed at the ankles, as if it were possible to relax in a straight-backed chair. The corn popped.

After a while her father said, "Best two out of three! I know when I am outflanked."

"Are you sure?" Jack asked.

"'Sure'? If I do this, you do that. And if I do this, you do that," he said, tapping the board with his finger. "It seems odd, in the circumstances, that I should be the one to point it out!"

"If you hadn't, I might not have thought of it."

"Well, then, we'll call it a draw."

Jack laughed. "That's fine with me."

"Whipped!" his father said. "Technicalities aside. It has taken the starch out of me! Glory, I've got the board warmed up. Let's see what you can do with this fellow."

So she sat down opposite her brother. He smiled at her. "This is very fine popcorn," he said.

"Extra butter."

He nodded. They played a polite game, distracted by their father's palpable hope that they would enjoy it a little. There was no trace in Jack's expression of anything at all except a readiness to oblige, which was only emphasized by the promptness with which he took his turns. "Oh," he said, when she triple-jumped him.

Then his father said, "I believe you have an opportunity there, Jack." And he reached over and made the move himself, a double jump. "Now you have a king, you see."

Glory said, "No fair," and Jack laughed.

"Old times, yes! It's very good, but I can't deal with all this excitement. I'm off to my room. No, you two finish your game," he said, when Jack stood up to help him with his chair. "There's time enough to get me to bed. I'm not going anywhere."

So they went on with their game. Glory said, "I don't recall that we ever did play checkers, you and I. I always played with the younger kids."

Jack began to make his move, but his hand trembled and he dropped it into his lap.

"What is it," she said.

He cleared his throat and smiled at her. "You never sneaked me upstairs with a bottle of aspirin. You were a little girl."

"No, I didn't mean I did it myself. I just meant I knew that it happened."

"Sorry. I didn't realize that. I didn't realize at the time. That you would have been aware of it." He cleared his throat.

"It was a stupid thing for me to say, Jack. I apologize. I hope you will forget it."

He said, "It just makes things sound worse than they were. They were bad enough."

"All right. I will never say it again."

He considered. "Say what, exactly?"

"Well, you're right. I didn't say that I personally was the one who sneaked you upstairs. That's just what you heard."

He said, "I wouldn't mind if we dropped the subject entirely. All that happened a long time ago."

At that point she lost her temper. She thought, Why am I apologizing to this man for something I did not say, and also for what I did say, which was only the truth?

"Well." She hoped she was controlling the quaver of anger in her voice. "At just that moment it was not obvious that all that had ended a long time ago."

He put his hand to his face. Oh, she thought, this is miserable. Dear God, I have made him ashamed. How will we live in the same house now? He will leave, and Papa will die of grief, and the fault will be mine. So she said, "Forgive me."

"Yes," he said, "of course."

Their father called, "Could one of you children come and give me a little help?"

"I'll go," Jack said. She put away the checkerboard, and then she looked down the hall, and there was Jack, kneeling to unlace the old man's shoes. And his father regarding him with such sad tenderness that she wished she could will herself out of existence, herself and every word she had ever said.

THAT WAS THE DAY A PHONE CALL CAME, A WOMAN ASKING
to speak to Jack Boughton. Glory said he was in the garden and
she would call him, but he wasn't there, so she went to the barn,
where she found him leaning into the engine of the car. "There's
a telephone call for you."

"Who is it?"

"She didn't say. A woman."

"Jesus," he said, and he stepped past her and ran down the
path and up the steps into the house. When she came into the
kitchen the phone was back on its hook. "She hung up." He said,
"Sweet Jesus, I'm out of the house twenty minutes—"

"I'm sorry—"

He shook his head. "It's not your fault. Did she tell you her
name? What did she say?"

"She said she was calling from St. Louis. The connection was
very bad. There was a lot of noise. She was calling from a phone
booth, I think."

"From St. Louis? She said that?"

"Yes."

He sat down at the table. "St. Louis! Did she say she would
call back?"

"Well, no. I thought I would be able to find you. I guess I
thought she'd stay on the line. I should have asked."

He drew a very deep breath and rubbed his eyes. "None of
this is your fault," he said. His hands were greasy, so he went to
the sink and washed them, and washed his face, then he took a
dishcloth and wiped down the telephone. "None of this is my
fault, either, I suppose. There's absolutely no comfort in that
thought." He sat down at the table. "I hope I'm not in the way
here. I cannot be farther than an arm's length from the telephone
into the indefinite future. Jack Boughton in chains. All I need is
an eagle to peck at my liver, such as it is. Ah," he said, and he
laughed. "At least I got a call. That's something." The thought
seemed to lift his spirits.

"Can't you call her? I mean, I know she was calling from a phone booth. But couldn't you call her family and ask how to reach her?"

He shook his head. "I have been warmly encouraged not to do that. By her father, no less."

She brought him the book she meant to read next, *The Paths of Glory.*

"Your memoirs?"

She said, "The girls in this family got named for theological abstractions and the boys got named for human beings. That's bad enough without our having to be teased about it for the rest of our lives."

"Sorry. It just slipped out. No more jokes."

"'The paths of Glory lead but to the grave.' Now you don't have to struggle with the urge to say that, either."

"Thank you," he said. "What a relief!"

So he sat in the kitchen reading, drumming his fingers. He turned the book to the last few pages and read the ending. "Sad!" He put it aside. She gave him a bowl of walnuts and he shelled them. And he paced. And he stood on the porch, just outside the back door, and smoked.

Two hours passed and the phone rang.

Her father called, in his sleep, "Could you get that, Glory?"

"It's probably for Jack, Papa."

"No, Faith said in her note she'd be giving me a call. She hasn't called in a number of days."

"You talked to her yesterday."

The phone rang again. She whispered to Jack, "Answer it!" because he was just standing there, looking at her. She took the phone off the hook and handed it to him, and then she went to her father's room. He was sitting on the edge of the bed. He looked drowsy, but he seemed set on getting up, so she brought his robe.

She heard Jack clear his throat. "Hello?"

82

Her father said, "That's a very good thing. He should talk with all his sisters and brothers. Every one of them. They are anxious to hear from him."

Jack said, "What's that? I can't quite hear you! He did? When? I am talking louder! No, it's not your fault, I know that! Yes, they do get upset!"

Her father said, "Well, I can't imagine that there could be any reason to shout like that!"

Glory said, "It's a bad connection, someone calling from a phone booth."

"Well, I hope so. Otherwise I'll have to call Faith and explain. And I really don't know how I could explain his shouting at her like that. I really don't. She has always been very fond of him." His eyes were closed, but she combed his hair and helped him into his slippers.

"He would never shout at Faith, Papa. So it has to be someone else."

"Yes," the old man said. "I suppose I should have realized that."

Glory was trying to distract her father from the conversation, and she was trying not to hear it herself, though Jack did sound alarmed, or aggrieved, and she could not help but wish she knew what the matter was.

"If the boys could keep looking!" he shouted. "I'll pay them! I'll send money!" A pause. "No, I wasn't suggesting that! I mean, I'm sure you are all doing your best, Mrs. Johnson! Believe me! I certainly don't blame you!"

Her father said, "Yes, he mentioned a Mrs. Johnson. He's shouting at someone we don't even know."

"Please, if he turns up, call any time! Call collect! Yes, thank you, thank you!"

She followed her father down the hall to the kitchen. Jack was sitting on the floor with his back against the wall and his knees drawn up, rubbing his face. He stood up and smoothed back his hair. He was pale and his eyes were red. He said, "It's nothing. A dog ran off. I promised someone I'd look after his dog."

"Oh yes," his father said. "All that shouting was about a dog." He shook his head. Her father woke up gruff sometimes, or confused. Sometimes he needed an hour or so to come into himself. Jack couldn't know that.

"It *was* about a dog," he said softly, and he smiled at her, because they had spent those long hours together and she would understand the bitterness of his surprise. "I can't be trusted with a *dog*."

She said, "They do come back sometimes. I think you'd better sit down."

He nodded and smiled, pale as she had ever seen him. "I'll get past this," he said. "I'll be all right." He took the chair she pulled out for him. "Thank you." She gave him a glass of water. "Maybe I can make it up to him." He shrugged.

His father was gazing at him, and Jack glanced up and then looked away, uneasy. The old man said, "Well, whatever the trouble is, I'll help if I can. I think you must know that by now."

"Yes, sir, I do."

"At this point I'm pretty much reduced to praying for you. Of course I do that anyway. If anything else comes to mind, let me know."

"Yes, I will."

When they were children their father had always avoided fault-finding, at least in the actual words he spoke to them. But there was from time to time a tone of rebuke in his voice that overrode the mildness of his intentions. She had not heard him speak that way in any number of years, and she watched Jack accept it now, patiently, as if he were hearing something necessary and true, something chastening. So she said, "None of this is your fault, Jack. The phone woke Papa out of a sound sleep, and he's a little cross. That's all there is to it."

Jack said mildly, as if he found the fact interesting, "It never seems to make much difference. Whether I'm at fault or not."

"Yes, if Glory says I was cross, I suppose I was cross. It wasn't my intention, not at all. I don't know what it was I said. I believe I said I'd help if I could. That seems all right to me. I don't know." He shook his head.

Jack said softly, "It was all right. It was very kind."

"Yes," the old man said, "I meant to be kind to you. I certainly did."

More often, as the days went by, Jack sought her out to talk with her, and when the talk drifted into silence, sometimes he would smile at her as if to say, You and I, of all people, here, of all places, killing time for lack of anything else to do with it. A stranger might look at her that way, past the tedium of their situation, past the accidental companionship that came with their whiling it out together, to let her know in a decorous and impersonal way how glad he was she was there.

And sometimes, when they were working in the garden or doing the dishes, she would notice that he had drawn back to watch her, appraisingly, as if he had suddenly dropped every assumption about her, as if she were someone who figured in an intention of his and about whom he realized he knew nothing to be relied upon, or nothing that mattered, someone he must consider again carefully. She did not remember from her childhood the habit he had now of running the tip of his tongue across his lower lip, but she thought she did remember that estrangement of his gaze, that look of urgent calculation, of sharply attentive calm. It could only be fear, and she wanted to say, You can trust me, but that is what they had always told him, and he laughed and pretended to believe them, and wished to believe them, she was sure, and never did. Her father always said, "That loneliness of his," and when she saw it in him now, she felt lonely, even abandoned for the moment it lasted, until the banter of comfort and familiarity took up again. He'd say, "Hey, chum," to coax her out of her thoughts. They were indeed very sad thoughts, as his must have been, too, and he would smile with fellow feeling, her bemused and improbable companion.

He would ask her advice about how to live in that house, and usually he would take it. He asked her if she thought it would be all right if he trimmed back the vines that grew on the front of the porch, and she said, "Better not. Those are there to attract hummingbirds."

"The old fellow can hardly see who's going by in the road."

"Well, he doesn't seem to mind that. He loves those birds. So did Mama. That's part of it."

Jack said, "Right." Then he said, "When we were kids, we'd have thought crazy people must live in a house that looked like that. All overgrown."

She laughed. "I remember the Thrushes. Teddy used to make you go with him to collect for the newspaper, because those old shrubs had grown up and buried the house."

"I was thinking about that. She used to stand on her porch on Halloween night and call to the kids in the road. She'd say she had cookies and apples for them, and they'd take off running."

"Everybody knows about Papa and his trumpet vines, though. And the house is pretty strange-looking, anyway. In my opinion."

Jack said, "True." But later she saw him appraising the vines again from the edge of the road, and the next day he began cutting back at the spragglier branches, more of them the next day and the next. She noticed the trimmings stacked out of sight behind the shed. Against her advice and to her surprise, he had undertaken a furtive campaign to make the house look a little less forbidding. He even found a flower pot in the barn and shoveled up some petunias to put in it and set it on the step.

"I didn't think anyone would mind," he said, when he saw her notice it.

GRADUALLY HE GAVE UP ON THE HOPE THAT THERE WOULD be another telephone call. He began spending time in the barn again, leaning into the engine of the DeSoto. To work on a car where anyone might see was considered unseemly by the Boughtons, not different essentially from setting it up on blocks. And Jack was aware of the likelihood of failure and therefore careful to provide as little opportunity as possible for anecdote or, worse, for offers of help or advice. Glory mused from time to time on how often the starchy proprieties observed in her family overlapped more or less precisely with Jack's strategies for avoiding humiliation. In any case, he spent a good part of every day in earthy, dank concealment, oiling some memory of resilience into stiffened leather upholstery, or sinking inflated inner tubes into the horse trough to find the leaks in them.

They had had a horse once, mottled white with a grayish face and stockings. They called him Snowflake for a dingy splat of near-white on his brow. He was docile when her father bought him for the first two of his children. There were photos of Luke and Faith as toddlers astride the horse and her father holding the reins. Docile meant old, and in the photos his weariness and bewilderment are already visible. But in fact what the photos captured was only the onset, in fact the spring, of a terrible longevity. Even Glory remembered the ancient, moldy horse standing in the barn or the pasture with his legs splayed out as if he expected the earth to tilt abruptly and was braced for it. It was his misfortune to be a horse, with enough persisting horse-like attributes, for example a mane and most of a tail, to have, in the eyes of children, a chivalric dignity and romance. So, year upon year, the matter of bringing an end to the tedium and confusion of his interminable life could not even be broached. Then finally one day he was gone. The boys made horrible jokes about how he had made a run for it, had charged through Gilead overturning matrons and baby carriages on his way to the freedom of the high plains. They took to calling glue and all that was gluelike Snowflake, to the irritation of their father and the bafflement of the younger children. Still, there was something about the fact that there had been a horse in that barn, that his trough still stood by the wall and his bridle still hung from a nail above it, that gave the barn itself a certain melancholy romance. A few motes of straw still managed to scintillate in any shaft of sunlight. It seemed sometimes as if her father must have meant to preserve all this memory, this sheer power of sameness, so that when they came home, or when Jack came home, there would be no need to say anything. In the terms of the place, they would all always have known everything.

JACK STILL HAD A LETTER TO MAIL ALMOST EVERY DAY. HE TOOK the letters to the post office, at the back of the drugstore. He dressed carefully before every venture into town, jacket, tie, and hat. It was a louche sort of respectability he achieved, she thought, but it was earnestly persisted in, with much attention to the shine on his shoes. He would sometimes tell her whom he had met on the street, if he recognized anyone, or, more precisely, if anyone recognized him. He reported brief conversations as if they were heartening, proof of something. Once he said, "I believe I could see myself here. Jack Boughton, honest working man. Little wife at home, little child—frolicking with his dog, I suppose. Not unthinkable." And sometimes he came back drawn and silent, as if he had been shunned or slighted, perhaps. All those letters, and never a word about whomever it was he sent them to, and never a word of reply.

One day when she was in the parlor, dusting among the clutter of gifts and souvenirs that crowded the mantel, he said, "Well, Glory, I did as I was told. I stopped by Ames's, paid my respects. Met the wife." He laughed. "You know, after all these years he still can't stand the sight of me."

She said, "He's a kind old fellow. He was probably just tired, probably up all night."

"No doubt you're right." Then he said, "I'm an insensitive brute for the most part. But if there is one thing I know I can recognize, it is dislike. If he allows himself such thoughts, he was sitting there on his front porch thinking, Here comes Jack Boughton, that son of a bitch."

"Maybe. Maybe not."

"Sorry."

"For what?"

"The language."

"Never mind."

He shook his head. "It's hard, coming back here." He opened the piano and touched middle C. "Did somebody tune this?"

"Papa had it tuned when I told him I was coming home. Back. That was the first thing he wrote to me, after his regrets and prayers and so on. 'It will be wonderful to have music in this house again.' I haven't played, though. I haven't really felt like it."

Jack slid onto the bench. "I can't do it without squinting one eye," he said. He took a sip from an imaginary glass, set it down again, and sang, "'When your heart's on fire, you must realize, smoke gets in your eyes.'"

"I hate that song," she said.

"'I'll be seeing you, in all the old familiar places . . .'"

"Stop it," she said.

He laughed. "Sorry. I really am sorry." He shrugged. "Limited repertoire."

"How can you even have a repertoire? You never practiced!"

"I thought playing piano had something to do with being Presbyterian. Nobody told me you could get paid for it."

Their father's voice rose from the next room, reedy and perfectly pitched. "'This robe of flesh I'll drop and rise, To seize the everlasting prize . . .'"

Jack said, "I guess that's a hint," and he played the hymn through, embellishing a little but respectfully enough. "'And sing while passing through the air, farewell, farewell, sweet hour of prayer.'" He knew the words, and he whispered them as he played. Well, that always was their father's favorite hymn.

"Yes!" the old man said. "And I would also very much enjoy

'Shall We Gather at the River.' Or 'The Church's One Foundation,' if you prefer that one. It's all the same to me." And he began, rather lustily, "'Shall we gather at the river, the beautiful, beautiful river—'" Jack plunged in after him. "That was rousing, Jack! Yes, the old songs. I believe I've worked up an appetite. Four o'clock. Well, I might have a cookie—"

Jack said, "I'll get one for you. Milk?"

"If you don't mind."

Jack brought him a plate and a glass. "Here you are, sir."

His father said, "It's always 'sir,' isn't it? Never Papa. Or Dad. Some of the others call me Dad now, some of the boys do."

"It's a habit, I suppose. Do you mind?"

"Oh no, Jack, I don't mind! Call me whatever you like! It's just so good to hear your voice. To hear your voice in this house again. It's just wonderful. If I could tell your mother, she'd never believe me." He took Jack's hand and stroked it.

Jack said, "Thank you, sir. It's good to be here."

And his father said, "Oh yes. Well, I hope so. That's another matter entirely, isn't it. Yes, it is." He patted Jack's hand and released it. "There's not much I can do about it. That's how it is." He said, "I know Glory got her feelings hurt something terrible. Terrible." He shook his head.

Jack looked at her, almost as if he had just learned something about her that was not perfectly obvious. Or maybe it was to see her reaction, to confirm his sense of things. How should she react? Her father understood much more than his happiness could abide with, and he was very old.

"I'll start supper," she said.

THE NEXT MORNING JACK WAS OUT IN THE GARDEN EARLY, cutting back weeds and spading up the soil. The old prairie came back the minute a spot of ground fell into neglect. Suddenly there would be weeds head high, gaunt shafts of plants with masses of tiny flowers on them, dusty lavender, droning with bees. And there would be black-eyed Susan, and nettles and milkweed and jewelweed and brambles and some avid vine that wilted in sunlight and broke at the slightest touch, leaving tiny whiskers of thorn in the hand that touched it. The roots they put down were deep and tough. It was miserable work to get them up. And here was Jack outside in the new morning light wrestling weeds out of the ground for all the world as if something depended on it. Glory made a pot of coffee and carried a cup of it out to him.

"I am working up an appetite," he said. "Today I will eat. Tonight I will sleep." He stood the spade in the ground and sipped the coffee. "Excellent. Thank you." They saw the little Ames boy in the road, walking along with his friend Tobias, the two of them elaborating a tale or a joke of some sort, to judge by the laughter. Robby saw them and shouted, "Hey, Mr. Boughton!"

Jack said, "I guess that's me." He handed her the cup and walked down to the foot of the garden. He said, "Whatcha got there, kiddo? Is that a baseball?"

"No," he said, holding it up. "It's just a ball."

Jack said, "Close enough. Chuck it here."

The boy threw the ball a few feet into the garden. Jack dropped down on one knee in the dirt and scooped it up, and made as if to fire it back to him, then lobbed it gently into the road. The boys laughed. Tobias said, "My turn. Let me throw it this time." And again, the ball fell into the garden. Jack picked it up, then drew himself up sidelong, formal as a matador, held the ball to his chest in both hands, and sited at Tobias along his shoulder. The boys giggled. Jack lifted his foot—"The windup, the pitch"—and lobbed the ball into the road. They laughed and stamped and shouted, "Do that again!" and threw him the ball, but he tossed it back and said, "Sorry, gentlemen. Another time. There is work to be done."

Tobias said, "Are you his cousin?" and Robby said, "I already told you he isn't my cousin!" and the two of them said goodbye and went off down the road, talking and laughing.

Jack watched them. "They seem like good kids. Nice kids."

Then he brushed at the dirt on his pant leg. "I really shouldn't have done that," he said.

Glory thought, That strange and particular grace a man's body seems never to forget. Scooping up grounders and throwing sidearm. When her brothers were at home, even Jack would play baseball. That may have been why they were all so taken up with it. Even Jack could be drawn into arguments about records and statistics. He would sit around the radio with the rest of them to listen to the games. And sometimes when he played on a team he would make a beautiful catch or lay down a perfect bunt, exactly sufficient to circumstance as he never was elsewhere, and there would be a general happiness that included him, for a little while at least. She had forgotten all that.

She said, "It's good of you to clear this out. I had more or less decided to let it go back to nature." He had even cleared the weeds out of the place by the fence where gourds reseeded themselves year after year.

"Well," he said, "at least now it will be a lot easier for the birds to find the strawberries." He had always had a kind of hectic high-spiritedness that came over him when he ought to have been sad, and there it was, the strange old glitter in his eyes, the old brusqueness in his manner. What could have made him sad? He brushed again at the smudge on his knee and shrugged and said, "'When Adam delved and Eve span, who was then the gentleman?'"

"But you do need some work clothes."

"Oh yes," he said. "Bib overalls. I have always admired them."

"You know what I mean. Something I could throw in the wash. Or you could."

He nodded, and took out a cigarette and lighted it. He said, "I am a stranger in a strange land. I might as well look like one, don't you think?"

"It doesn't matter to me. They're your trousers."

"Yes," he said. "So they are. Good of you to point that out." And he tossed his cigarette and went back to delving. That was a little flippant, she thought. She went into the kitchen to peel potatoes for a salad.

After a while he came into the porch and the kitchen and stood by the door.

"I'm sorry," he said.

"What for?"

"When we were talking just now. I think I may have seemed—flippant."

"No. Not at all."

"That's good," he said. "I didn't mean to. I can never be sure." Then he went outside again.

When she went out to the garden for chives and parsley, she saw the Reverend Ames strolling up the street. Jack said, "I guess he's decided I'll be around for a while. No point trying to avoid me."

Glory said, "Papa's been storing up so many grievances against John Foster Dulles I was beginning to wonder if he could survive another day without Ames to grumble at."

"Then he won't expect us to contribute to the conversation. That's good," he said. "I'm filthy."

GLORY WENT UP TO THE ATTIC, THE LIMBO OF THINGS that had been displaced from current use but were not in the strict sense useless. If civilization were to collapse, for example, there might be every reason to be glad for this hoard of old shoes and bent umbrellas, all of which would be better than nothing, however badly they might fare in any other comparison. Other pious families gave away the things they did not need. Boughtons put them in the attic, as if to make an experiment of doing without them before they undertook some irreparable act of generosity. Then, what with the business of life and the passage of time, what with the pungency of mothballs and the inevitable creep of dowdiness through any stash of old clothes, however smart they might have been when new, it became impossible to give the things away. From time to time their mother would come down from the attic empty-handed, brushing dust off herself, and write a check to the orphans' home.

So, Glory thought, the shirts her father had worn before he began to lose weight and height were no doubt in the attic, too. She found them in a cedar chest, laundered and ironed as if for some formal event, perhaps their interment. They had changed to a color milder than white, and there was about them, besides the smell of time and disuse, of starch and lavender and cedar, a hint of Old Spice that brought tears to her eyes. She took six of them, the newest, to judge by the cut of the cuffs and collars, and brought them down to the kitchen, hoping to get them washed, at least, before Jack saw them. But he was there, in the kitchen, rummaging in a drawer. He closed it. He said, "I was just looking for a tape measure. I thought I might get some chicken wire and fence in that garden." It made her uneasy that he always seemed to feel he had to make an account of himself to her.

"I found these shirts of Papa's in the attic. I thought you could use them if you wanted to. Around the house. They're good broadcloth."

He stepped back and smiled. "What is that? Cedar? Starch? Lilies? Candle wax? Isn't the phrase 'the odor of sanctity'? I would not presume."

She said, "I'm pretty sure the odor of sanctity will come out in the wash," and he laughed. "I'll try the effects of detergent and sunshine and then I'll ask you again."

"I've put you to a lot of trouble."

"It's no trouble."

He nodded. "You really are kind to me," he said, almost objectively, as though he finally felt he could justify that conclusion.

"Thank you," she said.

SHE DECIDED TO WALK TO THE GROCERY STORE WHILE THE shirts were in the washing machine and her father was content with the new issue of *Christian Century*. It was time she stopped avoiding ordinary contact with people. If Jack could brave it, certainly she could, too. It was a beautiful afternoon, bright, warm, and the leaves still had a glitter of newness about them. She had almost forgotten weather, between her father and her novels and her unaccountable insistence on reading them in the darkest room in the house, excepting only the dining room, beside that tedious radio. The store was almost empty, the cashier was cordial. She started home again through the radiant day with a brown paper bag in her arms, redolent of itself and the cabbage she had bought and the Cheddar cheese, thinking she had done herself a little good, just getting out. She decided to put *Andersonville* aside for a day or two.

Jack was standing on the pavement with his hands on his hips, looking in the window of the hardware store. There were always two television sets in the window, a portable and a console, and they ran all day, test pattern to test pattern. This had been true for years, from the time television was a curiosity. A woman stopped beside him and watched for a minute. She said something to him, and he nodded and spoke, and then she went on. Glory walked up to him and stood beside him. He touched his hat brim, never looking away from the screen.

She said, "Is that Montgomery?"

He nodded. "Yes, it is." Then the screen showed a tube of toothpaste.

Glory said, "Lila told me their church was planning to get a TV set so that Ames can watch baseball. I suppose that means Papa will want one, too."

He looked at her. "That's an idea." He took her package from her and they began to walk home. He said, "A portable is a couple hundred dollars. But you could ask him about it."

"I could just have them deliver one to the house. If he doesn't like it, they'll take it back."

He cleared his throat. "You could do that now."

"Yes, I could. Do you want to help me choose one?"

"Not really. I'll wait here." He laughed. "I've already spent about an hour in there looking at them. They all seem to work."

So she went back to the store and chose an eighteen-inch Philco with a rabbit-ear antenna. The clerk asked after her father and her brothers and sisters and after Jack, too. "Is he home for a visit, or is he thinking he might stay?"

Glory said, for brevity's sake, "He's just visiting for a while." If she'd said she didn't know what had brought him back to Gilead, the strangeness of his situation would have interested the clerk, and the owner of the store, who came out of the back room wiping machine oil from his fingers. Interested them more than it did already. She imagined Jack standing among the bins of nails and tool belts and the ranks of crowbars, unspoken to beyond the ordinary courtesies, seeming unaware of their awareness of him, watching flickering television in that cave full of the smells of leather and wood and oily metal, idle among all those implements of force and purpose, citified among the steel-toed boots and the work shirts. An odd place for a man to loiter who was so alive to embarrassment, so predisposed to sensing even the thought of rebuke. And when he did leave the store, standing on the pavement, looking in at the window, at the silently fulminating authorities and the Negro crowds.

Well, the clerk told her, the Philco would be delivered that afternoon, and if the Reverend decided to keep it, an antenna would be installed on the roof whenever he gave the word. The owner reassured her on precisely these same points. People had always been eager to accommodate her father, and to give even ordinary transactions like this one the aspect of exceptional kindness. So she was obliged to answer every question and to accept every assurance twice at least. They told her that many of the older folks find television a great comfort. They agreed that the baseball season was shaping up. And she was obliged to hear a little gossip.

Jack had stood a long time with his arms full of groceries

96

when she could finally leave the store. "So that worked out," he said. "Good. Thank you." He let her take a bottle of milk to make the bag less awkward, and they walked home.

Jack set the television on a lamp table in the parlor. He plugged it in, turned it on, and moved the antenna around one way and another until a passable image presented itself. Their father came in and sat down in an armchair Jack had turned and pushed into place in front of the set.

"So here it is," the old man said. "We're very modern now." He watched without comment a woman in high heels running back and forth across a stage carrying eggs in a teaspoon while a gigantic clock ticked.

Glory said, "The news will be on soon, Papa."

"Well, yes, I was about to say there isn't much to this. But you can hear people laughing. I hope there's money involved. To get a grown woman to act like that."

The phone rang and Jack came into the kitchen while she answered it, but it was Luke, so he went back to watch the beginning of the news. He was standing in the middle of the room with his hands on his hips. On the screen white police with riot sticks were pushing and dragging black demonstrators. There were dogs.

His father said, "There's no reason to let that sort of trouble upset you. In six months nobody will remember one thing about it."

Jack said, "Some people will probably remember it."

"No. It wasn't so long ago that everybody was talking about Senator McCarthy. Watching those fellows argue. It's television that makes things seem important, whether they are or not. Now you never hear a word about Senator McCarthy."

Jack said, "Well, that's important, isn't it?"

"I can't disagree. I don't know. I never admired him."

Police were pushing the black crowd back with dogs, turning fire hoses on them. Jack said, "Jesus Christ!"

His father shifted in his chair. "That kind of language has never been acceptable in this house."

Jack said, "I—" as if he had been about to say more. But he stopped himself. "Sorry."

On the screen an official was declaring his intention to enforce the letter of the law. Jack said something under his breath, then glanced at his father.

The old man said, "I do believe it is necessary to enforce the law. The Apostle Paul says we should do everything 'decently and in order.' You can't have people running around the streets like that."

Jack snapped off the TV. He said, "Sorry. I was just kind of—"

"No need to be sorry, Jack. Young people want the world to change and old people want it to stay the same. And who is to judge between thee and me? We just have to forgive each other." After a moment he said, "But I hope we don't have to argue. I don't like the shouting and I don't like the swearing. Especially the swearing." He said, "I know those words don't mean much to you. They do to me. You could respect that."

"Yes, sir." Jack stepped away and felt in his shirt pocket for his pack of cigarettes. His hand trembled. He stopped in the doorway and looked back at his father. The old man sat bowed in his chair, his head forward, the deeply cleft nape of his neck exposed under the thin tousle of hair. He might have been praying, but anyone who did not know him well could think he was simply sad and frail. Jack glanced at Glory. "Did I do that to him?" The scar under his eye was white.

"He's tired."

He said, "I shouldn't have said what I did. But things keep getting worse—"

"He'll be all right when he's had some sleep."

"No. No, I mean the dogs. The fire hoses. *Fire* hoses. There were *kids*—" He gave her that distant, appraising look, as if to see the effect of trusting her so far.

"Are you thinking of going back to St. Louis? None of that will be a problem for you if you stay here."

He laughed. "Oh, Glory, it's a problem. Believe me. It's a problem."

He went upstairs, came down again for a book, brought the book back down in half an hour and put it by the radio. He stood in the porch and smoked, and then he said, "Back in a while," and left. She kept his supper warm. Her father could not be persuaded to take even a bite of his. "I have never heard him speak that way. No, he was always respectful, as far as that goes. Here in my house. I may have made too much of it. No, it's something I don't feel I should tolerate."

When Jack came in, his father was still at the table, brooding over his cold soup. "Don't bother," he said, when Jack offered to help him with his chair. "Glory is here. She will look after me."

When she came back into the kitchen, Jack was standing in the porch. He said, "It's nice out here. Dark."

She went out and stood beside him.

He cleared his throat. "Can I ask you something?"

"Probably."

"It's nothing personal."

"All right."

"Say you do something terrible. And it's done. And you can't change it. Then how do you live the rest of your life? What do you say about it?"

"Do I know what terrible thing we're talking about?"

He nodded. "Yes. You do know. When I was out walking the other day I took a wrong turn and ended up at the cemetery." He said, "I'd forgotten she was there."

"She was part of the family."

He nodded.

"All I can tell you is what Papa would say. He'd say repent, and then—you can put it aside, more or less, and go on. You've probably heard him say that as often as I have."

"More often." Then he said, "Regret doesn't count, I suppose."

"I don't claim to know about these things. It seems to me that regret should count. Whatever that means."

"But if you just found out about it, no matter whether I regretted or repented—what would you think of me?"

"What can I say? You're my brother. If I were someone else, and I knew you and thought you were all right, then that would matter more to me than something that happened so many years ago."

"Even though I had never told you about it. And I should have told you."

"I think so."

He nodded. "You're not being kind."

"I don't really know."

"Well, I might have a chance. Things could work out." He said, "It will be bad at best. A miserable thing to have to hope for. Pain all around. Ah, little sister. It's no wonder I can't sleep."

The television set stayed on the lamp table. Jack turned it on for the morning, noon, and evening news, and turned it off again if there was nothing about Montgomery. His father ignored it completely.

FOR YEARS, BEFORE GLORY CAME HOME AND WITHOUT regard to the occasional pious attentions of family returned for holidays, Lila had gone up to the cemetery to look after the Boughtons as well as the Ameses. Glory noticed a special tenderness toward the first Mrs. Ames and her child, who had passed from the world together so long ago, and toward the other little girl about whom, in that gentle, worldly way of hers, Lila seemed neither to know nor to wonder. Snowdrops, crocuses, jonquils. Jack might have seen late tulips or creeping phlox. That was probably good, Glory thought. She would tell him, if he asked, that the flowers were Lila's, so he would not think they meant endless mourning so much as the wish to somehow compensate a child for missing seventy springs, or perhaps to offer delight to her perpetual childhood—she wondered if Lila would ever tell her what all the flowers meant, except kindness, and love of the lives, past and present, into which she had chosen to adopt herself, as if finally at home. She would probably smile and say, The soil is better there, or That spot gets more sun. But Glory was pleased that Jack must first have thought how pretty the place was, and then have looked to see who was cared for so lovingly. It must have been some comfort to him, though she knew no comfort was ever sufficient.

Maybe great sorrow or guilt is simply to be accepted as absolute, like revelation. My iniquity/punishment is greater than I can bear. In the Hebrew, her father said, that one word had two meanings and we chose one of them, which may make it harder for us to understand why the Lord would have pardoned Cain and protected him, and let him go on with his life, marry, have a son, build a city. His crime was his punishment, which had to mean he wasn't such a villain after all. She might mention this to Jack sometime, if it ever seemed to her a conversation had arrived at a point where she could dare, could summon delicacy enough, to compare him to Cain. She laughed at herself. What a thought.

GLORY HAD KEPT MOST OF THE HABITS OF HER PIOUS youth. Morning and evening she took her Bible out to the porch and read two or three chapters. When the others were at home for the holidays, they would sit around the table in the dining room and one of them would read aloud from the Psalms or the Gospels. Like most of their obligations and many of their pleasures, this was, whatever else, a performance meant to please their father, to assure him that they loved the old life, that they had received all the good he had intended for them. To please him was so potent a motive that it displaced motives of her own, which no doubt would have included piety. During the years she lived alone she had read the Bible morning and evening with the thought that her father would be pleased if he knew, and also to remember who she was, to remember the household she came from, to induce in herself the unspecific memory of a comfort she had not really been conscious of until she left it behind. Now, back in her father's house, as she read she remembered that same comfort, and remembered as well the privilege of distance and solitude, the satisfactions of that other life.

What a strange old book it was. How oddly holiness situated itself among the things of the world, how endlessly creation wrenched and strained under the burden of its own significance. "I will open my mouth in a parable. I will utter dark sayings of old, which we have heard and known, and our fathers have told us." Yes, there it was, the parable of manna. All bread is the bread of heaven, her father used to say. It expresses the will of God to sustain us in this flesh, in this life. Weary or bitter or bewildered as we may be, God is faithful. He lets us wander so we will know what it means to come home.

What does it mean to come home? Glory had always thought home would be a house less cluttered and ungainly than this one, in a town larger than Gilead, or a city, where someone would be her intimate friend and the father of her children, of whom she would have no more than three. Then she could learn what her own tastes were, within the limits of their means, of course. She would not take one stick of furniture from her father's house, since none of it would be comprehensible in those spare, sunlit rooms. The walnut furbelows and carved draperies and pilasters, the inlaid urns and flowers. Who had thought of putting actual feet on chairs and sideboards, actual paws and talons?

She had dreamed of a real home for herself and the babies, and the fiancé, a home very different from this good and blessed and fustian and oppressive tabernacle of Boughton probity and kind intent. She knew, she had known for years, that she would never open a door on that home, never cross that threshold, never scoop up a pretty child and set it on her hip and feel it lean into her breast and eye the world from her arms with the complacency of utter trust. Ah well.

Once, Jack had come into the porch and found her sitting there reading the Bible. He seemed pleasantly embarrassed and asked pardon for interrupting, and she said he was more than welcome to stay if he liked, so he took the chair next to hers and opened the newspaper. But he leaned over to see where she was reading. "Psalms," he said. "An excellent choice."

"Yes," she said.

"Sorry."

"I'm almost finished." She could feel that he was aware of her, restless enough to distract her, so she put the ribbon to mark her place and closed the book. He recrossed his ankles and rustled the paper. So she said, "What is it?"

"Oh. Sorry. Really just a sort of interest, I suppose. In the fact that you still do that sort of thing. That you always used to do. Not that I wouldn't expect you to. I don't mean that. In fact, I'm always a little surprised by things I would have expected. When they happen. If that makes sense."

"I think it does."

"Do you still, um, pray"—he gestured at the floor— "down on your knees?"

She laughed. "None of your business."

"I remember when you were little, you'd kneel by your bed and close your eyes and whisper things into your hands. Secrets. Hope's cat threw up on the rug. Johnny said a bad word. And we would sit there and listen to it all and try to be very serious about it." He laughed.

"You listened to my prayers?"

"Hope did, and Dan. I heard them laughing about it. So I came in a few times."

"I can only apologize."

"No point in it. The damage is done. The Lord will use the information as he sees fit, come Judgment."

She said, "I'm surprised you remember so much."

He shrugged. "I lived here, too."

"All I mean is that when everybody comes home for holidays we go over the old stories again. I doubt that we would remember half of them if we didn't remind each other three or four times a year."

"I've thought about this place. Sometimes I've even talked about it."

There was a silence. Then he said, "So. Are you going to try to save my soul, little sister?"

"What? Save your soul? Why would I do that?"

"Why not? It seems like a genteel occupation for a pious lady. I thought you might want to do me that kindness. Since you have a little time on your hands."

She looked at him. He was smiling. She knew him well enough to know that he smiled when he thought he might offend, whether intentionally or unintentionally. He could seem to be laughing at himself, or at her.

She said, "I'd be happy to oblige, but I have no idea how to go about it."

"Well," he said, "I'm willing to confess to a certain spiritual hunger. I think that's usually the first step. So that's out of the way."

"And then?"

"Then I think it is usual to ponder great truths. That has been my experience."

"Such as?"

"The fatherhood of God, for one. The idea being that the splendor of creation and of the human creature testify to a gracious intention lying behind it all, that they manifest divine mercy and love. Which sustains the world in general and is present in the experience of, you know, people whose souls are saved. Or will be." After a moment he said, "It is possible to know the great truths without feeling the truth of them. That's where the problem lies. In my case." He looked at her.

She said, "I'm flummoxed. I'll have to give this some thought."

"Yes. Well, it is a lot to spring on you, I know. I always nourish the suspicion that pious folk are plotting my rescue. Now and then it has been true. Not so often, really. But you are my sister. So it seemed worthwhile to inquire. Just to save time." He smiled.

She said, "I think I like your soul the way it is."

He looked at her and laughed, and his color rose. "Thanks, Glory. That's no help at all, but I do appreciate it. I really do."

GLORY MADE UP A BATCH OF BREAD DOUGH. BROWN BREAD was her father's preference. Something to lift the spirits of the household, she thought. The grocer brought her a roasting hen. She opened the windows to cool the kitchen and air out the dining room a little, and the breezes that came in were mild, earthy, grassy, with a feel of sunlight about them.

Jack came in from the barn, bringing with him a whiff of old straw and sweat and crankcase oil. He took a deep breath. "Ah! Bread!" She lifted the towel so he could see the speckled belly of the rising dough. Then he held up his hands to her, which were oily and grimy, and said, "Don't touch those potatoes!" He went upstairs. There were sounds of haste and ablution, and then he came back down with his shirt half buttoned and his hair wet. He found a knife. "Blunt as a poker," he said, but he set to paring. "It is art that keeps the demons at bay!" This was to bring home to her the significance of a long spiral of peeling he had removed intact.

"Amazing," she said.

He said, "Practice."

"Were you quoting?"

He nodded. "*La Sagesse de Jacques Bouton*. Bouton de la Rose, that is. *Poète maudit. Poète malgré lui.* Roué and—kitchen help. For some reason they didn't teach the French for that in college." He held up another spiral of peel. "Pity," he said. "Things sound so much better in French—*pomme de terre, fait-néant, voleur*—" He smiled. "My intellectual lady friend was set on keeping up her French. So I summoned what little I could of mine. We read

105

L'Education sentimentale. My enthusiasm for the project was almost unfeigned."

"Your friends are more interesting than mine."

"You must know where to find your friends, *ma petite*."

"And where is that?"

"If you are very, very good I might tell you. Someday. But you must be exceptionally good."

She laughed. "God knows I try."

He said, "That's a beginning, I suppose. Though not in every case."

She raised the tea towel and punched the dough, and a great sigh of yeasty air breathed out of it. After a minute he said, "I've been into the cash drawer again. I bought some spark plugs and a tire pump. The old one leaked so much it was almost useless. And a fan belt."

"You don't have to tell me about these things."

"And a baseball glove."

"That money isn't mine, either, Jack. And Papa doesn't care about it."

He nodded, delicately gouging out a potato's eye. He smiled at her. "A diligent and humiliating search for employment has persuaded me that I have to look beyond Gilead," he said. "I'll need a car. If I'm ever to become a respectable family man."

"So you're thinking that woman friend might come here?"

He shook his head. "Only when I'm trying to find a way to make myself go out and shop my miserable aspirations around town one more time. Or keep tinkering with that damn car. She'd probably hate it here, anyway."

"You've never told me her name."

"Her name is Della."

"I'd like to know her."

He said, "Would you be kind to her?"

"What a question!"

"Swear to God?"

"Of course! I'd be a sister to her!"

He laughed. "I'm going to hold you to that someday. If my wildest hopes are fulfilled. Which they won't be."

After a minute she said, "Jack, there's something I've been wondering about."

"Hmm?"

"What do you act like when you're happy?"

He laughed. "I forget."

"Seriously. When you came in just now, I thought something good must have happened."

"Oh. How to account for the high spirits. Gasoline fumes? And I have replaced so much of that engine that I must be closing in on the problem by now. With any luck. When I turned the key this time it—chortled. And that triggered a fantasy of charging off in my father's DeSoto to rescue my lady love from a smoldering Memphis."

"I thought she was in St. Louis."

He shrugged. "I'm a little tired of St. Louis. I'd rather rescue her from Memphis."

"I see."

"On second thought, her father is in Memphis. He's very protective, and he has a car that actually runs. And he thinks I'm damn near worthless—'damn near,' because he's professionally obligated to take a charitable view. She has three brothers in Memphis. So I guess I'd better rescue her from St. Louis." He began to peel another potato. "Joking aside, maybe she would come to Gilead for a while, to give it a try. It's possible."

They had an early supper. She had meant to serve the chicken cold, but she decided it was better to serve the bread while it was still warm, and what difference did it make when they did anything, anyway. Her father enjoyed the warm bread and the chicken, too, and the peas with potatoes in cream sauce. He grew voluble, talking about his own boyhood in Gilead, how, he said, he couldn't even draw water from the well to his grandmother's satisfaction, let alone split kindling, so he didn't have as many chores as other children did. "She never trusted me to bring the eggs in, either," he said. "It was her way of spoiling me. Yes. I used to go over to Ames's and help him out a little, and then we'd have the whole day, in the summer. The whole day by the river. I don't know how we passed all that time. It was wonderful. Sometimes his grandfather would be down there, fishing and talking to Jesus, and then we'd be pretty quiet, or we'd wade upstream a little way. He was a strange old fellow, but he was just a part of life, you know. Like the birds singing."

Jack said, "I spent time at the river. I liked to do that."

His father nodded. "I always thought this was an excellent place to be a child. Not that I had anything to compare it with."

"It is a good place."

"Well, Jack, I'm glad you think so. Yes. Some things might have worked out better than they did, I know that. But there was always a lot to enjoy. That was my feeling, at least. And there still is. I watch the children, and they seem happy to me. I think they should be happy."

AFTER SUPPER JACK CAME DOWNSTAIRS WITH THE NEW baseball mitt, flexing it and folding the pocket. He said, "I thought I'd see if the Ames kid would like to play a little catch. Is that a good idea? He's old enough. He seemed interested."

She said, "I think it's a good idea."

He went out to the porch and stood there for a while, and then he came into the kitchen again. "No," he said. He shrugged. "I'm disreputable. I forget that from time to time. But I have it on excellent authority." He smiled. "The good Reverend wouldn't approve. I'm pretty sure they'll give you your money back." He handed her the glove. "Those high spirits," he said. "They can get me in trouble."

She said, "I don't understand any of this. I think you worry too much. I'll keep the glove until you want it."

"You have to help me think things through, Glory."

"Does that mean remembering that you're disreputable?"

"'Fraid so."

"I think you're imagining."

"It is the central fact of my existence," he said. "One of three, actually. The one you have to help me keep in mind."

"Well, really, Jack. How on earth am I supposed to do that?"

He laughed. "Don't be so kind to me," he said.

SHE THOUGHT ABOUT THE THING JACK HAD SEEMED TO ask of her, some attempt to save his soul. Dear Lord. How could that idea haunt her with a sense of obligation, when she really did not know what it meant. There are words you hear all your life, she thought. Then one day you stop to wonder. She would not bring it up again, but if he did, she should have some way to answer him. She was not at all sure that he had been serious, that he was not teasing her. She might even have taken offense at the time, if there had seemed to be any point in it. A genteel project for a pious lady with time on her hands. How condescending. But that was what he did whenever he felt vulnerable—he found some way to sting, to make it clear that vulnerability was not all on one side. Poor man. But he was so practiced at reciting what he was also practiced at rejecting. He might have meant to draw her into some sort of argument and reject it, too, just to show her he could do it. He was uneasy. That was natural enough. And in fact he had made her embarrassed about that pleasant old habit of hers. Now she had to read the Bible in her room to avoid feeling like a hypocrite, like someone praying on a street corner. When Jack came out to the porch with his newspaper the next day and found her reading *The Dollmaker* he gave her a wistful, inquiring look, but he said nothing.

She did not know what it meant to be pious. She had never been anything else. Remember also thy creator in the days of thy youth. She had done that. She could hardly have done otherwise.

Her father never let a day pass without reminding them that all goodness came from the Lord, all love, all beauty. And failure and fault instructed us in the will of God in the very fact of departing from it. Then there were grace and forgiveness to compensate, to put things right, and these were the greatest goodness of God after creation itself, so far as we mortals can know. Her father's rapt delight in this belief put it beyond question, since it was so intrinsic to his nature, and they loved and enjoyed his nature, and laughed about it a little, too. Yes! He would achieve some triumph of extenuation and emerge from his study, eyes blazing, having solved the riddle, ready to forgive heroically, to go that extra mile. True, the slights and foibles for which he found extenuation necessary may have been minor or even questionable in some cases, evidence of a certain irritability on his part. But the gallantry of his response to them was no less handsome on that account.

As for herself, she did still pray on her knees. She also said or heard or thought a grace at every meal, even at a lunch counter or when she was with the fiancé. Train up a child in the way he should go and even when he is old he will not depart from it. The proverb was true in her case. And being at home only reinforced every habit that had been instilled in her there. Faith for her was habit and family loyalty, a reverence for the Bible which was also literary, admiration for her mother and father. And then that thrilling quiet of which she had never felt any need to speak. Her father had always said, God does not need our worship. We worship to enlarge our sense of the holy, so that we can feel and know the presence of the Lord, who is with us always. He said, Love is what it amounts to, a loftier love, and pleasure in a loving presence. She was pious, no doubt, though she would not have chosen that word to describe herself.

MAYBE SHE KEPT THE BIBLE OUT OF SIGHT BECAUSE SHE was afraid that if he spoke to her that way again she would have to tell him she had no certain notion what a soul is. She supposed it was not a mind or a self. Whatever they are. She supposed it was what the Lord saw when His regard fell upon any of us. But what can we know about that? Say we love and forgive, and enjoy the beauty of another life, however elusive it might be. Then, presumably, we have some idea of the soul we have encountered. That is what her father would say.

Maybe she had never before known anyone who felt, or admitted he felt, that the state of his soul was in question. Whatever might transpire in her father's study, there had been only calm and confidence among his flock, to all appearances. Granting the many perils of spiritual complacency, and her father did grant them as often as Pharisees figured in the text, complacency was consistent with the customs and manners of Presbyterian Gilead and was therefore assumed to be justified in every case. Christian charity demanded no less, after all. Among the denominations of Gilead, charity on this point was not granted by all and to all in principle, but in practice good manners were usually adhered to, and in general the right to complacency was conceded on every side. Even her father's sermons treated salvation as a thing for which they could be grateful as a body, as if, for their purposes at least, that problem had been sorted out between the Druids and the centurions at about the time of Hadrian. He did mention sin, but it was rarefied in his understanding of it, a matter of acts and omissions so commonplace that no one could be wholly innocent of them or especially alarmed by them, either—the uncharitable thought, the neglected courtesy. While on one hand this excused him from the mention of those aspects of life that seemed remotest from Sabbath and sunlight, on the other hand it made the point that the very nicest among them, even the most virtuous, were in no position to pass judgment on anyone else, not on the sly or the incorrigible, not on those who trouble the peace of their families, not on those who might happen to have gotten their names in the newspaper in the past week. The doctrine of total depravity had served him well. Who, after all, could cast that first stone? He could not, he least of all. But it was hard to get a clear view of something so pervasive as to be total, especially if, as her father insisted, it was epitomized in his own estimable person.

She did remember once, when Ames was at dinner years earlier, his mentioning to her father that a local man, unchurched, noted for bursts of rage and for a particular hostility toward children, his own included, had come to the parsonage at midnight to consider his soul. Ames had said, "It's like a bad tooth—it acts up when everybody else is sleeping, and it's not the kind of problem you want to deal with by yourself," and they had laughed together, quietly. Who could know what they knew, what restive hearts had opened to them, how many midnights had brought the sleepless to their doors. She should ask Jack what a soul is, since he seemed to feel the presence of a soul. Cankered, perhaps, but that was what gave him his awareness of it. Either of those prayerful old men, Ames or her father, could probably tell her, too. But it was late to put such a question to them. Jack would laugh at her and tease her, which would be much preferable to their sober, gentle surprise.

HER FATHER WANTED TO GO TO BED EARLY, BUT THEN HE was restless and asked to get up again. She helped him to his chair. "Where is Jack?" he said.

"I think he's working on the car."

After a minute he said, "I thought you might read to me. I'd like you to read from Luke."

She brought the Bible and opened it and began the greeting to Theophilus.

"Yes," her father said. "That's fine. He gives a world of attention to that car. I wish he'd play the piano. Then at least I'd know where he is."

Glory said, "I'll go find him. He'll be happy to play for you, Papa."

"Yes. I'm Saul in his madness. I want some music around here."

She went out to the barn and Jack was there, sitting in the driver's seat of the DeSoto. In the earthy, perpetual evening of the place he was reading a book by flashlight. She hesitated, but he saw her in the sideview mirror and put the book and the flashlight in the glove compartment and closed it. She saw him take the little leather folder, which had been standing open on the dashboard, and slip it into his breast pocket.

"Sorry," she said. "I didn't mean to intrude. Papa's awfully restless and he thought it would help if you played for him a little."

"Always glad to oblige," he said, standing up out of the car and closing the door. He smiled at her the way he did when she had become privy to something he had no intention of explaining. He said, "My home away from home."

"Fine. I wouldn't have bothered you, but he seems to be really uncomfortable this evening. He asked me to read to him, and that lasted about two minutes. I'd have played for him, but he wanted you to do it."

He said, "You never bother me, Glory. It's remarkable how much you don't bother me. Almost unprecedented."

"I'm so happy to know that."

He glanced at her, and when he saw she really was pleased, he smiled.

"Well, Reverend," he said, "Glory tells me you'd like to hear a song or two. Any special requests?"

"Yes. 'Blessed Assurance' and also 'Whispering Hope.' But I think I would be more comfortable lying on my bed, if you don't mind."

"We can take care of that." Jack helped him up, took him to his room, and settled him among his covers.

"First 'Blessed Assurance,'" the old man said. "If you know that one."

"I believe I do." Jack sat down at the piano, tinkered at the keys for a moment, found the tune, and played it through. His father did not sing.

"Now 'Whispering Hope.'"

"Yes, sir."

When the song ended, his father said, "'Making my heart in its sorrow rejoice.' That can actually happen. I have had that experience. Hope is a very valuable thing, since there is not always so much to rejoice about in this life."

Jack went to stand in his father's doorway, to spare him the effort of raising his voice. The old man said, "Come here, Jack. Bring the chair over here. There's something I need to say to you. You're probably going to have to forgive me for this."

"I'll do my best."

"Well, I know that. I can count on that. And you're a grown man now."

Jack laughed. "True."

"So I want to put a question to you. All right?"

"Go ahead."

"I feel I didn't do right by you. I wasn't a good father to you."

"What? Really?"

"No, it's a feeling I have always had, almost since you were a baby. As though there was something you needed from me and I never figured out what it was."

Jack cleared his throat. "I really don't know what to say. I've always thought you were a very good father. Much better than I deserved."

"No, but think about it now. You were always running off somewhere. Always hiding somewhere. Maybe you don't even remember why you did those things. But I thought you might be able to give me some idea."

"I can't explain it. I don't know. I was a bad kid. I'm sorry about all that."

The old man shook his head. "That isn't my meaning at all. You see, I feel as though you haven't had a good life."

Jack laughed. "Oh! Well, I'm sorry about that, too."

"You misunderstand me. I mean your life has never seemed to have any real joy in it. I'm afraid you've never had much in the way of happiness."

"Oh. I see. Well, I've been happy from time to time. Things are a little difficult now—"

"Yes, because you wouldn't be here otherwise. That's all right. I just never knew another child who didn't feel at home in the house where he was born. All the others, you know, they come back for the holidays. It was always like a big party in here, all the games they would play, all the noise they made, and your mother laughing at the endless pranks and the nonsense. And if you could find a way to leave, you'd be gone."

"I can't explain that. I'm sorry about it—"

"And then you really were gone, weren't you. Twenty years, Jack!"

Jack drew a deep breath and said nothing.

"And why am I talking to you about this? But it was always a mystery to me. Be strict! People would say that to me. Lay down the law! Do it for his sake! But I always felt it was sadness I was dealing with, a sort of heavyheartedness. In a child! And how could I be angry at that? I should have known how to help you with it."

"You helped me. I mean, there are worse lives than mine. Mine could be worse." He laughed and put his hand to his face.

"Oh yes. I'm sure of that, Jack. I see how kind you are now. Very polite. I notice that."

"These last years I've been all right. Almost ten years."

"Well, that is wonderful. Now, do you forgive me for speaking to you this way?"

"Yes, sir. Of course I do. I will. If you give me a little time."

The old man said, "You take your time. But I want you to give me your hand now." And he took Jack's hand and moved it gently toward himself, so he could study the face Jack would have hidden from him. "Yes," he said, "here you are." He laid the hand against his chest. "You feel that heart in there? My life became your life, like lighting one candle from another. Isn't that a mystery? I've thought about it many times. And yet you always did the opposite of what I hoped for, the exact opposite. So I tried not to hope for anything at all, except that we wouldn't lose you. So of course we did. That was the one hope I couldn't put aside."

Jack withdrew his hand from his father's and put it to his face again. "This is very difficult," he said. "What can I do—I mean, is there something I can do now?"

"That's true," his father said. "Not a thing to be done. I'm sorry I brought it up. I thought it was troubling my sleep. I guess it was. Why did that make me think it was important? I don't know. All that old grief coming back on me. I'm tired now, though. It seems like I'm always tired." And he settled into his pillows and turned onto his right side, away from Jack, toward the wall.

GLORY CAME OUT TO THE KITCHEN AND WAITED, AND after a few minutes Jack came out, too. "Would you mind just staying here with me for a few minutes, Glory?" he said. "Till I've had some time to check for broken bones." He laughed and rubbed his hands over his face. "Ahh. I'm feeling the impulse to do something unwise. You don't have to sit here until the bars close. Unless you want to."

She said, "I'm happy to sit here as long as you like."

"When do the bars close in this town, on a weeknight? It used to be ten."

"I'm not the one to ask, I'm afraid."

"It's not quite eight o'clock now. Two hours, maybe three. That's a long time."

"Believe me, I have no plans for the evening."

He laughed. "Good."

"Would you like coffee?"

"Coffee? Sure. Do you mind if I smoke?"

"Not at all."

He said, "You should be impressed that I don't know when the bars close. That means I haven't even gone near enough to one of them to read the sign on the door."

She laughed. "I am impressed. Now that you point it out."

"Yes, I think I should draw up a list of my accomplishments. That would be number one. Then: I am not incarcerated. And: I nearly finished college—"

"I thought you finished. We were all going to come to your graduation."

"And then the Reverend got a phone call from St. Louis."

"He said he should have expected that you wouldn't want to go through the ceremony."

"Well, there were some other considerations—some problems, shall we say. Omissions, mainly. Does that surprise you?"

"Not at all," she said.

He shook his head. "I am a monster of consistency, little sister. Though increasingly I realize that the consistency was mostly alcohol. But now I am a changed man, most of the time. For example, I have just told you the truth about something. I owe it all to the influence of a good woman."

She laughed.

He said, "What? Is that so hard to believe?"

"No, no. That's a phrase I used to hear a lot, that's all." She said, "Should I tell you the truth about something?"

"Sure. But you don't have to. This doesn't have to be an exchange of hostages or anything."

"I am giving you a hostage, though. I'm trusting you with this. You have to take it to your grave."

"Will do. On my honor, as they say. If you really want to tell me."

"I think so. I do want to tell you."

"Why?"

"Why? Because you're my brother, I guess. Because I want to see how it sounds when I say it out loud."

"How it sounds to me, or to you? There could be a difference."

"I suppose so. Does that matter?"

"Well, you know, I'm not the ideal sounding board. Especially if there's moral complexity involved. That was never my strong point. You might reveal some embarrassing deficiency in me. One more deficiency—" He laughed. "I'm in enough trouble as it is."

"All right," she said. "No secrets, no confidences." Then, after a minute, she heard herself say, "I was never married."

"Oh?" and he began to laugh, wearily and uncontrollably. "Is that the secret? I'm really sorry. It's because I'm tired," he said, wiping tears from his face.

"My fault," she said. "You gave me fair warning."

"I did, didn't I." The laughter persisted, somewhere between a sob and a cough. "I'm really sorry. The thing is, you know, I'm not married either."

"But no one ever thought you were. I mean, you didn't make people believe that you were."

He laughed into his hands, miserably. "That's true. I never did." Then he said, "I hope you're not mad at me, Glory. I don't know why you wouldn't be. Please don't be mad." He was struggling to catch his breath.

"Oh heck," she said. "I'm going to get you some coffee."

"Heck, yes! Bring on the coffee!" he said, and he laughed.

"I say 'hell' sometimes. If I'm mad. But I'm not mad. I'm just sort of flummoxed."

He said, "I do that. I flummox people. It's really about the best I can hope for, in fact."

"Well, I've gotten pretty used to it. It's actually a little bit interesting, in a way."

"Thank you," he said. "Seriously. I know I did the wrong thing, laughing like that." He shook his head ruefully, and laughed. "You're a good soul, Glory."

"I am," she said.

"I know that what happened to you was bad. I was an idiot to laugh."

"It was very bad. One midnight I went out and dropped four hundred fifty-two letters down a storm drain."

He laughed. "Four hundred fifty-two!"

"It was a long engagement. A policeman saw me and came over to ask me what I was doing. I told him I was throwing away four hundred fifty-two love letters and one cheap ring. He said, 'Well, I sure hope things work out for you.'" They laughed. "I'm all right," she said. "It was all horrible enough to be funny, I suppose. Now that it's over."

"Yes, there's always that to look forward to." Then he shrugged and said, "It's enough to make me hope there's a minute or two between death and perdition."

"Oh come on, Jack. I don't really think you get to believe in perdition unless you believe in all the rest of it."

"No? But perdition is the one thing that always made sense to me. I mean, it has always seemed plausible. On the basis of my experience. And I don't think this is a good time to try to talk me out of it. I'm tired. I'm sober—" He laughed, and she glanced at her watch. "Let me guess," he said. "Eight-twenty-eight."

"Eight-seventeen."

"If you tire of my company, I'll understand."

"No, not at all. Could I make you some supper?"

"I just had supper."

"No, you didn't. I watched. Six bites of potato."

"I haven't had much appetite, I guess."

"Well, I have news for you, Cary Grant. Your pants have begun to bag."

"Ah. You have mastered the art of persuasion. A scrambled egg then?"

"And toast."

"And toast."

Jack sat at the table, twitching his foot. He cleared his throat. "What?"

"Nothing," he said. "Not a thing." Then, after a minute,

"Correct me if I'm wrong, but I believe I have just been told that I am not the only sinner in this family." And then he laughed and put his hand to his face. "Now, that was probably a mistake. What a fool I am."

Glory said, "Well then, let's just say you're not the only fool in the family." She broke an egg into the frying pan.

"But you haven't told the Reverend about this, I take it."

"How can you even ask?"

He nodded. "That's what I thought."

"Stupidity isn't a sin, so far as I know. But it ought to be one. It feels like one. I can forgive myself all the rest of it."

"You can forgive yourself."

"Yes, I can."

"Interesting."

She glanced at her watch.

He said, "We'll change the subject."

Then he said, as if taking upon himself the effort of sustaining conversation, "That woman in St. Louis I mentioned—she sang in the choir at her church, of course. And sometimes, if the lady who played piano for them couldn't come to practice, I'd fill in for her. I'd come anyway, just to listen. That old lady could really play, but she was kind. She taught me as much as I could learn. I played for their service a few times. I used to come into the church on weeknights to use the piano, and so long as the music wasn't too worldly, they didn't mind. I could have made a decent living playing in bars, but they were—well, they were bars. So I hung around at her church. It was all right. I mean, I was happy then." He looked at her, smiled at her. "Why are you laughing? You don't believe me."

"Sure, I believe you. I've been wondering where you learned to play those hymns so well."

"There it is. Proof of my veracity. And you're laughing anyway."

"It's because I met, you know, the man I didn't marry, at a

choir rehearsal. He was passing in the street, he said, and he heard the music, and it took him back to the sweetest moments of his childhood. He hoped we would not mind if he stood very quietly and listened for a while."

"Why, what a cad. 'Sweetest moments of his childhood.' I could have warned you. That one phrase would have given him away."

"Yes, no doubt. But at the time I didn't know if you were alive or dead. So I couldn't avail myself of your wisdom."

"True." Jack cleared his throat. He cleared it again. "I wouldn't want you to think I was hovering around choir rehearsals looking for vulnerable women. I met my—the woman I mentioned—as I was walking by her apartment building one day. It was raining and she was coming home from school—she was also an English teacher. She dropped some papers and I helped her gather them up. And so on. I'd found an umbrella on a park bench a couple of days before, and here was a lady needing rescue. We became friends almost without calculation or connivance on my part. It was all very respectable. It was."

She said, "'Looking for vulnerable women.'"

"Oh well, that isn't quite what I meant."

"That is what he was doing, though. You're exactly right. It's only that I had never put it to myself in just those words."

"Sorry." He smiled and touched his hand to his face. She thought, Why has he turned pale? Then he said, "You know, by vulnerable I suppose I really meant—religious. Yes. Pious girls have tender hearts. They believe sad stories. So I have heard. All to their credit, of course. And they usually lead sheltered lives. Little real knowledge of the world. They are brought up to think someone ought to love them for that sort of thing, their virtue and so on. And they are ready to believe anyone who tells them about, you know, his angel mother, and how the thought of her piety has been a beacon shining through the darkest storms of life. So I have been told. And often, on a cold night, there will be cake and coffee, absolutely free of charge. That can bring out the hypocrite in a fellow, if he has a thin coat or a hole in his shoe. As I understand." Then he said, "If I had a daughter, I wouldn't let her go anywhere near a choir rehearsal."

She said nothing.

Jack stood up. "Yes," he said, "well. There's still a little bit of daylight. I'd better go make myself useful, hadn't I. Earn my bread in the sweat of my brow, as they say." He stopped by the door and stood there, watching her. After a long moment he said, "I know I should leave this town. But I can't leave yet."

"Sit down, Jack. No one wants you to leave. Papa doesn't, and I don't."

He said, "Well, that's good of you. Good of you to say."

"Not really. I appreciate the company." She laughed. "All my life I've wanted your attention. I've wanted to talk with you. It's the curse of the little sister, I suppose. I knew it would be hard. That was always clear enough."

He shrugged. "I'm glad to know I'm living up to expectations."

She said, "Papa's right, of course. Neither one of us would be here if we weren't in some kind of—difficulty. So there's not much point in pretending otherwise, at least when he's asleep. I'd have been afraid of the word 'vulnerable,' but it didn't kill me to hear you say it. So now I know that."

"You're welcome," he said.

Then she said, "She's the one you write to, the woman you mentioned?"

He smiled. "Why, yes, I write to her. I did just this morning. Dropped a tear where I had signed my name. It was tap water, really, but the thought is what counts. That was letter two hundred eight."

"All right," she said. "Sorry I asked."

"I'm afraid," he said, very softly, "that sometime you really might be sorry. I mean, if you got to know me well enough, you might not want me around. You might even ask me to leave." He smiled. "Then what would I do? Who would keep me out of trouble?"

"Well, Jack," she said, "I don't think I have to tell you where I've heard that before."

"That, too!" He shrugged. "In my case at least you know there is an element of truth in it. There probably was in his case as well."

She thought, How very weary he looks. So she said, "Do you remember the time you paid me a dime to stop crying? I was home with the mumps, and I was wretched with boredom. I thought everyone else was at school. But you came out of your room, and you took a dime from your pocket, and you said you would give it to me if I stopped crying. So I did. And then pretty soon you came back and paid me a nickel to stop hiccuping. And then you gave me another nickel after I promised not to tell where I got the money."

"Well," he said, "good for me, I suppose. Is that your point?"

"Yes, it is. I was very pleased—I meant to keep those coins, in fact, but I believe I spent them on gum. I'm sure I did keep them for a week or two."

"So. It sounds as though I bought myself some time. Maybe a little patience."

"Some loyalty."

"Excellent. What a bargain." He laughed. "If you think of anything else that redounds to my credit, let me know."

"And you taught me the word 'waft.'"

"Well, don't tell me everything at once. I wouldn't want to exhaust my capital."

"Then sit down," she said. She gave him the egg and toast and refilled his coffee cup and sat down across the table from him. He ate dutifully and said no thank you when she asked him if he would like more. They were silent for a while. "It's almost nine," she said.

Jack washed his plate and cup and put them away, and he sat down again.

Glory said, "How could you think you were the only sinner in the family? We're Presbyterians!"

"Yes, 'we have all sinned and fallen short.'" He laughed. "Talk is cheap." Then he said, "I mean, you have to admit that there is a difference between my tarnished self and, say, Dr. Theodore D. W. Boughton."

She said, "Teddy's all right. He means well."

"Despite his virtues and accomplishments."

"Yes. In a way, that's true."

They laughed.

Jack said, "Maybe there is no justice in the world after all. What a wonderful thought."

She shrugged. "Depending on circumstances."

Jack put his hand to his face. "Ah yes. Circumstances. The scene of the crime. The corpus delicti."

She glanced at her watch.

After a minute Jack said, "I suppose I should look in on the Reverend. I miss the old fellow. Two weeks ago he'd have been out here by now with the checkerboard. And on his way back to bed again."

She nodded. "I really don't think we'll have him much longer."

"Well. What will you do then?"

"Teach. Somewhere. Not here, I hope. I like teaching." Then she said, "You've seen Teddy since you left home?"

"Oh yes. Once. He came to St. Louis and hunted me down. He walked around the back streets with a couple of photographs until he found someone who recognized me. It took him days. That was a long time ago. He was just out of medical school. And I was—not in very good shape. That may have been my nadir, in fact. We sat on a bench and ate sandwiches together. He asked me to come home with him, but I declined. He offered me some money, and I took it. A miserable experience for both of us. He never talked about it?"

"Not so far as I know."

"I made him promise he wouldn't. And wouldn't come looking for me again. He didn't do that either. At least he didn't find me." He laughed. "Those photographs wouldn't have been much use after a while."

"He's a man of his word."

Jack nodded. "There's a lot I could regret," he said. "If there were any point in it."

"He'll be here at Christmas. Thanksgiving, too, if he can get away. With Corinne, who never stops talking. The children are nice."

Jack shuddered. "So many strangers. People whose names I wouldn't know."

"Six in-laws. Twenty-two children. And six of them are married, so six more in-laws. Five grandchildren."

"All in this house?"

"A good many of them."

"Whew!" He pondered this. "So you have been coming home all these years?"

"Most of them."

"With—hmm—with your fiancé?"

She looked at her watch.

He laughed and pushed back his chair. "Yes, I was going to check on the old gent, wasn't I."

He got up and went down the hall, and after a few minutes she heard the front door open and, quietly, close. Oh! she thought. Of course. I should have known. Now I sit here and wait till he comes back. No. I sit here for twenty minutes. Why do that? Because he might come back by then, and if I have gone upstairs, he will know what I was thinking, and that would not be good. Still, why would he sneak off like that? But what can it hurt to wait twenty minutes? Half an hour? I will not go looking for him.

That would be ridiculous. Especially if he went outside for some other reason. As if there were any other reason, at this time of night. I will give him half an hour.

In twenty minutes she heard the door open and close. He came in and sat down, smiled, shrugged. "I stepped out for a smoke," he said.

"I don't mind if you smoke in the house. Papa wouldn't mind."

He said, "I stepped out for a stroll."

"Fine."

He said, "I stepped out for a drink. But I never actually left the porch."

"Good for you."

"Yes," he said. "Good for me." He smiled.

"And how is the old gent?"

He shook his head. "Well, you know, he's old. I don't know why, but I can't quite get used to it. When we were kids, he was taller than Ames, wasn't he? He was very impressive. He used to seem to me to loom over everybody. And he had that big laugh. I was proud of him, I really was."

"We were all proud of him."

"Of course."

"And we were proud of you."

He looked at her. "Why do I find that hard to believe?"

"No, really. Not always. And it got a little harder over time." He laughed. "But we thought you were, I don't know, chimerical, piratical, mercurial—"

He said, "I was a nuisance and a brat. I was a scoundrel."

"Well," she said, "you know more than I do about the particulars. I'm just telling you how you seemed to the rest of us."

He smiled. "What a pleasant surprise." Then he said, "Ames always saw right through me. And when he looks at me he still sees a scoundrel. The other day I had the terrible feeling that maybe he wasn't quite wrong. So I began to be charming, you know. A little oily." He laughed. "I called him Papa. He deserved it, too. He hadn't even mentioned to the wife that my father had honored him with a namesake. Can you imagine?"

"You did bring out the crotchety side in him."

"The poor old devil." Jack shook his head. "I tried his patience. Like I would have teased a cat or stirred an anthill. Once I blew up his mailbox. He was walking up the street from Bible study. He just put his books down on the porch step and went and got the garden hose. I don't believe he ever told anybody a thing about it." He laughed. "It really was quite a spectacle. It was dark. I'd had to climb through my window to be out so late."

"You know, they moved you into that room, with the porch roof under the window, so that you could make your escape without killing yourself. You remember that time the trellis broke and Mama thought you were dead because you'd gotten the wind knocked out of you."

"I thought they'd just moved me away from the trellis."

"That, too, of course. They thought of telling you that you could leave through the door if you were so intent on leaving. But they were afraid that might seem like encouragement."

He looked at her. "What right did I have to be so strange? A good question. I've lost my watch. It must be ten o'clock by now."

"Yes, five after. I was a child when I said that to you. I hoped you had forgotten it. It didn't mean anything."

He laughed. "Out of the mouths of babes and sucklings. Good night, now."

She went up to her room and sat down at the dresser to brush out her hair. She heard the front door open and, quietly, close.

Jack came downstairs late the next morning and asked if he could borrow an envelope.

"Do you need a stamp?"

"Yes. Thank you." He took a folded letter from his jacket

127

pocket and slipped it into the envelope and sealed it, affixed the stamp, and then went into the dining room to write the address. When he came back into the kitchen, he picked up the coffeepot. "All gone."

"I'll have a fresh pot for you when you come back."

"Thanks, Glory." Then he said, "I'm sorry if I kept you awake last night. I was restless. I needed to take a walk."

"No, I went right to sleep," she said, which was not true.

"I tried to be quiet."

"I didn't hear a thing." That also was not true. She had heard him come through the door at a little after three. A five-hour walk. Well, he was always a mystery.

Her father had been grave that morning, having heard the furtive opening and closing of the door, she supposed, and again, the opening and closing of it and the cautious steps on the stairs. "No Jack for breakfast this morning, I see," he said. "Things don't change, I guess. People don't. So it seems." He picked up the newspaper, looked at it for a minute or two, and put it down again. "I guess I'm off to my room, Glory, if you don't mind helping me here."

"You haven't touched your cereal, Papa."

"That's a fact. I just don't feel up to it. If you don't mind." So she took him to his room and helped him into bed again. She would speak to Jack, when the time seemed right, and when she could think of a tactful way to broach the subject. There was no knowing what the old man heard, or what he knew, but it was clearly anxiety that made him so unaccountably aware. Jack troubled his sleep even when he didn't leave the house in the middle of the night. Five hours, she thought, imagining her father awake in the darkness. She sat down with the crossword puzzle. Before she was done with it, Jack had come downstairs with his letter and had left for the post office.

SHE SAW HIM COMING UP THE ROAD AGAIN, LOOKING A little dejected, she thought, but he smiled when he came in the door and set his hat on the refrigerator and a can of coffee on the table. "I thought we might be running out," he said. "The Reverend isn't up yet?"

"I guess he didn't sleep well. He didn't want any breakfast. I put him back to bed."

"Oh," Jack said. "I'm sorry. It's probably my fault."

"No way of knowing. Sleep isn't always easy for him."

Jack said, "Yes," and nodded, as if he were accepting a rebuke.

He poured himself a cup of coffee, sat down at the table, and opened the newspaper. Then he put it aside. "Did he see this?"

"What?" She looked at the headline. RASH OF BURGLARIES. "I don't know. I suppose he did. Why?"

He rubbed his eyes with the heels of his hands. "No reason, I suppose. When I walked into the drugstore this morning, the conversation stopped. You know that feeling you have when you're the reason people aren't talking." He laughed. "So I went into the grocery store, just to see if it would happen again. And it did. I was trying to tell myself it didn't mean anything."

"Well," she said, "I doubt that it did, Jack. Why should anyone think this has anything to do with you? Papa wouldn't think that."

He laughed into his hands. "I'm sorry," he said. "This is humiliating."

"I don't understand."

"I did that once. I did exactly that. I went out at night and tried doorknobs. And I found a couple of doors that were unlocked and took some money and some beer. Teddy saw it in my room. He said he'd tell the Reverend if I didn't. He gave me an hour. I used the time to drink the beer. Then the old gent came upstairs and gathered up the money and took me off to return it, drunk as I was. I couldn't stop laughing—ah!"

"Really, Jack. That must have been—what? —thirty years ago?"

"Hmm. More like twenty-eight."

"How can you think anyone would remember?"

"You don't think he remembers?"

"He probably does, I suppose. But that doesn't mean anyone else would. And it doesn't mean he thinks you did this, for heaven's sake."

He looked at her. "Would you be willing to vouch for my whereabouts?"

"Willing," she said. "Of course I'd be willing. But I don't know a thing in the world—your whereabouts are always your best-kept secret."

He nodded. "That'll change. But you see my point."

"No, I don't. Besides, this must have happened night before last, to be in the paper this morning."

"Did I leave the house night before last?"

"I don't know."

He shrugged. "You see what I mean."

"Did you?"

He nodded. "I can't sleep," he said. "I can't walk around in the house. He hears me. I can't stay in that room. Well, now I will." He looked at her. "I'm not going to leave yet."

"Leave? But maybe nothing has happened, Jack. Maybe Papa was reminded of that other time, but he'll forget it again—"

"What will I say to him? By the way, Dad, I sure haven't been out stealing petty cash from the dime store?" He laughed.

"You won't say anything. Things like this happen. It has nothing to do with you."

"Right. I have to remember that. I will keep that firmly in mind."

"Now, what would you like for breakfast?"

"A little more coffee."

"No. You're going to eat something. If you want to look like Raskolnikov, all right. Otherwise, you had better start eating. It would probably help you sleep. I'm going to make pancakes."

He laughed. "Oh, please no. Not pancakes. You have to let me work up to this."

"French toast. Oatmeal. Eggs and toast."

"Now I'm Raskolnikov. Just yesterday I was Cary Grant."

"You don't eat and you don't sleep. That's what happens. I'll make French toast."

"Yes. I have to keep my strength up, I suppose. I have to try to look employable."

She said, "So you really are thinking of staying here?"

He shrugged. "The thought has definitely crossed my mind."

"Well. I'm surprised."

"And you want to leave."

"Yes, I do. I hate this town."

"Why?"

She said, "Because it reminds me of when I was happy."

"Oh. So I suppose there isn't much chance that you might reconsider."

"Probably not. Should I?"

He laughed. "I believe you may be the only friend I have in the world at the moment, Glory. Nobody else would bother to force breakfast on me. So my motives are selfish. As always."

She stirred the milk and eggs and heated the griddle. "I know that could be charm," she said. "I'll believe you if you actually do what I tell you to do. Eat, primarily. And stop worrying about everything."

"I'll do my poor best. Seriously. I will."

"Then I might reconsider, after all."

"It's kind of you to say that, Glory. Everything would be so much harder if you weren't here. Impossible, in fact. I know that doesn't put you under any kind of obligation—"

Their father called from the next room, "Something smells very good. Yes, a late breakfast. That will be wonderful."

"Coming, Papa," Glory said. She helped the old man pull himself together and brought him into the kitchen. Jack had set the table and was standing, waiting for them. That deference, that guardedness. The newspaper was nowhere in sight.

"So, Jack. Up and about early today. Yes."

"Yes, sir. I had a letter I wanted to get in the mail."

"Well, that's fine." Then he said, "Could you say the grace for us, Jack? I think I'm not quite awake yet. Not up to it."

"Perhaps Glory—"

"No, no, Jack. I want to hear you say the grace. Humor an old fellow."

"All right." He cleared his throat. "For all we are about to receive, help us to be truly thankful. Amen."

His father looked at him. "That will do, I suppose. I have heard that grace any number of times. 'Bless these gifts to our use and us to Thy service'—that's another one. Perfectly all right. And the Lord is forgiving. So we can start our breakfast now."

Jack said, "Sorry."

"Yes, it doesn't matter. Prayer, you know, you open up your thoughts, and then you can get a clear look at them. No point trying to hide anything. There is a great benefit in anything the Lord asks of us, especially in prayer. I should have done more to encourage that habit in you."

Jack said, "You did a great deal, as I remember."

"Not enough, I'm afraid."

Jack smiled. "So it would seem." He glanced at Glory.

She said, "Would you like syrup on your toast, Papa? We also have honey and blackberry jam."

"Syrup is fine. Here I am trying to sort out things I should have seen to forty years ago. Well, just take it as fatherly wisdom, Jack. Prayer is a discipline in truthfulness, in honesty."

Jack said, "Yes, sir. I will bind those words for a sign upon my hand. They shall be for frontlets between my eyes."

His father looked at him. "That may be sarcasm, but at least you know your Scriptures."

"I didn't intend it as sarcasm, really."

"Very good. But here is the other thing I want to see to. It came to me in my prayer this morning. There is an account at the bank, some money from your mother's side of the family. I was going to just leave it there for all of you to share when I died. But I will tell the bank to give the two of you access to it. There is no reason why you should want for money. No need for problems of that kind."

Jack blushed darkly. He put his hands to his face.

"Yes," his father said. "We're Boughtons because my father's grandfather was an Englishman, but except for him we're Scots. You know about all that. But I mention it because I was always told by my grandmother, and my father, too, that you can't be too careful with money. But I think you can be, and I think maybe I have been a little too careful with it. My father, you know, he was a man of God, a very good man, but he was shrewd in ways I thought were not always becoming to him. My intention was to be openhanded, especially toward my children. As I could have been, because my poor old father left me the farm and this house and the furnishings. But I think I may have been more like him than I realized. I have money that just sits there in the bank, year after year."

Jack said, "You've always been generous."

"But not like I could have been. So I want to change that now."

"I don't think there's any real need."

"Reason not the need, Jack. Yes. If it lightens your burden a little, that's reason enough. I hate to think that any trouble might have come to you because your father was a tight-fisted old Scotsman!"

"I can reassure you on that point, sir."

"Good. That's fine. But there is that other vice of the Scots, you know. Drink."

Jack smiled. "So I understand."

"It is a plague among them, my grandmother said. They have no defense against it. She said she had seen many a good man wholly destroyed by it."

"Remarkable."

"Yes, it is. It is. When you're old like me you will understand. These are serious things, with grave consequences."

"I'm sorry. I didn't intend any disrespect. I really didn't."

His father looked at him. "I know that, Jack. And I see that the fault here is mine. I have been speaking to you as if you were a very young man, and you are not young at all."

Jack smiled.

"I've been saying things to you I should have said many years ago."

"You did say them, sir."

The old man nodded. "I thought perhaps I had."

Glory said, "Neither one of you has eaten a bite. You are both wasting away before my eyes, and the dogs in this neighborhood are getting too fat to walk. It is ridiculous."

"Yes, Glory, well, I'm very tired now."

"I'm sorry, Papa, but no one is leaving this table until he has eaten breakfast."

Jack smiled and stretched and looked at her as if to say she had no idea of the difficulty of what she was asking of him, but then he took a few bites. "Excellent, Glory. Thank you." He pushed back his chair.

"You haven't finished yet."

"That's true," he said, and he rested his head on his hand and ate what she had put on his plate, mock docile. "There," he said. "Now may I be excused?"

"No. You can wait for Papa to finish. Where are your manners?"

"A full-fledged domestic tyrant," her father said. "You see what I have had to put up with."

"Stop grumbling and eat."

Her father said, "I wouldn't mind if you cut this up a little for me, Glory. You could help me out here."

"I'm sorry. I should have thought of that."

"Too busy barking orders!" he said, and laughed.

Jack sat back with his arms folded and watched the old man struggle to close his hand on his fork. The scar under his eye was whiter, as it was, she knew by now, when he was weary.

WHEN SHE HAD SETTLED THE OLD MAN FOR SLEEP, SHE went out to the garden. Jack was at work already, chopping weeds. He stopped to watch the mailman pass on the other side of the street, then he lighted a cigarette.

She said, "Beware the Thane of Fife."

"Yes," he said. "This being a Scotsman is no bed of roses. A Scotsman!" He laughed. "I don't think I've ever even seen one of those."

"I suspect Scottishness is another name for predestination. It explains everything, more or less."

"The poor old bastard. Sorry. I wouldn't want to have me for a problem. At his age. Not that I won't." Then he said, "You know, if there has been another break-in, the cops might come by."

"The cop. This is Gilead."

"I'm serious, Glory. That could be very bad. For the old gent. For me, too. He already thinks I did it."

"You're making too much of this, Jack. If he thought you were a thief, would he give you the keys to the family coffers?"

"Yes, he would. That is exactly what he would do. He would think I might have needed money. He would give me money to keep me from stealing again. That's what he was talking about in there."

"Maybe."

He nodded. "You know I'm right." He said, "I don't want you to comfort me, Glory. I want you to help me. This could ruin everything. I deal with things like this very badly. I've gotten worse with practice."

"Of course I'll help you. But you have to tell me what I should do."

He said, "Just think it through with me. Help me think what

135

to do if things go wrong. It probably seems crazy to be so scared, but I am scared." He laughed. "I've done—I've done a lot of hard things in my life, but another— If I had to do thirty days, that would pretty well finish me up." He said, "I fear I am not in my perfect mind, little sister. I don't know how to deal with this." Then he said, "You have to keep me sober. That's the first thing."

"I'll do my best, Jack. I will. I swear to God. But if you want me to help you think this out, you'll have to give me a little time. And you'll have to promise me that you'll try to ignore Papa. He shouldn't talk to you the way he does. He isn't himself. He's always loved you more than any of us."

"I do try to—"

"If he were himself, he would be grateful to you for ignoring the things he's been saying."

He wiped his face with the heel of his hand. "Thank you, Glory. That's good of you."

They saw the mailman stop and put letters in the box, and they began walking down from the garden together.

He laughed. "It's amazing. I'm in hell over a miserable thirty-eight dollars."

She looked at him.

"Oh," he said. "Oh." Then, "It was in the newspaper, Glory. In the article." He was ashen. He stopped and rubbed his eyes. "I can show you. I have the paper in my room." Then he smiled at her, that weary, bitter smile of his, as if he knew her far too well, and did not know her at all.

She said, "Forgive me, Jack."

He said, "Sure, I forgive you. What choice do I have?" He took the mail from the box, a bill and a letter from Luke to their father, glanced at it, and handed it to her. "Do you ever hear from him? Your, um, fiancé?"

"What? No."

"Do you want to?"

"No."

"Do you write to him?"

"No."

He said, "Five years. That's about eighteen hundred days. So you'd have been getting letters at the rate of one every four days, more or less."

"He traveled."

Jack laughed. "Yes. Of course he did. Still, he was a prolific son of a bitch."

"Sometimes he just clipped poems out of magazines and signed his name."

"Which was?"

"What does it matter?"

"Oh, I don't know. I'm your big brother. I might want to stalk him down someday. Give him a black eye. Recoup some remnant of the family honor."

"Well," she said, "you'd better start eating a little, then."

"A big fellow, is he."

"No."

"I get it. Another crack about my physique."

"Yes. You deserve it. You know I don't like to talk about any of this."

He seemed to consider. "One sinner to another," he said. "I have never found comfort in confession, either. It just unleashes every bad consequence you might have avoided by keeping your transgressions to yourself. That has been my experience, at any rate."

She said, "So I guess I have that to look forward to."

He shrugged.

She said, "I promised I would help you, and I will. But you probably don't want me to be mad at you. I don't think as well when I'm mad."

He smiled. "Fair enough. I'll forget I ever heard of what's-his-name."

"Good."

"Well, maybe I won't forget the part about clipping out poems. That could come in handy. And the number four hundred fifty-two just seems to have lodged in my brain." He watched her face. "And then there is such comfort for me in the thought that there has been some minor smirching of your soul, I doubt I will forget that. Though I promise I'll make the attempt." Then he said, "What is this? Ah, tears! One friend in the world and I've made her cry!"

She said, "I'm not crying. Do you want my help?"

He laughed. "I need your help. I want it—abjectly."

"I've told you. I've promised you."

"You are crying."

"So what? Look after Papa. I'm going up to my room. We can talk about things when I've had some rest."

He opened the door for her and followed her inside. He said, "Glory."

"What?"

"I know this is a lot to ask. I know that. But I wish you wouldn't leave me alone just now." He put his hand to his face. He laughed. "What was that expression you used a minute ago? Ah yes. 'I swear to God.'"

She stepped closer to him so that she could speak softly. "Has it ever, ever occurred to you that you are not the only miserable person in this house? That must be fairly obvious. The least we can do is avoid making things worse than they have to be."

He smiled. "You think I'm a petty thief."

"How on earth can I know what to think?"

"Children!" their father called. "I could use some help here!"

"Coming, Papa!"

The old man was propped on one arm in a tangle of covers. "Such dreams I've had this morning! I've used a day's worth of energy just wrestling around in my sheets! Is Jack still here? Yes, there he is, there you are." He sank back on his pillows.

Jack smiled from the doorway. "Still here," he said. "You're not rid of me yet."

"Oh yes, rid of you! Come here where I can look at you, son. That's how it was in the dream. I could never get a clear look at you." He said, "Do you remember when you were about thirteen and you got the new suit for Easter? And some of the others grumbled a little, because they said you would never come to church anyway? But that day you did. The suit was big on you, but you looked so fine in it. You had your tie hanging around your neck, and you came to me, and I tied it for you. Do you remember that?"

"Yes, sir. I believe I was late."

"No, you were almost late. That's an important difference. You came running around the side of the church and sort of vaulted over the railing and landed on the steps, just as quick and graceful as could be. And then you looked at me, and I think you hoped I would be pleased, and of course I was, very pleased, and so was your mother. Yes. Bring that chair over here and sit down for a minute. Let me look at you for a minute."

Jack laughed. "Maybe I should shave first. Comb my hair."

"You just come here and sit down like I told you."

"Yes, sir."

"You just mind for once."

Jack put the chair beside his father's bed and sat down.

His father patted his knee. "Now you see how easy it is," he said. "I've never asked you for very much, have I?"

"No, sir, you haven't."

"Just take care of yourself. That's the one thing I ask. Don't do yourself harm. Don't neglect the things God has given to you for your comfort. Your family. Your brothers and sisters. The others tell me they haven't heard a word from you."

"Sorry. I'll see to that."

"Luke called yesterday. He asked if you would like to speak to him and I had to say I didn't know. He told me to give you his love. He said they all sent their love."

Jack laughed. "Thanks," he said.

"You were off at the post office anyway. But that is a thing I don't understand. A man with three fine brothers doesn't have to deal with the world on his own, like some kind of lone wolf. They'd all be glad to help. I would, too, if there were anything left of me."

"I'm all right."

"Well, that's just not true, Jack. I've still got eyes in my head. You're bone weary. Anyone could see that."

Jack stood up. "As I said, things are hard right now. I'm doing the best I can. Glory is helping me, aren't you, Glory?"

"That's good," his father said. And then, as if to explain himself, "I just woke up from the saddest dream! My grandmother always said you can trust a morning dream. I hope she was wrong about that."

"It sounds like I'd better hope so, too."

"Well, you're still here. You're alive." He closed his eyes.

JACK WAS RESTLESS, SO SHE GAVE HIM A SHOPPING LIST. IT surprised her that he was willing to brave Gilead again, and he was gone long enough to make her begin to worry, but then he came back with a bag of groceries. She saw him from the garden and followed him into the kitchen. He had put his hat on the refrigerator and loosened his tie. "One pork roast," he said. "One pound of butter. One loaf of bread. Two yellow onions." He put a carton of cigarettes on the table. "I owe you for these. And"—he said—"one small present for Glory." He reached into the bag again and produced an elderly book. "*The Condition of the Working Class in England in 1844.* Friedrich Engels. It was the best I could do. There was nothing by Marx. Nothing by DuBois, either. Plenty of Norman Vincent Peale, but I thought you might already have read him." He smiled.

She picked up the book and opened it. "This hasn't been checked out since 1925."

"I suppose that's why it was there at all. It has just stood quietly on the shelf for a quarter century, waiting to tantalize my sister's budding interest in Marxism." He unswaddled the pork from its butcher paper. "The best piece of meat in the store, so the grocer told me. Pretty fine, don't you think?"

"Yes, very nice."

He wrapped it up again and set it in the refrigerator. "You don't seem pleased."

"Well," she said, "the card is still in the book, and 1925 is still the last date on it."

"Oh. Hmm. Are you suggesting that I might have stolen it?"

"No. Just that you might have failed to satisfy the library's expectations before you walked off with it."

"I certainly do intend to return it. If you really want me to."

"Of course."

"A minor infraction."

"No question. But they would have let you borrow it. They might have asked you to sign your name."

"I'll confess, I considered that. But then I thought, Jack Boughton, noted rake and scoundrel, is observed in the Gilead public library checking out a virtual malcontent's bible. Here I am trying to rehabilitate myself, as they say, to cut a moderately respectable figure in this town. So that seemed out of the question. I could have told the truth, that the book was for you because you had mentioned to me your interest in exploring Communism, but then I would have been exposing you to every consequence I dreaded for myself. And why do that, I thought, when there is so much room for it in this grocery sack? If slipping it in with the butter and onions resembles petty theft, I will not lower myself in Glory's estimation, since that is the sort of thing she expects of me anyway."

"Oh," she said.

"What!?"

"I'm still being punished."

"No, I meant that as a little joke, I believe." He looked at her. "You don't seem to see much humor in it." He laughed. "You're right. A relapse. It all seems a little crazy, doesn't it. In the cir-

141

cumstances. Best not to seem light-fingered just now. You're absolutely right." Then he said, "When I walked into the store,
there was that same silence I mentioned to you last time. If Gilead
had forgotten any of the particulars of my troubled youth, it's
been reminded of them again. As if Jack Boughton were the only
thief in the world. God help me if anything catches fire around
here." He looked at her. "I'll take Herr Engels back tonight.
There's a slot in the door."

"No, you aren't going out at night anymore, remember? Not
before the bars close. And not after the bars close."

"Oh. Right. I forgot." He smiled. "I'm under house arrest. But
I don't want to leave here," he said. "Not just yet. The way things
are going, though, I suppose I might as well leave."

"You have to remember, nothing has happened. As far as
you're concerned."

"Yes, that is so true. Jack Boughton is in hell over nothing at
all. And it serves the bastard right, I'd say."

"I'll take the book back tomorrow," Glory said. "I can just slip
it onto a shelf. Not that anything would ever come of it, but it's
one less thing to think about."

"Tomorrow," he said. "All right. I was going to ask you if I
could borrow it, though. I've never read it myself. I thought it
might help me pass a night or two."

"Well," she said, "I'll take it back day after tomorrow. Next
week. It won't make any difference. I might read it."

He laughed. "Good girl. We might even be able to work up a
disagreement, one of those ideological differences I read about in
the news from time to time. Shouting and arm waving. In the
heat of it all I might come up with a conviction or two."

"That sounds wonderful," she said, "except we'd better forget the shouting, for Papa's sake. But we could still do the arm
waving."

He shook his head. "That would be so—Presbyterian,
somehow."

"There are worse things."

142

"Oh yes, I'm well aware that there are." Then he said, "I had no right to come back. It's a terrible worry to him, having me here. He worries in his sleep."

"He dreamed about you before you wrote to him, before he knew you were coming. You were always on his mind, all those years. It isn't having you here that makes him worry."

"Then it's—what?—my existence, I suppose. My hapless, disreputable existence. And from his point of view I can't even put an end to it. There is no end to it. I'll always be somewhere in eternity, rotting, or writhing. The poor old devil feels responsible for my soul."

"He never said one thing in his life about rotting or writhing!"

"True. It was always 'perdition,' wasn't it. I finally looked the word up in the dictionary. 'The utter loss of the soul, or of final happiness in a future state—semicolon—future misery or eternal death.'" He said, "This does all seem a little cruel, don't you think? He's a saint, and I believe he's afraid to die because of me. To leave me behind, still unregenerate—I know that's what he has on his mind. I can tell by the way he looks at me."

"You told him things have been different."

He laughed. "He thinks I'm a thief, Glory. He thinks I'm going to disgrace us all again. And that could happen, too. I mean, that I could be accused—that could happen." He put his hands to his face.

"It won't. Not over something so minor. No one is going to upset Papa over a robbery at the dime store. You know I'm right, Jack. We've worried about this way too much."

"Yes," he said. "Perspective. Thank you, Glory. I'd forgotten what it's like to have anyone give a damn who my father is."

She said, "If you feel he's so worried about you, have you ever considered—just to ease his mind—?"

He looked at her. "Lying to the old fellow? About the state of my soul?" He laughed and rubbed his eyes. He said, "Ah, Glory, what would I be then?"

"Forgive me. It was just a thought."

After a minute he said, "You remember that lady I mentioned, the one who had a good effect on my character. She was very pious—still is, no doubt. Very virtuous. I actually asked her father for her hand in marriage. He was aghast. Really horrified. Religion was one part of it. My not having any. I wished very much at the time that I could have been, you know, a hypocrite. But I just didn't have it in me. My one scruple. And it has cost me dearly." He considered. "No, if I were being honest, I'd have to say he despised me on other grounds as well. Religion first and foremost, of course. He was a man of the cloth. Is." He laughed. "I fell a little in my own estimation. I don't know what I could have expected his reaction to be. Something less emphatic, I suppose." He said, "I don't know why I told you that story, except maybe to let you know I do have one scruple. I'm not sure I should be as confident as I am that there is a difference between hypocrisy and plain old dishonesty. Though I have noticed that thieves are crucified and hypocrites seem not to be. And from time to time I have taken up my cross—" He laughed. "Not lately, you understand." He looked at her. "Sorry. No disrespect intended. I'm not a hypocrite. That was my point."

"I know you aren't. I shouldn't have suggested—"

"A fraud, perhaps. I'll have to grant you that." He smiled.

"I didn't accuse you of anything. If I were in your place I might be tempted, but you're right. I'm sorry I brought it up."

He nodded. "If I thought I could get away with it, I might be tempted, too," he said. "But I've been taking stock. These gray hairs. This battered visage. These frayed cuffs. I've had to admit that I'm not a very good liar, Glory. A lifetime more or less given over to dishonesty, and I have very little to show for it. It wouldn't be a kindness for me to lie to him, because I know he wouldn't believe me. If he still has a shred of respect for me—well, you see what I mean. I wouldn't want him to lose it."

"I find it hard to believe these things you say about yourself, Jack."

He laughed. "'All Cretans are liars.' Feel free to doubt me, if you want to. It gives me a sort of reprieve, I guess. But you see my problem. I can never persuade anyone of anything."

"I'm persuaded," she said. "Not of anything in particular, I suppose. Except that you're very hard on yourself."

He nodded. "Yes, I am. For all the good it does me." There was a silence.

"Well," she said, "I wouldn't care if you were a petty thief."

He smiled. "That's very subjunctive of you."

"All right. I don't care if you are a petty thief."

He said, "Thanks, Glory. That's kind."

He did not show her the newspaper article, the mention of thirty-eight dollars, and she did not ask to see it.

GLORY WENT TO THE HARDWARE STORE TO TELL THEM they would keep the Philco, and to ask them to install an antenna. When she came back she looked for Jack around the house, then found him in the barn, oiling the blade of a scythe, of all useless and forgotten things. She said, "I went to the hardware store to ask them to put up an antenna. They kept me there for an hour. But they did tell me who it was that stole that money from the dime store. Some high school kids. Good kids, they said. That's why there was never anything about it in the paper. It was a prank, I guess. Then one of the boys had an attack of conscience and fessed up."

Jack laughed. "How nice of them to tell you! I wonder how they knew you would be interested."

"Oh well. It's one less thing to worry about."

"True," he said. "In a sense that's true. For the moment."

THE NEXT MORNING JACK OFFERED TO READ TO HIS father, and the old man was pleased. "Yes!" he said, "that will

145

pass the time!" So they thought they might make a custom of taking him into the porch early every morning, after he was bathed and shaved, when the warmth would be tolerable to him, and the breeze would be pleasant.

"What would you like to hear?" Jack asked. "We've got *The Condition of the Working Class in England.*"

The old man shook his head. "Read it in seminary," he said. "It was very interesting, but as I remember, the point was clear. I don't feel I need to return to it. I'm surprised we still have it. I thought I gave my copy to the library."

Jack laughed and glanced at her. He said, "Here's one Luke sent. *Something of Value.* It's about Africa."

His father nodded. "I had a considerable interest in Africa," he said. "At one time."

Glory said, "Luke sent me a note about that one. He says the critics raved."

Jack said, "I'm a little bit interested in Africa, myself."

"Yes, well, Mozambique, Cameroon, Madagascar, Sierra Leone. Beautiful names. When I was a boy I used to think I'd go there someday. We can read that one."

"It's about Kenya."

"Well, that's fine, too."

Jack lowered his head and began to read, leaning over the book almost prayerfully. He smiled at the parts he liked— "'Somewhere out of sight a zebra barked, and along the edge of a stream a baboon cursed.'" Teddy used to say Jack was the bright one, that he, Teddy, was only conscientious. And in fact there was a kind of grace to anything Jack did with his whole attention, or when he forgot irony for a while. It was always a little surprising because it was among the things about himself he shrugged off, concealed when he could. But his voice was mild and warm, courteous to the page he read from, and his father looked at her and lifted his brows, the old signal that meant, He is wonderful when he wants to be. Really wonderful.

The old man laughed over the cook's pagan version of "Jesus Wants Me for a Sunbeam," listened with interest to the household arrangements of the McKenzies, marveled at the killing of the elephants, and nodded off. Jack continued reading to himself. He said, "I think I can see how this is going to end." He turned to the last few pages. "Yes." He read, "'Peter hunched his shoulders close to his neck and took a deep, sobbing breath and squeezed. Kimani's tongue came all the way out past his teeth, and his eyes suffused in blood as the tiny vessels broke. There was a slight crick and then a sharp crack, as if a man had trodden on a dry stick, and Kimani's body went limp.'"

Their father roused himself. "Kimani is that child he's playing with at the beginning, isn't he? Those two children are playing together."

Jack nodded.

"I guess he killed him."

Jack closed the book. "I guess he did."

"A pity," the old man said. "That seems to be how it is, though. So much bad blood. I think we had all better just keep to ourselves."

Jack laughed. "I have certainly heard that sentiment before," he said. "I know a good many people who agree with you about that, believe me."

"Yes. We might want to try another book, Jack, don't you think? It seems there's nothing in that one that's going to surprise us."

"Not a thing."

He nodded. "The fellow writes well, though. The elephants were very interesting."

THE DAY SEEMED TO BE PASSING IN THE WAY THAT HAD become customary, Glory tending to household things while her father slept and Jack made himself useful around the place, making small, patient inroads on dishevelment and disrepair. Or so she assumed. Then she realized that she hadn't seen him for a while. Usually he found some reason to speak to her from time to time, to joke with her a little, as if to assure himself again that she was kindly disposed toward him. She looked out at the garden, then she walked to the shed, looked into the barn. Jack was nowhere to be found. This is ridiculous, she thought. I can't worry this way. An hour passed, then two. She had glanced through the mail and the new *Life* magazine. She had answered letters from Dan and Grace. Then the screen door closed and there was Jack, coming through the porch, looking disheveled and yet a little pleased with himself. He was in his undershirt, having made his shirt into a bundle of some kind which he set on the table and opened. "Mushrooms!" he said. "Morels! Right where they always were!" Sand and leaf mold and that musky smell.

"Where were they?"

"In a remote area, my dear. Far from the haunts of men."

"Honestly! I'm your sister! Your only friend in the world!"

"Sorry. No dice. Just look at these beauties. We eat mushrooms tonight, Glory!"

"What is that?" their father called. "What are we talking about?"

Glory said, "Go show Papa. He loves morels."

"I think I'd better clean up a little."

"You don't have to clean up. Just go show him."

So Jack carried the bundle into his father's room and spread it open on the old man's lap. "Ah," his father said. "Ah yes. You've been out foraging." He drew a deep breath and laughed. "'See, the smell of my son is as the smell of a field which Jehovah hath blessed.' Morels. Dan and Teddy used to bring me these. And blackberries, and walnuts. And they'd bring in walleye and catfish. And pheasants. They were always off in the fields, down by the river. With the girls it was always flowers. So long ago."

Jack stood back and watched the old man study the mushrooms, sniff them, turn them in the light. He rubbed his bare arms as if he felt the way he looked, thin, exposed. He said softly, "Bless me, even me also."

"No," his father said, "that's Esau. You're confusing Esau and Jacob."

Jack laughed. "Yes, I am the smooth man. How could I forget? I'm the one who has to steal the blessing."

His father shook his head. "You have never had to steal one thing in your entire life. There was never any need for it. I have been searching my memory on that point."

Glory said, "Papa, while I was in the hardware store the other day—"

But Jack said, "No, don't. Don't." And smiled at her, and she knew she had come near shaming him. He had not robbed the dime store. How painful for this weary man to need exoneration from the mischief of bad children. "So good to be home," he said to her afterward. "No place like it, the old song says."

"Can I get something for you? Coffee?"

"Sure. Coffee. Why not?" He said, "You are a good soul, Glory. That fellow who did not marry you was a very foolish man."

She shrugged. "Not altogether. He was a married man."

"Oh."

"So he said."

"Oh."

"Of course I didn't know it at the time. Particularly."

He laughed. "Particularly."

"You know what I mean. I could have figured it out if I'd wanted to."

He nodded. "Ah, that's hard. I'm sorry." After a moment, "And no child was born of this union, I take it."

She shook her head. "No."

"So you were spared that, at least."

She drew a deep breath.

He said, "I'm sorry! Why did I say that? Why don't I just stop talking? Why don't you tell me to stop?"

"Well, Jack, you didn't know her. So I suppose it isn't surprising that you'd think about her that way. As something we might have wished to be spared."

"Yes, the little girl."

"Your little girl."

"My little girl." He stood up. "I'm not much good at— I stayed away all that time—it was the best I could do—"

"That's not what I mean. I mean we're glad she was born. We enjoyed her life. I believe she enjoyed it, too. I know she did."

He put his hand to his face. "Thank you. That's good to know, I suppose. I'm probably saying the wrong thing—I've never known how to deal with this. Shame. You'd think I'd be used to it."

"But I'm trying to tell you, there was so much more than shame in all that, or wrongdoing or whatever. Anyone could have been proud of her. That's what I tried to say in those letters I sent you."

"Oh. Then I guess I should have read them." He laughed.

"Dear God," she said. "Dear God in heaven, I give up. I throw up my hands."

"Please don't say that, Glory. I'm alone here—"

"Well," she said, "you know I don't mean it."

After a moment he said, "Why don't you mean it?"

"Well, I'm your sister, for one thing. And for another thing—" He laughed.

"—I'm your sister. That's reason enough."

He nodded. "Thank you," he said. "That's very kind."

JACK HAD ADDED TO THE GARDEN, SUNFLOWERS AND SNAP-dragons and money plants, several hills of cantaloupe, a pumpkin patch, three rows of corn. He rescued the bleeding-heart bushes from a tangle of weeds and tended the gourds with the tact of a man who believed, as all Boughtons did, that they throve on neglect. When her brothers and sisters were children they had made rattles of the gourds when they dried, and bottles and drinking cups, playing Indian. They had carved pumpkins and toasted the seeds. They had pretended the silver disks of money plants were dollars. They had pinched the jaws of snapdragons to make them talk, or pinched their lips closed to pop them. They had eaten the seeds of sunflowers when they were ripe and dry. They had opened the flowers of bleeding hearts to reveal the tiny lady in her bath. Corn on the cob they had all loved, though they hated to shuck it, and they had all loved melons. Jack tended these things with particular care. When he was restless he would sometimes walk out into the garden and stand there with his hands on his hips, as if it comforted him to see their modest flourishing. Once, when he saw her looking at it all, he said, "Have I forgotten anything?"

"No, I don't believe you have."

"I'm no farmer," he said, clearly pleased that his crops were doing well enough just the same.

His father watched from the porch day after day and asked him what it was he was planting, and then whether the corn was up and the sunflowers, and whether the melons were setting on. Jack brought him a sprig of bleeding heart, the bud of a pumpkin blossom.

"Yes," the old man said, as he did when memory stirred. "Those were good times."

ONE EVENING JACK CAME IN FROM THE LATE TWILIGHT while Glory was settling her father for the night. They heard him in the kitchen getting himself a glass of water. The air had cooled. Insects had massed against the window screens, minute and various, craving the light from the tilted bulb of her father's bedside lamp, and the crickets were loud, and an evening wind was stirring the trees. It always calmed her to know Jack had come inside for the night. She knew he would be propped against the counter, drinking good, cold water in the dark, the feel and smell of soil still on his hands. But her father was restless. He had something in mind, an intention he meant to act upon even in violation of this sweet quiet. He said, "I want a word with him. If you wouldn't mind, Glory."

So she called him, and she heard him shift himself upright and set his glass in the sink, with that little delay that meant reluctance overcome. When he came into the room he smiled at her. "Well, here I am."

His father said, "Bring that chair over here. Sit down."

"Yes, sir."

"There's something I want to say to you." He reached a hand out of the covers and patted Jack's knee. He cleared his throat. "I've given it a lot of thought, and I feel I know what is troubling you, Jack. I believe I always did know, and I just haven't been honest with myself about it. I want to talk to you about it."

Jack smiled and shifted in his chair. "All right. I'm listening."

"It's that child of yours, Jack."

"What?"

"Yes, and I want you to know that I realize how much I was at fault in it all."

"What?" Jack cleared his throat. "I'm sorry, sir. I don't understand."

"I should have baptized her. I have regretted many times I didn't do at least that much for her."

"Oh," Jack said. "Oh, I see. Yes."

His father looked at him. "Maybe you didn't realize that, that she died without the sacrament, and maybe I shouldn't have said anything about it, since it might only add to your grief. I was reluctant to mention it. But I wanted to be sure you understood the fault was entirely mine." He put his hand to his face. "Oh, Jack!" he said. "There I was, a minister of the Lord, holding that little baby in my arms any number of times. Why didn't I just do the obvious thing! A few drops of water! There was a rain barrel right there by the house—who would have stopped me! I have thought of that so many times."

Glory said, "Papa, we're Presbyterians! We don't believe in the necessity of baptism. You've always said that."

"Yes, and Ames says it. He'll take down the Institutes and show you the place. And Calvin was right about many things. His point there is that the Lord wouldn't hold the child accountable—that has to be true. As for myself, well, 'a broken and contrite heart Thou wilt not despise.' I must remember to believe that, too."

They were silent. Finally Jack said, "Everything that happened was my fault. It was all my fault. It is hard for me to believe that you could find any way to blame yourself for it. I'm—I'm amazed."

"Oh," his father said, "but you were young. And you didn't know her. Glory was always trying to get a good picture to send to you, she'd dress her all up, put bows in her hair. But you couldn't really tell much from the pictures. She was such a clever little thing, such a sprightly, funny little thing. She couldn't wait to get up and start walking. Remember, Glory? When she was no bigger than a minute she'd be tagging after her mother, they'd be playing together—I've often thought I should have baptized her mother, for that matter." Then he said, "To know a child like that, and then not to do just anything you can for her—there's no excuse." He said, "The Lord had the right to expect better of me, and you did, too. I understand that."

Jack pushed back his chair and stood up. "I—I have to—" He laughed. "I don't know. Get some air." He smiled at Glory. "If you'll pardon me, I—" and he left the room.

Glory kissed her father's forehead, and then she said, "You get some sleep now," and turned his pillow and smoothed it. She followed Jack into the kitchen. He was sitting at the table with his head in his hands. "I'm sorry," she said.

He said, "Do you mind if I turn off the light?" So she turned it off. After a long time he said, "If I were an honest man I'd have told him I have never given a single thought to—any of that. Not one thought. Ever."

"Well."

"I mean, to whether or not she was baptized. I have thought about the rest of it, from time to time. I have." He laughed. "Never because I chose to."

She said, "That was all so long ago. You were young."

"No. I wasn't young. I don't believe I ever was young." Then he said, "Excuses scare me, Glory. They make me feel like I'm losing hold. I can't explain it. But please don't try to make excuses for me. I might start believing them sometime. I've known people like that."

She paused. "You did know that she died."

"That envelope had a black border. I thought it might be—"

"What? Someone who mattered?"

"I didn't say that. I didn't mean it. You just never expect a child to die—" He said, "I never thought of it then. Now I do. I think of it now, all the time." He laughed and put his hands to his face. "That can't be justice. It would be horrible to think it has anything to do with justice."

What could she say to comfort him? "These things are hard to talk about. I say things I shouldn't. I'm sorry." And after a moment, "I don't really think justice can be horrible."

"Really? Isn't that what vengeance is? Horrible justice? What would your papa say?"

"Well, I don't know for sure, but grace seems to answer every question, as far as he's concerned."

Jack looked at her. "Then he shouldn't have to worry about his reprobate son, should he. I wish you would point that out to him. I mean, it does seem like a contradiction, doesn't it?"

She said, "It does. I think we're beyond the point where we can raise questions about his theology, though. If I pointed out a contradiction in his thinking, I would probably upset him. He's gotten touchy about that kind of thing. Well, he has been for years. Anyway, I don't think he worries about all that any more than you do."

He shrugged. "Like father, like son."

THE OLD MAN SEEMED TO HAVE ALARMED HIMSELF WITH his candor. He was suddenly anxious to be with Jack, at companionable, fatherly peace with him. He mustered a sociable interest in television, especially baseball, and he and Jack talked about the teams and the season as passionlessly as anything of great moment could be talked about, as if they were summer weather, drought and lightning. He always seemed to nod off if there was news of turbulence anywhere.

Jack must have taken his father to be in fact asleep, because when the news turned to the troubles in the South, he said, softly, "Jesus Christ."

The old man roused himself. "What is it now?"

"Oh, sorry," Jack said. "Sorry. It's Tuscaloosa. A colored woman wants to go to the University of Alabama."

"It appears they don't want her there."

Jack laughed. "It sure doesn't look like it."

His father watched for a moment and then he said, "I have nothing against the colored people. I do think they're going to need to improve themselves, though, if they want to be accepted. I believe that is the only solution." His look and tone were statesmanlike. He was making such an effort to be mild and conciliatory, even after Jack's misuse of the name of the Lord, that Jack simply studied him, his hands to his mouth as if to prevent himself from speaking.

Finally he said, "I'm a little unimproved myself. I've known a good many Negroes who are more respectable than I am."

His father looked at him. "I don't know where you get such a terrible opinion of yourself, Jack."

"Well, I guess that's something we should both be grateful for."

His father said, "I'm serious. There's a lot you could do if you put your mind to it."

Jack laughed. "True enough. I could stay in a hotel. I could eat in a cafeteria. I could hail a cab. I could probably exercise my franchise. Unworthy as I am."

"You're a college graduate," his father said firmly.

Jack smiled and glanced at Glory. She shook her head. So he

said, "True." Then he said, "Most people don't have that advantage, however. I mean, white people."

"All the more reason you should take some pride in yourself."

"Oh, I see. Yes, sir. I'll bear that in mind."

After a moment his father said, "I know I strayed from the point a little there. But I've wanted to mention that to you. I've wanted to say you should think better of yourself."

"Thank you, sir. I'll give it a try."

"The colored people," his father said, "appear to me to be creating problems and obstacles for themselves with all this—commotion. There's no reason for all this trouble. They bring it on themselves."

Jack looked at him. He drew a long breath, then another. He asked softly, "Have you heard of Emmett Till?"

"Emmett Till. Wasn't he the Negro fellow that—attacked the white woman?"

Jack said, "He was a kid. He was fourteen. Somebody said he whistled at a white woman."

His father said, "I think there must have been more to it, Jack. As I remember, he was executed. There was a trial."

Jack said, "There was no trial. He was murdered. He was a child, and they murdered him." He cleared his throat to recover control of his voice.

"Yes, that is upsetting. I had another memory of it."

Jack said, "We read different newspapers."

"That might be the difference. Still, parents have a responsibility."

"What?"

"They bring children into a dangerous world, and they should do what they have to do to keep them safe."

Jack cleared his throat. "But they can't always—they might really want to. It's very hard. It's complicated—" He laughed.

"So you know some colored people, there in St. Louis."

"Yes. They've been kind to me."

His father regarded him. "Your mother and I brought you children up to be at ease in any company. Any respectable company. So you could have the benefit of good friends. Because people judge you by your associations. I know that sounds harsh, but it's the truth."

Jack smiled. "Yes, sir, believe me, I know what it is to be judged by my associations."

"You could help yourself by finding a better class of friends."

"I have made a considerable effort in that direction. But my associations have made it very difficult."

"Yes." His father was wary of this concession. The readiness of it sounded like irony. After a minute he said, "It seems to me you always think I'm speaking of that child of yours. You regret that you weren't a father to her, I know that. And if you had it to do over again, you'd want to be there with her, I know that, too. And the Lord knows it."

Jack covered his face with his hands and laughed. "The Lord," he said, "is very—interesting."

"I know you don't mean any disrespect," his father said.

"I really don't know what I mean. I really don't."

"Well," the old man said, "I wish I could help you with that." Then he turned his face resolutely toward the television screen. Jack sat down beside him and watched it with him. In the gray light he looked saddened and spent and oddly young, a man whose father was still his father, and impossible, and frail. The old man patted his knee. Cowboys and gunfire. Glory fixed them a supper and they ate quietly, carefully polite. "I believe this is Thursday. Am I right?"

"Yes, sir."

"I'd like roast beef for Sunday dinner. I want the whole house to smell like roast beef. I'll put on a necktie. We'll light the candles. Maybe Ames and his family will join us. We could have a sort of a good time, you know. Will you be there, Jack?"

"Sure."

"You could play a little piano for us."

"I could do that."

"Let me see your hand, where you had that splinter in it."

"It's healing."

"Let me see."

Jack gave his father his right hand, and the old man took it in his hands and stroked it and studied it. "There will be a mark there." Then, "Twenty years," he said, "twenty years."

Jack settled his father for the night, dried the dishes, and went to his room.

WHEN GLORY CAME DOWNSTAIRS THE NEXT MORNING, Jack was at the stove, preparing to fry bacon. He said, "I believe I may have undergone a conversion experience." He looked at her sidelong.

"Interesting. Tell me more."

"Nothing dramatic. I was brushing my teeth, and a realization came to me. The gist of it was that Jack Boughton might become a Congregationalist. You know, at least try it on for a few weeks."

"That's a little bit dramatic. I mean, if you're actually thinking of going to church."

"I intend to do exactly that, little sister. Unless I change my mind. This coming Sunday. If it wouldn't be inconvenient for you, which is why I thought I'd mention it. We can't leave the old gent here on his own, I know that—"

"So that you can go to church? I might have to tether him to the bedpost to keep him from floating out the window. Aside from that, I doubt there would be any problem."

"Well, that's actually a concern of mine. He might make too much of it. It's just a thought I had. I might not even go through with it."

"I'll stay with him. It'll be all right."

"I thought maybe I could talk with Ames about a few things.

158

If I got on better terms with him. That's all it really amounts to. A gesture of respect." He looked at her. "You would tell me if you thought this was a bad idea."

"I really don't know what could be wrong with it."

He nodded. "Ames will be sure to mention it. So there's no point being secretive about it. I wondered if you wouldn't mind—"

"I'll just bring him his coffee, and he'll ask me why I'm not dressed for church, and I'll say, Jack wanted to go this morning."

"And then—" Jack said, and they laughed. "Ah," he said, "help me think this through. Maybe you should just say Jack went to church this morning. If you say I wanted to go, he'd read a lot into that. Maybe—Jack decided to go. No, that's almost as bad as wanted."

"All right. Jack went to church this morning."

"And then what?"

"Who knows. I'll improvise. This is uncharted territory."

"So it is." He looked at her. "You don't think this will seem too cynical, do you? Hypocritical? Unctuous? Calculating?"

She shrugged. "People go to church."

"Other people do. I mean, I'll hardly be inconspicuous. And old Ames doesn't think the world of me." After a moment he said, "Well, nothing to be done about that, hmm? That's why I thought of going in the first place. I can't think of another approach. I have tried. I will sit under his preaching, as they say, and maybe his feelings toward me will soften a little. I'll be very attentive." He smiled. He said, "It's worth a try. Then he and the wife will come to dinner, I'll play a few of the old favorites. It could work."

"All this is fine, Jack. But I can't quite convince myself that it's necessary."

He nodded. "I've been a torment to his dearest friend for forty-three years, give or take. He's sick of me. He doesn't want to be, but he is. I would be, too. But I want to talk to him."

She said, "It's a good idea. Very good, I think."

"All right, then. If you say so. I'll probably do it."

Jack put on his tie and his hat and went off to the store to buy groceries for Sunday dinner with two ten-dollar bills from the household money Glory kept in the drawer in the sideboard. She could have called the grocer's and ordered them, as she usually did, but Jack said he needed to get out of the house for a while. So she went down to the Ameses'. Lila was in the garden picking lettuce into a basin and Robby was fooling around on his swing, lying across the plank on his stomach, pushing and pivoting and sweeping the grass with his fingertips. Lila stood up when she saw Glory at the fence and smiled at her and called the little boy to come say hello, so he came and said hello and then ran off to look for his friend Tobias, who had been called in for lunch.

Glory said good morning, and Lila answered, "It is. It's a fine morning." She brushed her hair back with her hands. "Could you use some salad? It's coming in faster than I can eat it myself, and my men aren't much for greens, neither one of them." She handed the basin to Glory. "I was just picking it because it's so pretty. I'd be glad if you could use it."

Lila was wide at the shoulders and hips, and her hands were large, tentative, competent. Sometime, somewhere, it had seemed good to her to pluck her brows thin and arched, and so they remained, a suggestion of former worldliness at odds with her stalwartly maternal frame. Sunlight seemed a bother to her, like a friendly attention she might sometime weary of, though for now she only smiled and shrugged away from it, holding up her hand to shield her eyes. Glory said, "Papa asked me to invite you to dinner tomorrow."

She nodded. "Jack stopped by a few minutes ago. I told him I'd speak to the Reverend about it. Preaching wearies him more than he likes to admit."

"It could be an evening dinner. That would give him time to rest."

THAT AFTERNOON, WHEN SHE WAS OUT IN THE GARDEN weeding the strawberries, picking the handful of ripe ones, she heard the DeSoto's starter straining twice, then again, and then the roar of an automobile engine, the sound robust for a moment, then trailing away. Again the starter and the engine, and after a minute or two the rattle and pop of gravel as the DeSoto eased backward out of the barn. It gleamed darkly and demurely, like a ripe plum. Its chrome was polished, hubcaps and grille, and the side walls of the tires were snowy white. There was a preposterous beauty in all that shine that made her laugh. Jack put his arm out the window, waving his hat like a visiting dignitary, backed into the street, and floated away, gentling the gleaming dirigible through the shadows of arching elm trees, light dropping on it through their leaves like confetti as it made its ceremonious passage. After a few minutes she heard a horn, and there were Jack and the DeSoto going by the house. A few minutes more and they came back from the other direction, swung into the driveway, and idled there. Jack leaned across the front seat to open the passenger door. She walked across the lawn to the car and slid in.

"Wonderful!"

He nodded. "We're doing all right so far. I smell strawberries."

She held out her hands. "I haven't washed them."

He took one, eyed it, and gave it back. "How about a little spin around the block?"

"Papa will want to come."

"Yes, well, I'm working up to that. I'd like to put a couple of miles on this thing, so I'll know it can be trusted. We wouldn't want to make the old fellow walk home."

So she closed the door and they pulled into the street.

He said, "You must have a license. You used to drive."

"I do. Somewhere. Do you?"

He looked at her. "Why do you ask?"

"Never mind. Just making conversation." They completed a

decorous circuit of the block, and when they pulled into the driveway, they saw their father standing in the screen door.

"Something very exciting!" he called. "I thought I might come along, if it's no trouble." He seemed even about to attempt the front steps.

"Wait!" Jack ran across the lawn and took him by his arms and helped him down to the sidewalk.

"Thank you, dear. This is very good." He leaned on his cane and gazed appraisingly at the DeSoto. "Yes. It's a fine-looking car. I knew I must be saving it for some reason." He chuckled. There was a barely restrained glee about him, as though he felt he had done something, or had done nothing, to excellent effect. "I had offers for it, you know. Several of them. Yes." He regarded the gleaming DeSoto with something warmer than pride of ownership. "And now, look what you have done with it! Jack, this is wonderful!"

Jack was watching all this with his hands on his hips and a look of grave, distant pleasure, as if it were a moment proposed to him by imagination, an indulgence he could not finally allow himself. "It seems to run all right," he said. "I suppose we could take a little drive." He helped his father into the front seat. "I'll go in and get a couple of dollars for gas, just in case." He walked toward the house, then came back. He held out his cupped hands to Glory and she emptied the berries into them. "Two minutes," he said. When he came back he had the berries in a cereal bowl, rinsed and glistening with water. He handed the bowl to Glory and climbed into the driver's seat. He turned the key, turned it again, and the engine caught, and the three of them backed out and sailed off down the street. When a neighbor waved, the old man made the merest gesture of his hand in reply, as if this were all foreseen and intended, too perfect a vindication to be in any way remarkable. Jack laughed.

Glory said, "Have a strawberry."

Jack took one and handed it to his father, then took one for himself. He popped it in his mouth and spat the stem out the window.

"Yes," his father said, as they passed through the countrified outer reaches of Gilead into country itself, "this is the high life."

The sky was blue, the terraced hills glittered with new corn, and in the pastures the cows were standing with their calves or lying in the mingled, muddied shade of oak trees. "Well, I'd almost forgotten it all," the old man said. "It's good to get out of the house from time to time. Ames will enjoy it." He talked for a while about the old Gilead. It was the smell that reminded him. There used to be chicken coops and rabbit hutches behind every house almost, and people kept milk cows, and there was enough open land right in town to be plowed with a horse or a mule and planted in corn. You knew the animals around town just like you knew the children, and if some old she-goat was grazing in the flower garden, well, you knew her and she knew you and you could just walk her home. But the geese could be mean, and noisy. They'd follow you along and nip at you, pinch your heels. There was no sleeping through the racket all those roosters made in the morning. But at night you could hear the animals settling, and that was very comforting. Jack drove with such solemn caution that the dogs that ran out to the car were a long time in giving up the chase and falling back.

They turned onto another road, and then Glory and her father were silent for a while, watching the landscape grow uneasily familiar. Then Jack said, "Oh." He said "I—" and pulled off onto the shoulder to turn the car around, so close to a shallow ditch that the rear wheels slid in the sand. A hundred yards ahead of them was the bridge across the West Nishnabotna, and a little way beyond it that small white house. Jack gunned the car and it lurched into the road and stalled. "Sorry. I can deal with this," he said. "Give me a minute." He put his hands to his face and took a breath. Then he put the car in gear and turned the key and touched the choke and it started, and he maneuvered it very carefully, reversing twice before he eased onto the right side of the road. "I guess it's time to go home," he said.

Through all this his father maintained a serene, high-minded

163

expression, as he always did when he sensed emergency. "Yes," he said. "Yes. I have been keeping an eye on events in Egypt. In that one case I have felt that the policies of Eisenhower are appropriate to the situation. But time will tell."

Jack said, "True."

"Kenya is another matter."

"That's true, too."

After another mile or so he pulled onto the shoulder and stopped. "Glory, would you mind driving the rest of the way? It isn't far. I forgot to get gas. I'm not sure the gas gauge is working, and it distracts me to worry about it. And that worries me." He laughed. "I haven't driven a car in twenty years."

So she changed places with him. He held the door for her, ceremoniously, smiling at her, wry and weary. "Thank you so much," he said.

She looked to see where the pedals were, and the clutch, and then she put the car in gear and it lurched and died, and she tried again and it started. Jack said, "There's still something wrong with the—with the blasted thing. It doesn't sound right. This was stupid of me. I knew I should have stayed in town." He lit a cigarette and rolled down the window.

Glory said, "We'll be fine," having no particular grounds for confidence except that as they approached town the houses were less scattered. Rural people might or might not have telephones, but they were certain to have gasoline, and, if it came to that, to have practical experience with balky machines. That is what Jack dreads most, she thought. Having to knock at a door. Out here someone might know about him, without mitigating acquaintance with his estimable father. Well, she would spare him that, one way or another. And the car was running well enough. Her father appeared to be dozing, though still maintaining that statesmanlike expression that meant he could be counted on not to add difficulty to a situation, even by seeming aware of it.

When the DeSoto had brought them home, Jack stood up out

of the backseat and stretched, and then opened his father's door. The old man roused himself. "I will telephone Ames," he said. "After I've had some rest." He handed Jack his cane. "If you don't mind, dear. I'm a little bit stiff." Jack lifted him out by his arm, and then he seemed at a loss how to help him, because his father had made a sharp little cry, and then laughed. "Ouch!" he said. Jack looked at Glory, tired.

She said, "Let me help." She took her father's other arm, and they walked him into the house, slowly, carefully. Her helping did nothing to lessen her father's pain, but it did spare Jack from being the sole immediate cause of it. She took off the old man's tie and shoes and bundled him into his chair. She went to the kitchen to get him aspirin and a glass of water, and she heard the car start and went out to the porch. She saw the beautiful old plum-colored DeSoto disappear into the barn, and then she heard the barn doors close. When Jack came in, he held the keys out to her.

"It's your car," she said.

"I'm making you a gift of it." He shook the keys so they jingled. "Here. I don't want the damn thing."

"Tell me that in a week and I might believe you."

He dropped the keys on the piano and smiled at her. "Whatever you say, Pigtails."

She said, "Jack, you can't leave."

"Well, I can't very well stay, can I." He rubbed his eyes and laughed. "No point in it. I can see myself giving my lady love a tour of the scenes of my youth. Not that she has so many illusions about me. But the few she does have might just be crucial."

"Maybe they are. Who knows. But we have to think about Papa. We don't want to kill him."

"No, we don't. And if we were to leave, we would be forever alienated from our little sister, on whom we have become surprisingly dependent."

"Yes, we would. You would. And I mean it, Jack. If I've ever meant anything in my life."

"Such ferocity," he said, and laughed and rubbed his eyes. "Thank you. A good brisk threat can orient a fellow. But what is this? Now you're crying!"

She said, "Never mind."

"You forgive me."

"Of course."

He said, "There are all the others, Glory. The old fellow would love to have them around, and they'd be a lot more help to you than I am." He said, "This might be too hard, you know. I'm not exactly a pillar of strength. And if I went wrong, it would be better if I did it somewhere else. Better for Papa. I do think about that."

"Yes, you thought about that for twenty years, didn't you."

He laughed. "In fact I did. And maybe I wasn't wrong, Glory. Not altogether wrong."

"You know more about that than I do. But you said that for ten years you had been all right."

"That's true. Almost ten."

"Then you could at least have come home for Mama's funeral." Her voice trembled. "That would have meant so much to him. I'm sorry. I shouldn't have mentioned it. I don't know why I did."

He smiled. "I'm a scoundrel, Glory. Let's leave it at that." He said, "I'm sorry. I'm going to have to lie down for a while. Please excuse me."

"Wait." She went to him where he stood with his hand on the stair railing, his face so weary, and she kissed his cheek. He laughed.

"Thanks," he said. "That was kind. That might even help me sleep."

He slept, and he came down to help set the table for supper. "I can stick around for a while. If that's still all right."

"It's all right," she said.

He watched a baseball game on television with his father when the dishes were done.

Sunday morning Jack came downstairs dressed and shaved, in his stocking feet, carrying his shoes, to avoid waking his father. He looked at her and shrugged as if to say, What have I got to lose, and she handed him a cup of coffee. He sipped it, leaning against the refrigerator. Then he went to the money drawer and took two dollars. "For the collection plate," he said softly. "I owe you." He brushed at the brim of his hat. "Do you mind if I borrow your watch? Then I can take a little walk before the service begins." She gave him the watch and he glanced at it and then slipped it into his jacket pocket. "Well," he said, "here goes." He stopped in the porch to put on his shoes and adjust his hat, and he left.

Half an hour later she heard her father stirring, and she took him his tray of coffee and applesauce and buttered toast and the aspirin tablets with a glass of water. She was still in her robe and slippers and wearing a hairnet. He said, "Aren't you feeling well, my dear? No church today? Maybe I should call Ames and tell him we'll have to have dinner another time—"

"No, Papa, I'm fine. I stayed home today so Jack could go."

"Go to church? Jack?"

"Mmhmm."

"Jack went to church?"

"Ames's church. As a gesture of respect, he said."

"Yes, well, that's very good. John can give a fine sermon. That new fellow we've got now, I'm not so sure about him. I might go to the Congregationalists myself. If I went anywhere. Well." He laughed. "This is something. This is quite a day."

He sat perfectly still for a minute, smiling into space, considering. "Just when you're about to give up entirely! The Lord is wonderful!"

"Maybe you shouldn't read too much into it, Papa."

"Read into it! It's just a fact! You go to church and there you are!" He said, "I thought I must have turned him against it all. I really did. I've heard of that in preachers' families. More than once."

"Well, he seems to have had some contact with a church in St. Louis. He says he played piano for them."

"Did he! I wouldn't know that. He doesn't talk to me very much. Never did." He laughed. "Your mother used to ask me, Why do we keep paying for piano lessons for that boy? Because he wouldn't practice, you know. If you tried to make him, he'd just walk out the door. But I said I thought something might come of it. He'd go to the lessons when Teddy went. Yes. I told her I thought we should treat all the children the same, Jack, too." He sat there smiling, his face bright with vindication. "It's wonderful. You make some sort of decision, just a little choice you can't even quite explain, and years later— Well, I knew he was clever. That was clear to me. He was always paying more attention than he would let on. But I knew it, I did." He laughed at the thought of his own shrewdness. "Yes."

Glory said, "He seems to have friends in the church there."

"Friends! Well, I suppose he would. That just happens in a church, doesn't it. He didn't really have friends as a boy, though. He never seemed to want them. I've prayed his whole life that he'd have a friend or two. It often came to my mind, you know, that loneliness of his. And it didn't really occur to me—it honestly never occurred to me—that off in St. Louis somewhere my prayers were being answered! Isn't that something!" He shook his head. "It would have been a weight off my heart, I'll tell you that. I could have spared myself years of grief, just by having a little trust. There's a lesson in that." Then he said, "I do wonder what happened, though. I mean, right now he doesn't strike me as a man who feels he has friends. Then I could be wrong."

"He doesn't tell me very much either."

"Well," he said, "here I am worrying, and this is a remarkable day! I have to bestir myself. Would you mind giving my hair a little trim, Glory? I've been feeling sort of shaggy. It's probably my imagination, mostly." He laughed. "Not much there anymore, I know. Still."

So she brought her father into the kitchen, sat him down, wrapped a towel around his shoulders and tucked it close around his neck. She got a comb and the pair of shears and set to work. His hair had vanished, or was on the point of vanishing, not through ordinary loss but by a process of rarification. It was so fine, so white and weightless, that it eddied into soft curls. Wafted, she thought. She hated to cut it off, since there seemed very little chance that it could grow back again as it was. It was like cutting a young child's hair. But her father claimed to be irked by the prettiness of it. Fauntleroy in his dotage, he said.

So she clipped and trimmed, making more work of it than it was in order to satisfy him that some change had been accomplished, combing it down a little with water so he would feel sleek and trim. The nape of his neck, the backs of his ears. The visible strain of holding the great human head upright for decades and decades. Some ancient said it is what makes us different from the beasts, that our eyes are not turned downward to the earth. Most of the time. It was Ovid. At the end of so much effort, the neck seemed frail, but the head was still lifted up, and the ears stood there, still shaped for attention, soft as they were. She'd have left all the lovely hair, which looked like gentle bewilderment, just as the lifted head and the ears looked like waiting grown old, like trust grown old.

"Yes," her father said, "whenever I thought of him, he was always alone, the way he used to be, and I would wonder what kind of life he could have, with no one even to care how he was, what he needed. I realize that was the one thing I thought I knew, that he would be alone." He laughed. "Yes, that cost me a lot of grief, and I never thought to question it. I prayed about that more than any one thing, I believe."

The screen door opened and Jack came into the porch, then into the kitchen. He looked at her and shrugged. "My courage failed," he said. "I thought if you were dressed you might be able to go late. Sorry."

After a moment her father said, "Come here, son," and held out his hands. Jack set his hat on the table and came to the old man and let him take his hands. "There is nothing surprising in this," the old man said. "Not at all." There was a quaver in his voice, so he cleared his throat. "Many people find it hard to go to church if they've been away for a while. I've seen it very often. And I'd say to them, It's because it means something to you. The decision is important to you. As it should be! So, you see, there's no reason at all to be disappointed. I used to say, The Sabbath is faithful. In a week she'll be here again." And he laughed, sadly, and patted Jack's hands.

Jack looked down at him, tender and distant. "Next week," he said.

Glory combed through her father's hair and then kissed it where it was whitest and thinnest, just at the top of his head. "All done," she said, and took the towel off from around him.

Jack said, "I don't suppose you'd have time for another customer."

"Well, sure." She was surprised. They had always been so careful of him, almost afraid to touch him. There was an aloofness about him more thoroughgoing than modesty or reticence. It was feral, and fragile. It had enforced a peculiar decorum on them all, even on their mother. There was always the moment when they acknowledged this—no hugging, no roughhousing could include him. Even his father patted his shoulder tentatively, shy and cautious. Why should a child have defended his loneliness that way? But let him have his ways, their father said, or he would be gone. He'd smile at them across that distance, and the smile was sad and hard, and it meant estrangement, even when he was with them.

Her father was also surprised. He said, "Well, I'll get myself out of your way here." Glory helped him up from his chair. "I've got to give the paper a little going over, if Ames is coming. I have to be up to the minute in case he starts talking politics." She settled him by the window, and when she came back, Jack was still standing there, waiting.

"You're probably busy," he said.

"Not especially. But I have to warn you, I don't make any claims for myself as a barber. I really just pretend to cut Papa's hair."

Jack said, "If you could trim it a little. I should have gone to the barbershop yesterday. I might have felt a little less—disreputable."

"This morning? You looked fine."

"No." He took off his jacket, and she wrapped the towel around his neck and around his shoulders. "I could feel it. It was like an itchiness under my skin. Like—scurrility. I thought it might be my clothes. I mean that they made it obvious. More obvious."

He shied away from her touch. "You're going to have to sit still," she said. "Is it Ames?"

"Him, too. But I can't really say the experience is unfamiliar. It has come over me from time to time. It rarely lasts more than a few months." He laughed. "I shouldn't have asked you to do this. You don't have to."

"Sit still."

"You can't commiserate. You have never felt disreputable."

"How do you know?"

"Am I right?"

"I suppose."

"I am right." He said, "In case you're wondering, scurrility seems to be contagious. Be warned. I should wear a leper bell. I suppose I do."

"You're imagining."

"No, I'm only exaggerating."

"You didn't actually go inside the church."

"I didn't even cross the street."

She put her hand under his chin and lifted his head. Had she ever touched his face before? "I can't really see what I'm doing here. You'll have to sit up."

"I suppose old Ames must have seen me there. Loitering. Lurking. Eyeing his flock." He laughed. "What a fool I am."

"Sit still."

"Will do."

"I'm going to trim around your ears. I've got to get it even."

He crossed his ankles and folded his hands and sat there obediently while she snipped at one side and then the other. She tipped up his face again to judge the effect. There were tears on his cheeks. She took a corner of the towel and patted them away, and he smiled at her.

"Exasperation," he said. "I'm so tired of myself."

HE ASKED HER TO CUT HIS HAIR SHORTER ON THE TOP SO it wouldn't fall down on his forehead. He said, "I look like some damn gigolo."

"No, you don't."

He eyed her. "How would you know?"

"I suppose I wouldn't know."

He nodded. "One brief stint as a dance instructor. The old ladies loved me. But I was drinking at the time, so I never really mastered the samba."

She laughed. "That's a sad story."

"Yes, it is. I thought I was doing all right. But my employer frowned on, you know, improvisation. I did some very interesting steps, but you really have to be able to do them again, at least once. That was his major criticism."

"Ah, Jack."

"Jack indeed. I spent that winter at the library. It was such a miserable winter that I seized the opportunity to improve my mind. The old ladies loved me there, too. A gentleman fallen on hard times. I subsisted on bran muffins and white cake. These were not the same old ladies. Less rouge, no henna."

"I've noticed how well-read you are."

He nodded. "I have been a frequenter of libraries over the years. It's the last place people think to look for you. The sort of people who come looking for you. Much better than a movie theater. So I thought I might as well read what I was supposed to have read in college. Insofar as memory served. Awfully dull work, a lot of it. I'd never have lasted a week in college if Teddy hadn't been there to do it for me."

"Oh."

"He's never mentioned that."

"Not a word, so far as I know."

"That precocity of his? It came from years of doing my homework. He is deeply in my debt. I would never mention this, of course. Except to you."

"That's good of you."

He nodded. "We are brothers, after all."

"But you have to sit still."

"I'm trying."

"Maybe calm down a little."

"An interesting suggestion," he said. "A really good idea."

"I will not touch another hair of your head unless you sit still."

"Fair enough. Just let me have the scissors and I'll finish it up myself."

"Not a chance, buster."

He laughed.

"Not in the mood you're in."

He nodded. "You're right to worry. I just want to be rid of this damn forelock. What do they say? Seize Fate by the forelock?"

"Time, I think. It's Time that has the forelock."

"Well, something's got me by the forelock. Nothing so dignified as Fate, I'm pretty sure. If thy forelock offend thee, cut it off. Sorry."

"Then sit still."

"Did you ever wonder what that means? If thy right eye offend thee? As if it were not part of thee? It's true, though. I offend me—eyes, hands, history, prospects—"

"Did you have any breakfast?"

He laughed.

"You didn't. I'm going to make you a sandwich. You're worried about seeing Ames tonight at dinner."

"Yes, well, it seems I've done as much as one man could do to make the experience embarrassing."

"Nonsense. Really. If he did see you on the street, what of it?"

"Good point, Glory. Perspective. Just what is called for here. Would he have noticed my discomfort with myself from that distance? Well, so what? A law-abiding citizen has a perfect right to feel wretched on a public sidewalk, on a Sabbath morning. Even to pause as he does so. Near a church, too. There's poetry in it, of a sort."

"You don't really know that he saw you."

"Right you are."

"Meat loaf or tuna salad?"

"Meat loaf. Just a little catsup."

She started to move his jacket away from the table and he stood up and took it out of her hands, smiling. It was another sensitivity, like the privacy of that bare, orderly room upstairs. Fine. She was sorry she had forgotten. He felt for the slight weight in the left breast pocket, about which she did not let herself wonder, and put the jacket on. "I'll shake out this towel," he said. "Then I'll sweep up a little."

JACK BROUGHT HIS FATHER'S ARMCHAIR INTO THE KITCHEN so he could be present for the paring of apples and the rolling of pastry. "I have always enjoyed that," the old man said, "the sound of a knife slicing through an apple." He asked for a look at the pie before the top crust went on—"More fragrant than flowers!"—and for a look at it afterward, when the edge had been fluted and the vents were cut. He said, "My grandmother used to go out and gather up windfall apples. Our orchard was too young to produce much, but she'd pick them up wherever she found them and bring them home and make a pile of them out there in front of the shed, and they'd stay there till they fermented, and then she'd make them into cider. She said it was medicinal, tonic for her achy bones, she said. She'd give me a taste sometimes. It tasted terrible. But when the morning was chilly, the steam would pour off those apples like smoke. A smoldering pyre of apples. The chickens would roost on it, for the warmth." He laughed. "The cats would sleep on it. She always had her own little projects. She'd eat kidney when she could find it. Tongue. Mutton. In spring she'd be out in the fields, along the fences, picking dandelion greens as soon as the sun was up. She'd come in with her apron full of purslane. My mother thought it was embarrassing. She'd say, 'You'd think we didn't feed her!' But she always did what she wanted to do." He talked on with the intermitted constancy of a pot simmering. Jack trimmed mushrooms he had brought in and washed them, and washed them again until he was sure there was no trace of sand left in them. He chopped the onion. The kitchen began to smell of pie baking.

"This is wonderful," his father said. "So much going on and me right in the middle of it. In the way, too, I suppose. It was kind of you to set me up like this, Jack. You're very good to me."

Jack laughed. "You deserve it," he said.

His father said, "Yes, the pleasures of family life are very real."

"So I understand."

"Well, you would remember them yourself, Jack. Your mother was always baking something. Ten of us in the house, and there were people dropping by all the time in those days. She felt she had to have something nice to offer them. The girls would be out here helping her, making cakes and cookies. All the talking and laughing. And a little fussing and scuffling now and then, too. Yes. But you were always off somewhere."

"Not always."

"No, not always. That's just how it seemed to me."

"Sorry."

"Well, we missed you, that's all."

And now here he is, Glory thought, haggard and probationary, with little of his youth left to him except the wry elusiveness, secretiveness, that he did in fact seem to wear on his skin. He stood propped against the counter with his arms folded and watched his father while his father pondered him, smiling that hard, wistful smile at what he knew his father saw, as if he were saying, "All those years I spared you knowing I wasn't worth your grief."

But the old man said, "Come here, son," and he took Jack's hands and caressed them and touched them to his cheek. He said, "It's a powerful thing, family."

And Jack laughed. "Yes, sir. Yes, it is. I do know that."

"Well," he said, "at least you're home."

WHEN THE PIE WAS DONE AND THE ROAST WAS IN THE OVEN AND the biscuits were made and set aside and the old man had nodded off in the warmth of the kitchen, Jack went upstairs and Glory sat down to read for a while. The table was set, the kitchen was in reasonable order, Lila was bringing a salad.

She heard Jack washing up, shaving again, no doubt. That was how he nerved himself. By shaving and by polishing his shoes. He ironed his own shirts, very carefully, though not as well as she could have done it for him. He never let himself be a burden to her if he could avoid it, or accepted help he did not immediately repay with help. When she laundered her father's shirts for him, he in return mopped the kitchen floor and waxed it, too. He did such things with a thoroughness and flair he always quite plausibly ascribed to professional experience. She tried to assure him that it wasn't necessary to maintain this careful reciprocity, but he only raised his eyebrows, as if to say he might know more about that than she did. She realized it was not only proud but also prudent in a man so disposed as he was, by habit and experience, to doubt his welcome. It calmed him a little to know he had been useful.

And his self-sufficiency was also guardedness, as if his personal effects could be interpreted, or as if, few as they were, worn as they were, they were saturated with the particulars of his secretive life and could mock or accuse him, or expose old injury, or old happiness, which seemed to be the same thing, more or less. Once, when he had been home for a week or so, she had gone out to hang the laundry and had found two of his shirts on the line, already dry. So she took them in to iron them, since she would be ironing anyway. Collar, yoke, sleeves—this was the proper order of things, so her mother had said, and she did not depart from it. When she began to iron the first of the sleeves, she noticed that it was spangled with stars and flowers, an elaborate embroidery of white on white from the cuff to the elbow, and one final flower near the shoulder.

Jack came into the porch, stopped abruptly when he saw what she was doing, and smiled at her.

"Sorry," she said. "I guess I've intruded again."

He said, "Careful. That's my best shirt."

"I'm always careful. The embroidery on it is really beautiful."

"A friend of mine said she would mend it for me, and that's what she did instead. It was a kind of joke."

"Very pretty, though."

He nodded.

She said, "You can finish. You've made me nervous."

He shrugged. "I'm touchy. I know that."

"No, this is beautiful. You're right to worry about it."

He said, "I almost never wear it. But I lost that other suitcase." He came just close enough to look sidelong at the flowers and stars, pressed smooth, softly bright like damask. "I never ex-

177

pected anything like that. She did it years ago. Years ago." That was the first she had heard of Della.

JACK CAME DOWNSTAIRS TO HELP PREPARE THEIR FATHER for his dinner, wordlessly, since the old man slept on in the vapors and perfumes of Sabbath. He polished the old man's shoes and brushed his jacket and rummaged through his ties. He brought out two, one a dark blue stripe and one maroon and ruby. Glory touched the gorgeous one, Jack nodded and draped it over the shoulder of the jacket. Then he rummaged again and found the tie clasp that looked like a dagger with a St. Andrew's cross on the hilt, and the matching cuff links. She shrugged. Allusions to Scotland aroused in their father a wistful indignation, and a readiness to defend the proposition that history in general ought to have unfolded otherwise, with that one sad instance as case in point. Ames, being no Scot, nor much interested in history after the sack of Rome and before the Continental Congress, heard him out with a patience their father found trying. "Then what does matter?" their father would ask the air, once Ames was out the door. So Jack returned them to the dresser. He came back with the Masonic set, Scottish Rite, of course, but a reminder of power and prosperity won despite all. Ames was no Mason, either, so their father's vows of secrecy forbade conversational forays that might otherwise have become tedious. She nodded.

She brought out his best new shirt. Jack touched the sleeve and whispered, "Very nice!" Their father had always said it was a false economy to buy clothes of poor quality because he was, in his decorous, ministerial way, a dandy. From time to time, in their childhood, boxes arrived from Chicago. Suits and shirts and ties emerged from them, ordinary enough to pass unnoticed, except as they gave his lanky body an air of composure and grace. A new dress or suit, which also arrived from Chicago, was the reward for the child who gained the most height as a percentage of his or her height the previous Easter. This began as a ploy of their mother's to get them to eat vegetables. The figuring of percentages was added as a concession to Teddy's notions of equity. It was he who reflected on the fact that the girls would be sure to grow less than the boys did in absolute terms. Jack never turned up for the measuring ceremony, which was a boisterous business of cake and cocoa and argumentative calculation. But that one year the suit was for him anyway and he did come to Easter service. Looking so beautiful, his father said when he mentioned it.

So SHE AND JACK MADE A SORT OF PIECEMEAL SIMULACRUM of their dozing father. Jack played solitaire beside him while Glory dressed, then Jack went upstairs while Glory finished the vegetables and the gravy. Half an hour before the Ameses were to arrive, Glory roused her father and helped him into his clothes, washed his face and brushed his hair into a fine white tousle that went handsomely with his glorious tie and the irascible look he assumed to conceal his pleasure at these attentions to his vanity.

"Jack is here," he said, as if to exclude other possibilities.

"He went upstairs a few minutes ago."

"He will be back downstairs in time for dinner."

"Yes."

Then Ames arrived with Lila and Robby, the three of them in their church clothes, and she took her father into the parlor with them, the company parlor, where they sat on the creaky chairs no one ever sat on. It had been almost forgotten that they were not there just to be dismally ornamental, chairs only in the same sense that the lamp stand was a shepherdess. Ames was clearly bemused by the formality her father had willed upon the occasion. The room was filled with those things that seem to exist so that children can be forbidden to touch them—porcelain windmills and pagodas and china dogs—and Robby's eyes were bright with suppressed attraction to them. He leaned at his mother's knee, lifting his face to whisper to her now and then, bunching and twisting the hem of her dress in his hands. There were remarks on the weather. Her father said, "Egypt will have consequences," and she went into the kitchen to sauté the morels, since Jack had still not appeared.

Just when his absence began to seem conspicuous and awkward, when she had gone into the parlor to tell them that Jack would certainly be down in a minute or two, they heard him on the stairs, and then there he was, standing in the doorway. He was dressed in one of his father's fine old dark suits. There was a silence of surprise. He brushed at his shoulder. He said, "The cloth is a little faded. It looks like dust." Then no one spoke until his father said, "I was quite a tall fellow at one time."

Jack was wearing one of the creamy shirts she had brought down from the chest in the attic and the blue striped tie, and his hair was parted high and combed straight to the side. He looked very like his father in his prime, except for the marked weariness of his face, his mild and uninnocent expression. Aware of the silence, he smiled and touched the scar beneath his eye. But he would have looked elegant, after a decorous and outmoded fashion, if he had not been Jack, and if they had not thought, therefore, What does this mean? what might he do next? And there was something moving in the fact that the suit fit him almost perfectly, or would have if he were not quite so thin. He was the measure of the failure of his father's body, and also perhaps a portending of the failure of his own.

Ames said, "Well," and looked at him for a moment before he remembered to rise.

Glory had noticed that men who were on uncertain terms with each other will take one step forward, leaning into a space between them as if the distance had been arrived at by treaty and could be breached only for the moment it took them to shake hands. "Jack," he said.

Jack said, "Reverend. Mrs. Ames." And then he laughed and

smoothed his lapels and looked at Glory sidelong, as if to say, "Another bad idea!" He was wearing the dagger tie clasp. The brightness in his face meant anxiety. When he was anxious a strange honesty overtook him. He did understandable things for understandable reasons, answering expectation in terms that were startlingly literal, as if in him the skeletal machinery of conventional behavior, the extension and contraction of the pulleys of muscle and sinew, was all exposed. And he was aware of this, embarrassed by it, inclined to pass it off, if he could, as irony, to the irritation of acquaintances and strangers, and, she could only imagine, employers and police.

She said to her guests, feigning the same slight strangerliness they feigned, too, "Please come into the dining room. Jack will help me serve."

"Oh, good," Jack said. "I was feeling a little at a loss." Then to Lila he said, "No gift for small talk, polite conversation. None at all."

Lila smiled. "Me neither." She had a soft, slow, comfortable voice that suggested other regions, and suggested, too, in its very gentleness, that she knew a good deal more about the world than she would ever let on. Jack looked at her with pleasant interest, with a kind of hopefulness, Glory thought. Clearly Ames noticed, too. Poor Jack. People watched him, and he knew it. It was partly distrust. But more than that, the man was at once indecipherable and transparent. Of course they watched him.

He followed her into the kitchen. He said, "Maybe I should go change."

"No, no. You're just fine. You look nice." She put serving dishes into his hands. "I'll bring the condiments. Come back for the roast."

He carried in the huge, chipped semi-porcelain platter on which roasts and hams and turkeys had always made their entrances in that house and, after a moment's hesitation, set it down in front of his father, in keeping with what was once family custom. But the old man was still a little grimly bemused by the apparition he had seen of himself in his relative youth. He said, "I don't know what I'm supposed to do with that. It might as well still be on the hoof for all the luck I'd have with it. Give it to Ames."

Jack said, "Yes, sir," and after Lila had rearranged the serving dishes, he set the roast in front of Ames, who said, "I'll do my best."

Jack took the chair next to his father, and then Robby left his mother's side and came around the table and leaned into the chair beside Jack's.

"I could sit here," he said shyly.

Jack said, "You could, indeed. Please do," and helped him pull the chair a little way from the table. Ames glanced up from the roast.

Lila said, "He's taken to you. He don't often act that friendly. Doesn't."

Jack said, "I'm honored," as if he meant it. Then he stood up from the table. "Excuse me. One minute. An oversight," and left the room. They heard him leave the porch.

His father shook his head. "He's up to something, I suppose. No idea in the world what it could be."

They sat waiting for him, and in a few minutes he came back with a handful of sweet peas in a water glass, which he put down in front of Lila. "We can't have Mrs. Ames as our guest and no flowers on the table!" he said. "It's not much of a bouquet. A little better than nothing, I hope."

Lila smiled. "They're nice," she said.

Ames cleared his throat. "Well, Reverend Boughton, since I have carved, maybe you could offer the blessing."

Boughton said, "I was thinking you might do that, too."

There was a silence.

Jack took a slip of paper from his pocket. "In case of emergency," he said. "I mean, in case this should fall to me, the grace. I've written it out."

His father looked at him a little balefully. "That's excellent, Jack. Perhaps it won't be necessary."

Jack glanced at Ames, who shrugged, and he began to read. "'Dear Father,'" he said. He paused and studied the paper, leaning into the candlelight. "My handwriting is very poor. I crossed some things out. 'You are patient and gracious far beyond our deserving.'" He cleared his throat. "'You let us hope for your forgiveness when we can find no way to forgive ourselves. You bless our lives even when we have shown ourselves to be utterly ungrateful and unworthy. May we be strengthened and renewed, to make us less unworthy of blessing, through these your gifts of sustenance, of friendship and family.'" And then, "'In Jesus' name we pray, amen.'"

Again there was a silence. He looked at Ames, who nodded and said, "Thank you."

"Jack, that was fine," his father said.

Jack shrugged. "I thought I'd give it a try. I should have noticed I had the word 'unworthy' down twice. I thought 'sustenance' was good, though." He laughed.

After a moment Boughton said to Ames, "We have had some conversation about family over the last few days, and I believe Jack has brought the conversation to a point here. It is in family that we most often feel the grace of God, His faithfulness. Yes."

Jack nodded. He murmured, "Amen."

Heartened, his father launched into an account of his views on Dulles's policy of containment. "It is provocation!" he said. "Pure and simple!" Ames thought Dulles might be proved right in the long term, and Boughton said "the long term" was just a sort of feather pillow that was used to smother arguments.

Ames laughed. "I wish I'd known that sooner."

Boughton said, "You've always enjoyed a good quarrel as much as anybody, Reverend."

Jack asked his father if he thought the long-term consequences of the violence in Montgomery would be important, and his father said, "I don't believe there will be any consequences to speak of. These things come and go. The gravy is wonderful, by the way." Jack absently spindled the slip of paper in his fingers. When he realized Ames had noticed, he smiled and smoothed it out again and slipped it into his pocket. Ames cut Robby's roast for him, and Jack split and buttered a biscuit and set it on the boy's plate.

Whatever part of her father's hopes for the evening could be satisfied by fragrance and candlelight and by food consecrated to the rituals of Boughton celebration, that part at least had been seen to. The roast beef was tender, the glazed beets were pungent, the string beans were as they always were so early in the year, canned. But she had simmered them with bacon to make them taste less like themselves. She waited for someone to remark on the biscuits, but it was the gravy they admired, and she was proud of that, too.

Still, there was something strained about it all, as if time had another burden, like humid air, or as if it were a denser medium and impervious to the trivialization which was all they would expect or hope for on an evening like this one, now that grace was said. Her father gazed at Jack from time to time, pondered him, and Jack was aware of it. His hand trembled when he reached for his water glass, and ordinarily the old man, gentle as he was, would have looked away. But instead he touched Jack's shoulder and his sleeve. Ames, his expression pensively comprehending, watched his friend take the measure of his erstwhile youth.

Jack said, "Dinner with Lazarus."

His father drew his hand away. "Sorry, Jack. I didn't quite hear that."

"Nothing, it just came to my mind. 'And Lazarus was one of those at table with him.' I've always thought that must have been strange. For Lazarus. He must have felt a little—'disreputable' isn't the word. Of course he'd have had time to clean himself up a little. Comb his hair. Still—" He laughed. "Sorry."

Boughton said, "That's very interesting, but I'm still not sure I see your point."

Ames turned a long look on Jack, almost the incarnation of his father's youth. It was a reproving look, as if he suspected that he did see the point and he felt the conversation ought to take another turn. Jack shook his head. "I just—" he said. "I don't know what I was thinking about." He glanced at Glory and smiled.

FOR A WHILE TALK DRIFTED GENTLY AND PREDICTABLY from the world situation to baseball to old times. Then there was a lull in the conversation, and Jack turned his gaze on Robby, who had sat beside him quietly, using his spoon to make a fort or embankment of his mashed potatoes.

"Robby for Robert," Jack said.

He nodded.

"Robert B."

He nodded and laughed.

"B. for Boughton."

He nodded.

Jack said, "I believe that is the best name in the world."

Ames said, "Your father was always naming his sons after other people. He didn't have a Robert of his own."

"No," Boughton said. "Glory would have been Robert, but she wasn't a boy."

Jack looked at her.

His father, afraid he had been rude, said, "It worked out very well—four of each."

Jack shrugged. "Faith. Hope. Grace. Roberta—"

"No," his father said. "Charity was my first thought. But your mother sort of put her foot down. She thought it would make her sound like an orphan or something. The word is actually *agape*. *Caritas* is the Latin. Nothing you would name a child."

Glory said, "I think we should change the subject."

"Your mother wanted to call her Gloria, the usual spelling, but I couldn't see that, when all the other names are in English."

Jack said, "*Fides, Spes, Gratia, Gloria.*"

"Ah, the old jokes," Glory said.

"Yes, it was Teddy who came up with that one," the old man said. "Everything was high school Latin around here for a while, wasn't it." He looked at Jack. "Teddy called yesterday, by the way."

Jack nodded. "Sorry I missed him."

"Well, I suppose he's used to it by now. I guess he'd better be."

Jack smiled at his father. "Yes, well, there's something else I forgot. If you'll excuse me for a minute—" And he put down his fork and stood up and left the table and left the room.

Boughton shook his head. "First he was off picking flowers. Now he's left the table in the middle of dinner. I suppose because I mentioned Teddy. I don't understand it. They used to be close, when they were boys. At least he'd talk to Teddy now and then. I believe he did. That was my impression."

Glory said, "You might lower your voice a little, Papa."

"Well, sometimes I just don't understand his behavior," he said in an emphatic whisper. "I thought after all this time he might be—"

Glory touched her father's wrist, and Jack walked into the silence of interrupted conspiracy, or so he must have thought, smiling as he did, guilelessly, eyebrows raised. "Sorry," he said. "If you'd like, I could just wait out here in the hall for a minute or two. Until you've finished."

"No. You'd better sit down," his father said. "Your dinner is cold enough already."

Jack smiled. "Yes, sir." He was holding a baseball in his hand. When he had sat down, he held it up for Robby to see. "What have we here?" he said.

Robby said, "Um, fastball!"

Jack laughed with surprise, and looked at his hand. "Right you are!" He shifted the ball in his fingers. "And what is this?"

"Knuckleball!"

"And this?"

"Um. Curveball."

He shifted the ball again.

"Um. I forget that one. Let me think. A slipper!"

"Well," Jack said, "when I was a boy we used to call it a slider. Same idea."

Robby put his hands to his face and laughed. "No, a slipper is, like, a shoe!"

Jack nodded. "I suppose you could get in trouble with the umpire if you were out there throwing slippers," and then he watched the child with grave, pleasant interest until he had finished laughing. "So I guess you want to be a pitcher."

Robby nodded. "My dad was a pitcher."

"A very fine pitcher, too," Boughton said. "I don't think people play that game as much as they used to anymore. They're home watching it on television."

"My dad taught me all those pitches," Robby said. "With an orange!" He laughed.

Ames said, "We were just talking baseball over lunch the other day. I thought I'd show him a few things."

"He's a quick study," Jack said.

Ames nodded. "I'm a little surprised he remembered all that."

Robby said, "We have a real baseball, but it's up in the attic somewhere. My dad hates to go up in the attic."

"Well," Ames said. "I see I have been remiss."

Jack put the baseball beside Robby's plate. "This one is for you. It's a present. I knew you probably had one of your own, since your dad was a pitcher. But an extra one can come in handy."

Robby looked at his mother. She nodded.

"Thanks," he said. He took up the ball, shyly, tentatively.

"It's brand new, so you'll have to take care of it. Do you know how to take care of a new baseball?"

"No, but my dad'll tell me."

Jack said, "It's pretty simple. You just rub dirt all over it. Scruff it up a little."

"Rub dirt on it—" the boy said, doubtful. "I guess I'll ask my dad, anyway."

Jack laughed. "That's always a good idea." And he glanced at his own father. "My dad and I used to play a little ball."

The old man nodded. "Yes, we did. We had some good times, too, didn't we?" He looked at his hand. "Hard to believe it now, when I can't even tie my own shoes! I think back to those times, when I was just an ordinary man, not even a young man, and it's like remembering that I used to be the sun and the wind! Taking the steps two at a time—!"

Ames laughed.

"Well, it all just seemed so natural, like it could never end. Your mother would be there in the kitchen, cooking supper, singing to herself. And she'd have a cup of coffee for me, and we'd talk a little. And I could tell just by hearing all the voices who was in the house. Except for Jack, of course. He was so quiet."

Ames said, "The sun and the wind!"

"Oh yes, you can laugh. A big brute like you wouldn't even know what I'm talking about. It seems to me I've gotten old for both of us."

"I beg to differ, Reverend. I feel I've done my share of getting old."

Robby said, "He told me he's too old to play catch."

Ames nodded. "And so I am. It's a sad fact."

Glory saw her brother glance at her, as if an intention had begun to form, and then he looked away again and smiled to himself.

THEY ATE THEIR PIE. "I SUPERVISED," HER FATHER SAID. "Jack pared the apples and Glory made the pastry, and I made sure it was all up to my specifications." He laughed. "Jack put my chair out there in the kitchen, right in the middle of everything.

It was very nice. We've had some good times, we three. I told you that he's almost got the old DeSoto running. Yes. Good times. And he plays the piano! I must say, that came as a surprise."

"Yes," Jack said, "I could play a little now, if you'd like." And he excused himself. They heard him from the next room, trying one hymn and then another—"'I come to the garden alone, while the dew is still on the roses,' then 'Sweet hour of prayer! sweet hour of prayer! that calls me from a world of care.'" Glory brought him a cup of coffee. "Thanks," he said. "'If I have uttered idle words or vain, if I have turned aside from want or pain.'" He laughed. "If only I knew how you do that!" Then "'Love divine, all loves excelling'—they're all waltzes! Have you noticed that?" Lila and Robby came to listen, then Ames, who had stayed behind a little to offer Boughton help, should he admit to needing it.

Lila said, "I like waltzes." So Jack plunged into a brief and distinctly Viennese "There's a Garden Where Jesus Is Waiting."

Ames looked on without expression. Her father's expression was statesmanlike.

And then Jack played, "'I want a Sunday kind of love, a love that lasts past Saturday night.' I've forgotten the words. 'I'm on a lonely road that leads to nowhere. I want a Sunday kind of love.'"

Lila said, almost sang, "'I do my Sunday dreaming, and all my Sunday scheming, every hour, every minute, every day. I'm hoping to discover a certain kind of lover who will show me the way.'"

Jack said, "Why, thank you, Mrs. Ames!" and she smiled.

His father said, "I thought we might enjoy something a little more in keeping with the Sabbath."

Lila said, "That's a good song, though."

"If you wouldn't mind, Jack."

He nodded. He played "Our God, Our Help in Ages Past" and "Faith of Our Fathers" with a kind of exuberant solemnity, and they sang, and then Ames said he was weary after a long day and it must be after Robby's bedtime, too. The boy had climbed up on the

189

piano bench beside Jack and was shyly touching the keys. Jack went to see the guests to the door, but Robby stayed behind, plinking tentatively. When his mother called him and he climbed down from the bench, he noticed that the seat could be lifted, and he opened it. He said, "There's money in here!"

Ames reflexively took Boughton's arm. Glory said, "Oh, I put it there," but her father crept toward the bench to peer into it as if it were a chasm opening. Glory said, "It's just leftover money from the household allowance. I take it out of the other drawer so I can keep track of what I'm spending," but her father, with Ames holding his arm, continued to stare at it. Jack looked in at it, too, and then he started to laugh. "Good try, Glory. A likely tale!" He said, "If there are thirty-eight dollars in there I will have to believe in—something." And he put his hands to his face and laughed.

His father was bewildered to the point of indignation. "Now that," he said, "is a remark I simply do not understand!"

Robby said, "Well, it is kind of funny to have all those dollar bills in there!"

Ames smoothed the boy's hair. "Yes, it is. You're right about that. Now, you go home with your mother. I'll be along pretty soon."

When Lila and the boy were out the door, Glory slammed the piano shut, so hard that the strings rang. "Everyone is ignoring me!" she said. Her anger startled all of them. "Wait." She went into the parlor and came back with the big Bible. She closed the bench and set the Bible on it. "Now watch. Everyone watch." And she knelt and put her right hand on the Bible. "I solemnly swear, so help me, God, that I personally put that money in the piano bench. It looks as if I were hiding it, but it was just a lazy kind of bookkeeping. That's all it was. And I did it. No one else. If I'm lying, may God strike me dead."

Her father said, "That kind of language isn't really necessary, dear," but he was clearly impressed, and also relieved. "You're good to your brother," he said, and Jack laughed. "I only meant—" he said, and looked so weary that Ames took him into his room and helped him lie down. Before he left, Reverend Ames said goodbye to them both, and shook Jack's hand again. His cordiality seemed heavily compounded with regret, with suppressed irritation. Still, Jack was clearly grateful for it.

When he was gone Jack said, "That thing you did with the Bible was great. I'm going to have to remember that." And he laughed. Then, "If you hadn't rescued it, the whole thing would have been a disaster, but as it was, I thought, well, I didn't think it was a disaster, all in all." He looked at her as though he had asked her a question.

Amazing, she thought, but she said, "No, it went well enough."

He nodded. "I believe it did. My expectations were low. Reasonable in the circumstances. Still. His kid seemed to like me. And the Mrs. That part of it went pretty well." He went upstairs and came back down again in one of his own shirts and began to help her clear the table.

She said, "Jack, can I ask you something? No, I'll tell you something. I'm beginning to think your Della can't be worth all this misery."

"What? She's worth it. If I could be any more miserable, she'd be worth that, too. You'll have to take my word for it."

"She doesn't write to you—"

He smiled at her, stung.

"I'm sorry. I don't know what the problem is."

He said, "That's true. You don't."

"But I know you a little now, and you're really not so hard to forgive."

"Why, thank you." Then he said, "But you don't know how much she's had to forgive. You can't even imagine. And there's more every damn day." He looked at her. He said, "And I think that's enough about Della."

THE NEXT DAY GLORY WENT TO THE HARDWARE STORE and bought two pairs of the tan cotton pants and three of the blue denim shirts local men wore when they were not farming or fishing or dressed for a funeral. They were folded over cardboard, stiff when they were new, but she would put them through the wash twice and press them a little and they would be fine. She guessed at Jack's size. Anything long enough was too wide, but he would have to make the best of that.

While she was hanging them on the clothesline, he walked over from the garden and stood with his hands on his hips, watching. He said, "Those for me?"

"If you think you can use them."

He laughed. "I'm pretty sure I can." He said, "Thanks, Glory," and he reached over and touched a sleeve appreciatively. There was no irony in the gesture. "I'll have to owe you for this."

"You don't owe me for anything. I took some money out of the piano bench. I'm as broke as you are."

"I lost that other suitcase."

"I know."

He was quiet for a minute. "You had a pretty good job."

"I did."

"That bastard took your money."

She shrugged. "I gave it to him. It doesn't matter. I didn't have any real plans for it."

He nodded. "The old fellow thinks you had to quit teaching because you got married."

"And you know differently."

"Yes. None of my business." He took a cigarette from his shirt pocket and tapped it on his thumbnail.

"What?"

"I've often thought—" he said. "I mean, it's been my experience—that women can be too kind. Too kind for their own good."

She laughed. "I've thought so, too, from time to time."

"You're kind."

"Case in point."

He studied her face, wincing against the smoke from his cigarette. Then he said, "Could you forgive him?" He glanced away. "Sorry. None of my business." He said, "You brought it up last night. I was just wondering."

She smiled at him.

"Right," he said. "You don't like to talk about it."

There was something that charmed her in the fact that her brother, the one true worldling in the whole tribe of Boughtons, seemed to be asking her for advice, or for wisdom, standing there in the sunlight with the wind hushing in the dusty lilacs of their childhood and laundry swaying on the lines where their school clothes used to hang. He looked older in sunlight. It brought out a sort of toughened frailty in him. But, standing at a little distance, looking away at nothing in particular, he had that oblique and hesitant persistence about him that meant he was in earnest, so far as she could tell.

So she said, "Could I forgive him? I'm not sure I understand the question. But the answer is no."

He nodded.

"I don't wish him any harm, and I'm glad I'll never see him again. I don't enjoy being reminded of him."

"Sorry. I wouldn't have mentioned it, but you did bring it up. You said I'm not hard to forgive. Something like that."

"Were you good to her?"

"I tried to be." He shrugged.

"Then if she's a kind woman she'll probably forgive you. Of course I don't know what you did, what she'd have to forgive you for."

He laughed and tossed away his cigarette. "I'm not sure I do, either. There were so many things she put up with—it's what I am, as much as anything. What I'm not. She got tired of the problems. I should have been more protective somehow." He said, "I tried that. Once I sort of defended her honor. Not wise in the circumstances." Then, "It probably wouldn't matter if she did forgive me. I thought she might write, though." He said, "You get used to kindness. After a while you begin to count on it. You miss it when it's gone."

She said, "I know a little bit about that," and he nodded, and the lilacs rustled, and the sun shone, and there was quiet between them, a calm that came with being of one mind. So she had to say, "You shouldn't lose hope."

He laughed. "Sometimes I really wish I could."

She said, "I know about that, too."

Why hadn't she bought clothes for him weeks ago? Because he was a stranger she was afraid of offending with so personal an attention. Because her buying clothes for him would allude to his poverty and offend him. Because it might seem like a subject of conversation for people who saw her buying them and this would embarrass and offend him. Because he was vain, and particular, and Jack. Cheap, sturdy work clothes were not the kind of thing he thought he should wear, and they would offend him. But in fact she saw him check the shirts on the line several times, and when one of them was dry enough, he brought it in and ironed it and put it on. The pants were heavier and took longer to dry. She saw him check them, too, then walk over by the orchard, pick a fallen apple off the ground, throw it up on the barn roof, and wait and catch it when it came down, and throw it again. Her brothers all did that when they were boys. Jack looked a little stiff, as if he were making an experiment in attempting this lonely game after so many years. Tentative as he was, it might have meant happiness.

AMES STROLLED OVER THAT EVENING AFTER SUPPER, FOR a game of checkers, he said, but he and their father sat in the porch with the board between them and talked quietly together, the way they did when advice of some kind was being sought and given. Glory brought them ice water and left them to themselves. It was a courtesy Ames paid to his friend to seek out pastoral wisdom even though he must have had wisdom of his own to spare after so many years, and since he was, by temperament, the more obliging of the two and therefore seldom in particular need of wisdom, his own or Boughton's. All the same, he would offer up some soul to her father's contemplation and then they would consider together, as they did in the old days, how to mollify, comfort, instruct. Boughton had resigned his pulpit ten years earlier, under circumstances that made Ames especially careful to respect his views. The Sunday-school children were marrying, and the married couples had settled into difficult, ordinary life, and the grave old men and women who had taught the Sunday-school children about bands of angels and flying chariots were themselves crossing over Jordan one by one. So he helped Ames think through whatever question might have arisen among the Congregationalists, whom he knew better than his own former flock now, through these murmured consultations. "Yes," he would say, "a good deal of tact will be called for in dealing with that fellow," and Ames would say, "That's for sure." During these conversations her father's expression assumed its old sagacity, that gentle shrewdness of the practiced shepherd of souls. "But I'd tell him where matters stand. I'd be frank about it." His eyes would kindle with the thought of firmness and candor, the memory of those old pleasures. Ames always watched him with a kind of bemused and wistful respect, as if he were now the younger man and his friend had aged past him into a venerability he might never attain. "Yes," he would say, "I will certainly be frank."

Jack came upon them there, talking together. She heard them greet him, and a word or two, and then he came into the kitchen with cucumbers from the garden. His shirt bloused and his pants gathered a little under his belt, but she was pleased all in all with the way he looked and she could tell he was, too. He managed to seem a little dapper, somehow, a thing his pride required. She knew this was a relief to him. He washed the cucumbers. "Cucumbers smell like evening," he said. "Like chill. Need any help?" When she said no he went to the piano and sat down and began to play "Softly and Tenderly," a favorite hymn of his father's. He played it softly, and, she thought, very tenderly. She went into the hallway to listen, and he glanced up at her sidelong, as if there were an understanding between them, but he played on pensively, without a hint of detachment or calculation. "Come home, come home, ye who are weary, come home." The old men fell silent. "Earnestly, tenderly, Jesus is calling, calling for you and for me." Her father sang, Ames with him. Then "Rock of Ages," then "The Old Rugged Cross," and when that song was over, it was night. It had begun to thunder and rain, one of those storms that come after dark and change the weather. The old men sat there, silent for a long time. She brought Ames an umbrella, and after a while she heard him take his leave. She was afraid the damp might make her father uncomfortable, but he asked her, very kindly, to leave him alone for a little while. He said, "Tell Jack that was wonderful. I was proud of him."

She found Jack in his room, the door open, lying on his bed reading a book. She said, from the doorway, "Jack, Papa told me to tell you it was wonderful that you played for them. He said he was proud of you."

He considered. "Was Ames still here when he said that?"

"Not when he said it to me. Ames would have known it anyway."

Jack nodded. "I suppose he would. Good. Thanks, Glory."

IT RAINED SOUNDLY AND SATISFACTORILY OVERNIGHT. There was talk of drought, and one good rain would not end the worry, but it did make a beautiful morning, a mild and fragrant wind and shimmering trees loud with birds. Jack had left the house early. Glory heard the creak of the screen door before the sun was well up. His restlessness took on the aspect of virtue, rousing him out of bed in the dark and sending him out into the garden to expend the sour energies of failed sleep. She went down to the kitchen and started a pot of coffee, and sat in the porch while it brought itself to the kind and degree of fragrance her family had always preferred. Then she poured a cup for Jack. She found him out by the clothesline. He pulled a line down and released it, and raindrops flew up, brilliant in the morning light. He did the same with the next one, and the next.

"Thanks," he said, as he took the cup from her. She saw that he had brought the gasoline can out of the barn. He said, "Back in a minute," and went into the house, and came out again with his suit on hangers and a dishtowel over his shoulder. "I'm going to do a little dry cleaning." He poured gasoline into an empty coffee can and soaked the cloth in it, and then sponged the sleeve of his jacket, saturated the bulge at the elbow and the creases at the inside of the elbow, and pulled it straight. He glanced at her. "This sort of works," he said. "After a while the smell goes away. Here," he said, and handed her his cigarettes and his matches. "I can be absentminded."

She said, "I've heard that people did this. I've never actually seen anyone do it before."

He said, "Sheltered life."

The whole of that morning he worked at his suit. She saw him stand back finally and study it as it swung there in the wind and apparently decide it was good enough, since he emptied the coffee can out on the ground and carried the gasoline back to the barn. She went out to see for herself, and it did look to her as if it had fewer of the signs of hard use than it had had before, that it looked more impersonal, less conformed to one particular life. In the breeze there was something game about it, even a little jaunty. No wonder he was pleased.

He came inside, washed up, and made himself a peanut butter

sandwich. "Want one? I'll give you half of mine. All of it. I washed my hands." He said, "What is the French for sandwich?"

"I'm pretty sure the French for sandwich is sandwich."

He nodded. "I was afraid of that. So I am at a loss to make this slightly gaseous object more appealing to you. To me, for that matter."

"Jelly?"

"Hate the stuff. It can be good in doughnuts." He lifted the top slice of bread and looked under it. "An ugly food, peanut butter. If I struck a match, perhaps I could serve it to you flaming, madame. As they do in the finer restaurants. Mademoiselle."

"No, thanks. I'm having soup. Want some?"

He shook his head. "I am hungry in general. It is the particulars that discourage me."

"Then you might as well just eat your sandwich."

"True." He said, "Do we still have that baseball mitt?"

"Yes, we do. I put it in my closet. I was afraid you might find some way to swap it for a hair shirt."

He nodded. "That was prudent of you. I was thinking, if you still had it, I might borrow it back."

She said, "Sure. As soon as you finish your sandwich."

"I do this," he said, "only because I trust you to have my best interests at heart." He ate it in eight bites and washed it down with a glass of water. "Well, now I've fed the beast," he said. "It should stagger through till supper. It is an oddly patient beast, my carnal self. I call it Snowflake. For, you know, its intractable whiteness. Among other things. A certain lingering sentiment attaches to it. It reminds me of my youth."

She brought him the mitt. He said, "Kids his age are always losing things, so I bought another baseball. I mean, I was always losing things. At his age."

"That's fine."

He put the mitt on his hand and popped the ball into the pocket with a flick of his wrist. That ancient gesture. "I thought

Ames might appreciate— A kid ought to learn how to play catch. I was good at baseball. I thought he might remember that."

"It's a good idea, Jack. I don't think you need to worry so much about what Ames thinks of you."

"I know what he thinks of me. It can't get much worse. So that doesn't worry me."

"Then what does?"

"You're right. Deranged by hope. I guess I thought he might look down upon me from his study window and say to himself, 'He's a cad and a bounder, but I appreciate his attention to my son.'" He laughed. "That won't happen. No need to worry about that. What a stupid idea."

Glory said, "I've been meaning to ask you to take the new *Life* and *The Nation* over to the Ameses'. They don't subscribe. Ask Lila if Robby might like to play a little ball. If she says yes, the Reverend won't object."

He nodded. "All right. I'll do it. Nothing ventured and so on."

AFTER HALF AN HOUR SHE WALKED OUT JUST FAR ENOUGH to see Jack and Robby in the road in front of Ames's house, Robby encumbered with the big stiff glove, scrambling after the ball when Jack tossed it and throwing it back halfway and in something like the right direction. "That's the idea!" Jack called. The child squared off and punched his mitt, ready for anything. The next toss bounced off his shoe. Jack laughed, very kind laughter that she had not heard for decades if she had ever heard it. He ran forward to field Robby's throw, and when he turned around he saw her. He waved. "Home soon," he called.

She called back, "No hurry," sorry she had distracted him. He looked like a man full of that active contentment that makes even ordinary movement graceful. He looked at ease in sunlight. She hoped old Ames had indeed gazed down upon him. He might have seen him as his father did, for once.

After another half hour Jack came in through the porch. He smiled when he saw her. "That was all right," he said. "What a funny kid. He's a nice kid. I don't think I'm grooming him for the majors, though. He wants to play for the Red Sox. I'm not saying he has no chance at all. You have to be black to have no chance at all."

"There's Jackie Robinson."

"Ah yes. Jackie Robinson of Dodger fame. There's Larry Dobie, Willie Mays, Frank Robinson. Roy Campanella, Ernie Banks. Satchel Paige. I'll give you a nickel if you can tell me which one plays for Boston."

"I confess, I haven't given much thought to baseball lately."

"Clearly. There are those in St. Louis who think of little else. I have had many earnest conversations on the subject."

She looked at him. "With Della?"

"One or two of them with Della. She knows what matters in this world."

Glory laughed. "Well, I'm pretty sure I don't. Here I've been wasting my time worrying about radioactive fallout. About strontium 90."

He said, "Believe me, she worries about that, too."

JACK LET A DAY PASS, AND THEN IN THE AFTERNOON HE took his ball and glove and went to Ames's again. When he came back he seemed pleased. "The kid's shaping up. He actually caught one on the first bounce." He said, "It was all right. They even asked me to stay for supper. Lila asked me. But I don't think the Reverend objected. He didn't seem to."

"Why didn't you stay?"

He shrugged and smiled. "They were being polite."

"Of course they were being polite. That doesn't mean they weren't really inviting you."

After a moment he said, "I have learned, in the tedious course of my life, that it is safer not to presume on these courtesies. I have taken the bait often enough to know how it feels when the trap shuts. Better to forgo the pleasures of, you know, pot roast and mashed potatoes."

She said, "You want to get yourself on better terms with Ames. How can you do that if you don't let him—well—treat you like a friend? Ask you to supper? It's the most ordinary thing in the world."

He nodded. "There it is. My lifelong exile from the ordinary world. I have to learn the customs. And somehow persuade myself that they pertain to me." He looked at her. "That's where it gets tricky."

"No, you just have to relax a little and remind yourself that you are dealing with a very kind old man."

He said, "It really is more complex than that, Glory. The other day I gave his kid my glove to use, so he ran upstairs and took that old glove Ames keeps on his desk and brought it down to me. I guess it once belonged to the long-departed Uncle Edward. It seemed harmless enough to me to put it on. I mean, it wasn't as if I were going to be catching anything with it. But, you know, I stole it once. Temporarily. I don't know why. And Ames knew I had stolen it, because who else would bother. And I was the town thief. So today when he came up the road from church there I was with that thing on my hand and nothing to do but stand there. He looked at it and looked at me and he didn't say anything about it and neither did I, but I could tell that he was reminded of all that, my troubled youth, and it was embarrassing. For him, too."

"I think you forget how long ago all that happened."

"Yes, and here I am today, John Ames Boughton, solid citizen. A miraculous transformation." He laughed. He was thoughtful for a while, and then he said, "If I had it all to do over again, I mean adolescent criminality, I'd try to restrict myself to doing things that were explicable. Or at least appeared to be explicable. I'm serious. It's the things people can't account for that upset them. The old gent used to ask me, 'Why did you do that, Jack?' And I couldn't even tell him I did it because I felt like it. Even that wouldn't have been true. What did I want with an old baseball mitt? Nothing. But there wasn't really much to steal in this town. It would have been hard to find anything to want, anything that might make it seem as though I had a motive. So all my offenses were laid to a defect of character. I have no quarrel with that. But it is a problem for me now."

Glory said, "If the Ameses ask you to supper again, say yes. And stay. Promise me."

He laughed. "Will do. On my honor." He said, "You have a feeling for these things."

AND THE VERY NEXT DAY, HAVING TOILED EARNESTLY IN the vegetable patch and the flower beds from dawn till noon, and having tightened the joints of the three Adirondack chairs that had always slouched together under the kitchen window as if to be indolently serviceable in the event that something in the yard between them and the barn should attract spectators, and having restrung the clothesline, he came into the house, ironed a shirt, and polished his shoes. "I'm feeling useful," he said. "Productive. That's good for morale. So is the tan." He pushed up his sleeve to show her. "There's a definite line there."

"So there is." She had learned to worry about these hectic outbursts of purposefulness, and to know there was no point in trying to damp them down.

He said, "I believe this is Thursday. So tomorrow is Friday, and Ames will probably be working on his sermon. He won't welcome interruption." He said, "I will probably go to church on Sunday. I can do that. My suit no longer smells combustible. Just slightly automotive. I wouldn't want to alarm anyone." He laughed.

So all this was in preparation for supper at the Ameses', for which he had not been invited. But he left the house in the early evening, pausing in the door to look at her and shrug, as if to say, Wish me luck. When he was not home for supper, she told her father that she thought he might have been invited by Ames and Lila.

"Yes," her father said. "I hope John will take some interest in him. That is a thing I wished for many years. When you give a man a namesake, you do expect a certain amount of help. Ames was a help to me, of course. Not to Jack so much. I don't mean to criticize. I guess I wasn't much help to him either, as far as that goes."

The old man wanted to wait for him in the porch, so they sat there together in the mild night. "You can't see the lightning bugs through these screens," he said. "You can't see the stars. But at least you get the breeze. You hear the crickets."

After a little while he said, "Ames will need his rest. Old fellows can't tolerate these late nights. I hope he will realize that." And then they heard footsteps and Jack came up the walk and up the steps.

"Nice evening," he said. His voice was soft and calm. Glory knew that her father noticed, too.

"Yes," the old man said. "Yes, it is. A fine evening."

Jack said, "They were very kind. The boy likes me. And Mrs. Ames seems to think I'm all right."

"I suppose you talked a little politics, Jack?"

"Yes, sir. He says, 'Stevenson is a very fine man, no doubt.'"

His father laughed. "There's no persuading him. He'll agree with anything you say. But when the chips are down, it's Eisenhower. Yes, I know what it's like, trying to reason with him where politics are concerned. He hasn't been around so much lately. Maybe I've been trying too hard."

Jack said, "He talked a little bit about his grandfather."

"Yes, he likes to tell the old stories. The Boughtons weren't here for most of that. We left Scotland in the fall of 1870, so we missed out on the war and the rest of it. There was a lot of what you might call fanaticism around here in the early days. Even among Presbyterians. That old fellow was right in the middle of it, from what I've heard. And then in his old age he was about as crazy as it's possible to be and still be walking the streets. I would never have named you after that John Ames. We were used to him, of course. We felt sorry for him. But he was crazy when I knew him, and before that, too, I believe."

Jack was quiet for a while. Then he said, "Ames seems to have a lot of respect for him."

His father said, "The old settlers, you know, the old families, they used to tell stories they thought were just wonderful, and then I think they began to realize that the world had changed and maybe they should reconsider a few things. It's taken them awhile. Ames was pretty embarrassed about the old fellow while he lived. Always talking with Jesus. I suppose he didn't tell you about that."

"He told me. He told me the story about his grandfather leaving Maine for Kansas because he had a dream that Jesus came to him as a slave and showed him how the chains rankled his flesh. I'd heard the story before, of course. I always thought it sounded enviable. I mean, to have that kind of certainty. It's hard to imagine. Hard for me to imagine."

"Certainty can be dangerous," the old man said.

"Yes, sir. I know. But if Jesus is—Jesus, it seems as though he might have shown someone his chains. I mean, in that situation."

"You might be right, Jack. I'm sure Ames would agree. But when you see where we are now, still trying to settle these things with violence, I don't know. Live by the sword and die by the sword."

Jack cleared his throat. "The protests in Montgomery are non-violent."

The old man said, "But they provoke violence. It's all provocation."

There was a long silence. Then Jack said, "This week I will go to church. I will definitely go to church."

"That's wonderful, Jack. Yes."

He helped his father to bed, and then he came into the kitchen. "You were right," he said. "It was fine. I said the grace. I'd practiced this time. I was polite, I believe, and I didn't talk enough to get myself in trouble. I don't think I did. I'm not saying anything changed, but it wasn't a disaster. Macaroni and cheese. I cleaned my plate." He laughed.

THEN JACK TOOK THE AMESES SOME EARLY APPLES, AND some plums he said could be ripened on a windowsill, and he played a little catch with the boy, and he even helped Lila move the Reverend's desk and some of his books down to the parlor so that he would not have to deal with the stairs. "Very neighborly," he said. "Friend-like."

Glory had no reason for concern about all this, except that Jack was intent on it. He seemed to have invested so much calculation in it that it bordered on hope, now that the Reverend and his family had warmed to him a little. Dear God, she thought. They are the kindest people on earth. Why should I worry? She had talked him into trusting them, which would have been entirely reasonable in any other circumstance. But his reservations were the fruit of his experience, and his experience was the fruit of his being Jack, always Jack, despite these sporadic and intense attempts at escape, at being otherwise. Dear God in heaven, no one could know as well as he did that for him caution was always necessary.

Sunday came and Jack rose early, loitered in the kitchen drinking coffee, refused breakfast, brushed his suit and his hat. He came downstairs at a quarter to ten looking as respectable as he ever did, tipped his hat, and walked out the door. She got her father up and brought him into the kitchen, where he lingered over his eggs and toast, then over the newspaper, then over a *Christian Century* he had read weeks before, then over the Bible. Finally he fell into that sleep or prayer that was his refuge in times of high emotion. At two o'clock Jack still had not come home, so she told her sleeping father that she was going out to look around a little and he nodded, abruptly, as if to say it was high time. She couldn't hunt her brother down as if he were a lost child, or an incompetent of some kind. There was nothing he, therefore she, dreaded more than the possibility that he might be embarrassed in any way that could be anticipated and avoided. Enough that there was an incandescence of unease about him whenever he walked out the door or, for that matter, whenever his father summoned him to one of those harrowing conversations. Or while he waited for the mail or watched the news.

She went to the barn and there he was, in the driver's seat of the DeSoto, with his head tipped back and his hat over his eyes. She tapped on the window, and he roused himself and smiled at her, an effort. Then he reached over and opened the passenger door. "Hop in," he said. "I was just collecting myself. Couldn't face your papa quite yet." Then he said, "Ah, little sister, these old fellows play rough. They look so harmless, and the next thing you know, you're counting broken bones again."

"What happened?"

"He preached. The text was Hagar and Ishmael, the application was the disgraceful abandonment of children by their fathers. And the illustration was my humble self, sitting there beside his son with the eyes of Gilead upon me. I think I was aghast. His intention, no doubt. To appall me, that is, to turn me white, as I am sure he did. Whiter."

"Well," she said, "I find this hard to believe. It just doesn't seem possible."

"Yes, yes, such a kind old man. I don't think I'll be asking your advice any time soon, Pigtails." He laughed. "I left through the chancel. I had half a mind to pull my jacket up over my head."

Then he said, "Sweet Jesus, I am tired. And now you're crying. Don't do that, please."

"It's just tears," she said. "They don't matter. I'll leave you alone if you want me to."

"No," he said. "Don't do that either. Maybe you can help me sort this out."

There was a silence.

"Well, for one thing," she said, "I know he wouldn't have mentioned you by name. He would never do that."

"He didn't say, 'Jack Boughton, the notorious sinner in the first pew. The gasoline-scented fellow.' That's correct."

"And he'd have prepared his sermon days ago. I'm sure he had no idea you would be there this morning."

"Excellent point. In fact, I thought of that myself. But through the worst of it he wasn't even speaking from notes, Glory. The old devil was extemporizing. Very effectively, I might add, for a man of his age. Anyway, I would have been on his mind while he worked on it. All that ingratiating behavior just beneath his window." He laughed. Then he said, "Don't cry." He produced a handkerchief from the breast pocket in which he also carried the little leather case. One of her father's beautiful handkerchiefs.

She said, "I'll never forgive him."

He looked at her. "I appreciate the sentiment."

"I mean it. It could be senility, I suppose. I still won't forgive him. He was always like a father to me."

"It's sad."

"It's terrible."

Jack drew a long breath. "Consider our situation, Glory. Two middle-aged people in decent health, sane and civilized, generally well disposed toward the world—perhaps I am only speaking for myself here—sitting in an abandoned DeSoto in an empty barn, Snowflake not far from our thoughts, pondering one more thoroughly predictable and essentially meaningless defeat. Does this strike you as odd?"

She laughed. "It's just ridiculous."

"I had no plans when I left Gilead," he said. "Survival on terms I could convince myself were tolerable. That was the pinnacle of my aspirations. I did not anticipate failure. I have awakened in the occasional gutter from time to time—figuratively speaking, of course—and I have thought to myself, Just a little effort would improve my situation dramatically. So there was that optimism. It may have been youth."

"You were all right for ten years."

"Almost ten. Seven and a half, if we are speaking of sobriety. Nine and a half, if the measure is a sometimes pleasurable engagement with life."

"Della."

"Della."

They were quiet for a while.

He said, "I used to think we might slip into Gilead under cover of night, throw a little gravel at Ames's window, say our I-do's, get his blessing. Or at least his signature—"

"You'd have asked Ames to marry you?"

He shrugged. "He's always awake at odd hours."

"You'd have tipped your hat to the family homestead on the way out of town, I suppose."

"No doubt. I never really thought through the fine points. I'm sure I would have tipped my hat."

"That's good to know."

Then he said, "I came back thinking we might be able to make a life here, she and I. Why did I think that? I came here because everything had fallen to pieces and she had run off to her family." He looked at her. "I wasn't particularly at fault. I personally. Don't get the wrong idea. But I was clutching at a straw, coming to Gilead. No doubt about that. I've had some experience with them. Straws."

He looked at her sidelong. Bemused, worldly, sad, spent.

"You've never just talked to Papa about this."

He laughed. "Some things are sacred, Glory. You've never talked to him about old Love Letters." Then he said, "Our father is not a man of the world, shall we say, but he would no doubt assume that a nine-year relationship with my sullied self might have involved some degree of—cohabitation. I hope I haven't offended you." He glanced at her. "He might, never meaning to, only by implication, cast an aspersion. I don't know how I would deal with that. I'm trying to stay sober."

She said, "How do you know I didn't do that? Cohabit."

He said, very gently, "Call it a wild guess."

Condescension, she thought. But kindly meant. Brotherly.

He said, "I don't recommend it. There are laws. A person could end up with the cops at his door." He smiled.

"Sorry." Poor Jack.

The truth was, she wished there had been more to her endless supposed engagement. That there was not her fiancé's extremely scrupulous respect for her to, in retrospect, embitter her sense of the fraudulence of it all. Still, she wished she had the letters back, and the ring. Sacred, she thought. Strange to think of it that way. Time and again she had read through the half dozen letters that moved her, and even they sometimes seemed so commonplace that it frightened her, as if a precious thing had been lost and she could not find it, search as she might. Then she would notice a phrase, something about loneliness or weariness or the view from a train window, the intimacy of the ordinary, and her heart would stir. She had ticked the margins beside these lines to spare herself the vertiginous sense that there was nothing in the letters at all worth cherishing, and then when she looked at them again she could not always see why she had chosen these passages, and again she would be frightened. He was at the center of her life, and who was he, after all? Why did it comfort her to trust him? The letters were so precious to her, and what were they? They were bland and prosaic, three readings out of four. But when they touched her, she was suffused with joy. There was no other word for it. She knew that if she

had kept them, she would still look at them to see if there was anything in them to account for the sweet power they had had for her,
and that if she did not find it, she would read them again. When
she thought of them, she put aside all bitterness and folly and disil-
lusionment, as no one else ever could, no one who listened to her
with compassion. Sympathy would corrupt something wonderful,
which secrecy and a kind of shame kept safe for her.

She said, "I've wondered if it might not be easier to be somewhere else. Where my life would be my own, at least."

"My thought, too. And I gave somewhere else a pretty good
try. Now I'm home again in Iowa, the shining star of radicalism.
It is the desire of the tattered moth for the shining star that has
brought me home, little sister."

She said, "Well, Iowa is a pretty big state."

He laughed. "Yes, why am I here when I might be in An-
keny? Ottumwa?"

"That strikes me as a fair question."

"Maybe because I have no sister there."

"I'd visit."

He nodded. "Kind of you." Then he said, "I knew I would
need help. I thought the old gent might help me, but I didn't
realize—that he was so old. I couldn't find work on my own. So I
decided to place my hopes in the kindly Reverend Ames. Which
brings us to the present moment." Then he said, "And I just
wanted to come home. Even if I couldn't stay. I wanted to see the
place. I wanted to see my father. I was—bewildered, I suppose."
He laughed. "I was scared to come home. It was as much as I
could do to get on the bus. And stay on it. I was largely successful
at that, all in all. Too bad. Too bad for the old man. It's amazing to
me that I can still disappoint him. I knew I would." He touched
the scar beneath his eye.

"Well," she said, "he's worried. I left him at the kitchen table.
He's probably uncomfortable. I should go inside."

"What will you tell him?"

"What should I tell him?"

"Oh, let me think. Tell him my life is endless pain and difficulty for reasons that are no doubt apparent to anyone I pass on the street but obscure to me, and that I am flummoxed and sitting in the DeSoto but will probably be in for supper."

"It would be simpler if you just came inside with me now."

He sighed. "No doubt you're right. And I do know why my life is the way it is, Glory. I was joking about that. I wouldn't want you to think I don't. I'm fresh from a sermon on the subject." He glanced at her.

Glory said, "I'll never forgive him."

Jack said, "Thank you. I'm touched." Then he said, "I'll forgive him. Maybe I've forgiven him already." When she looked at him he shrugged and said, "He might take it as a sign of character. It might look like generosity or humility or something. Anyway, neither one of us can risk upsetting the old man by holding a grudge against Ames. I mean, one that he or Ames might be aware of." He said, "I have thought this over pretty carefully. Either my manly pride insists that I confront him, which even I would not descend to. Or it obliges me to leave town—in a huff of some kind to avoid that whipped-cur impression even I dread. Or else I seize upon the only undamaging choice left to me. Which might also have the look of virtue, I believe."

"Then I suppose I'll have to forgive him, too."

"I would appreciate that. It would make things easier."

They walked up to the house together. Their father was still at the table, a little fierce with the tedium of his situation, which had compounded his anxiety. "Ah, there you are!" he said, as they came through the door. "I was beginning to think—" and then he saw Jack's face.

Jack smiled. He said, "A powerful sermon. It gave me a lot to consider."

"Well, that's all right," his father said. "No harm in that, I suppose. I'm sure he must have meant well. Nothing I would have expected. He seems to have squandered a wonderful opportunity." His voice became softer and his gaze more fixed as realization settled in.

Jack said, "Please don't worry about it. It really doesn't matter," and went up to his room.

Days passed without any word from Ames. Their father read and prayed and brooded, and every time the telephone rang he said, "If it's Ames, tell him I'm dead."

HER FATHER HAD SUFFERED A TERRIBLE SHOCK. IT WAS his habit to consider Ames another self, for most purposes. And here his son, for whose spiritual comfort and peace he had prayed endlessly, often enough in Ames's kitchen, in his hearing, and in full confidence that his friend seconded his prayers—his son had made himself vulnerable to him and had been injured, insulted. That Jack was a wound in his father's heart, a terrible tenderness, was as fully known to Ames, almost, as it was to the Lord. And here the boy had put on a suit and tie—he had borrowed one of his father's ties—and gotten himself to church, for heaven's sake, despite reluctance, despite even fear, to judge by the potency of his reluctance. Glory could read her father's thoughts as they sat together over their breakfast that morning—the look of vindication, of confidence that things were miraculously about to come right. He had stood at the front of his own church year after year, hoping to be able to preach again about grace and the loving heart of Christ to his aloof, his endlessly lonely son. When he smiled to himself, he was certainly imagining himself in that pulpit, amazed and so grateful. Who better than Jack's second father, his father's second self, to say the words of welcome and comfort he could not say? It would never have occurred to him that Ames would not speak to the boy as if from his own heart.

Then this incomprehensible disappointment. The old man muttered and stared, his eyes flickering over the memory of the kindnesses he had done Ames through all those years, the trust he had placed in him. He frowned as he did when he was rehearsing grievance and rebuke. Never since the darkest storms of his retirement had she seen him so morose.

Over the decades there had been actual shouting matches between Ames and her father, set off by matters so abstruse no one dared attempt mediation. Once, when her mother tried to say something emollient about the communion of saints, her father, in the persisting heat of disputation, said, "That's just foolish!" and she terrified them all by packing a bag. Sometimes the older children tried to soothe, to make peace, but in fact the friendship was not threatened but secured by a mutual intelligibility so profound it enabled them to sustain for days an argument incomprehensible to those around them, to drop it when they wearied of it and then to take it up again just where they had left it. No one could predict when the warmth of their pleasure in argument would kindle and flare into mutual irritation, though weariness and bad weather were factors.

But in all those years neither of them had ever done the other any harm. This particular injury, utterly unexpected, to the old man's dearest affection—it was without question the costliest of them all, therefore most precious to him—was hardly to be imagined. Her father was in mourning, and Ames stayed away, no doubt waiting for a sign that he had not alienated the Boughtons forever. He would be in mourning, too.

Something had to be done. Ames already had their copies of *Life* and *The Nation*, and he had his own subscriptions to *Christian Century* and the *Post*. So far as Glory knew, there were no books around the house that he had lent their father, or that he had said he would like to borrow. Every vegetable and flower they grew Lila grew more abundantly. Glory decided to make a batch of cookies. But Jack came downstairs with a faded copy of *Ladies' Home Journal*. He tapped the note on the cover: *Show Ames*. "I've been up in the attic a few times. All sorts of

things up there. I found an article in here about American religion. Pretty interesting."

"Nineteen forty-eight. It's so old he's probably seen it."

He nodded. "It's so old he's probably forgotten it."

"Well, I think I'll just make cookies."

"Whatever you say." Jack put the magazine on the table. Then
he stood looking at it with his hands on his hips, as if he were relin-
quishing something that mattered. "Interesting article, though."

"All right," she said. "I'll need a minute to comb my hair."

"Sure." Then he said, "My idea was that you would give it to
the old gent first, before you take it to Ames. Then they'll have
something to argue about. I mean, conversation might be strained.
In the circumstances. So I thought this might help." He shrugged.

She put away the mixing bowl and the measuring spoons.
"Any further instructions?"

"Not at the moment. Well, he's awake and dressed. I thought
maybe you might read it to him over breakfast. I've eaten. I'm—"
He made a gesture toward the door that suggested he had some
sort of intention to act upon. Some hoe blade to whet. He had
already oiled the horse collar.

"All right," she said. "Should I tell him this is your idea?"

"Yes. Tell him that. Say I'm afraid I might have offended
Ames, and I'd like to put things right."

"Why don't you tell him yourself? I suppose he'd want the
particulars."

"Bright girl," he said. "Thanks, Glory." And he left.

HER FATHER TOOK INSTANTLY TO THE IDEA OF RECONCIL-
iation. He relaxed visibly at the very word. There was nothing
improbable in the idea that Jack was somehow at fault, though,
after allowing himself the thought a few times, he still had no
specific notion of how he could have been. A skeptical look, perhaps, but that was to be expected. Still, Jack was Jack, and there

was nothing disloyal about accepting that Jack might be at fault in some degree, since forgiving him was deeper even than habit, since it was in fact the sum and substance of loyalty. Yes. The old man always interpreted any pleasing turn of events as if he were opening a text, to have a full enjoyment of all reassuring implications and all good consequences. "It's very kind of Jack to recognize his part in this, and to want to make amends. Christian of him. I believe he may be doing this to please his old father, too. So I have something to think about that might not have been so clear to me otherwise." He laughed. "That sermon was for my benefit. Yes. The Lord is wonderful." He said, "Old Ames says he remembers me in skirts and a lace bonnet, and that could be true. My grandmother took my infancy in hand and she made it last as long as she possibly could. Longer, I guess. She meant well. My mother's health failed after I was born. That was Mother's opinion, anyway. But you just can't give up a friendship that goes back as far as that!" He loved to reflect on the fact that grace was never singular in its effects, as now, when he could please his son by forgiving his friend. "That is why it is called a Spirit," he said. "The word in Hebrew also means wind. 'The Spirit of God brooded on the face of the deep.' It is a sort of enveloping atmosphere." Her father was always so struck by his insights that it was impossible for him to tell those specific to the moment from those on which he had preached any number of times. It had made him a little less sensitive than he ought to have been to the risk of repeating himself. Ah well.

So she read the article to her father, and he chuckled over the passages by which Ames was certain to be exasperated, his eyes alight with the pleasure of knowing he and the Reverend were, for Jack's purposes, entirely of one mind. "Very thoughtful of him to find this for us," he said.

When they had finished reading it, Glory took the magazine to Ames's house and left it with Lila, since the Reverend was out calling. A day passed. Jack came in from the garden to ask if she had delivered it, then to ask if there had been any response. Finally, weary of all the anxiety, she went again without gift or pretext and found Ames at home. He opened the door, and when he saw her there, his eyes teared with regret and relief. "Come in, dear," he said. "I'm very glad to see you. How is your father doing these days?"

"As well as can be expected. Jack helps me take care of him. Or I help Jack." She said, "We've missed you."

Ames rubbed his eyes behind his glasses. "Yes. I know it has been wonderful for Robert to have him home again." He looked tired and moved and as if he needed to recover himself, so she said that her father had asked her to look in but she really couldn't stay.

"I haven't been sleeping very well so I'm not worth much right now, but I'll come by tomorrow or the next day." He said, "Give Jack my regards."

He seemed so robust beside her father that it was hard to remember Ames was old, too.

The next day Ames strolled up the street with Robby tagging after him, running ahead of him, pouncing at grasshoppers. "Like a puppy," her father said. "Into everything." Glory went inside to make lemonade and allow the two old gentlemen time to follow out the protocols of renewed cordiality. Jack came downstairs to the kitchen and leaned against the counter with his arms folded. Together they listened for a while to the voices, firmer as talk proceeded. There was laughter and the creaking of chairs, and there were silences, too, but there were always silences. When she was no longer afraid of disrupting any delicate work of reparation, Glory took them their lemonade and sat with them a while. Robby went to the garden and came back with a toy tractor he had brought on another visit and forgotten to take home with him. He drove it here and there around the porch floor, under his father's chair and around his shoes.

The conversation turned to the article Jack had found, "God and the American People." It was contemptuous of the entire enterprise of religion in the United States. But it was awkwardly reasoned, so the two old clergymen could enjoy refuting it. They had labored earnestly at propagating the true faith, which had never seemed to them to have national traits or boundaries. Nor did they feel directly implicated in whatever eccentricities and deficiencies in the local practice of it they might be obliged to grant.

Jack came out on the porch with a glass of lemonade and took a chair. There was a little silence. "Reverend," he said.

Ames said, "Jack, it's good to see you," and he glanced away, at Boughton, at the glass in his hand.

Jack watched him for a moment. Then he said, "I heard you two laughing about that magazine. It's pretty foolish, all in all. Could I see it for a second? Thanks. I thought he made one interesting point in here somewhere, though. He said the seriousness of American Christianity was called into question by our treatment of the Negro. It seems to me there is something to be said for that idea."

Boughton said, "Jack's been looking at television."

"Yes, I have. And I have lived in places where there are Negro people. They are very fine Christians, many of them."

Boughton said, "Then we can't have done so badly by them, can we? That is the essential thing."

Jack looked at him, and then he laughed. "I'd say we've done pretty badly. Especially by Christian standards. As I understand them." Jack sank back into his chair as if he were the most casual man on earth and said, "What do you think, Reverend Ames."

Ames looked at him. "I have to agree with you. I'm not really familiar with the issue. I haven't been following the news as closely as I once did. But I agree."

"It isn't exactly news—" Jack smiled and shook his head. "Sorry, Reverend," he said. Robby brought the tractor to show him, let him work the steering wheel, ran the tractor along the arm and over the back of his chair.

Boughton said, "I don't believe in calling anyone's religion into question because he has certain failings. A blind spot or two. There are better ways to talk about these things."

Ames said, "Jack does have a point, though."

"And I have a point, too. My point is that it's very easy to judge."

That was meant to end the conversation, but Jack, who was studying the ice in his glass, said, "True. Remarkably easy in this case, it seems to me."

"All the more reason to resist that impulse!"

Jack laughed, and Ames looked at him, not quite reprovingly. Jack's gaze fell.

Boughton said, "If there is one thing the faith teaches us clearly it is that we are all sinners and we owe each other pardon and grace. 'Honor everyone,' the Apostle says."

"Yes, sir. I know the text. It's the application that confuses me a little."

Ames said, "I think your father has shown us all a good many times how he applies that text."

Jack sat back and held up his hands, a gesture of surrender. "Yes, sir. Yes, he has. For which I have special reason to be grateful."

Ames nodded. "And so have I, Jack. So have I."

There was a silence. Her father averted his face, full as it was of vindication and conscious humility.

Lila came up the walk. Jack saw her first and smiled and stood. Ames turned and saw her and stood, also. When she came through the screen door, Boughton gestured toward his friend and his son and said, "I'd stand up, too, my dear, if I could."

"Thank you, Reverend." She said, "I can't stay. I just come to tell John I fixed a supper for him. It's cold cuts and a salad, so there's no hurry about it."

Boughton said, "Join us for a few minutes. Jack will get you a chair."

Jack said, "Please take mine, Mrs. Ames. I'll bring one from the kitchen." And he seated her beside his father with that gal-

lantry of his that exceeded ordinary good manners only enough
to make one wonder what was meant by it.

Glory thought Jack might have made an excuse to have a word
or two with her about how she thought things were going, so she
went into the kitchen after him. She was ready to tell him it might
be time to mention the weather, baseball, even politics. But he
pointedly did not meet her gaze and went out to the porch again.

Ames said to his wife, "We were just talking about the fact
that the way people understand their religion is an accident of
birth, generally speaking. Where they were born."

Jack said, "Or what color they were born. I mean, that is a
subject of the article. Indirectly. It seems to me."

Lila could never really be drawn into these conversations,
though Ames tried to include her. She seemed more interested by
the fact that people talked about such things than she was by anything they talked about, and she watched the currents of emotion
pass among them, watchful when they were intent and amused
when they laughed.

Boughton said, "Yes, that's very interesting." Then he fell
back on his experience of Minneapolis, his closest equivalent to
foreign travel. "Mother and I went up to the Twin Cities from
time to time, and we saw Lutheran churches everywhere. Just
everywhere. A few German Reformed, but the Lutherans out-
number them twenty to one, I believe. That's an estimate. Minneapolis is a large city. There may be Presbyterians in areas we
didn't visit."

Jack said, rather abruptly, "Reverend Ames, I'd like to know
your views on the doctrine of predestination. I mean, you mentioned the accident of birth."

Ames said, "That's a difficult question. It's a complicated
issue. I've struggled with it myself."

"Let me put it this way. Do you think some people are intentionally and irretrievably consigned to perdition?"

"I'm afraid that is the most difficult aspect of the question."

Jack laughed. "People must ask you about this all the time."

"Yes, they do."

"And you must have some way of responding."

"I tell them there are certain attributes our faith assigns to God—omniscience, omnipotence, justice, and grace. We human beings have such a slight acquaintance with power and knowledge, so little conception of justice, and so slight a capacity for grace, that the workings of these great attributes together is a mystery we cannot hope to penetrate."

"You say it in those very words."

"Yes, I do. More or less those very words. It's a fraught question, and I'm careful with it. I don't like the word 'predestination.' It's been put to crude uses."

Jack cleared his throat. "I would like your help with this, Reverend."

Ames sat back in his chair and looked at him. "All right. I'll do my best."

"Let's say someone is born into a particular place in life. He is treated kindly, or unkindly. He learns from everyone around him to be Christian, say. Or un-Christian. Might not that have an effect on his—religious life?"

"Well, it does seem to, generally. There are certainly exceptions."

"On the fate of his soul?"

"Grace," his father said. "The grace of God can find out any soul, anywhere. And you're confusing something here. Religion is human behavior. Grace is the love of God. Two very different things."

"Then isn't grace the same as predestination? The pleasanter side of it? Presumably there are those to whom grace is not extended, even when their place in life might seem suited to—making Christians of them." He said, "One way or the other, it seems like fate."

Jack had put his glass down and sat slumped, with his arms

folded, and he spoke with the kind of deferential insistence that meant he had some intention in raising the question.

His father said, "Fate is not a word I have ever found useful."

"It is different from predestination, then."

"As night and day," his father said authoritatively. Then he closed his eyes.

Glory thought she saw trouble looming. Ames and her father had quarreled over this any number of times, her father asserting the perfect sufficiency of grace with something like ferocity, while Ames maintained, with a mildness his friend found irksome, that the gravity of sin could not be gainsaid. Could Jack have forgotten? She stood up. She said, "Excuse me. I hate this argument. I've heard it a thousand times and it never goes anywhere."

Her father said, "I hate it a good deal, too, and I've never seen it go anywhere. But I wouldn't call it an argument, Glory."

She said, "Wait five minutes." She looked pointedly at her brother. He smiled. She went into the house. Then she heard him say, "I was thinking about your sermon last Sunday, Reverend. A fine sermon. And it seemed to me another text very relevant to your subject would have been the story of David and Bathsheba."

Glory thought, Dear God in heaven.

There was a silence while the old men pondered this. Then Ames said, "Robby, you'd better run along. Go find Tobias. Take your tractor now, and run along."

There was another silence. Jack cleared his throat. "As I read that story, the child died because his father committed a sin." Glory thought she heard an edge in his voice.

Ames said, "He committed many grave sins. Not that that makes the justice of it any clearer."

"Yes, sir. Many grave sins. Still. I'm not asking about the justice of it. I'm asking if you believe a man might be punished by the suffering of his child. If a child might suffer to punish his father. For his sins. Or his unbelief. If you think that's true. It seems to me to bear on the question we were discussing before. Predestination. The accident of birth." Jack spoke softly, carefully, touching the tips of his fingers together in the manner of a man whose reasonableness approached detachment. Glory thought, Either he has forgotten that Ames also lost a child all those years ago, or he is implying that Ames was being punished when he lost her, that he was a sinner, too. Jack's impulse to retaliate when he felt he had been injured was familiar enough, and it always recoiled against him. She coughed into her hand, but he did not look up.

After a moment Ames said, "David's child returned to the Lord."

Jack said, "Yes, sir. I understand that. But you do hope a child will have a life. That is what David prayed for. And you hope he will be safe. You hope he'll learn more than—bitterness. I think. You hope that people will be kind." He shrugged.

Ames said, "That is true. In the majority of cases." His words seemed pointed.

There was a silence.

Then her father said, "Oh!" and covered his face with his hands. "Oh! I am a very sinful man!"

Lila made a low sound of commiseration. "Dear, dear."

Jack said, "What? No, I—" He looked up at Glory, as if she could help him interpret the inevitability, the blank certainty, of painful surprise.

His father said, "The night you were born was such a terrible night! I prayed and prayed, just like David. And Ames did, too. And we thought we'd pulled you through, saved your life, didn't we? But there's so much more to it than that."

Jack smiled with rueful amazement.

Ames leaned over and patted Boughton's knee. "Theology aside, Robert, if you are a sinful man, those words have no meaning at all."

Boughton said, from behind his hands, "You don't really know me!"

This made Ames laugh. He thought it over and he laughed again. "I think I know you pretty well. I remember when your granny still pushed you up the road in a perambulator. Of course your arms and legs might have been hanging out of it. You might have been ten or twelve at the time. With that lace bonnet sitting on the top of your head. My mother used to say it would make more sense if the old lady was in the perambulator and you were pushing."

"Oh, now, it wasn't as bad as all that. I think I climbed out of that contraption when I was about six. I used to run when I saw it coming. God bless her, though. She meant well."

The two old men sat for a moment gazing at nothing in particular, as they did when memory arose between them. Jack watched them, the privilege of ancient friendship enclosing them like a palpable atmosphere. "We pulled him through, Robert, and he's here with you. He's back home."

Boughton said, "Yes. So much to be grateful for."

After a moment Jack said, "'Behold, all souls are mine; as the soul of the father, so the soul of the son is mine; the soul that sinneth, it shall die.' That's Ezekiel. But Moses says the Lord 'will by no means clear the guilty, visiting the iniquity of the fathers upon the children, upon the third and upon the fourth generation.' I wondered if you could explain that to me. It seems like a contradiction."

There was a silence. Then Boughton said, "He knows his Scripture."

"Yes, he does."

Boughton cleared his throat. "If you look at the Code of Hammurabi, I believe that's Davies—"

Ames nodded. "Davies."

"—you will find that if a man kills another man's son, then his own son will be killed. That was the punishment. Ezekiel was writing in Babylon, for the people living there in exile. So I think he was probably referring to the way things were done in that country, by the Babylonians."

Ames said, "Ezekiel does mention the proverb among the Israelites, the fathers have eaten sour grapes, and so on."

"But the language of the proverb does not by itself imply anyone should exact a punishment of the sons. I believe at the time Ezekiel wrote, that proverb must have been interpreted in a way that justified the Babylonian practice." Boughton rallied when he made arguments of this kind, spoke in the language of the old life, and wearied even to crankiness if the discussion went on very long.

Ames said, "Yes, Reverend, that may well have been the case."

Jack said, "Thank you. So the law can't punish a child for his father's sins, but the Lord will."

His father said, "There is the passage in John, the ninth chapter, in which the Lord Himself says, 'Neither this man nor his parents sinned.' Speaking of the man born blind."

"Yes, sir. But how do we know what He says is not specific to that case? Or that what He means is that sin can't always be inferred from—misfortune? He doesn't really say that if the parents had sinned, they would not be punished through the child. As I read it."

Silence again. Then Ames, clearly irritated, said, "It is true that children suffer when their fathers aren't good men. Anyone can see that. That's common sense. It's a grave error, I think, to interpret their suffering as an act of God, rather than as a consequence of their fathers' own behavior."

Boughton said, "We tried to do right by her. We should have done much more, I know that."

Jack smiled. He said very softly, "I really am a sinful man. Granting your terms." He shrugged. "Granting my terms."

Boughton waved this off, a gesture that discouraged elaboration. There was a long silence. Then he said, "Nonsense. That had nothing to do with it."

"And I don't know why I am. There's no pleasure in it. For me, at least. Not much, anyway."

Boughton covered his face with his hands.

Ames said, "I think your father is tired."

But Jack continued, very softly. "I'm the amateur here. If I had your history with the question I'd be sick of it, too, no doubt. Well I do have a history with it. I've wondered from time to time if I might not be an instance of predestination. A sort of proof. If I may not experience predestination in my own person. That would be interesting, if the consequences were not so painful. For other people. If it did not seem as though I spread a contagion of some kind. Of misfortune. Is that possible?"

Ames said, "No. That isn't possible. Not at all."

"No," his father said. "It just isn't."

Jack laughed. "What a relief. Because that visiting of the sins, it seems to describe something. It works the other way, too. The sins of the sons are visited on the fathers."

There was a silence. Then Ames said, "'If our heart condemn us, God is greater than our heart.' That's from the First Epistle of John."

Jack nodded. "He is writing to the 'beloved,' the church. I do not enjoy the honor of membership in that body."

"I don't know why you want to insist on that," his father said. "Why you want to set yourself apart like that. You were baptized and confirmed just like anybody else. How can you know all this Scripture when all you do is reject it?"

Ames said, "He doesn't exactly reject it, Robert. He's clearly given it a good deal of thought."

"Still. It seems almost like pride to me."

Jack said, "I'm sorry. I don't mean to be disrespectful. My question is, are there people who are simply born evil, live evil lives, and then go to hell?"

Ames took off his glasses and rubbed his eyes. "Scripture is not really clear on that point. Generally, a person's behavior is consistent with his nature, which is to say that his behavior is consistent. The consistency is what I mean when I speak of his nature."

Boughton chuckled. "Do I detect a little circularity in your reasoning, Reverend Eisenhower?"

Jack said, "People don't change, then."

"They do, if there is some other factor involved. Drink, say. Their behavior changes. I don't know if that means their nature has changed."

Jack smiled. "For a man of the cloth, you're pretty cagey."

Boughton said, "You should have seen him thirty years ago."

"I did."

"Well, you should have been paying attention."

"I was."

Ames was becoming irritated, clearly. He said, "I'm not going to apologize for the fact that there are things I don't understand. I'd be a fool if I thought there weren't. And I'm not going to make nonsense of a mystery, just because that's what people always do when they try to talk about it. Always. And then they think the mystery itself is nonsense. Conversation of this kind is a good deal worse than useless. In my opinion."

Glory said, "Your five minutes aren't up yet."

Jack glanced up at her blandly, not quite smiling, touching his fingertips together as if there were no such thing in the world as a hint. So she went into the parlor and turned on the radio and took up a book and tried to read, and tried to stop wanting to make sense of words she was doing her best not to hear. The Presbyterian Church. Redemption. Karl Barth. She read one page over three times without giving it enough of her attention to remember anything about it, and the radio was playing the *William Tell Overture*, so she set the book aside and went to stand in the doorway.

Lila said, "What about being saved?" She spoke softly and blushed deeply, looking at the hands that lay folded in her lap, but she continued. "If you can't change, there don't seem much point in it. That's not really what I meant."

Jack smiled. "Of course I myself have attended tent meetings only as an interested observer. I would not have wanted to find my salvation along some muddy riverbank in the middle of the night. Half the crowd there to pick each other's pocket, or to sell each other hot dogs—"

Lila said, "—Caramel corn—"

He laughed. "—Cotton candy. And everybody singing off key—" They both laughed.

"—to some old accordion or something—" she said, never looking up.

"And all of them coming to Jesus. Except myself, of course." Then he said, "Amazing how the world never seems any better for it all. If I am any judge."

"Mrs. Ames has made an excellent point," Boughton said, his voice statesmanlike. He sensed a wistfulness in Ames as often as he was reminded of all the unknowable life his wife had lived and would live without him. "Yes, I worried a long time about how the mystery of predestination could be reconciled with the mystery of salvation."

"No conclusions?"

"None that I can recall just now." He said, "It seems as though the conclusions are never as interesting as the questions. I mean, they're not what you remember." He closed his eyes.

Jack finally looked up at Glory, reading her look and finding in it, apparently, anxiety or irritation, because he said, "I'm sorry. I think I have gone on with this too long. I'll let it go."

Lila said, never looking up from her hands, "I'm interested."

Jack smiled at her. "That's kind of you, Mrs. Ames. But I think Glory wants to put me to work. My father has always said the best way for me to keep out of trouble would be to make myself useful."

"Just stay for a minute," she said, and Jack sat back in his chair, and watched her, as they all did, because she seemed to be mustering herself. Then she looked up at him and said, "A person can change. Everything can change."

Ames took off his glasses and rubbed his eyes. He felt a sort of wonder for this wife of his, in so many ways so unknown to him, and he could be suddenly moved by some glimpse he had never had before of the days of her youth or her loneliness, or of the thoughts of her soul.

Jack said, very gently, "Why, thank you, Mrs. Ames. That's all I wanted to know."

THE NEXT MORNING THE MAIL CAME EARLY, SO SHE SAW it first. Jack was upstairs. Once he would have been waiting somewhere, lingering, even an hour before the usual time for it to come, but that sharp old hope seemed to have dulled a little. Notes to her from her sisters. And four of Jack's letters, addressed to Della Miles in Memphis. They were unopened, and the words *Return to Sender* were written across each one, in bold print and underlined. She put the envelopes facedown on the hall table and went into the kitchen to collect herself.

Glory had begun to despise this Della. The woman had to have a fairly good idea of the misery she was causing, if she knew Jack at all. Granted that she had no obligation to be in love with him, simply because he was in love with her. Granted that his persistence must seem irksome, unwelcome as it was—by now she had certainly made that clear. But she had read French novels with him, and had embroidered his sleeve with flowers, for heaven's sake. Don't laugh while you're smoking, he had said, if you're carrying a birthday cake. He had showered himself with ashes. Then all that whimsical, meticulous embroidery, not mending but commemoration. What was it that had made them laugh? Whoever Della was, she knew him too well to treat him this way. She could ignore his letters if she wanted to. But this was cruelty.

Since Glory had seen the letters, she would have to tell him they had been returned. She thought of putting them back in the box and letting him find them himself. But what was the point of that? He might think he could keep them a secret from her, since that was always his first impulse, and then she couldn't speak with him about them, which she thought she should do, at least to offer him comfort, if she could think of any comfort to offer. Four letters! If any more came back like that, she would burn them. The point was made. She thought she might take three of these, or two, and hide them somewhere and burn them when she had the chance, since two would be sufficient for this Della's purposes. Two would be unambiguous but not quite so insulting.

She might say, How do you know it was Della who sent them back? It might have been her father. The printing was very bold, even allowing for the emphasis intended. Her impression of Della had been of someone with a lighter touch, a kind of delicacy she would not depart from if only because she herself was not quite aware of it. But what did she know about Della, except that Jack had courted her as if she were the virtuous lady in an old book? Poetry. Flowers, no doubt. All with a fresh shave and polished shoes and that air of mild irony he assumed whenever his sincerity embarrassed him.

Jack came down the stairs and went out to the mailbox, then came back in again. She went into the hallway. He found the letters lying where she had put them. His back was turned to her, but she could see the shock travel up his body. His weight on his heels, the setting of his knees, and then the recoil in his shoulders. He turned the letters over in his hands. He knew she was watching, and he said, "Have any more of these come back?"

"No."

"You wouldn't keep it from me if they did."

"No, I wouldn't do that. I wish I could."

He nodded.

She said, "I wanted to think a little before I gave them to you."

He nodded. "Any ideas?"

"Well," she said, "you haven't told me much about all this, but

229

from what you have told me, I thought it might not be Della who sent them back. I thought it might be her father or someone else in her family. You said she's living with her family. This doesn't really seem like her, my impression of her, anyway."

He shook his head. "Mine either." He dropped the letters on the table again. He turned around and smiled at her. "Not much to do, is there."

Glory said, "I was wondering if you had a mutual friend you could write to. Maybe the friend could send a letter from you, and she would read it. I mean, if her father or someone is keeping her from reading your letters, that might be a way to reach her. It could be worth a try."

He nodded. "I'll give it some thought." He said, "I don't blame her, though. I don't blame her father, if he did it. I understand it. They're good people. I should just—respect her judgment. Or his. I'm pretty used to the idea by now." He said, "I've sent a couple more letters. I suppose they'll come back, too. If you'd burn them, I'd be grateful."

"Should I burn these?"

He nodded. He touched the table as if it reminded him of something that had mattered once, and then he shrugged. "I don't really know what to do with myself. Any suggestions?"

OVER THE NEXT FEW DAYS THREE MORE LETTERS CAME back. She made careful fires of small kindling in the fireplace and tended them until each of the letters was burned to ashes. Jack saw her kneeling there, Jack who had taken to wearing his suit again, jacket open and tie loose to acknowledge the late-summer heat. He watched from the door, smiled and nodded to her, and stepped away when she tried to speak to him. There was still courtesy, taken back to what was for him its essence, the dread and certainty of being unwelcome, a bother, out of place. He had fallen back on estrangement, his oldest habit. As if he knew his unease made him seem aloof, he left the house in the morning and stayed away until evening, too late for supper but in time to spare his father his darkest fears. She left biscuits on the counter with the thought that he might pocket a few of them, and he did. She set out oatmeal cookies and hard-boiled eggs. She left coffee for him in a thermos bottle and a cup beside it, which he washed and put away. While he was gone she was very careful to see to everything he might have helped her with, so that he would not have to choose between the embarrassment of imposing on her and the forced familiarity of her company. And she prayed for him and prayed for him, she and her father, in long, silent graces that were grateful in anticipation of their relief at hearing him come through the door.

At supper the third night her father said, "I don't know what it is, Glory. I don't know what has happened."

She said, "He is in love with a woman he knew in St. Louis."

"Well, I figured out that much. All those letters."

"Yes. The last week she's been returning his letters."

"Oh." He took off his glasses and blotted his face with his napkin. After a moment he said gruffly, "I thought that might happen. Something like that. He doesn't have a job. I don't believe he ever graduated from college. He's not a young man, not likely to change his life, and I don't think it's been a very good life. I can see why a woman might—" He cleared his throat. "Well, I can't say I'm surprised."

"He's known her for years. Those ten good years he talks about. He says she has helped him."

Her father looked at her. "And they were never married at all?"

"I don't know," she said. Her father looked somber. A failed lie meant his suspicions were correct, and she had probably never lied to him successfully. In fact, lying in that family almost always meant only that the liar would appreciate discretion. So the transparency of a falsehood was very much to the point. She had cordoned off her own embarrassments from inquiry by means of a few explanations that were false on their face and never tested or returned to for that reason. As a matter of courtesy they treated one another's deceptions like truth, which was a different thing from deceiving or being deceived. In fact, it was a great part of the fabric of mutual understanding that made their family close.

She told some truth in this case because she was offended for Jack's sake by the suggestion that he had simply thrown himself at a woman and been rejected, as if he were not ruefully aware as anyone could be of his utter ineligibility. It must have been this Della who kept him safe despite everything they feared, who may have kept him alive, and in any case who had made the world a tolerable place for him for a while, as they had somehow never managed to do. Jack had said that he worried about the casting of aspersions on Della and on their relationship, told her about trying to defend her honor, and Glory knew even as she did it that she should not have mentioned those ten years. Still, Jack should not be made to seem like a fool. And Della, whoever she was, had not reckoned his worth in terms of his prospects, for heaven's sake. That much had to be said for her.

She knew she had made a grave mistake in giving her father's anxieties some grounding in fact. She said, "The woman is a minister's daughter."

Her father nodded. "And Jack is a minister's son." Then he said, "There are no children involved." This was a statement of the kind that meant he did not want his hope contradicted.

"No," she said. From time to time she had wondered, too.

His face settled into that grave look it took on when he felt some sort of moral intervention was required of him. It was a sad, even a bitter look, because only the lack or failure of other approaches could induce him to fall back on this one, and because he knew it had never yielded any wholly good result. It might be that Jack had obligations he could not meet. If he did, then the family must act on behalf of those to whom he was obligated. Especially since they were no doubt also family. The old man would have to know what he was dealing with here, even though Jack was sure to be offended. His questions would inevitably sound like accusation. Such misery, just to learn what he did not want to know.

IF JACK HAD MARRIED THAT FRECKLED CHILD, OR AT LEAST if they had managed to bring her and her baby into their household, then he could have gone back to college and the girl could have finished school and gone to college herself, if she wanted to. "She seems bright enough," Glory's mother had said. That was her interpretation of the precocious, intractable hostility toward the Boughtons that would not be moved or swayed by any kindness they could contrive. She was a hard, proud, unsmiling girl, and she may well have hated them all for their benevolent intentions, which were indeed condescending, reflecting as they did their awareness that her circumstances could be improved, that she might benefit from being gently instructed in the proper care of an infant even though this would involve overruling her mother.

Once, Glory had talked that freckled child into coming to her house to pick apples, she said, and bake a pie. Annie was her name. Annie Wheeler. She came out to the gate dressed the way schoolgirls dressed on Saturdays, in dungarees and an oversized shirt. She carried the baby on her hip. They sailed off to Gilead, the girl acknowledging no pleasure at all at having the top down on a bright afternoon, or at stopping for ice cream cones to eat as they drove. The baby gummed at the ice cream and put her hand in it, and her mother said, "Now look at you!" and licked a smear of ice cream off the baby's chin and the palm of the baby's hand.

It was all Glory's idea. Her parents were gone for the day to a wedding in Tabor. She had not spoken to them about her plan. She drove very carefully.

They went out to the orchard, and the girl stood silently with the baby on her hip and watched Glory pick apples. When she said she had picked enough for the pie but would pick a few more for the girl to take home, she said, "We got apples." Well, of course they would have them. There were apple trees everywhere anyone had ever thought to plant them, like lilac bushes and gooseberries and forsythia and rhubarb. She and the girl went into the house and set the baby in the sunlight on the kitchen floor. Her mother gave her a toy she pulled out of her pocket, buttons on a string, and said, "At home she's got a milk bottle." So Glory decanted a pint of cream into a drinking glass and rinsed it out and put it on the floor by the baby's knee. The girl knelt beside her and poured the buttons from her hand into the bottle, then out again, and the baby laughed and did awkward and purposeful things for a while with her toys, and Glory started to make pastry, talking aloud as if to remind herself of the fine points of the process, the need for careful measurement. The girl sat at the table, sipping a root beer.

Then the baby's back began to round with the weight of her head, and she pitched over on her side and began to kick and fuss. Glory said, "Oh, poor thing!" and took her up and swayed with her and kissed her teary cheek. And the baby struggled and wept and yearned away from her with a weight and strength that surprised her, holding out her arms to her mother. The girl took her and settled her on her hip, and the baby leaned her head against her shoulder, sucked her hand, and drew her breath in gasps of relief. "You just ain't her mama," the girl said. "No use crying about it." She never gave any sign that Glory's efforts at befriending her were more than an irritation till that morning when she called her and said, "I wish you'd come over to my house. My baby's got something the matter with her." She had walked three miles down the road to ask the use of a telephone.

It was an infection a little penicillin could have cured, but there was no penicillin then, or for years afterward. No one was at fault, really. Something like it could have happened even if those two children had come to live in Gilead. Every family had a story that would have ended differently if only there had been penicillin. Chimerical grief—now guilt, now blame, now the thought that it could all have been otherwise.

But how had Jack ever involved himself with that girl? That was where fault lay, impervious to rationalization, finally even to pardon. Such an offense against any notion of honor, her father had said, and so it still seemed to her, and to him, after all those years. She had followed her father's thoughts back to that old bitterness, and bitterness simmered in his half-closed eyes as he reflected on the inevitability of his disappointment.

IT WAS LATE EVENING WHEN THEY HEARD JACK COME INTO the porch. He might have expected his father to be in the parlor, reading in his Morris chair. The other evenings he had spoken to Glory as he passed, called good night to his father, and gone up to his room. But this time the old man would not leave the table. "I'm going to wait for him. I'm going to stay right here."

Finding the old man still in the kitchen when he came in, Jack paused, reading the situation as he had always done, aware of having fallen into some frail web of intention. He looked at Glory, then he simply stood there, hat in hand, and waited. Distant, respectful and tentative.

"Jack," his father said.

"Sir."

"I think we need to have a conversation."

"A conversation."

"Yes. I think you had better tell me how things stand with you." Jack shrugged. "I'm tired. I hope to sleep."

The old man said, "You know perfectly well what I mean. I want you to tell me if there are—obligations that require the help of your family. Things that might have happened there in St. Louis that you haven't told me about. That trouble you."

Jack looked at Glory. There it was, however mild and kindly meant, the aspersion he dreaded. He put his hand to his face and said, very softly, "Another time."

"Sit down, son."

He smiled. "No." Then he said, "My obligations are my problem, I'm afraid." It was his sadness that made him so inaccessibly patient.

His father said, "Your obligations are your problem if you can meet them. If not, they become my problem. Things must be seen to. It's only decent."

Fealty to kin, actual and imagined, and the protection of them, possible or not, were their father's pride, his strongest instinct, and his chief source of satisfaction, frustration, and anxiety. He had drawn himself up so that his words would have the force and dignity of their intent, but his eyes were closed and his mouth had turned down and the rectitude of his posture exposed his narrowed shoulders and his fallen throat. Jack gazed at him as if his father were the apparition of all the grief and weariness he had cost him, still gallant in his weakness, ready to be saddened again, ready to be burdened again.

"No. No, sir. Another time."

"You know there won't be another time. You're planning to leave now."

"I might not be here much longer. I'm trying to make some decisions."

His father's head fell to the side. He said, "I hope very much you will decide to stay. Stay for a while."

Jack said, "That's very kind."

"No, it is just a hope of mine. It will be kind of you to give it a little consideration, if you can. Now Glory will help me to bed."

THE NEXT MORNING THE OLD MAN POKED HIS SPOON AT his cereal for a little while, and then he said, "I want to talk with Ames. You can take me there in the DeSoto."

The car worked well enough for errands, and Glory had used it to drive the Ameses to the river for a birthday picnic. Her father had not felt comfortable enough to go along that day, and when she mentioned it to Jack, he laughed at the idea—"*Et ego in Arcadia*"—but at least everything had gone well enough with the car to encourage her to make more use of it. Her father thought often about the DeSoto. In his mind it was an open promise of mobility, a puissance that could also be a boon to his good friend. So his thinking about it was generous and agreeable, tonic. He had not, however, consented to ride in it since the day Jack took them out to the country.

"Mrs. Ames and the boy will be there," he said.

"I'll take them to the matinee."

"Very good."

Glory arranged the day to her father's specifications, and after lunch she helped him down the stairs and into the car. There was a ringing loneliness in the house with Jack always away somewhere, and it felt good to her to leave it for a while, to take her father away from it. She drove him past the church and past the war memorial to let him admire the gardens and the trees, and then she took him to Ames's house and helped him again, out of the car, up the walk, up the steps. Ames seemed startled to find him at his door.

"Yes," the old man said, "I thought you and I could look after each other while the women are out at the movies. I came over here in the DeSoto."

Ames pulled a chair away from the table. "Unless you would rather sit somewhere else."

Boughton said, "No, this has always been my chair, hasn't it. My pew." He sat down and hung his cane from the edge of the table and closed his eyes. Lila and Robby came downstairs, Robby with his hair neatly parted and his cheeks pink with scrubbing. Glory took them off to the musty little movie theater, where they watched good triumph over evil by means of some six-shooters and a posse. "Say your prayers!" said the bad guy to the harmless citizen trapped against a canyon wall. And in the moment he so graciously allowed his captive, horses came clattering up from behind him and he was made to drop his gun. Robby was amazed and gratified by this turn of events, which was as much as Glory could hope for. With previews and newsreels and a cartoon, and a short second feature in which good triumphed once again, more than two hours had passed by the time they came blinking out into afternoon sun.

The old men were still sitting at the table, and Jack was with them. He looked at Glory and smiled. "There was no one at home, so I thought something must be the matter. I came here—" She had not seen him for three days, except when he walked past her on the way to the door, saying nothing, tipping his hat as he left, or walked through the kitchen on the way to his room, saying only good night. It had never crossed her mind that he would come looking for them. If they had been there, it might have been the beginning of better times. Just the thought gave her a twinge of blighted joy. She wanted to look at him, to see how he was, but his smile was cool. He might be angry. He must think she had betrayed him. Well, she had betrayed him. Dear God, she hadn't meant to, and what did that matter, when her father was here confiding in Ames again, telling him under the seal of old friendship what he suspected and what he feared, just as he had done in the endless, excruciating past. It was bad enough last night, the way he spoke to Jack. And now this. If her brother had had one surviving hope, she knew it was that he could find some way to speak to Ames himself, in his own right. She was so glad to get her father out of the house, to give him the comfort of a visit to Ames's kitchen—how long had it been? She hadn't thought it through. Her father just sat there with his eyes closed.

Ames was visibly relieved to see the three of them. Robby scrambled into his lap full of the unspent energy the movie had summoned up in him. "You should've gone, Papa. You should've seen it." He slapped the bottom of his Cracker Jack box and a few sticky morsels fell out on the table in front of his father. "I'm saving some for Toby." Then he said, "Here," and slid off his lap and went to Jack and dug out a few morsels for him. "There's supposed to be a prize in here," he said. "Do you see any prize?"

Jack took the box and tilted it to the light and looked into it. He said, "I believe you must have eaten it."

Robby laughed. "No, I didn't."

"You were so interested in that movie you didn't notice. It could have been a silver dollar and I bet you wouldn't have noticed it."

"Oh yes, I would. I'd notice a silver dollar!"

"It was probably a rubber snake. I bet it was a tarantula."

"No, it wasn't," Robby said. "Let me see," but Jack held the box away from him, peered into it, then extracted something between two fingers. "You're a pretty lucky kid," he said. "I'd like to have one of these."

"What is it? What?"

Jack laid the little toy on the table. "That," he said, "is a magnifying glass."

Robby looked at it. "It isn't very big."

"Well, you have to start somewhere."

"Start what?"

"Looking for clues. Here. I think I have a spot on the cuff of my shirt. What does it look like to you?"

Robby peered at it through the little lens. "It just looks like a spot."

Jack shrugged. "Well, there you are. Case closed."

Robby laughed, and so did Lila.

Ames said, "Robby, why don't you run off and find Tobias. He'll want to see what you've got there. Maybe you can find a bug to look at. Now run along." The boy hesitated, and then he left.

Jack turned to look at Ames, a bland, weary look that meant, "I understand why you do that, why you send your child away." No doubt Ames and Boughton had just prayed for his soul, probably slandering before heaven whatever life he had had, and had lost, the life he mourned. Deploring it under the name of sin, or some milder word they had agreed on. Transgression. Dishonor. Unmet obligation. He had walked in upon this conjuration of himself in the bleak light of his father's suspicions, which were innocent and uninformed and therefore no doubt exaggerated to ensure the sufficiency of his intercession. Jack had walked in on a potent thought of himself, like Lazarus with the memory of cerements about him no matter how often he might shave or comb his hair.

"Mrs. Ames," he said, "did you enjoy the movie? I've seen it a few times myself. The newsreel was interesting. A little strange for a matinee, I thought."

Lila said, to Boughton and Ames, "The newsreel was terrible. It showed an atom bomb going off, and all the buildings that would have been burned down by it. There were dummies inside, like families eating their supper. They shouldn't be showing that to children."

"They shouldn't be doing it in the first place," Boughton said. "They love those mushrooms. All that racket." He still had not opened his eyes. "Dulles."

Jack said, "Yes, Dulles. A Presbyterian gentleman, as I understand."

Boughton snorted. "So he says."

Jack had settled back in his chair and folded his arms, as he did when he wanted to seem at ease. He said, "They make it hard to bring up children these days. Hard to protect them. I suppose. Fallout in the milk they drink. You'd expect a Presbyterian gentleman to give these things a little more thought. In St. Louis they did a study of what they called 'deciduous teeth.' Baby teeth. There was radioactive material in them. It was alarming. To people trying to bring up children. So I have read."

Ames looked at Jack, a little reprovingly. "Your father certainly has no brief to offer for John Foster Dulles. Neither have I."

Boughton muttered, "But he'll vote for Eisenhower."

After a moment Jack cleared his throat. "Granting that responsibility is not a standard I myself have adhered to, particularly—"

His father opened his eyes.

"Granting that I have been a disappointment. Worse than a disappointment. Still."

His father looked at him. "No, you haven't. What's your point?"

Lila said, "I know what he means. Things don't make much sense. It's hard to know who you're supposed to look up to. That's true."

"Yes. No disrespect intended. I just feel I should put in a word for the reprobate among us. For their relative harmlessness. Being their sole representative, of course." He smiled. "I'm not making excuses. But those of us who take a moment from our nefarious lives to read the news can find it all a little disorienting. Our fault, no doubt." Then he said, "Reverend Ames, I would appreciate any insight you could give me."

Ames glanced at him to appraise his sincerity, as if surprised by the possibility that it might be genuine. He said, "That's a lot to think about."

"It comes up fairly often. Among people I know. People living at close quarters, with time on their hands—" He laughed.

There was a silence. Boughton had closed his eyes again. His head fell. After a moment Glory said, "I think Papa must be getting tired."

"I'm right here. You can ask me. I still exist in the first person."

"Are you tired?"

"Yes, I am. I will want to go home soon. Not just yet." No one said anything for a minute, and then the old man lifted his head. "Yes, we should be going home."

Glory would have expected Jack to come with her, hoped he would, but he stayed where he was, as if at ease in his chair, and did not meet her eyes. She walked her father to the car and helped him into it, with Lila, who went along to help him out of the car and up the steps of his own house. After she had settled the old man for a nap, Glory phoned Ames to tell him that Lila would stay and help her make dinner. Robby was having supper with Tobias. Dinner would be ready in an hour or so, but he and Jack could walk over whenever they felt like it. In half an hour Ames came in by himself. He said Jack would be along in a little while, and they waited dinner until it was slightly ruined, and ate in silence.

Her father asked, "Did you and Jack have any kind of talk, the two of you?"

Ames said, "Not really. I think he wanted to talk, but he couldn't bring himself to say what he had on his mind. He only stayed for a few minutes after you went home."

"He didn't give any indication where he might be going?"

"He said he might be late."

Glory listened all night for the sound of the door opening. Twice she put on her robe and shoes and went outside to look in the barn, in the car, the shed, the porch, but her father heard her and called out, called to Jack, thinking, no doubt, that it was Jack he heard. Better to let him think so. She crept upstairs and stayed in her room until morning.

Her father told her not to bother with breakfast, but she made coffee for him and put toast and jam on the lamp table next to his chair. And the newspaper, as if this were an ordinary morning. She did what she could to make him comfortable. He was irritated by the delay.

"I'll be gone a little while," she said, and he nodded. He asked nothing, which meant he knew everything.

He said, "You'd better go."

She dressed and brushed her hair. Then she looked into Jack's room. The bed was neatly made, his books and clothes were still there, and his suitcase. She found the car keys where she had left them, on the windowsill in the kitchen.

She thought Jack might have found his way out of town somehow, hitched a ride with someone passing through, and if she did not find him in Gilead, she would drive to Fremont to look for him, just to see if he might be on the street. If she was delayed, she would telephone Lila and ask her to look in on her father. Two hours there and back, at best. Her father would be as patient as he could, knowing as he clearly did why she had to leave him.

She put the keys in her pocket and walked out to the barn. She opened the door and stepped into the humid half-darkness. And there he was, propped against the car, with the brim of his hat bent down, holding his lapels closed with one hand. He held the other out to her, discreetly, just at the level of his waist, and said, "Spare a dime, lady?" He was smiling, a look of raffish, haggard charm, hard, humiliated charm, that stunned her.

"It's your brother Jack," he said. "Your brother Jack without his disguise."

"Oh dear Lord! Oh dear Lord in heaven!" she said.

He said gently, "No reason to cry about it. Just a little joke. A kind of joke."

"Oh, what are we going to do?"

He shrugged. "I've been wondering about that myself. He can't see me like this. I know that much."

"Well, where is your shirt?"

"I believe it's with my socks. I seem to have stuffed them into the tailpipe. The shirt is hanging out of it, the sleeves. Not much good to me now."

She said, "I have to sit down." She could hear herself sobbing, and she couldn't get her breath. She leaned against the car with her arms folded and resting on the roof and wept, so hard that she could only give herself over to it, though it kept her even from thinking what to do next. Jack hovered unsteadily at a distance from her, full of drunken regret.

"You see, I was right to give you the key," he said. "I guess I tried to start the car without it." He gestured toward the open hood. "It looks like I did some damage. But I'm glad I didn't bother you for the key. I'm not always thoughtful. When I'm drinking."

She said, "I'm going to put you in the backseat, and then I'm going to get some soap and water and a change of clothes, so we can get you back into the house. You can lie down here and wait for me. Stay here now. I'll be right back."

He was docile with embarrassment and weariness and relief. He lay down on the seat and pulled up his knees so she could close the door.

When she went into the house her father called to her, "Is Jack here?"

"Yes, Papa, he's here." She could not quite control her voice.

There was a silence. "Then I suppose we'll see him for supper tonight."

"Yes, I think we will." Another silence. The old man was giving them time, a reprieve, restraining curiosity and worry and anger and relief, too, while she tended to whatever the situation required. She took a sheet and a blanket and a washcloth and towel from the linen closet at the top of the stairs, and she took a pail from the broom closet, rinsed it out, and filled it with hot water. She had worried about her father's hearing all this haste and urgency, but clearly he had mustered the courage of patience—yet again, dear Lord, she thought. She dropped the bar of laundry soap into the water and carried the things she had gathered out to the porch step.

Now what. She dragged an Adirondack chair from the side yard to the back of the barn. It was concealed from the neighbors by the lilac bushes. The sunlight was full there, but it was mild enough. She took the sheet with her into the barn through the side door.

"Jack," she said, "Jack, I want you to take off your clothes and wrap yourself in this sheet and come outside. We're going to get you clean. Did you hear what I said?"

He moaned and roused himself and squinted up at her.

She said, "I'll help you. I'll get you a change of clothes. You'll feel so much better."

He shook his head. "I think I ruined my clothes."

"I'll take care of that. But you have to give them to me. Then I can try to clean them up."

He looked at her. "You're still crying."

"Don't worry about it."

"I'm sorry. Terribly sorry."

"It doesn't matter." She took his arm and helped him up, leaned him against the side of the car. "Give me your coat." Under his coat he was bare-chested. He crossed his arms and laughed with a bitter sort of embarrassment.

"Maybe I should get a little more sleep." He started to open the car door.

She pushed it shut again. "I don't have all day. I have Papa to think about. He's worried half to death. Hold this." She gave him a corner of the sheet and bundled the rest around him, just under his arms. "Now, I'll wait for you outside. I have a chair for you out there where no one will see you."

"I managed to smell like death, at least," he said. "This seems a little too—appropriate. What is it called? A winding sheet."

"Oh!" she said. "What should I do with you? Tell me what to do!"

"I wish you wouldn't cry," he said. "Give me a minute here. I know you want to help me, Glory."

She went outside and waited, and in a little while he emerged, barefoot, wincing, abashed by daylight, startlingly white and thin. He lowered himself into the chair and she brought the bucket and the soapy water and the cloth and began to wash him down, starting with his hair and face and neck and shoulders, wringing out the cloth again and again, scrubbing his arms and his hands, which were soiled with grease and were injured, marred. Her father would notice that.

"Lavender," he said.

She leaned him forward to wash his back. His head lolled on her shoulder. He said, "I once worked in a—mortuary. Briefly."

"That's fine," she said.

"Yes. I didn't mind. It was quiet."

"You don't have to talk."

"Then a citizen came in. Wrapped in a sheet. Complete stranger. There was a piece of paper tied to his toe, tied on with a red ribbon. It was an IOU with my name on it. My—signature. People sell those for a—fraction of their value." He looked at her. "Have you ever heard of that? Someone else has your note. You don't know who to be afraid of."

"That's a shame," she said, since he seemed to hope she would share his sense of injury.

He laughed. "I never even knew how much I owed. On those notes. I never wrote one when I was sober. Couldn't have been much. I wasn't, you know, a good risk."

"Probably not." She would have to try to shave him. His beard made his face look pallid, and his pallor made his beard look dingy.

"I think they just liked to see me jump," he said. "I'm high-strung. Never let people know that about you. They figure it out anyway."

She said, "You should have come home."

He laughed. "Maybe." He said, "I failed as a lowlife. But not for want of—application."

"I'm sure," she said.

She settled him back against the chair and toweled him down and bundled the blanket around him. She put one of his feet and then the other into the soapy bucket. "That's the best I can do for now. Are you comfortable? Does the light bother you?"

"I'm all right. Much better. Maybe a glass of water?"

"Yes. I'll find some clothes for you. I'll have to go into your room. Is that all right?"

He seemed to drift off and then to startle awake. "My jacket—" he said.

"It's right here." She brought it out and hung it on the back of the chair. Then she took the slim leather case out of the breast pocket and, being careful first to dry the place very thoroughly, put it down on the arm of the chair.

"Thank you, Glory," he said, and he covered it with his hand and closed his eyes again.

"I'll just get some clothes out of your room. If you don't mind."

He said, "You might notice a bottle or two in there." He laughed. "I've been getting into the piano bench lately."

"You stay right here. I'll be back."

She had stopped crying, but she had to sit down in the porch. She put her head on her knees. She imagined him in that bleak old barn in the middle of the night, stuffing his poor socks into the DeSoto's exhaust pipe, and then, to make a good job of it, his shirt. He'd been wearing his favorite shirt, the one with the beautiful mending on its sleeve. All the drunken ineptitude and frustration, his filthy hands, everything he could reach in the engine pried at, pulled loose. She couldn't leave him alone for more than a few minutes, but her father needed her, too. She might call Lila. Not yet. Her family was slower to forgive a failure of discretion than they were to forgive most things actually prohibited in Scripture. If Jack's notions of privacy were generally indistinguishable from furtiveness, there was only more reason to be cautious about offending them.

Was this what they had always been afraid of, that he would really leave, that he would truly and finally put himself beyond the reach of help and harm, beyond self-consciousness and all its humiliations, beyond all that loneliness and unspent anger and all that unsalved shame, and their endless, relentless loyalty to him? Dear Lord. She had tried to take care of him, to help him, and from time to time he had let her believe she did. That old habit of hers, of making a kind of happiness for herself out of the thought that she could be his rescuer, when there was seldom much reason to believe that rescue would have any particular attraction for him. That old illusion that she could help her father with the grief Jack caused, the grief Jack was, when it was as far beyond her power to soothe or mitigate as the betrayal of Judas Iscariot. She had been alone with her parents when Jack left, and she had been alone with her father when he returned. There was a symmetry in that that might have seemed like design to her and beguiled her with the implication that their fates were indeed intertwined. Or returning herself to that silent house might simply have returned her to a state of mind more appropriate to her adolescence. A lonely schoolgirl at thirty-eight. Now, there was a painful thought.

She recalled certain moments in which she could see that Jack had withdrawn from her and was looking through or beyond her, making some new appraisal of her trustworthiness, perhaps, or her usefulness, or simply and abruptly losing interest in her, together with whatever else happened just then to be present and immediate. She found no consistency in these moments, nothing she could interpret. He was himself. That is what their father had always said, and by it he had meant that Jack was jostled along in the stream of their vigor and purpose and their good intentions, their habits and certitudes, and was never really a part of any of it. He had eaten their food and slept beneath their roof, wearing the clothes and speaking the dialect of their slightly self-enamored and distinctly clerical family and, for all they knew, intending no parody even when he was old enough to have been capable of it, and to have been suspected of it. A foundling, she thought, even though he had been born in that house at memorable peril to himself and their mother, alarming her two older sisters so severely that for years they had forsworn the married life. Oh, it was the loneliness none of them could ever forget, that wry distance, as if there were injury for him in the fact that all of them were native to their life as he never could be. She was almost disappointed that she couldn't be angry at him. He had very nearly brought a terrible conclusion to his father's old age. It would have been an inexpressible, unending grief to the whole family to have the old man's patience and his hope recoil on him so mercilessly. How resigned to Jack's inaccessible strangeness she must be to forgive him something so grave, forgive him entirely and almost immediately. They all did that, and he had understood why they did, and he laughed, and it had frightened him. She thought, I will not forgive him for an hour or two.

She took Jack his glass of water. He was dozing in the sunlight, lacquered with sweat. He opened his eyes, only a little, but she saw a glimmer of his familiar, wry despair at himself. "I'd forgotten how much I sweat," he said. "It's disgusting."

She set his feet on the towel and dumped the filmy water out of the pail and went into the house and filled it. She found a sponge. She took them outside and began to bathe him again, his hair, which looked surprisingly thin when it was wet, and his face, his beloved and lamented face. Ah, Jack, she thought. He looked like destitution. He looked like the saddest fantasy she had ever had of the worst that might have become of him, except that he was breathing, and sweating, and a little tense under her touch.

"I can do this," he said. "You don't have to."

So she handed him the sponge and went inside and brought back a razor and shaving cream. "Excuse me," she said, and lifted his chin. She squirted the foam into her hand and lathered his jaw.

He studied her face. "You're furious."

"That's right."

"I can't say I blame you."

"Don't talk."

He looked away. There was grief in his expression, a kind of bewilderment. Could he be surprised? Or was it only the shock of finding himself back in the world, with all his defenses ruined and his one friend lost to him?

She said, "Do that thing with your lip." So he pulled his lip taut over his teeth and she shaved it. "Now your chin." And he did the same. She lifted his chin and shaved his throat. Then she wiped away the foam with the sponge and inspected him.

"Good enough," she said. It was a relief to see him looking more like himself. She smoothed his hair away from his brow. The gentleness of the gesture seemed to come as a relief to him. So she kissed his cheek.

He said, "I'd never have done that if I'd been sober. I don't even remember—anything about it." He looked at his hands, as if to confirm to himself that it had happened.

"It's over now."

He smiled at her as if to say, No, it isn't, and it won't be. "I'm sorry you saw me like that," he said.

"I'm glad it wasn't worse."

He nodded. "Now you know me—some other aspects of my character."

She said, "Let's not talk."

"All right."

"I still haven't brought clothes for you. You've made me nervous about going into your room. Do I have your permission?"

He laughed. "Yes, you have my permission."

So he went into the barn and dressed himself and came out in his father's dark pants and beautiful old shirt, the sleeves rolled for lack of cuff links. It bothered her that she had forgotten to bring him socks. They walked together up the path to the porch, he behind her, the two of them no doubt looking very unlike two ordinary people who had not passed through fearful and wearying hours together. If anyone saw them, which God forbid.

She could hear Jack's breathing and his footsteps in the grass, neither of which she could take for granted anymore, if she ever had.

They heard voices from the road. He stopped. It was as if he turned to face some last, unimaginable trial. But she said, "It's nothing to do with us," and he nodded and followed her again, up the step, into the porch.

"Is that Jack with you?" their father called, and she said, "Yes, Papa," and Jack smiled at her and shook his head. He was sober enough to know that speech was not a thing he could risk. They went up the stairs, and she drew his blinds and brought a glass of water to set on the night table. She found a ball of socks in the dresser and put it beside the water. He rolled onto his stomach and hugged the pillows to his face. He was relieved to lie down on his own bed, as if he had been too long away from home and had come back again to a kind of rest that meant, That's all over now, or Now at least I know it will be over sometime.

She washed her face, brushed her hair, and changed her dress and went downstairs to tend to her father. She said, "He's getting some rest."

The old man was rigidly wakeful. She knew he had been sitting there, interpreting noises, interpreting her haste and her strained assurances, then Jack's slow steps on the stairs behind her. He would have interpreted her reddened eyes, too, if he had looked at her. "He's all right," he said.

"Yes, he's all right."

He closed his eyes. He was as still as if he had expended all the life that remained to him composing himself to accept this cross. His jaw slackened a little, and she thought for a terrible moment that he might have died, but then his hands adjusted themselves on the quilt and she knew it was only sleep.

Tired as she was, she could not possibly sleep. She felt lonely, lonely. She found a wire coat hanger in the front closet and straightened it, and went out to the barn. She pulled Jack's shirt out of the exhaust pipe. He had managed to jam in the tails of it only. The body and the sleeves were lying on the ground, a greasy clay of perpetual dank and animal waste and vehicle seepage, old life and old use whose traces outlasted the memory of them. She caught one sock and then the other with the hanger. So, the proof of what he had intended was removed, and that was a comfort to her, as if she could now stop believing it entirely herself. She put the socks in the fireplace on a pyre of kindling. They made a smoldering fire. Then she filled the sink with water and scrubbed at the shirt, careful of the embroidery. It might be best to let it soak for a while. She went up the stairs as quietly as she could, and into Jack's room. She found two pints of whiskey in the bottom drawer, as he had said. He stirred and raised his head and looked at her, irritated, but it was troubled sleep, not awakening. She took the bottles out to the orchard and emptied them on the ground, and put the empty bottles in the shed. Then she went back to the silent house. That shirt. It had to be put out of sight. She squeezed the water out of it and put it on a hanger, carried it out to the shed, and hung it from a nail in the wall behind the door.

How to announce the return of comfort and well-being except by cooking something fragrant. That is what her mother always did. After every calamity of any significance she would fill the atmosphere of the house with the smell of cinnamon rolls or brownies, or with chicken and dumplings, and it would mean, This house has a soul that loves us all, no matter what. It would mean peace if they had fought and amnesty if they had been in trouble. It had meant, You can come down to dinner now, and no one will say a thing to bother you, unless you have forgotten to wash your hands. And her father would offer the grace, inevitable with minor variations, thanking the Lord for all the wonderful faces he saw around his table.

She wished it mattered more that the three of them loved one another. Or mattered less, since guilt and disappointment seemed to batten on love. Her father and brother were both laid low by grief, as if it were a sickness, and she had nothing better to offer them than chicken and dumplings. But the thought that she could speak to them in their weary sleep with the memory of comfort lifted her spirits a little. There was a nice young hen in the refrigerator, and there were carrots. There were bay leaves in the cupboard. Baking powder. Lila would send Robby over with whatever she lacked, knowing better than to ask why Glory or Jack didn't go to the store themselves. Good Lila. She might know some simple, commonplace treatment for hangover, some cool hand on the brow that would wake Jack from his sweaty sleep, as if penance were swept aside by absolution. If there were such a thing, Jack would know and would have asked for it, unless misery was the way he spoke to himself, unless he had meant to recruit his whole body to the work of misery. There would be a rightness in his grieving in every nerve. However slight her experience, she did know that. And she knew he would sleep for hours, and awake vague and somber.

So she bathed the hen and set it in water with the carrots and an onion and the bay leaves. Some salt, of course. And she turned on the heat. Poor little animal. This life on earth is a strange business.

She had sat by the sputtering radio, trying to interest herself in *The High and the Mighty*. She went into the kitchen to turn the little hen onto her belly, and she saw that a blue Chevrolet had pulled into the driveway. Teddy. Of course, Teddy would come just now. Glory felt anxiety, and relief, and resentment. If he had come even a week earlier, he'd have found everything much better, another atmosphere in the house. Instead, he was walking in on failure and shame. She should have called him weeks ago, asked him to come while her father was still a little sprightly and Jack was still all right, even, she had thought, healthy. At least not unhealthy, not miserable. She had felt, she knew now, that she was sustaining a familial peace—fragile, certainly, and only more remarkable for that. Jack, who had never trusted any of them, trusted her. Not always, not wholly, not without reservations of a kind he did not divulge and she could not interpret. Still, even Teddy would have envied the talking and joking and the moments of near-candor, the times they were almost at ease with each other. She had been so proud of all that, pleased to believe it was providential that she should be there, having herself just tasted the dregs of experience, having been introduced to something bleaker than ordinary failure—it was a sweet providence that sent her home to that scene of utter and endless probity, where earnest striving so predictably yielded success, and Boughton success at that, the kind amenable to being half-concealed by the rigors of yet more earnest striving. Not that she could entirely forget the bitterness of her chagrin, not that she preferred the course her life had taken to the one she had imagined for it. But she did feel she had been rescued from the shame of mere defeat by the good she was able to do her brother.

Teddy walked into the porch, into the kitchen, threw his arms around her, and kissed her forehead. "Hiya, babe," he said, making a brief study of her face, noting and ignoring the weariness of it. "Good to see you! How's it going? Do you mind if I make a few phone calls?"—all this in a very soft voice, since he knew his father was probably asleep. He leaned in the hallway, giving advice and assurance, making three attempts to reach someone who didn't answer. Then he hung up the phone and came back and hugged her again, comforting her, though he said nothing. Teddy used to be just Jack's height, a slightly sturdier version of him, without the tentativeness that made Jack always seem to be taking a step back. Now Teddy was taller, she thought, no doubt the effect of quiet purposefulness on the one hand and evasiveness and generalized reluctance on the other. Once again he studied her face. She had been frightened so recently, and she was sad, and so tired, and it was all surely visible to him. "I hope I haven't come at a bad time," he said. "It's been hard to stay away. I finally gave in."

"This is a good time. As good as any, I suppose." What excuse was there for keeping him, all of them, away while their father dozed through whatever time remained to him, even though the old man himself did not ask her to send for them? Teddy could have blamed her for letting things get worse without calling him. It was pride, or it was shame that had made her hope Jack would recover himself enough to let the others see that things had been good between them. Though there was their father, too. But she saw nothing of anger or accusation in Teddy's manner. A calm, affable man who went about his doctoring with scrupulous detachment and a heavy heart, he saw enough misery in the ordinary course of his life to avoid adding to it, except when compelled to on medical grounds.

"Is he here?"

She said, "He's upstairs."

"Would he mind if I said hello to him?"

She said, "Why should he mind?" and they laughed, ruefully. "I'll tell him you're here."

JACK WAS LYING ON HIS BACK WITH AN ARM ACROSS HIS face, to shield his eyes from the light that came through the drawn blinds. When he heard her at the door he rolled away from her.

"What," he said. "What is it."

"Teddy's here."

He laughed. "I wondered when you were going to get around to that. Calling Teddy."

"I didn't ask him to come. He just came on his own, as far as I know."

He turned to look at her. "You're whispering. So he must be downstairs."

"Yes."

"I didn't hear his car. I guess I was asleep."

"Well, he'd like to see you."

"Have you told him?"

"No. Should I?"

"Please don't. Don't, Glory. It will never happen again, I swear." He rubbed his face. "I'll have to wash up. I shouldn't have slept in this shirt. I could use an aspirin." He swung his legs over the side of the bed and sat up. "Where did I leave my shoes?" He rubbed his eyes. "Teddy," he said. "That's just what I need right now."

She brought him the bottle of aspirin and a glass of water. Then she brought him a washcloth and a towel.

"Thanks," he said.

"I'll tell him you'll be down in a few minutes. I'll start some coffee."

"Yes, coffee," he said, scrubbing his face and his neck, then his face again. "Sorry," he said. "Sorry about all this."

She went down to the kitchen. Teddy was standing in the porch looking out at the garden. "You've been busy," he said.

"Jack did most of it."

He looked at her, to gauge the ratio of truth to loyalty in what she said, ready to be pleased with either of them, just wanting the information. "Then he must be doing all right."

"He was for a while."

"I see." Teddy with his crisp hair and his groomed hands, his soft brown sweater and his tortoiseshell glasses. He was mild and reassuring in every way he could be, by nature, habit, and intention. There was something of the scent of rubbing alcohol about him, so faint that he must have known it suggested illness or emergency and have scrubbed it off as carefully as he could. That would account for the cologne he wore, his only departure from decorous simplicity. After a few minutes he said, "I can leave, if that's what he wants. I knew he wouldn't be too happy to see me. You can tell him I won't stay long."

"Give him a few more minutes. He'll be down. He probably wanted to clean up a little."

Teddy laughed. "And polish his shoes, I suppose. Has he changed a lot?"

"I didn't know him as well as you did. He's still Jack."

"Dad told me you and he get along. He worried about that."

Jack came down the stairs in his stocking feet, wearing one of his own shirts, still trying to button a sleeve. He stopped by the door, glanced at Glory, and smiled. He folded the cuff over twice, then unbuttoned the other sleeve and rolled it up, too.

His brother said, "Jack."

Jack said, "Teddy."

"How are you, Jack? It's good to see you."

Jack propped himself against the counter and folded his arms. It was fairly obvious how he was. Still, Glory wished he were not so thin, that he'd put on a better shirt, that it was not so hard for him to raise his eyes. "I'm all right," he said. He smiled and shrugged. "I've been looking for work."

Teddy drew a breath. He said, "I'm your brother, Jack! Jesus Christ!"

Jack laughed.

"I mean, it's fine if you're looking for work. But it's none of my business, is it." Then he said, "Hey, Jack. Can we shake hands, at least?"

Jack shrugged. "Of course."

Teddy went to his brother and took Jack's hand in both his hands and held it. "So it's true. You're really here. I've seen it with my own eyes. I've hardly been able to believe it."

Jack laughed. "I could show you the wound in my side if you like." Then, "Sorry." And his head fell, and it was real regret. He was so tired of himself.

Teddy didn't study him, exactly, though there was always something of the doctor in his kindest attention. They teased him about it. Once, when he had looked too intently into Hope's eyes, she pulled down a lower lid to accommodate his scrutiny. Now he could not help but notice Jack's color, notice how thin his hand was, that it trembled. How could he help but notice these things, and how could Jack not step back from him, with a smile of irritation?

"You're a good man, Teddy. I remember you said that time I talked with you in St. Louis that you wouldn't come looking for me again. I appreciated that."

"Well, the fact is, I did. I just didn't find you. I came back six times altogether. The last time was about two years ago." He said, "Once, I thought I'd found your hotel. The fellow at the desk said you were staying there. That was a long time ago. My third trip, I think. I left an envelope with a note in it and some money. I guess it never got to you."

Jack shook his head. "No." Then he said, "Did the fellow have a bad eye?" He touched his face.

"Terrible," Teddy said. "Did he ever see anybody about it?"

Jack smiled. "I wouldn't know. The bastard evicted me. Sorry."

"Well, I promised to leave you alone, and then I made a pretty good try at going back on my word. Sometimes I'd just get the feeling I had to see you again, and I'd take off for St. Louis. A couple of times I called home from the road to tell them where I was. I'd think I was going to get a tank of gas and I'd find myself headed for Missouri."

Jack said, "I've put you to a lot of trouble."

"No, no. Looking for you was sort of the next best thing to finding you. It made me feel like we were still brothers, I suppose."

Jack said, "If we're being honest—I saw you there once. You were getting out of your car. It was a black Chevy. You were wearing a brown sweater that day, too. I stepped into a cigar store and waited until you drove away. I had to buy a magazine because I'd read most of it. That didn't make sense to me, but it did to the clerk. It took my last quarter."

Teddy laughed. "Okay," he said, and tears started down his cheeks. "I guess that doesn't surprise me." He took off his glasses and rubbed his eyes.

Jack said quietly, "I don't want you to give a damn about me. Any of you. I never did." He looked at Glory as if he might apologize, and then there was a silence. He laughed. "What an asinine remark that was. I'm really sorry. It sort of makes a point, though."

Teddy nodded. "There is clearly a good deal of truth in it."

"I'm not sure I understand it myself. I don't know why you'd put up with it. Me."

Teddy said, "That is an interesting question. For another time."

Jack laughed. He stood up. When they both looked at him he said, "Getting coffee. Would you like some more, Glory? Teddy?" He took up Glory's cup and saucer, but they chattered in his hand so he put them down. "I'll get the pot." When he had finished serving them he propped himself against the counter again.

"I'm doing all right, too," Teddy said. "Hanging together. No major problems at the moment. So far as I know."

Jack said, "Glad to hear it."

Then their father called, "Is that Teddy! I believe I hear Teddy!" His voice was urgent with relief and joy.

Teddy said, "Here I am, Dad. I'm coming." He went into the old man's room, sat down on the edge of the bed, and took him up in his arms. The old man put his arms around him, rested his head on his shoulder, and wept. "I'm so glad you're here, Teddy!" he said. He tried to speak in his reasonable, fatherly voice, but it was broken by sobs. "It's been hard, Teddy. I knew it would be. But it's been very hard!" And he wept. "I'm so old!" he said.

Teddy stroked his back and his hair. "It's all right. It'll be all right."

Jack looked at Glory and smiled. He was very pale. "What the hell have I been doing?" He said, "What a fool—" And he went upstairs. She heard his door close.

259

The old man said, "Glory has been such a help. He doesn't talk to me, but he talks to her. Sometimes I hear them laughing, and that's very good, but I don't think she can reason with him. I know I can't."

Teddy said, "I left my bag in the car. I'll get it and check you over a bit, listen to your chest, and then we can worry about Jack." He was the only doctor their father would allow anywhere near him, since the local fellow had suggested that brandy might ease his discomfort a little, and then had given him a tonic which the old man swore was concocted of whiskey and prune juice.

"No, no, Teddy, I don't care about my heart, that's very kind. What I want is just to see the two of you together. Is Jack here? I hope you find him, because it seems like I never even get a clear look at him. If you could just stand there beside him, I believe that might help me. I rest all the time, but I can't get my strength up. So I thought you might help me."

"Sure, Dad." Teddy came out to the hallway and called up the stairs, "Jack, would you come here for a minute." When there was no response, he raised his voice. "Hey, Jack, get down here. Dad wants to see you." A minute passed and Jack came down the stairs. Teddy said, "He wants to see us together."

Jack said, "You coming, Glory?" and paused to let her go ahead of him. He had that cautious, distant look, absent the calculation she had learned to recognize as hope. Her father seemed to have forgotten her, and Jack wanted her there, as if she could somehow support him or defend him. But there was a respect in the gesture that Teddy noticed, too, and he set the chair for her by her father's bed, as if to show that he had not meant to slight her.

"Yes," their father said, "this is wonderful. Could you stand a little closer, Jack?"

He shrugged. "Sure. If you say so."

"Yes, now I can see all of you." He glanced at Jack's face, then glanced away. "I want a picture of you in my mind, together like that." After a moment he said, "I have thought so often of when you were boys, and sometimes people would ask if you were twins. There was such a resemblance. That changes over time, of course."

Jack laughed.

Teddy said, "Somehow I got all the gray hair."

"Responsibility does that," the old man said. "You were always the one to take responsibility. Much more than your share."

"I was always the one to worry," Teddy said.

"Yes, it comes to the same thing. I've worried, myself, the Good Lord knows. That took a great part of my life, I realize, looking back on it."

Jack rested his hand on the back of Glory's chair.

"Now I have to put all that aside and stop tormenting myself with the thought that I can do anything about—anything. Yes. But the Lord does work through human beings, through families." He cleared his throat. "Part of it is giving care and another part is accepting it. That second part is difficult and very important. I know I've been a burden to everybody for years and years, and you have all been very good to me. And I've enjoyed that, even though I never enjoyed the suffering and the general uselessness that made it necessary. And I hope I have made it clear that I thank God for you, that you have been a great blessing to me. In the time he has been home, Jack has shown great kindness to me. Glory, too, of course. Yes."

He closed his eyes, and frowned with the carefulness he brought to forming his conclusion.

"That's what the family is for," he said. "Calvin says it is the Providence of God that we look after those nearest to us. So it is the will of God that we help our brothers, and it is equally the will of God that we accept their help and receive the blessing of it. As if it came from the Lord Himself. Which it does. So I want you boys to promise me you will help each other."

Jack laughed.

"And accept help, too. I want you to shake hands and promise me that, too."

Teddy held out his hand, and Jack took it and released it. Teddy said, "I promise."

Jack said, "All right."

His father looked at him. "What was that, Jack? I thought I heard you say 'All right.' I'm sorry, but that seems a bit evasive."

Jack said, "Yes, sir, I guess it was. I just don't see how I'm supposed to keep up my side of it. How I could help Teddy."

"Well, that's what I mean about receiving help. Teddy took a world of responsibility for you, every way you'd let him do it, and it was because his happiness depended on yours. So the greatest kindness you could ever have shown him was to accept the good he intended for you. You owed him that much. And I mean spiritual help, too. Particularly spiritual help."

Teddy smiled at Jack and shrugged, sorry for their father's candor and helpless to bring an end to it. He said, "I just liked Jack. I liked to spend time with him. He doesn't owe me anything."

"Oh!" their father said. "I am not in the mood to argue." His voice broke. "I asked Jack to promise, and he wouldn't do it. I don't want to hear you making excuses for him. That has happened far too often, in my opinion." He was weeping.

Jack said, "No, I was just asking a question. I'll promise. I mean, I do promise."

His father did not open his eyes, but he said with great dignity, "I believe I anticipated your question, Jack, and I believe I answered it. Now I'm tired." And he turned toward the wall.

Teddy went to him and smoothed his hair away from his face, and very gently and casually he laid his fingertips on his brow and his temple and the artery in his neck. He took a handkerchief from the drawer where his father kept them and touched the tears off the old man's face, lifting his head to dry the wetter, downward side. Then, still holding his head, he turned the pillow to make it dry and cool. He lifted the blanket and sheet to straighten them, and glanced at his father's slight and crooked body.

"Where's your stethoscope?" the old man asked.

"It's in the car."

"A good place for it. My heart will do whatever it wants to, and it has my permission. Same for my lungs." Then he said, "You might look in on Ames."

Teddy stood there, lightly caressing the old man's hair and face with the handkerchief. "How about some aspirin?"

"No harm in it, I suppose."

Jack said, "I think I just used it up. I mean, I used it up."

"I keep it in my bag. So that's no problem. I'll leave a bottle here for you."

Jack put his hands to his face and laughed. "I can't believe I did that."

"No matter." He glanced at Jack, took note of his color, the tremor in his injured hands. "There's plenty for everybody."

Glory went to the car, found the pebbly black bag in the passenger seat, and brought it into the kitchen. Opened, it smelled strongly of leather and rubbing alcohol. There were cotton balls and tongue depressors in glass bottles, and thermometers, and assorted pills and salves and syrups and the stethoscope and several bottles of aspirin. When Glory brought the glass of water and two tablets, Teddy looked at them and said, "Three." He watched her prop her father up to help him swallow. Then he tucked him in again and said, "You'll feel better when you've had some sleep."

He went into the kitchen, filled a glass of water, and set it on the table with three aspirin tablets next to it. "I use a lot of the stuff myself," he said, and held up his right hand. The fingers had begun to enlarge at the knuckles and twist out of line.

Jack said, "That's hard."

Teddy nodded. "I wish it was only my hands. You're okay?"

"So far."

"Glory?"

"I seem to be."

"Well," he said, "at least I know how tough the old fellow has been all these years. It's no wonder he gets cross. How's he eating?"

Glory said, "Not very well lately."

Teddy nodded. "What are you making, Glory? Chicken and dumplings? He'll enjoy that, if there's anything in the world he can still enjoy." He said, "It smells great. I'm sorry I can't stay for supper. I have another doctor covering for me, but when people are in trouble they like to see a familiar face. So I'd better get back to work." He hugged Glory, and he held out his hand to Jack. "It's been wonderful to see you," he said. "It really has."

Jack said, "Yes. Thanks." Then, "Teddy, you know, I'd like to ask you something, if you could spare a few more minutes. It'll probably be a waste of your time. I know you have to leave."

Teddy set his bag by his chair and sat down again at the table. "Are you kidding? I can spare the time! I see patients every day of my life. Seeing you is—very exceptional." Then he said, "I'll just make a few phone calls."

JACK SAT DOWN AT THE TABLE, NEXT TO HIS BROTHER, SO he could speak softly. He said, "What does he want me to tell him? I mean, I know what he wants, but how do I say it?" He looked at Teddy. "The problem is, I'll be lying. I thought that mattered. Well, I suppose it does matter. I'd know what to say otherwise." He laughed. "I flattered myself that I had a scruple. But I was just making the poor old devil miserable for no reason. Except that I didn't know how to end it. I realize that now. Glory said it would be all right. If I tried to, you know, talk to him."

Teddy took off his glasses and rubbed his eyes. "So you want to put him at ease about the state of your soul. That's a good idea, I think."

Jack laughed. "That may be more than I can hope for. I'd like to tell him I believe in—something. Maybe not the resurrection of the body and the life everlasting. But something."

264

"Well." Teddy toyed with his glasses. Then he sat back. "You know, I thought about the ministry for a while. Very seriously. But I had to face the fact that I wasn't good at talking about these things. It wasn't my calling, as they say. Have you spoken with Ames?"

Jack said, "I've tried, a couple of times. It doesn't matter. I just thought I'd ask."

"No, I don't mean we should give up on this. I'm just reminding you of my limitations. This will take some effort."

"You have to go."

Teddy shook his head. "This is for the old fellow's comfort. A legitimate medical concern."

"All right. Thanks."

There was a silence.

Teddy said, "It might help to take a few notes." He reached up under his sweater and took a pen and a prescription pad from his shirt pocket. He put his glasses back on. Another silence. Then he wrote, in the upper-left-hand corner, *Beliefs:* Jack leaned over to read what he had written, and he laughed. Teddy tore off the page and crushed it into a little ball. "My thought was," he said, "that if we found something you could say to him honestly, we could go on from there. We'd have something to start with."

Jack said, "That's a thought." Then he said, "What would you say if you were in my situation? I mean, he has never asked you to —give him any assurances. Has he?"

Teddy shook his head. "I never left the church. I guess that was assurance enough."

"But you still, I mean, you do—"

"Sure. I have patients in the polio hospital. Sometimes I pray about as often as I breathe."

"That helps—"

"It helps me. I can do my work."

Jack nodded.

Teddy said, "These past few years have been pretty hard. There aren't many new cases anymore, thank God."

"Yes, I've read about that vaccine they have now."

Glory said, "Lila's afraid of it. She saw an article that said it sometimes causes polio."

"Well, in a few cases it has. It's probably safe for her to wait a year, till they've improved it. I haven't vaccinated my own kids yet. I send them to the country in the summer, to Corinne's folks. That's where they are now."

Jack said, "So the safest thing is just to get them out of the city."

"I think so. For the time being."

Jack picked up the crumpled page and twisted it, pondering.

Teddy said, "But we've gotten off the subject here."

"Oh. Sorry. I guess my mind wandered."

"Do you want to go on?"

Jack said, "Yes. Let's go on." Glory could see that look of calculation in his face again, that oddly illusionless hope.

After a minute Teddy said, "I'll have to have some help with this."

"Sorry." Jack cleared his throat. "Have you thought of bringing your kids to Gilead? Would this be a good place for them?"

"Sure. It's just not a good situation, with Dad the way he is."

Jack nodded. He seemed to reflect a minute. Then he stretched and ran his fingers through his hair. "I do wish to God I were religious, Teddy. That's the Lord's truth."

Teddy said, "Well, that seems like a beginning."

"Yes. If I were religious some things might be easier. Possible, at least."

Under *Wishes to be religious*, Teddy wrote *to make things easier.*

Jack looked at the pad and laughed. "I'm not so sure that is a beginning. It looks to me like a heresy of some sort."

Teddy tore off the page and balled it up. "I didn't know we'd be worried about that. Interesting." Jack smiled and shrugged. "Okay," Teddy said. "What things would be easier?"

"Well, it's hard to talk to people. Religious people."

"Dad, for example."

"For example."

"Me."

Jack laughed. "Another example. Ames."

"Yes. Can you tell me why it's hard? I've never really understood."

Jack said, "Sometimes it seems as though I'm in one universe and you're in another. All of you." He shrugged. Then he glanced at Glory, as if he might want to apologize.

Teddy considered him for a moment with gentle objectivity. "How long have you felt that way?"

"Well, Dr. Boughton, I may always have felt that way. If I can trust the tales of my stormy infancy."

"Sorry."

"Don't be. There are things I think it may have helped me with. Helped me understand a little." He said, "There are separate universes, you know. I happen to have mine to myself. There are others. At least I know that."

After a moment Teddy said, "Well, when we began the conversation you said you intended to lie to the Reverend. That was your word, 'lie.' And I said I respected that decision, in the circumstances. And I also respect the fact that it was a hard decision for you to make. I really do. Then I complicated things by suggesting that we might find something for you to say that would be—not altogether false. Now I think it might just be best to tell him you believe in God. That you've given the matter serious thought, and you are persuaded of the truth of Scripture. Something like that. Short and to the point."

Jack nodded. "Do you think there's any chance he'll believe me?"

"I know he'll want to believe you."

Jack smiled. "Maybe this isn't a good idea. I don't exactly look like I've been washed in the blood of the Lamb recently, do I? He probably knows—the state I was in a few hours ago. He probably has some idea."

267

"Well, I think we have to remember, you know, that time is short. In a few more weeks he might not even hear what you say to him."

Jack said, "All right. Yes. I believe in God and I am persuaded of the truth of the Scriptures. After serious thought. I can do that. When I've had some rest."

Teddy stood up. "I don't know if I've been any help. But I really should go. If there's nothing more we need to talk about."

"It helps to know you think it's all right. If I lie to him."

Teddy nodded. "I think it's kind of you to do it, in the circumstances. I put an envelope on the refrigerator with my addresses and telephone numbers. Home and office. If you want to stay in touch. Pay us a visit."

"So you want old Uncle Jack to turn up on your doorstep someday."

"Nothing would make me happier."

Jack looked at Glory and smiled. "Maybe."

"I know you won't," Teddy said. He studied his brother's face. "I suspect I'll never see you again. In this life. I'd say take care of yourself, but I'm afraid you won't do that, either. Well, never hesitate—" He held out his hand. When Jack took it, he touched his shoulder, then embraced him.

Jack was patient with the familiarity. He said, "I wish things could have been better between us all these years. I do. There's a lot I regret."

"I know," Teddy said. "It's okay. Now you can get some sleep."

Jack went out to the porch with him. He stayed there after Teddy's car had turned into the street. Then he said to her, "Do you think that's what the ocean sounds like?" The wind was tossing the leaves of the oak tree, which were dense and heavy enough to roar and ebb and then roar again. "When I was a kid I liked to think so."

"Luke says it is."

He nodded. "Luke would know."

Jack took Teddy's envelope down from the refrigerator. He held it up to show her the thickness of it. "What do you think is in here? Want to guess?" He lifted the flap and showed her the edges of a stack of bills. He went to the piano bench, lifted the lid, and dropped the envelope into it. "Now we're even. I mean, where money is concerned. He's right, I have to get out of here. I will." He paused on the stairs. "But now I am going to write a letter." Then he said, "Glory, I know I haven't even begun to— I had no right to do that to you. You've been kind to me, and I— But you have to get those bottles out of my dresser. Now, if you don't mind. The bottom drawer. You should put that money somewhere, too. All of it."

Glory said, "Wait, Jack. Did Teddy say you should leave?"

"He said the old fellow doesn't have much more time. So he'll be back here in a few weeks, you know he will. They'll all be here. And he said he will never see me again. It adds up." Jack looked at her. "If I send this letter to the mutual friend, she sends it on to Della and Della writes to me here, that could take— twelve days, maybe two weeks. So I'm going to stay here for another two weeks, and then you'll be rid of me."

"Will you give me your address, in case I need to forward something to you?"

He laughed. "When I have an address, little sister, you'll be the first to know."

After a while Jack came downstairs with his letter, took an envelope and stamp from the drawer, and pulled a chair away from the table.

"Mind?" he asked. His eyes were still reddened, and the flesh of his face looked a little like wax, or like clay, creasing deeply when he smiled. If she had not known him she'd have thought, wistful and unsavory. He looked at her, as if he knew he did not seem the same to her, as if he had made some terrible confession and been forgiven and felt both shame and relief.

"Of course I don't mind."

He said, "My hands aren't very steady. That might make the wrong impression. I want her to open it, at least." So she wrote the address as he told it to her. He licked the flap of the envelope and winced. "Snowflake," he said, and she laughed, and he laughed. He placed the stamp carefully. Then he took a folded paper from his shirt pocket and put it on the table. He said, "That's for you."

She took the paper up and opened it. A map. There was the river, and a road, and between them, fences, a barn, woods, an abandoned house, all of them sketched in and carefully labeled, and in the woods a clearing, and at the upper edge of the clearing an X and the word "morels." In the lower-left-hand corner there was a compass, and a scale in hundreds of paces, and in the upper-right-hand corner a dragon with a coiled tail and smoking nostrils.

She said, "This is very pretty."

He nodded. "More to the point, it is accurate. I made it when I was stone sober. It was the work of several days, a number of drafts."

She said, "Now we really are even."

He laughed. "That's right." His face was mild and his voice was soft with weariness, but he was clearly moved and relieved to be joking with her.

"Except it doesn't say where these woods are. There are lots of fences and barns around here."

"My, my," he said. "What an oversight." And he smiled at her.

"Well, I'm going to ignore that. It's pretty. I'm going to frame it."

"You're a good soul, Glory."

"Yes, I am."

"Chicken and dumplings."

"Yes."

"I thought you probably needed some rest. I can keep an eye on things if you want to get a little sleep."

"No. I'm all right. If you don't mind the company."

"I'm grateful for the company, Glory." He laughed. "You have no idea."

She said, "Do you want the newspaper? I've done the puzzles. I'm grateful for the company, too."

He nodded. "That's kind of you to say."

Then they heard a stirring of bedsprings, then the lisp lisp of slippered feet and the pock of the cane. After a moment their father appeared in the doorway in his nightshirt, pale, with his hair rumpled, but solemnly composed. He looked first at Glory, then at the window, then finally, as if he had nerved himself, at Jack. "Oh," he said, a regretful, involuntary sound. Then he rallied. "I thought I might enjoy a little conversation. I heard the two of you talking out here and I've come to join you. Yes."

Jack helped him with his chair and sat down again.

The old man took his hand. "I think I was cross," he said.

Jack said, "I had it coming."

His father said, "No, no, it isn't how I wanted things to be. I promised myself a thousand times, if you came home you would never hear a word of rebuke from me. No matter what."

"I don't mind. I deserve rebuke."

The old man said, "You ought to let the Lord decide what you deserve. You think about that too much, what you deserve. I believe that is part of the problem."

Jack smiled. "I believe you may have a point."

"Nobody deserves anything, good or bad. It's all grace. If you accepted that, you might be able to relax a little."

Jack said, "Somehow I have never felt that grace was intended for me, particularly."

His father said, "Oh nonsense! That is just nonsense!" He closed his eyes and withdrew his hand. Then he said, "I was cross again."

Jack laughed. "Don't worry about it. Dad."

After a moment the old man said, "Don't call me that."

"Sorry."

"I don't like it at all. Dad. It sounds ridiculous. It's not even a word."

"I'll never say it again." Jack stretched and smiled at Glory, eyebrows raised, as if to say, Help would be appreciated.

So she said, "Would you like me to get your robe, Papa?"

"I'm fine as I am. You'd think we were living in the Klondike." Then he said, "I came out here for a little conversation and you've both stopped talking."

There was a silence. "Well," Glory said, "I'm making chicken and dumplings. Mama's recipe."

He said, "That can be very good, if the dumplings aren't wet. Heavy. I've had to eat some terrible dumplings in my life." Then, his eyes still closed, he said, "I can't look at Jack's hands. I don't want to know what he did to them."

Jack cleared his throat. "It's mostly just engine grease I haven't scrubbed off yet. I scraped them up a little, I guess." He folded his arms to conceal them, and he smiled.

His father looked at him, sharply. "I don't know what happened. Something happened last night."

"Nothing good. You really don't want to know. No point in it. Sir."

"So, are we going to have the sheriff coming around here?"

"No, sir," he said. "I have done nothing that would interest the sheriff." His voice was soft and sad.

"Papa, Jack's all right. Everything's all right. But he's tired now," Glory said. "I think we should talk about something else."

The old man nodded. "We're all tired now." Then he said, "So many times, over the years, I've tried not to love you so much. I never got anywhere with it, but I tried. I'd say, He doesn't care a thing about us. He needs a little money now and then, that's the extent of it. Still, I thought you might come home for your mother's funeral. That was a very hard time for me. It would have been a great help. Why did I think you might come home? That was foolish of me. Your mother always said, You imagine some happiness is going to come out of all this, all this waiting and hoping, but it never will. So I tried to put an end to it. But I couldn't."

Jack smiled and cleared his throat. "Maybe now you can. Maybe I should tell you what I was up to all those years. That might put an end to it."

The old man shook his head. "It couldn't be worse than what I've imagined. I've thought of every dreadful thing, Jack. Lying awake nights. But it only made me grieve for you. And for myself, since there was no comfort I could give you."

Jack said, "Well, I wouldn't want you to think—I mean, 'dreadful' is a strong word. There are worse lives than mine. I know that's not much to be proud of. But still."

Glory said, "We all loved him, Papa, all of us, and there were reasons why we did. Why we do."

"Could you expand on that a little, Glory?" Jack said. "I'd be interested."

His father said, "Well, it's just natural. What I'd like to know is why you didn't love us. That is what has always mystified me."

After a moment Jack said, "I did. But there wasn't much I could do about it. It was hard for me to be here. I could never—trust myself. Anywhere. But that made it harder to be here."

His father nodded. "Drink," he said.

Jack smiled. "That, too."

"Yes, well, maybe it's a joke, I don't know. Last night was about as bad a night as I have passed on this earth. And I kept thinking to myself, asking the Lord, Why do I have to care so much? It seemed like a curse and an affliction to me. To love my own son. How could that be? I have wondered about it many times."

Jack said, "I'm sorry. I couldn't be more sorry. But at least you know why I stayed away so long. I had no right to come home. I shouldn't be here now."

"No right to come home!" his father said, and his voice broke. "If I'd had to die without seeing your face again, I'd have doubted the goodness of the Lord." He looked at Jack. "That was a fear I had. So I was very happy, you know, there for a while."

Jack said, "What are your feelings now, about the goodness of the Lord?" He said, "I really don't think the Lord's good name should depend on my behavior. I'm not equal to the responsibility."

The old man shook his head. "Nobody is. I'm not equal to it, either, the way I've been talking to you here—"

"No matter. I knew most of it anyway."

His father pondered for a while. "You knew it, and it didn't make a bit of difference. I should have realized that. I suppose I did."

Jack pushed back his chair and stood up. "Yes, well, if you'll excuse me—"

Glory said, "No, Jack, you sit down. We've worried about you enough."

His glance at her was weary, even bewildered. "I just thought I'd go up to my room."

"No." She touched his shoulder. She could see him make the decision to trust her, at least not to offend her. He sat down again.

His father said, "Kindness takes more strength than I have now. I didn't realize how much effort I used to put into it. It's like everything else that way, I guess."

Jack said, "I can't leave quite yet. But I'll leave as soon as I can."

"Oh yes, you came for your own reasons, and you'll leave for your own reasons. And it just happened that I was here, I wasn't dead yet."

Glory said, "I'm sorry, Papa, but this has gone on long enough."

The old man nodded. "Maybe I'm finding out I'm not such a good man as I thought I was. Now that I don't have the strength— patience takes a lot out of you. Hope, too."

Jack said, "I think hope is the worst thing in the world. I really do. It makes a fool of you while it lasts. And then when it's gone, it's like there's nothing left of you at all. Except"—he shrugged and laughed—"except what you can't be rid of."

His father said, "I'm sorry you've had to know about that, Jack. And now we've got Glory crying."

Jack shrugged and smiled at her. "Sorry."

Glory said, "Don't worry. There's no harm in it."

Her father sighed. "Yes, well, I wish I could take it all back, everything I've just said. But I suppose you did know it already. Still, it's different when you say things like that out loud. It already seems like I didn't mean it. Now I know I'm going to just lie on my bed and worry about it, and wish I'd held my peace. I did that for so long."

Jack said, "You did. You were always very kind."

The old man nodded. "I hope that still counts for something."

"It's the only thing that counts."

"Thank you, Jack. And I know you want to be done with me now. I've worn us out, both of us. I'll just let the two of you get back to your conversation."

Glory helped him to his room and into his bed, and when she came back, Jack was slouched in his chair with his ankles crossed, laying out cards for solitaire.

He said, "Has a day ever passed when you haven't thought of him?"

"Who?"

"Whom. The old gent. Whom did you think I meant? Mr. 452 Love Letters?"

She said, "You're so jealous!"

He laughed. "True. It isn't fair. I never got even one. Just the other day in the *Post* I noticed a poem by Mrs. Lindbergh that I wouldn't mind getting in the mail. Much better than nothing. Though I've learned that nothing also has charms. It's more nuanced than 'return to sender,' for example."

She said, "I doubt I've gone a whole day without thinking of Papa. I'm sure there have been hours here and there."

"I've thought about this place so many times. When I was a kid I used to wish I lived here. I used to wish I could just walk in the door like the rest of you did and, you know, sit down at the table and do my homework or something."

"Why didn't you?"

He shrugged. "I actually tried it out once or twice." Then he said, "I know why people watched me. I'm not even sure that was what made me uneasy. I think it made me feel safer sometimes. I used to test it, stir up a little trouble to make sure the old fellow was still keeping an eye on me. Sometimes I'd be out in the barn, in the loft, listening to the piano, you all singing 'My Darling Clementine,' and I'd think, Maybe they've forgotten all about me, and it felt like death, in a way." He said, "I was usually closer to home than he thought I was. Where he didn't look for me." He glanced at her. "Don't cry, please. I'm just telling you how it was." He laughed. "How it is." Then he said, "There are a couple of bottles in the loft. If you want to get them down, I'll hold the ladder."

"I get tears. I can't help it. They don't mean anything."

"They're nice, actually. To be honest, I think I tell you my sad stories to see if they really are sad. And sure enough, the tears start, and I can relax about it. I mean, there's nothing sad about getting what you deserve. So I've been told. I feel a little vindicated when you cry."

"I don't know. Maybe getting what you deserve is the saddest thing in the world."

"Really? I think about little Annie Wheeler, the non-bride of my non-youth." He looked at her. "That's sad. You see, I just mention her name and here come the tears." Then he said, "I'm really sorry. I should have known better."

After a while Glory said, "I wouldn't mind talking about her. I think about her, too."

He cleared his throat. "Do you know where she is? You don't

have to tell me. I mean, I don't think she'd have any use for me. There are plenty of bums in Chicago. I just wondered if you knew."

"If her family knew, they wouldn't tell us. Papa talked to them about it a number of times, thinking they might hear from her. He has worried about her."

Jack said, "I really shamed him."

"It was a hard time."

He fiddled with the deck of cards, cutting it and squaring it and cutting it. "That last time I spoke to him, before I left, I knew I had done something he couldn't forgive. He thought he could. He said he had, but he's a terrible liar. It shocked me that I could hurt him so badly. It scared me. It was what I expected, but it scared me. It was like stepping off a cliff. And it was a relief, too. I thought, It's finally happened, I knew it would." He laughed. "I believe I was drunk for the next three years. Teddy found his vocation keeping me alive. The poor devil, when I think of what he went through with me. When he was nineteen, trying to study, trying to make varsity baseball, trying to get me to class. He was caught cheating once. Teddy. He took my place at an exam. I believe my sense of decency must have stirred briefly, because that was when I went off to St. Louis. Apparently the dean decided Teddy violated the honor code for honorable reasons, I don't know. But it could have kept him from finishing. It could have been a blot on his record, kept him out of medical school." He said, "St. Louis was stepping off another cliff. And that was a relief, too."

He shuffled the cards, laid them out, swept them up, and shuffled again. "None of this makes sense," he said. "It's all pretty ugly. For a while I thought I might have come to the end of it. No, I knew better than that. I knew better." He said, "Della's father asked around. He wanted—character references." He smiled.

"I'm sorry."

"He told me some things about myself I'd forgotten. He showed me a letter he had written to Della. He said he wouldn't give it to her if I let her alone. I couldn't do that. But she stuck with me. That was hard."

"But you were all right then, when you were with Della."

"'Can the Scotsman change his skin or the leopard his spots? Then may ye also do good that are accustomed to do evil.' He was just trying to look out for his daughter. I respect that. He's a lot like our reverend father, in fact. Always trying to look after everybody." He laid out the cards. "Anyway, I feel more like myself now. Wanting, hoping—it's like the old fellow said, those things take a lot out of you. But this—this I can do."

"You are going to send the letter."

He nodded. "There's no point in sending it. On the other hand, why waste a stamp?" He glanced at her. "Gloria Dolorosa. It's good of you to take it all so hard, chum. It really is."

She made up the dumpling batter and dropped it onto the stewed chicken. She, also, had eaten some terrible dumplings. It occurred to her to wonder if they were ever good in the ordinary sense, if at best they were not just familiar, inoffensive. They really were too inoffensive. It might have been the word "dumpling" she liked rather than the thing itself.

She said, "I have an idea, Jack. I could go to Memphis. I could talk to her. If you fix the car, we could drive down together. We'll call Teddy, and he'll come here to look after Papa for a few days. He would do that if you asked him to. And then I'd just go to her house. Or to her church. No one would notice me, and maybe I could get a chance to talk to her."

"That's kind. But let's just say they don't notice you." He laughed. "I'm pretty sure they would. But if they didn't. What would you say to her? That no one will give me a job, and I'm drinking again, and I recently failed to fire up the DeSoto and sail off to perdition? That I am metaphysically responsible for the floweriest little grave in all Gilead?"

"Don't talk like that."

"What would you say, though, Glory? You see my point."

"I'd say you were waiting in the car."

"With a dozen roses. And the engine running."

"And a box of chocolates."

Jack looked away and smiled. Then he said, very softly, "Don't, Glory. I have to deal with reality. Or at least accept the fact that reality is dealing with me." He touched his face. "I'm a rougher-looking bastard now than I was when I came here. And even then I was surprised that you'd let me in the door. I don't think I'd want her to see me now."

"You'll be better in a day or two. Then you can decide."

He laughed. "This is a terrible plan. I can't tell you how bad it is."

"Well, you can think about it."

"Yes," he said. "It is nice to think about. I'd like to show them what good people I come from. If I could get the radio working, we'd hear some music on the way to Memphis. I might as well take a look at that engine, anyway. You were getting some use out of the old crate. I'll try to get it running again." Then he said, "Is my shirt still out there?"

"No, I brought it in this morning. I tried laundry soap and that didn't do much. I doubt bleach would, either. I thought I might ask Lila. But that sleeve isn't stained very badly." She said, "Your suit is hanging in the porch. I burned your socks."

He looked at her. "Tears again." He laughed. "Regret is wasted on me, Glory. I do the damnedest things, and there's no help for it. I kept that shirt for a long time. I don't often manage to keep things."

She said, "I haven't given up yet. If I can't get those stains out, I'll sew the sleeve into your other shirt. That wouldn't be hard."

"Don't," he said. "Let me get used to things the way they are. That's the biggest favor you can do me, Glory." He smiled. "But thanks. You're a good kid."

"Yes. In the morning I'm going to take your letter to the post office."

"All right." He said, "You did get those bottles out of my dresser?"

"While you were asleep."

"Good. It would be a mistake to trust me. I'm sorry about that."

While she looked after her father, Jack set the table. She brought the old man out to the kitchen and seated him. He said, "Yes," and bowed his head and said no more for a little while, then, "If you wouldn't mind, Glory."

"All right. Dear Lord, bless these gifts to our use and us to Thy service, and keep us ever mindful of the needs of others. Amen."

"Yes, I've always objected to that prayer. If it were only a little easier to know what they are. The needs of others. A good deal more is required than just being mindful. That has certainly been my experience."

Jack served the chicken and dumplings with something of the wry decorum of former days, but quietly, calmly, the old suspense gone now. The dumplings were tacky on the outside and doughy on the inside, but that might just be how they are, she thought. How they have always been. Her father said, "Excellent," and ate half of one.

Jack said, "There's really nothing like a good dumpling."

"Except a bad one," she said.

He laughed. "True, they are pretty similar." Then he looked at her. "Ah, tears."

Their father said, sharply, "You shouldn't tease your sister. You boys think it's some sort of game, but I don't like it. A gentleman is always considerate of women. I have said this many times. That means your sisters, too, even the little ones. This is very important. I hope you will reflect on it." He did not appear to be asleep, though his eyes were closed.

Jack said, "Yes, sir," to calm his irritation, and then he sat there gazing at him, taking in what the old man had said.

"I was remarking to your mother about it just the other night. We should not allow this teasing."

Glory was aware suddenly that the weariness of the night and day had overwhelmed her, and her hope of comforting had not had anything to do with the way things really happen in the world. Her father was crouched in his chair, with his chin almost in his plate, drowsing and speaking from what she could only hope was a dream, and her brother was withdrawing into utter resignation, as if the old incandescence had consumed him before it flickered out. But he brought her a tea towel for her tears, and then he helped his father to his room.

THE HEAT OF THE MORNING WOKE HER, SO SHE KNEW SHE had slept late. There were no sounds in the house, there was no smell of coffee. Jack and her father must still be sleeping. Good for them. She felt stiff, as if some physical exertion had wearied her, and it was only the thought that she might miss the morning mail that induced her to get up, wash, brush, dress, make herself presentable to whatever passerby or clerk might otherwise notice her and wonder what new drama had unfolded in the poor old preacher's house. She had put the letter on her dresser the night before, in case Jack might have had second thoughts and chosen resignation over futile hope. She went down the stairs as quietly as she could and let herself out the door.

And here is the world, she thought, just as we left it. A hot white sky and a soft wind, a murmur among the trees, the treble rasp of a few cicadas. There were acorns in the road, some of them broken by passing cars. Chrysanthemums were coming into bloom. Yellowing squash vines swamped the vegetable gardens and tomato plants hung from their stakes, depleted with bearing. Another summer in Gilead. Gilead, dreaming out its curse of sameness, somnolence. How could anyone want to live here? That was the question they asked one another, out of their father's hearing, when they came back from college, or from the world. Why would anyone stay here?

In college all of them had studied the putative effects of dera-cination, which were angst and anomie, those dull horrors of the modern world. They had been examined on the subject, had re-hearsed bleak and portentous philosophies in term papers, and they had done it with the earnest suspension of doubt that afflicts the highly educable. And then their return to the *pays natal*, where the same old willows swept the same ragged lawns, where the same old prairie arose and bloomed as negligence permitted. Home. What kinder place could there be on earth, and why did it seem to them all like exile? Oh, to be passing anonymously through an impersonal landscape! Oh, not to know every stump and stone, not to remember how the fields of Queen Anne's lace figured in the childish happiness they had offered to their father's hopes, God bless him.

She had to speak to neighbors in their gardens, to acquain-tances she met on the sidewalk. Strangers in some vast, cold city might notice the grief in her eyes, even remember it for an hour or two as they would a painting or a photograph, but they would not violate her anonymity. But these good souls would worry about her, mention her, and speculate to one another about her. Dear God, she saw concern in their eyes, regret. Poor Glory, her life has not gone well. Such a nice girl, and bright. Very bright.

That odd capacity for destitution, as if by nature we ought to have so much more than nature gives us. As if we are shockingly unclothed when we lack the complacencies of ordinary life. In destitution, even of feeling or purpose, a human being is more hauntingly human and vulnerable to kindnesses because there is the sense that things should be otherwise, and then the thought of what is wanting and what alleviation would be, and how the soul could be put at ease, restored. At home. But the soul finds its own home if it ever has a home at all.

ROBBY AND TOBIAS WERE IN THE DRUGSTORE, EXTRACTING Fudgsicles from the smoking freezer chest. Each of them had a dime, earned pulling weeds in one of Lila's gardens. They showed them to her. She dropped Jack's letter in the slot, heard the clerk's views on the weather, and started home again, the boys tagging along with her, skipping and circling and taking a few steps backward, not yet resigned to the tedium of merely walking. They split their Fudgsicles as they are meant to be split, and Tobias dutifully offered her the second half of his, and she said no, thank you, which pleased him. Robby said, "I'm saving mine for Mr. Boughton."

Glory said, "You can call him Jack. He wouldn't mind."

Robby shook his head. "My dad says I have to call him Mr. Boughton."

He walked along at her elbow, engrossed in the Fudgsicle, coping as he could when the ice slid down the stick. When they came to his corner, Tobias took off for home and Robby went on with her. He said, "My mom likes it when I help out. Well, my dad likes it, too, but he just watches. He sits on the porch."

Lila had said to her once that the boy had to learn what it was to work. Glory knew she meant she would be his only support through most of his growing up, and life would be difficult for them. "We'll be leaving sometime," she said. "There's nothing to do around here." That was when they had been at the river for Ames's birthday, and had walked down to rinse the plates, and had stopped to watch Robby and Tobias racing leaves through an eddy between two ribs of sand. She said, "We hope he'll remember something of it." Then Glory had seen the place as if it were the kind of memory a woman might wish for her child, and it was exactly that, the river broad and shallow, the intricacies of its bed making rivulets of the slow water, bloom on the larger little islands and butterflies everywhere. And the trees meeting high above it, shading it, making the bottom earthily apparent wherever there was calm. They all loved the river, in all generations, Jack, too. She bent and dipped her hands in the water and pressed them to her face, to conceal the embarrassment of tears, but more than that, because the river was simply manifest, a truth too seldom acknowledged. When she had been on her own, sometimes she had thought of it.

Jack was sitting on the front step, his elbows on his knees, waiting for her. When he saw the two of them, he stood up, tossed his cigarette, and went into the house. Robby said, "Well, you can give him this," and handed her the half Fudgsicle, which had melted into its bag.

"He doesn't feel too well today," she said.

He nodded. "He wouldn't want me to catch anything."

"No, he wouldn't."

"Then my dad might catch it."

"True," she said. It was the thought of seeing Jack that had brought him along with her. Now he turned and waved and ran off toward home.

Jack was at the kitchen table, laying out a hand for solitaire.

"Sorry," he said. "Not up to small talk."

"He wanted me to give you this."

"Great. Nice kid."

She put the soggy packet in the sink.

He said, "I thought you might not have gotten the bottles out of the loft. So I couldn't start working on the car till you came back."

He followed her out to the barn and opened the door for her. "Stay here," he said. Then he dragged an empty crate out from the wall, climbed up on it, took hold of the edge of the loft with one hand, and with the other brought down a ladder that had been lying on the floor of the loft, out of sight. When the base of it hit the floor, there was a painful sound of crotchety wood and pulled nails. He said, "This is where I was last night when you came looking for me. I meant to say something, but I—didn't." He shrugged. "I wasn't out staggering the streets of Gilead, in case you were worried about that. I didn't disgrace the family."

He held the doubtful old ladder while she climbed up into the loft. It smelled airy, and like hay or burlap and desiccated wood, a place with a history of rain and heat, long abandoned by human intention. Her older brothers and sisters had stories of playing in it, but their father had forbidden them to play there years before she was born because of the splinters in the plank floor and the nails that had been driven through the shingles in the low roof, and he had taken away the ladder in order to baffle temptation. Nevertheless, from time to time the boys contrived to hoist one another up into that secret and forbidden place to act out stealth and ambush, an impulse too primordial for even Teddy to resist. It would never have occurred to them to bring her along, the baby sister whose indiscretions were notorious in the family for years after she had outgrown them. So this was the first time she was setting foot in that fabled space.

Jack had run a length of clothesline from beam to beam and thrown a tarp over it to make a low tent in the angle of floor and roof. She knelt and looked into it. The edges were neatly nailed down. There was a floor of newspapers, a rumpled blanket and a pillow. He had set a wooden box on its side as a table and shelf. A flashlight, a few books, a mayonnaise jar with a handful of her oatmeal cookies in it. The framed photograph of a river. A glass and an uncapped pint bottle, three-quarters empty. The dark little room smelled strongly of whiskey and sweat. It seemed almost domestic, and yet there was a potency of loneliness about it like a dark spirit lurking in it, a soul that had improvised this crude tabernacle to stand in the place of other shelter, flesh. She thought, What if he had succeeded in dying, and then she had found this, so neatly and intentionally made out of nothing anyone could want, with the fierce breath of his grief still haunting it, the blanket still tangled.

Jack said, "Are you all right? I'm sorry. I shouldn't have asked you—"

She said, "I'm fine." He would know from her voice that she was crying, but she had to say something, and he would expect her to cry, surely. She pulled the blanket out of the tent. An empty bottle dragged along with it. She put the bottle aside and folded and smoothed the blanket and put it back. Then she pulled the crate to her and took the bottle and the glass out of it and set them aside. The books were *The Condition of the Working Class*, *The High and the Mighty*, and a worn little Bible. The flashlight had burned itself out, but she turned it off and put it beside the books and slid the crate back into its place. It felt like piety and propitiation to calm the disorder this most orderly man had left in the confusions of his sorrow.

He said, "I think there are only two bottles up there. I'm pretty sure."

That meant he thought she was taking longer than she needed to. He would be embarrassed that she had seen and touched his secretiveness, which was so like shame, so like affliction, that they could hardly be distinguished. She said, "I'm coming," and stayed where she was, kneeling there, amazed at what was before her, as if it were the humblest sign of great mystery, come from a terrain where loneliness and grief are time and weather.

She held the bottles against her side with one arm and the glass in her hand, and with her free arm she held to the ladder and lowered herself onto it.

"I'm right here," Jack said, and held it steady for her. Then he stepped away and stood with his hands on his hips, looking at her with the distant and tentative expression that meant he felt she might be making a new appraisal of him. He said, "A little strange, hmm? A little squalid? Sorry."

"No matter," she said. "I think this is everything."

He nodded.

"I poured out the other bottles in the orchard."

"Fine." He said, "I made that to keep the bats off when I read with the flashlight. Bats are attracted by light, did you know that? Useful information. And it kept the rain off. That roof is just about worthless. So it made a kind of sense. To me."

HE WAITED FOR HER, AND WHEN SHE CAME BACK FROM the orchard and the shed he walked to the house with her, a few steps behind. He said, "I'll pull that down tomorrow. My shanty. I'll clean things up around here before I go. I've let a lot of things slide."

"It's still much better than it was when you came."

He opened the screen door for her. He said, "I'm going to try to get some of these stains off my hands. I can't help much with the old fellow until I do. I think he's scared of me, the way I look now."

"No, he just hates the thought that you hurt yourself."

He nodded. "You can hate thoughts. That's interesting. I hate most of my thoughts." He opened the cupboard under the sink and found a scrub brush.

Glory said, "You might rub your hands with shortening. That would probably dissolve the grease. Scrubbing will make them look inflamed." She took the can from the cupboard, scooped out a spoonful, and put it in his palm. She said, "Remember when you talked to me about your soul, about saving it?"

He shrugged. "I think you may be mistaking me for someone else."

"And I said I liked it the way it is."

"Now I know you're mistaking me for someone else." He did not look up from the massaging of his hands.

"I've thought about what I should have said to you then, and I haven't changed my mind at all. That's why it embarrassed me, because it would have been so presumptuous of me—I'm not even sure what it means." Then she said, "What is a soul?"

He looked up, smiled, studied her face. "Why ask me?"

"It just seems to me that you would know."

He shrugged. "On the basis of my vast learning and experience, I would say—it is what you can't get rid of. Insult, deprivation, outright violence—'If I make my bed in Sheol, behold, thou art there,' and so on. "'If I take the wings of the morning, and dwell in the uttermost parts of the sea.'"

"Interesting choice of text."

"It came to mind. Don't make too much of it."

"Well, your soul seems fine to me. I don't know what that means, either. Anyway, it's true."

He said, "Thanks, chum. But you don't know me. Well, you know I'm a drunk."

"And a thief."

He laughed. "Yes, a drunk and a thief. I'm also a terrible coward. Which is one of the reasons I lie so much."

She nodded. "I've noticed that."

"No kidding. What else have you noticed?"

"I'm not going to mention vulnerable women."

"Thanks," he said. "Very generous in the circumstances."

She nodded. "I think so."

He said, "I am unaccountably vain, despite all, and I have a streak of malice that does not limit itself to futile efforts at self-defense."

"I've noticed that, too."

He nodded. "I guess there's nothing subtle about it."

She brought a washcloth and began gently to soap away the dingy shortening from his hands. He took the cloth from her.

"So," he said, "we have made a list of my venial sins."

"Presbyterians don't believe in venial sins."

"I'm pretty sure I'm not described by the word 'Presbyterian.'"

"Oh, hush!"

He laughed. "All right. My lesser sins. Not that Presbyterians believe in them, either. Do you want a list of the grave ones? The mortal ones?"

"Not really."

"That's good." He said, "Reverend Miles, Della's father and my biographer, told me I was nothing but trouble. I felt the truth of that. I really am nothing." He looked at her. "Nothing, with a body. I create a kind of displacement around myself as I pass through the world, which can fairly be called trouble. This is a mystery, I believe." He said, "It's why I keep to myself. When I can. Ah. And now the tears."

"Don't you think everybody feels that way sometimes, though? I certainly have. While you had Della you didn't feel that way. If you weren't alone so much, I mean, Papa's right about that. If you'd just let us help you."

He said, "When Mama died I'd been out of jail for a couple days. So I could have come home. Strictly speaking. But it takes awhile to shake that off, you know. Wash it off. To feel you could blend in with the Presbyterians. And the old fellow doesn't miss anything. I wouldn't have wanted him to see me. I was terrified at the thought. So I used his check to buy some clothes. I knew what he'd think of me when he saw I'd cashed it." He smiled at her. "I was grateful for the check, I really was. I hadn't been at that hotel where he sent it for quite a while. I was surprised the letter found me. But the desk clerk was impressed by the black border, so he brought it to me. He hadn't even opened it. I spent part of the money in a bar. What was left of it."

Glory said, "You don't have to tell me anything you don't want to. Not that it matters. I don't care if you've been in jail."

He said, "No? It made quite an impression on me. I believe it's as congenial a place to be nothing as I could ever hope to find." He laughed. "In jail, they call it good behavior. Not a thing I've often been accused of." He said, "Jail reinforced my eccentricities. I'm pretty sure of that."

"Mama died more than ten years ago. So you were all right after you got out of jail."

"Yes, I was. And now I know it was an aberration. Nothing I can sustain on my own. I've found out I still can't trust myself. So I'm right back where I started." He smiled. "You forgive so much, you'll have to forgive that, too. Well, I guess you won't have to."

"You know I will."

After a moment he said, "You probably wonder what kind of woman Della is, shacking up with the likes of me."

"She reads French. She embroiders. She sings in a choir."

"There are things I haven't told you about her."

She shrugged. "Some things are sacred."

He laughed. "Yes, that's it. That's it exactly." He wiped his hands on the dishtowel and looked them over. "Not too bad," he said. He held them up to her inspection. "He should be able to stand the sight of my hands, at least. I wish there were something I could do about my face."

"You could get a little sleep."

"Not a bad idea. If you don't mind. There are a few things I meant to get done today."

"Sleep for an hour or two first."

"Yes," he said. "I'll do that. Thanks." He stopped halfway up the stairs. "I told you a minute ago that I was in jail. I should have said prison. I was in prison." Then he watched her to appraise her reaction.

She said, "I don't care if you were in prison," but the words cost her a little effort, and he heard it and smiled at her for a moment, studying her to be sure that she meant them.

He said, "You're a good kid."

It was suppertime when Jack came downstairs again. He said, "I slept a lot longer than I planned to. Sorry." He did look more like himself, she thought. An odd phrase, since he was always himself, perhaps never more so than he had been in the last two days. He was wearing his father's old clothes and the blue striped necktie, and he was conspicuously kempt and shaved. Old Spice. He buttoned the top button of the jacket, unbuttoned it again, then took the jacket off. "This is better, I think," he said, and looked at her for confirmation.

"In this heat," she said.

"Yes, but the tie's all right."

"It looks fine."

He had some intention, clearly. That was probably a good thing, all in all. There was a kind of tense composure about him that seemed like morale. He said, "What's for dinner?"

"Creamed chicken on toast. Leftovers. No dumplings this time. I made a peach cobbler, though."

"Well," he said, "I thought we might eat in the dining room. If that's all right. With candles. The light seems so bright in here. To those of us who fear the light and love the darkness." He laughed.

She thought, He doesn't want Papa to be pained by the sight of him. Of course. She said, "Whatever you like. I'll open the windows and put the fan in there. It gets stuffy in this weather."

"I'll take care of that."

She went into her father's bedroom and found the old man lying there pensively awake. When she spoke to him, he said, "I love hearing all the voices. Your mother says this house is like an old fiddle, what it does with sound, and I think that's true. It is a wonderful house." He was still worn from that long night, she thought, still half asleep.

"Would you like to get up now, Papa? I've made supper. Jack got some rest this afternoon, and he's up and setting the table."

He looked at her. "Jack?"

"Yes. He's feeling a lot better."

"I didn't know he was ill. Yes, I'd better get up." His concern was such that he seemed to have forgotten the recalcitrance of his body and to be surprised to find himself struggling to sit upright.

"Here, I'll help you," she said.

He looked at her with alarm. "Something's happened."

"It's over now. We're all right."

"I thought the children were here. Where are they?"

"They're all at home, so far as I know, Papa."

"But they're so quiet!"

She said, "Just a minute. I'll ask Jack to play something while we get you ready for supper."

"So Jack's here."

"Yes, he's here."

She stepped into the dining room and asked Jack to play, and then she went back to help her father. "'Softly and Tenderly,'" the old man said. "A very fine song. Is that Gracie?"

"No, it's Jack."

The old man said, "I don't believe Jack plays the piano. It might be Gracie."

She brought her father down the hallway. He stopped at a little distance from the piano, released her arm, and stood looking at Jack with puzzled interest. He whispered, "The fellow plays very well. But why is he here in our house?"

Glory said, "He's come home to see you, Papa."

"Well, that's very nice, I suppose. No harm in it."

Jack played the hymn to the end, then he followed them into the dining room. He had put the jacket back on. He helped his father with his chair, Glory with hers, then seated himself by his father. The old man looked at him as if he had taken a liberty, not offensive but surprising just the same, in sitting down with them. He said, "Glory, if you don't mind."

"Yes. All right." She closed her eyes. "Dear God in heaven, please help us. Dear God, please help everyone we love. Amen."

Jack looked at her and smiled. "Thank you," he said.

The old man nodded. "That pretty well sums it up."

Her brother leaned out of the candlelight while she served. He pushed back his hair and settled his tie down the front of his shirt, and then folded his hands in his lap, as if remembering to keep them out of sight. His father glanced at him from time to time, sidelong. Glory cut up her father's toast, and then they ate in silence, except when Glory asked if they would like more of anything. She hadn't read a newspaper in days or turned on the television set or the radio, so she could not think of a way to bring up Eisenhower or Dulles or baseball or Egypt, the things that focused her father's attention, lured him out of his dreams. At least he and Jack were eating.

Finally, Jack cleared his throat. Still, his voice was a throaty whisper. "Sir," he said, "there are some things I've wanted to say to you. If this is a good time. I thought it might be as good as any."

His father smiled at him kindly. "No need to be so formal. I have been retired for a number of years. Just call me Robert."

Jack looked at her.

She said, "Papa, can I get you some coffee?"

"Not for me, thanks. Our friend might want some."

After a moment Jack said, "If I could talk to you about something. I wanted to tell you that after considerable reflection, after giving the matter some careful thought—" He looked at Glory and smiled.

His father nodded. "Are you considering the ministry?"

Jack took a deep breath and rubbed his eyes. "No, sir."

"There's quite a return to the ministry these days. Many young men are drawn to it now. It's wonderful. You might want to think about it."

Jack said, "Yes, sir." He toyed with his water glass, reflecting. Then, "I've made an effort, for a number of reasons. To believe in something. I've read the Bible I don't know how many times. And I've thought about it. Of course I have been in situations where it's the only book they let you have, where there isn't much else to think about. That you'd want to think about." He looked at Glory. "I have tried, though. Maybe that just makes me— obdurate. Isn't that the word? I don't know why I am what I am. I'd have been like you if I could."

His father looked at him, solemnly uncomprehending.

Jack said, "I meant to tell you that I had—after careful thought, I had become persuaded of the truth of Scripture. Teddy said it would be all right to say that. I wanted you to stop worrying about me. But all I can really say is that I've tried to understand. And I did try to live a better life. I don't know what I'll do now. But I did try."

The old man looked at him intently. Then he said, "That's fine, dear. Have we talked before? I don't believe so. I may be wrong."

Jack leaned back in his chair and folded his arms. He looked at Glory and smiled. He said softly, "Tears!"

Glory said, "Jack wants to talk to you, Papa. He's trying to tell you something."

"Yes, you said Jack is here. That would be very surprising. He's never here."

After a long breath, "I'm Jack."

The old man turned stiffly in his chair to scrutinize his son. He said, "I see a resemblance." He reached out painfully and took hold of the candlestick, to move it closer to Jack, who put his hand to his face and laughed. His father said, "There is a resemblance. I don't know." He said, "If you could take your hand away—"

Jack dropped his hand into his lap and suffered his father's scrutiny, smiling, not raising his eyes.

The old man said, "Well, what did I expect. His life would be hard, I knew that," and he fell to brooding. "I was afraid of it, and I prayed, and it happened anyway. So here is Jack," he said. "After all that waiting."

Jack smiled at her across the table and shook his head. Another bad idea. Nothing to be done about it now.

Glory said, "It's been hard for him to come here. You should be kinder to him."

A moment passed, and her father stirred from his reverie. "Kinder to him! I thanked God for him every day of his life, no matter how much grief, how much sorrow—and at the end of it all there is only more grief, more sorrow, and his life will go on that way, no help for it now. You see something beautiful in a child, and you almost live for it, you feel as though you would die for it, but it isn't yours to keep or to protect. And if the child becomes a man who has no respect for himself, it's just destroyed till you can hardly remember what it was—" He said, "It's like watching a child die in your arms." He looked at Jack. "Which I have done."

"Oh. I didn't know that. I didn't—" He put his hands to his face.

Glory said, "No. This is terrible. I won't let this happen."

"Let it happen," Jack said softly. "I don't have anything to lose." And he dropped his hands, like a man abandoning all his defenses.

The old man was groping for his napkin, which had slipped to the floor. Jack gave him his. "Thank you, dear," he said, his voice ragged with tears, and he blotted his face with it.

"That wasn't Jack's fault," Glory said. "You know it wasn't."

Her father said, "Then why did you slap old Wheeler's face? She did, she slapped him. Because his house was no fit place for a child, that's why. Broken things, rusted things on the ground everywhere. Just everywhere! We could have brought her home! If Jack had owned up to her at all. He knew what kind of place it was," he said bitterly. "He'd been there."

Jack leaned back in his chair and shielded his eyes with his hand.

Glory said, "That was so long ago. Can't we put it aside, Papa?"

"Have you put it aside? We thought you never would get over it. It nearly scared your mother to death the way you mourned for that child."

She said, "But Jack is here now. His life has been hard. It's been sad. And he's home now. He's come home."

"Yes," the old man said, "and he's telling us goodbye. You know he is. He says he's read the Bible. Well, any fool could see that. He knows it better than I do. Why would he bother to say that to me? So I'll think maybe he's been working out his salvation. Well, maybe he has. I hope he has. But that isn't why he spoke to me about it. He doesn't think he should leave me here worrying about his soul. He has a few chores to finish up around the place. He's going to toss the old gent an assurance or two, and then he's out the door."

Jack laughed. He said, very softly, "That's not quite the way I thought of it." He cleared his throat. "But I probably will be leaving. That's true."

Her father hung his head. "All of them call it home, but they never stay."

After a moment Jack said, "You don't want me hanging around here. Reminding you of things you'd rather forget." His voice was still barely more than a whisper.

"I never forget them. Hard as I try. They're my life." He looked up at his son. "And so are you."

Jack shrugged and smiled. "Sorry."

His father reached over and patted his hand. "It worries me sometimes. I don't know what's become of my life." Then he said, fingering Jack's sleeve, in a tone of rueful admission, "I lost my church, you know."

Jack said, "Well, I knew you were retired."

The old man nodded. "That's one way to look at it." The candles had begun to flicker in an evening wind. The wind toyed with the crystal droplets on the light fixture. He said, "I lost my wife."

Jack shifted away as if he expected another rebuke, but his father just shook his head. "Why did I ever expect to keep anything? That isn't how life is. I'm"—he said—"I'm awfully worried about Ames. There he's got that little boy. I don't know." After a moment he looked up. "I've left the house to Glory. All the rest of them are settled. There's some money you'll each get a share of, and some for the Ames boy. It's not much. I know Glory will be glad to see you if you ever feel like coming home again."

Jack smiled at her across the table. "That's good to know."

The old man closed his eyes. "I can't enjoy the thought of heaven like I should, leaving so much unattended to here. I know it's wrong to think your mother's going to ask me about it." He was silent for a while, and then he said, "I was hoping I would be able to tell her that Jack had come home."

Jack sat pondering his father, and there was something in his face more absolute than gentleness or compassion, something purged of all the words that might describe it. Finally he said, whispered, "I hope you will give her my love."

The old man nodded. "Yes. I will certainly do that."

AFTER HE HAD PUT HIS FATHER TO BED JACK CAME OUT TO the kitchen. He said, "Feel like a few games of checkers? I really can't imagine going to sleep right now."

"Neither can I."

He said, "I'm sorry about that, Glory. These things never go the way I expect them to. You'd think I'd have learned by now. Not to expect."

"You meant well."

"I believe I did."

"You did."

"Yes," he said, and nodded, as if he had steadied himself against this minor certainty. "I checked with Teddy. And it was your idea to begin with."

"We both thought it was worth a try."

"I didn't try, though. Did you notice that? To lie to him. I lost my nerve."

"That's probably just as well."

He shrugged. "I wouldn't know."

They played three wordless games, Jack so distractedly that Glory won despite her best efforts. She thought, There ought to be a name for this. Boughton checkers. Gandhi checkers.

He said, "You probably want to get some sleep."

"Well, Jack, I just found out that I will inherit this house. I never meant to stay in Gilead. I mean I positively intended to leave Gilead. I don't want to sound ungrateful, but I'm—'horrified' is too strong a word, but it's the one that comes to mind. So I doubt I could sleep if I wanted to."

Jack leaned back in his chair and looked around him, almost objectively. "It's a pretty decent house. Free and clear. You could do worse."

She said, "This is a nightmare I've had a hundred times. The one where all the rest of you go off and begin your lives and I am left in an empty house full of ridiculous furniture and unreadable books, waiting for someone to notice I'm missing and come back for me. And nobody does."

He laughed. "Poor Pigtails." Then he said, "When I have that dream, I'm hiding in the barn hoping someone will find me, and nobody does."

"Well," she said, "I'm going to get that barn torn down. If I inherit this place, that's the first thing I'm going to do."

"Fine. Should I make some coffee?"

"Might as well."

Jack filled the percolator. Then he leaned against the counter. "It's your barn. Of course, if you had somebody work on the roof a little, it would last a few more years. That's just a thought. Paint would help."

She laughed. "So you want me to keep the barn. What else should I keep?"

"What else are you planning to get rid of?"

"Oh, the rugs, the drapes, the wallpaper, the lamps, the chairs and sofas—a few dozen of the souvenir plates. The figurines."

"Fine," he said.

"Some of the bookcases. And Grandpa's old theology books. There must be five hundred of them."

"You'll keep the Edinburgh books, I suppose."

"Yes, I will keep them."

"Some of the rest of it you could just put in the attic. I could move things around to make more room up there."

"That's a thought."

He went across the hall to the dining room and flipped on the light, and stood in the doorway, his hands on his hips. "I see what you mean."

"It looks like something out of *The Old Curiosity Shop*."

"True." But he kept looking around at it, the table and sideboard with their leonine legs and belligerently clawed feet, like some ill-considered, doily-infested species of which they were the last survivors. The wall sconces that were lotus blossoms with lightbulbs where their stamens ought to have been. She thought, Dear Lord, he is missing it all in anticipation. She thought, As long as he is alive in the world, or as long as no one knows otherwise, I will probably have to keep all that sour, fierce, dreary black walnut. That purple rug. And if he dies I will still have to keep it, because I have seen him look at it this way.

She said, "You want it to stay the same."

"What? No, no. It doesn't matter to me. Maybe I'll be back here sometime," he said, and it was clear from his tone that he doubted he would be. That he seemed to entertain doubt only for politeness's sake. He said, "I've thought about this place now and then," and he shrugged. The coffee was done and he gave her a cup and filled it and took one for himself.

She said, "No one will want me to change anything. When Papa's gone they'll come here twice a year or once a year or never, but they'll want it all to be the same."

He nodded. "You could sell it. Let someone else tear down the barn. Let the memory of Snowflake vanish once and for all. It would probably be best for everybody if you did that." He knew he was proposing the unthinkable, and he smiled.

"Ah!" she said, and she rested her head on her arms. "I don't want this to happen. Somehow I always knew this would happen to me."

"It doesn't have to. You could just light out, make a run for it. Let the others deal with it. No one would blame you. I wouldn't, anyway."

"No, I really couldn't do that."

"Sorry," he said. And then he said, "It's a relief to know you feel that way, Glory. I know I have no right to say this, but it is a relief to me. Of course, you can always change your mind." He got the deck of cards and laid out a hand of solitaire.

WHEN SHE DID FINALLY GO UP TO HER ROOM AND LIE down as if to sleep, she fell to pondering the fact that she had almost promised him she would stay in Gilead and keep the house as it was, the grounds as they were, more or less weedy, more or less un-pruned, but essentially the same. Even though he might never see it again. All that helpfulness of his, now that she thought about it, was restoration. Mother's iris garden reclaimed, the Adirondack chairs repaired, the treads replaced on the back porch steps. It was a little like having the family come to life again to have him there, busy about the place the way her father used to be. When he had first come home, fearful as he was that he had become a stranger, he still came around to the kitchen door, that old habit.

She had thought of pulling down the barn because the worst hours of his life, surely, had passed in it. And she couldn't walk into it without the thought of what might have happened, what she might have found, and then the terrible problem, the catas-trophe it would have been for her father no matter what she could think of to say or do. Having to tell Teddy. It would have been the final insult, the most unpardonable desecration of every-thing they had somehow managed to cherish about him. Dear God in heaven. And then that hiding place he had made, com-forting himself in concealment as he had always done. Or hiding his loneliness, or making his estrangement literal, visible. It was something a boy might do, that old game of hiding in the loft. He had done it as a boy and remembered, and maybe it made him feel at home. She should have pulled it apart herself, not left it for him to do. It was so profound a habit not to intrude on anything of his that she could hardly bring herself to do even what he had asked her. She wondered if he had taken it down, or if he might have left the house when she came upstairs and gone back to it again this very night. And then she wondered if he might not have another bottle hidden somewhere. In the DeSoto. She should have gone back to look around that afternoon, while he was sleeping. She hadn't been thinking clearly.

What had changed, after all? He had shamed himself in front of her, making her cover for his awful helplessness, defenselessness. Not that she could hold that against him, but that he could never forget what she had seen. She knew this by the way he looked at her now, by the chastened softness of his voice. He had made a generous attempt to lie to his father and failed, and in trying had dropped a stone into a very deep well of sorrow. The report of terrible particulars coming to him after so long, and for no reason except that his poor father seemed to forget everything else while he remembered them more bitterly. Jack promised her that he would never again try to end his life, but then he also told her he had done it only because he'd been drinking, and that must mean that if he happened to have another bottle somewhere—

In the course of time the dim glow of the lightening sky paled the curtains, and she heard Jack stirring in his room. Then finally she fell asleep, and gradually awoke again to the smell of bacon, of coffee.

JACK HAD BROUGHT IN HIS SUIT FROM THE PORCH, WHERE she had hung it to air, and he was brushing and pressing it. There were no really noticeable grease marks except one above a trouser pocket and a few on the underside of the lapels where he had held them closed with his hand. His solicitude for that suit must have sunk so far into him that he had been a little careful of it even in extremis. If he remembered to keep the jacket closed to hide the smudge on the trousers, it would be about as presentable as it ever was. This was clearly a relief to him. He asked her for a needle and thread and secured a hanging button. She enjoyed the wry seriousness with which he went about such things, these unlikely shifts and competences she knew she was privileged to witness. Still, there was something slightly hectic about it this morning, something disturbingly purposeful.

He hung the suit on the door frame and stood back to look at it. "Not too bad, considering. Hmm?"

"Not bad at all."

"There's toast in the oven. And I fried some bacon. I could scramble an egg for you."

"You're being very nice."

He nodded. "I called Teddy."

It took her a moment to understand what he had said. "You called Teddy?"

"Yes. I woke him up. But I thought I'd better make the call before my resolve faded."

"Just toast will be fine," she said.

"As you wish." He stacked toast on a plate and set it in front of her, and jam, and butter, and a cup of coffee. He said, "I went in to check on the old gent this morning, and he didn't know who I was. He didn't know who he was, either. No idea. He was very polite about it." He propped himself against the counter. "So I thought I'd better talk with Teddy. He's calling the others. He said he could be here by Tuesday." It was the first time he had looked at her directly, met her eyes.

"All right. I'll have to get the house ready. Make up the beds. I'll need some groceries."

Jack said, "I'll be here to help you with that. Until Tuesday. Then I'll be out of your way."

"What? But you said you'd be staying, let's see, ten more days. To wait for that letter."

He smiled. "There won't be a letter. I don't know what that was—a joke. Don't ask me to stay here, Glory, when all this is happening. You know I can't trust myself. I could do something—unsightly. I could make everything much worse." He said softly, "I really can't deal with the thought that he will die." Then he said, "Tears and more tears. But I won't be leaving you here by yourself. Teddy said he would call from the road, from Fremont, and I'll stay until he does. You won't be alone."

"Ah," she said, "but who will look after you?"

"It will be fine. Better for me, anyway. Better for everyone. You know that."

"But we won't even know where you are, Jack."

He said, "What does it matter?"

"Oh, how can you ask? How can you possibly ask? I can't deal with— I know what it is you're afraid of. It breaks my heart."

He shrugged. "You really shouldn't worry so much. I have an impressive history of failure. For what that's worth. And people can be surprisingly decent about it. Cops. Nuns. The Salvation Army. Vulnerable women."

She said, "Don't you dare joke with me."

He smiled. "I was pretty well telling you the truth just then."

"Then don't tell me the truth. You've worried us almost to death. You've scared us almost to death. But this really is your masterpiece."

Then he looked at her, his face pale and grave and regretful, and she knew there was no more to be said, that she should not have said what she did say, because the grief he always carried with him was as much as he could bear. He said, "I took care of him. I made oatmeal and fed it to him. I cleaned him up and changed his sheets and turned him over, and I think he went back to sleep. Last night was too hard for him. My fault."

"No. You were trying to comfort him. And this was coming. We all knew it would happen."

He nodded. "I suppose so. Thanks. Thank you, Glory. I'm going to go take care of that thing in the loft. It won't take long."

Glory went to look in on her father. He lay on his right side, his face composed, intent on sleep. His hair had been brushed into a soft white cloud, like harmless aspiration, like a mist given off by the endless work of dreaming.

She went to speak with Ames, to tell him the family was being asked to come home. He hugged her and gave her his handkerchief and said, "I see, I see, yes. I'll be by to look in on him when he's had his sleep. I have a few things to take care of at the church first. And how is Jack?" So she told him, though she had not meant to, that Jack was leaving. She said it was so hard for her that he should leave just then, and she said it with all the passion of her worry and grief, but she did not let herself violate the secrecy she had been sworn to, more or less. She did not mention his dread of doing something unsightly. Ah, Jack.

"Yes," Ames said, "his father would want him there with his family. It would be a pity for him to leave now."

"It would," she said.

There are very few comforts to be had from half-confiding, and Glory thanked him and went away before she could find herself giving in to habit and sadness and divulging her fears about Jack, the thing most offensive to him that they had done all through their childhood and his. That her father had done once again no doubt on his last visit to Ames's kitchen. She had left Ames with the impression, she knew to her deep chagrin, that Jack was just behaving badly, a scoundrel disappointing the standards of civility. Ah well. Nothing to do but go home and start preparing for the brothers and sisters.

She came into the kitchen and found Jack there, wearing his suit and tie, brushing at a smudge on the brim of his hat. He said, by way of explanation, "I have one last glimmer of hope, a merest spark of optimism. I want to make sure it is extinguished before I leave this town." He laughed. "I didn't mean that the way it sounded. I mean, I doubt that there's any life in it, but I thought, you know, I'd inquire, just to be sure. I'm going to go speak with Reverend Ames again. I thought I'd give it one last try." He shrugged.

Glory said, "Yes, fine. I just saw him. I told him about Papa. He said he would be at the church this morning, and then he would come by here. So you could wait and talk to him then."

"No, I think I'll stroll up to the church," he said. "That's more or less as I imagined it. It will be that kind of conversation. There will be a certain element of confession in it. I can do that." He smiled. "Don't look so worried. I won't let him hurt my feelings this time. I mean, at least he won't catch me off guard. For what that's worth."

Oh, she thought, dear God, let that be true! How to warn him. How to warn either of them. Jack would be walking into an embarrassment she had prepared for him. When Ames said to her, It would be a pity, his voice had a hint of that taut patience with which he had always heard out tales of Jack's scoundrelism. And Jack had a way of conceding ground he could not defend, taking on a manner of evasive deference when he felt he might be seen as a shady character, which meant that he certainly would be seen that way, however bright the shine on his shoes. That weary smile of his, as if he knew that between him and anyone he spoke to there was none of the trust that sustained the most ordinary conversation, as if between them there was an uneasy mutual understanding that almost obviated words. The jaded intimacy in his assuming so much seemed to startle people. Still, he had to assure himself that his last spark of hope was extinguished, so he checked the knot of his tie and tipped his hat, and went off to find Ames at his church.

Glory looked in on her father, and finding him still asleep, she went up to her room, got down on her knees, and prayed fervently in the only words that came to her—"Dear God in heaven, help him. Dear God in heaven, protect him. Please don't let him suffer for my stupidity, dear God, please." Then she lay on her bed and thought. More precisely, she fell to remembering something she had almost forbidden herself to remember. Something it seemed she had now fully and finally given up, though it had never been hers. A modest sunlit house, everything in it spare and functional, airy. Nothing imposing about it at all. In front a picture window looking out on a garden, a patio in back. The kitchen would be spacious and sunlit, with a white painted table, no, a breakfast nook, where morning light would fall on it. Sometimes she had talked about this house with the fiancé, and they had been in such agreement, they were so much of one mind, that it was amazing to them. No gilt frames, no beetling cornices. She had mentioned children, and he had said they would have to be very practical the first few years, there was time enough to think about children. So she imagined the children playing quietly, tiptoeing in from the patio now and then to whisper a secret or open a hand to show her an interesting pebble, then back out the door again so quietly, because Papa must not be disturbed. He must not know they were there at all. She had names for them, which drifted among them, and changed, as did certain of their attributes, ages, gender, number. For a few weeks one or another of them had a stammer, because she had spoken with a child at school who stammered, a sweet child. But then they were infants again, no traits particular to them yet, happy to lie in her arms. They wore flannel pajamas every cool night, and in her fantasies she sang to them the ballad of lost children. "The robins so red brought strawberry leaves and over them spread." They would weep in her arms and love her more, since she would keep them safe forever from abandonment and all bitter loss. She might have had doubts about dropping this tincture of sorrow into their hearts if they had been real children, though for herself she never could regret that her sisters had sung to her, making her feel so sharply the steadfast and effectual care of her family, while the great wind roared in the trees and rattled the windows. That wind, they all knew, could sweep up a town and scatter it hither and yon, houses and cattle and children. Robins so red. The words were bright as a prick of blood.

The fiancé had a habit of sitting with his heels together and his toes pointing outward. This was truer when he wished to seem content or ingratiating. She could never help feeling this meant something disheartening about him that would not be fixed even if she sometime mentioned to him that he might arrange his feet more gracefully and he complied. If she gave him a cup of coffee, he would lean there, elbows on his knees, holding the saucer under the cup, and he would grin at her, and those feet would seem to mimic the grin, which was excessive in itself. He told her she was a snob about her family, and that was true. And not without reason. They were all graceful people after their shambling style, and they did not grin.

The fact was, all the same, that she would have married him, that for years she had had no other intention, except when doubts emerged that reduced intention to hope. How miserable that was to remember, and how miserable the relief when a letter came, the phone rang, she heard his knock at the door. He was a pleasant-looking man, robust and ruddy, with clear blue eyes and red hair that crinkled against his scalp. If in person he did not altogether answer to the idea of him she took from his letters, he was agreeable enough. Sometimes he made her laugh. She would almost like to know how much money she had given him, only to be able to gauge the depth of an infatuation that seemed so remote to her now. It was for the children and the sunlit house that she had been diligent at discerning virtues and suppressing doubts, ready to give up mere money if it could put aside the obstacles to her happiness, or if it could keep the thought of happiness safe from disruption. God bless him, Jack had understood it all and laughed, a painful but companionable laugh, as if they'd been whiling away perdition together, telling tales of what got them there, to forestall tedium and the dread of what might come next.

The sweet thought of sunlight and children she had cherished in secret was now utterly dispelled. No, she wanted to tell Jack about them, to dispel them, as if they were spirits of the kind that perish in daylight. But for that reason she could not and never would betray them. Let some sleep of oblivion overtake them, finally.

So Glory would live out her life in a place all the rest of them called home, a place they would mean to return to more often than they did. If she spoke discreetly to the high school principal about the fact that the marriage she intended had not in fact taken place, the information would pass through town and be absorbed and cease to be of particular interest. She could start teaching again.

She heard Jack walk into the kitchen, put his hat on the refrigerator. She heard him go down the hall, speak to his father, then come back to fill a glass with water and take it to him. After a few minutes, he went to the piano and began to play a hymn. "'When all my trials and troubles are o'er, and I awake on that beautiful shore.'" Things must have gone well enough, thank God. So she went downstairs.

When he had finished the hymn he turned and looked at her. "It wasn't bad," he said softly. "He was very kind. He couldn't do anything for me, but he was kind. It was all right. Better than I expected, really. Ames's heart is failing, he said, so he won't be around much longer. I thought he might, I don't know, vouch for me. Help me overcome my reputation. But I have to leave here anyway. I don't know why I bothered him." He shrugged.

She said, "I'm glad it was a good conversation."

He nodded. "I called him Papa, and this time I think it may even have pleased him a little." He smiled to himself, and then he said, "I told him almost everything, and when I was done he said, 'You are a good man.' Imagine that."

"Well, I could have told you you are a good man. I've said it in so many words, surely."

He laughed. "You're a miserable judge of character. Mine, especially. No objectivity at all."

WHEN THEY HEARD THEIR FATHER STIR AND WAKE, JACK carried him to his chair on the porch and settled the quilt around him and read to him from the newspaper while Glory made potato soup almost the way he had always liked it, without onions but with butter melted into it and crackers crumbled on top. Jack fed him, held his cup for him. The old man accepted these attentions without comment. Then Jack changed into his work clothes and went out to the garden, where his father could watch him, as it seemed he did until he began to doze off. After a little while Jack came back and found him asleep and carried him to bed again, slipping the crooked body out of the robe with great care. It seemed to her there was a peacefulness about him that came with resignation, with the extinction of that last hope, like a perfect humility undistracted by the possible, the unrealized, the yet to be determined. He worked on the DeSoto, then sat in the porch and read till the sun went down. He went out for a stroll, just to look at the place, he said, and came back in an hour, stone sober. It may have been the saddest day of her life, one of the saddest of his. And yet, all in all, it wasn't a bad day.

THEN IT WAS SUNDAY AND JACK WENT TO CHURCH. THIS was to show Ames his respect and, he said, appreciation. He asked her for two dollars for the offering, since he had made her put all money away out of sight, and had even, despite their sentimental value, given her dollar bills he had hidden years before in the pages of the Edinburgh books, the proceeds of youthful thefts, which he had put where he knew no one would find them. Twelve dollars scattered through *The Monstrous Regiment of Women* and nineteen in *On Affliction*. From *The Hind Unloos'd*, which their father had told them to revere as a great work, he took a few desolate report cards and a note to his father from a civics teacher who saw only the darkest clouds on his moral and educational horizon and asked urgently for a conference. He shook his head. "I guess I was a pretty cynical kid," he said, and laughed. Glory suggested he put the money in the collection plate as a sort of penance, but he thought the amount was large enough to arouse suspicion. "Coming from me it would be, anyway."

She stayed with her father, who she thought had reacted to the news that Jack was at church with a brief and tentative cheerfulness. Jack came home as calm as he was when he left, to his father's apparent relief, and when she asked him what the sermon was about, he laughed and said, "It wasn't about me." Then he said, "Well, it was about idolatry, about the worship of things, on one hand the material world, in the manner of scientific rationalism, and on the other hand—chairs and tables and old purple drapes, in the manner of Boughtons and totemists. It did cause me to reflect."

"Don't worry," she said. "I won't change a thing."

"If you want to, feel free."

"Of course."

She made a beef roast and dinner rolls while Jack worked in the attic, clearing space for whatever in her hardness of heart she might decide to put out of sight. Again he was purposeful. The picture of the river was back in its old place, so she glanced through the open door of his room and saw the volumes of Kipling on his dresser between the Lincoln bookends. Nothing to be said, nothing to be done. Her father, who hardly spoke at all, watched their comings and goings with irritation and distrust. She served dinner in the kitchen, careful not to stir memories if she could avoid it. When they were seated and she had said the grace, her father sat impatiently with his hands folded in his lap until Jack offered to feed him his mashed potatoes and gravy. These last few days his gentleness had been especially striking to her, and why should it be? She had always known he could be gentle. She would tell the others in case they had forgotten, so that they would all hope someday to know him as well as she did. Then if he ever came to any of them he would be deeply and immediately welcome, however disreputable he might seem or be. Finally her father gestured at the meal she had made and said, "I guess this is goodbye."

Jack said, "Not quite yet."

The old man nodded. "Not yet," he said bitterly. "Not yet."

"Teddy will be here soon."

"I'm sure of that." His head fell. "With his stethoscope. As if that solved anything."

Jack cleared his throat. "It's been good to be home. It really has."

The old man raised his eyes and studied his son's face. "You've never had a name for me. Not one you'd call me to my face. Why is that?"

Jack shook his head. "I don't know, myself. They all seemed wrong when I said them. I didn't deserve to speak to you the way the others did."

"Oh!" his father said, and he closed his eyes. "That was what I waited for. That was what I wanted."

Glory had developed a new appreciation for the Sabbath because it was the day when no mail came. That Sunday had passed in sad tranquillity, her father a little stronger, she thought, and Jack full of solicitude for them both, regretful but not at all in doubt, embarrassed by his own undeviating will to be gone. Monday morning she heard him in his room, sorting through his dresser, putting aside, she was sure, everything of her father's she had given him, to suit his strangely rigorous notions of what indeed belonged to him. She had never known another thief, so she could not generalize, but she thought thievishness might involve some subtle derangement of the sense of mine and thine. Some inability to find the bounds of scrupulousness. That would account for his refusal to leave the house with a pair or two of his father's socks. The austerity of it all broke her heart. The handkerchiefs he had borrowed were washed and pressed and back in their father's drawer. He was becoming once again the Jack who had turned up at the kitchen door claiming to have lost a suitcase.

No, there was that other thief, the one who had kept an account of the money she gave him, perhaps even believing he might pay her back. Time enough to think about children, he said, and she had nodded, knowing it wasn't true. He needed a little money, a little more money, because he was going into business with an old army buddy of his. He couldn't wait for the two of them to meet, she would love him—in a manner of speaking, ha ha. She gave him the money so he would stop talking, maybe even so he would go away. He might have known this. He would go away and leave her with her thoughts of him. Those few things it still moved her to remember, how he took her hand. Luke and Daniel and Faith had all been there in the parlor waiting, the day she brought him home. They were perfectly cordial, not visibly surprised. She was fairly sure nothing sardonic would have passed among them when she and the fiancé left the room. There was no hint that they had any particular doubts about his character or his intentions. Still, there was a flicker of nerves in the glance he gave her. Then he took her hand.

She was thinking about all this when the mail came. Letters to her from Luke and Hope and a letter to Jack from Della Miles. She went into the kitchen and sat down. She had become used to the idea that nothing more of consequence would happen after the last of the letters Jack had sent came back to him. But if the woman named Lorraine—Glory had addressed the envelope— telephoned Della and read Jack's letter to her—no, this still would have arrived too quickly. It was sent from Memphis, not by air mail. She was light-headed. It is terrible that letters can matter so much. She thought of burning it. She even thought of opening it. Then she would burn it if need be. No, some things are sacred, even, especially, this wounding thing—wounding, how did she know that? She knew. She went to the stairs and called to Jack to come down, which he did very promptly. He would think she needed help with their father. When he saw her he said, "What's the matter?"

"Nothing. This letter came for you."

She had left it lying on the table. He picked it up and looked at it. "Jesus," he said. "Sweet Jesus."

"Would you like me to leave you alone?"

"Yes," he said. "If you don't mind. Thank you."

So she went into the parlor and sat down next to the radio, and waited for any sign that she might be wanted or needed. There was only silence. Finally she went to the kitchen door. Jack looked up at her and smiled. He said, "It doesn't really change anything." He cleared his throat. "It isn't unkind. I'm all right." Then he said, "Cry if you want to, chum. Feel free."

Glory sat there with him, ready to go away if he gave any sign that she should. From time to time he looked up at her, as if there were something he thought of saying and did not, or as if he knew she was of one mind with him though neither of them spoke. Finally he said, "I'm still planning to stay around until Teddy calls. I won't be good for much." And he said, "Anyone in the world would want a drink right now." When they heard their father stir he went with her to tend to him. The old man blinked at Jack and said, "Now she's crying. I don't know what to do about it. Jesus never had to be old." But he let them bathe him and dress him and shave him, and he let Glory brush his hair. Jack brought the Old Spice and touched it to his cheeks. They helped him to the parlor, to his Morris chair. Glory poached an egg, and Jack leaned in the door and watched while she fed him.

Then there was a knock at the kitchen door, and Ames came in, carrying the little case he brought with him when he visited the sick. Their father's eyes found it and remained on it while Ames said his hellos and remarked on the weather. Glory knew they were conspicuously miserable, the three of them, and that Ames would acknowledge this only by the gentleness of his voice. Her father tapped his fingers on the arm of his chair, as he did when he was impatient. Ames said to him, "Robert, I was hoping I might share communion with you," and the old man nodded. So he put the little case on the mantel and opened it and took out a silver cup. He filled the cup from a flask, and then he asked Glory for a bit of bread. She brought him a roll from their Sunday dinner on a linen napkin. He set the elements on the broad arm of Boughton's chair. He was silent for a while, and then he said, "'The Lord Jesus in the night in which he was betrayed, took bread and when he had given thanks, he brake it, and said, This is my body, which is for you, this do in remembrance of me.'" Boughton said, "Yes. 'In like manner the cup.' Yes. 'You proclaim the Lord's death until he come.'" And the two old men fell silent. They had said those words so many times. Ames broke the bread and gave a piece of it to Boughton, and to Glory, and offered it to Jack, who smiled and stepped away. Then he held the cup to Boughton's lips, gave it to Glory, drank from it himself. The two old men were silent together for some time.

When Boughton nodded off, Ames came into the kitchen. There seemed to be nothing he wanted to say to them, but he took a chair at the table when it was offered to him and he accepted a cup of coffee. His care of their father, bringing the Sacrament, would have been an enhancement of the sad quiet of the day. But he stayed, and he attempted conversation. Jack leaned back in his chair with his arms folded and watched him, too weary to help sustain it. Glory went to see that her father was comfortable, and brought his quilt, and when she came back, Ames was letting himself out the door, looking a little embarrassed and dejected.

She said, "What happened?"

"Well, he tried to give me money. To leave. I told him I was leaving anyway, he needn't bother."

"Ah, Jack."

"You know he wants me out of here. He can see what I've done. To my father."

"Did he say that?"

"Good Reverend Ames? Of course not. He said he thought I might want to go to Memphis."

"Well, why wouldn't he think that? You and I have talked about going to Memphis."

He reflected a moment, and then he laughed. "We did, didn't we. That seems like a million years ago. Another life." He said, "You're right. Poor old blighter. Trying to give away money he doesn't have. What a fool I am." He rubbed his eyes. "That was friendliness, wasn't it. I should have thought of that. He was starting to like me, I suppose."

The day passed. Glory wanted to value it, though of course she could not enjoy it. She would probably never see her brother again—in this life, as Teddy had said. Sweet Jesus, she thought, love this thief, too. After a while Jack roused himself and went about the work he had set for himself, putting things in order. He nailed a loose plank in the shed wall, and he cut some dead canes out of the lilac hedge. He split a pile of kindling. Then he came in and asked her for the car keys. He said, "I think I've got it back together well enough. I'll try to start it." She went to the porch and heard the engine start and idle. Jack opened the barn doors, and then he backed the DeSoto into afternoon light. He pushed the door on the passenger side open. "I was thinking we might go for a spin, take the old gent along." So they went into the house and Jack took their father up in his arms and carried him out to the car. And then he drove them past the church, which was, to their father's mind, the place where the old church had stood. And he drove them past the house where Mrs. Sweet had lived, and past the Trotskys' old house, and past the high school and the baseball field, and then out to the peripheries, where town gave way to countryside and the shadows of late day were blue between the rows of corn and on the evening side of trees and the swells of pasture and in the clefts of creek. The smell of ripe fields and water and cattle and evening came in on the wind. "Yes," their father said. "It was wonderful. I remember now."

When they came back to the house again, Jack smiled and handed her the keys. They settled their father for the night, sat together in the kitchen trying to read, then trying to play Scrabble. It was a habit of hers to stay up as long as Jack did, thinking he would be more reluctant to leave the house if he knew she was aware of his leaving. Finally he went upstairs, and in half an hour she did, too. She spent the night listening and worrying, dreading his absence, because the thought of it made her life seem intolerably long. She thought, If I or my father or any Boughton has ever stirred the Lord's compassion, then Jack will be all right. Because perdition for him would be perdition for every one of us.

She came downstairs at dawn and Jack was in the kitchen already, in his suit and tie, with his suitcase by the door. He said, "I hope I haven't been too much trouble. There's a lot I regret." He said it the minute she came into the room, as if it were the one thing he was determined to have said, the one thing he wanted her to know.

She said, "Ah, Jack," and he laughed.

"Well, I haven't been the perfect houseguest. You have to grant me that."

"All I regret is that you're leaving."

He nodded. "Thank God," he said. "I could have given you a lot more to regret. And myself. You've really helped me."

"Now you know where to come when you need help."

"Yes. Ye who are weary, come home."

"Very sound advice."

He said, "I'm not sure you should stay here, Glory. Promise me you won't let anyone talk you into it. Don't do it for my sake. I shouldn't have talked to you about it the way I did."

"Don't worry. If you ever need to come home, I'll be here. Call first, just to be sure. No, you won't have to do that. I'll be here."

He nodded. "Thank you," he said.

He helped her bathe their father and dress him and feed him, and then it was eight o'clock and the phone rang. Teddy had driven the whole night to make up for an emergency call and a late start. He was in Fremont, where he had stopped for coffee. Jack said, "I'm going to have to ask you for some traveling money. Not enough to get me in trouble. Just enough to get me out of town." She had set aside Teddy's envelope and put into it the ten-dollar bill Jack gave her when he had just arrived, and the money hidden in the Edinburgh books.

Jack hefted the envelope and handed it back to her. "Too much. You know how much liquor this would buy me? Perdition for sure. Unless I got lucky and somebody rolled me for it."

"Oh dear God in heaven, Jack. How much can I give you, then? Sixty? It's all your money. You won't owe me a dime."

"Forty will do. No need to worry. There are always more dishes to be washed, more potatoes to be peeled. Except in Gilead."

"I'll keep the rest for you. Call me. Or write to me."

"Will do." He picked up his suitcase, and then he set it down again and went into the parlor, where his father was sitting in the Morris chair. He stood there, hat in hand. The old man looked at him, stern with the effort of attention, or with wordless anger.

Jack shrugged. "I have to go now. I wanted to say goodbye." He went to his father and held out his hand.

The old man drew his own hand into his lap and turned away. "Tired of it!" he said.

Jack nodded. "Me, too. Bone tired." He looked at his father a minute longer, then bent and kissed his brow. He came back into the kitchen and picked up his suitcase. "So long, kiddo." He wiped a tear from her cheek with the ball of his thumb.

"You have to take care of yourself," she said. "You have to."

He tipped his hat and smiled. "Will do."

She went to the porch to watch him walk away down the road. He was too thin and his clothes were weary, weary. There was nothing of youth about him, only the transient vigor of a man acting on a decision he refused to reconsider or regret. No, there might have been some remnant of the old aplomb. Who would bother to be kind to him? A man of sorrows and acquainted with grief, and as one from whom men hide their face. Ah, Jack.

So Teddy arrived and settled in and became the one to read in the porch, to bathe his father and feed him and turn him, and to help prepare for the others, going off to buy groceries. He didn't ask much about their brother and she didn't offer much about him, except to say that he had been helpful and kind. Jack was Jack. There was little enough to say that would not seem like betrayal, even though Teddy knew him well enough to have a fairly good idea of the terms he had made with the world. In time she would say more, when the sense of his presence had dimmed a little.

Once, Teddy knelt by his father's chair to help him with his supper, and the old man reached out his hand to stroke his hair, his face. He said, "You told me goodbye, but I knew you couldn't leave," and there was a glint of vindication in his eyes.

The second day after Jack had left, Glory was out in the garden clearing away the cucumber vines and gathering green tomatoes. There had been a sudden change of weather, a light frost. She noticed a car passing slowly on the farther side of the street. She watched it, thinking it must be someone from the church, some friend or acquaintance wondering if the rumors were true, that her father was indeed failing and the family were coming home. But the driver of the car was a black woman, and that was a curious thing. There were no colored people in Gilead.

Glory bent to her work again, and the car came back on the near side of the street and stopped. She could see two colored women in the front seat and a child in the back. They looked at the house from the car for a few minutes, as if deciding what to do next, and then a woman stepped out of the passenger side and came up the walk. She was a dark, angular woman in a gray suit. Her hair was pulled back under a gray cloche. She looked very urban here in Gilead, and conscious of it, as if she felt the best impression she could make was one that would set her sharply apart. She turned and spoke to the child, "Robert, you stay in that car." So the boy stood on the edge of the grass with one foot inside the car door. He was wearing church clothes, a blue suit and a red tie.

Glory came down out of the garden to meet the woman on the sidewalk. She said, "Hello. Can I help you?"

The woman said, "I'm looking for the home of Reverend Robert Boughton." Her voice was soft and grave.

"This is his house," Glory said, "but he's very ill. I'm his daughter Glory. Is there something I can do for you?"

"I'm sorry to hear your father is ill. Very sorry to hear it." She paused. "It's his son I was hoping to talk to, Mr. Jack Boughton."

Glory said, "Jack isn't here now. He's been gone since Tuesday morning."

The woman looked over her shoulder at the little boy. She shook her head and he leaned back against the car. She turned to Glory again. "Would you happen to know if he was planning to come back?"

"No, I don't expect him to come back. Not any time soon. I don't know what plans he had. If he had any. I don't know where he was going to go."

The woman smoothed her gloves, trying to hide her disappointment. Then she looked up at Glory. "I'd think he might be here, if his father is sick. I'd think he might be coming back, at least." She looked at the house, with its tangled covert of vines and its high, narrow windows. Then she said, "Well, I thank you for your trouble," and she turned back toward the car. The little boy wiped his cheeks with the heel of his hand.

There was an unconfiding gravity in the woman's manner, a sense that she spoke softly across an immeasurable distance. Yet she had studied Glory's face as if she almost remembered it.

Glory said, "Wait! Please wait," and the woman stopped and turned. "You're Della, aren't you. You're Jack's wife."

For a moment she did not speak. Then she said, "Yes, I am. I am his wife, and I sent him that letter! And now I don't even know where to find him, to talk to him." Her voice was low, broken with grief. She looked at the boy, who had taken a few steps from the car to lay his hand on the trunk of the oak tree.

Glory said, "I didn't know—Jack didn't trust me well enough to tell me much about anything that mattered to him. It's always been that way. There's a lot I didn't tell him. Maybe that's just how we are."

"But he always said in his letters how kind you were to him. I want to thank you for that."

"He was kind to me, too."

Della nodded. "He is kind." There was a silence. She said, "This place looks just the way he described it. That tree and the barn and the big tall house. He used to tell Robert about climbing that tree."

"We really weren't supposed to do that. Even the lowest branches are so high."

"He said there were swings hanging from it, and he'd shinny up on the ropes and then climb up into the top branches. He'd hide up there, he said."

"Well, I'm so glad our mother didn't know that. She was always worrying about him."

Della nodded. She looked past her at the orderly garden, at the clothesline, and again at the porch with its pot of petunias on the step. Her eyes softened. It was as if a message had been left for her, something sad and humorous and lovely in its intimacy.

Glory could imagine that Jack might have drawn them a map of the place, orchard and pasture and shed. Maybe there were stories attached to every commonplace thing, other stories than she had heard, than any of them had heard. A mention of Snowflake. She said, "Would you like to come inside?"

"No, no, we can't do that. Thank you, but we have to get back down to Missouri before dark. Especially the way things are now. We have a place to stay down there. That's my sister driving the car, and I promised her I would only be a few minutes. We got lost looking for this place, and the days aren't so long anymore. We have the boy with us. His father wouldn't want us to be taking any chances."

Glory said, "Jack told me he would call me, or send an address. That doesn't mean he will. He might call his brother Teddy, so I'll tell him you were here. This is so sudden. I hope I'm not forgetting anything."

Della saw her tears and smiled. One more thing that was almost familiar to her.

"This happens to me," Glory said, and wiped her cheeks. "But I can't tell you how glad he'd have been to see you. Both of you. It would have been wonderful. If only I could have kept him here a little while longer."

Della said, "We'll go back to St. Louis. He might come there, to the old neighborhood." Then she said, "Was it because of my letter that he left? Because, you know, I'd be very worried about that." Her voice was almost a whisper.

"It was hard for him. But he said the letter wasn't unkind. And he was going to leave anyway. He had his own reasons. He didn't blame you for anything."

"Thank you. God bless you," Della said. Then she said, "We'd better leave now. It was so kind of my sister to come up here with me, and I don't want to upset her. She didn't think it was a good idea. My whole family thought it was a bad idea."

"If you could just wait another minute, though. I should give you something to take with you, since you've come all the way here—please wait." She went into the house, and there were all the books, there was the everlasting jumble of small things. She had meant to take anything at all. She had seen the little boy pocketing acorns. Anything would be a memento. A pagoda. A swan. But all the knickknacks were so odd and ridiculous. None of the big old books would do. She went upstairs to the room Jack had had as a boy and took the framed photograph of a river off its nail and brought it downstairs. When she gave it to Della she said, "Jack always liked this. I don't know why, really. But he kept it in his room."

Della nodded. "Thank you." The boy came up the walk to see what it was his mother had been given. She gave it to him and he studied it. She said, "It's a picture of the river."

Glory bent to the child and offered her hand and he took it. "You're Robert," she said.

"Yes, ma'am."

"I'm Glory. I'm your father's sister."

"Yes, ma'am." And then a long look, as if he were remembering, or preparing to remember.

Jack had a beautiful child, a beautiful son, who would some time turn Boughton, no doubt, and lose his prettiness to what they called distinction.

"Are you a baseball player, too?" she asked.

He smiled. "Yes, ma'am. I play some ball."

His mother said, "He thinks he's going to be a preacher," and she stroked his hair. The sister opened the door on the driver's side and stood out of the car to stare across the roof at them. Della said, "We have to be leaving now."

"Yes. Will Jack know how to reach you? If he does call here."

Della put the boy in the backseat, and then she took an envelope from the glove compartment and wrote on it, some numbers and some names. Her sister had started the car. Della handed her the letter. "It was a pleasure to meet you. I hope your father will be feeling better. If you have a chance to get this to Jack, I'd be grateful." Then she closed the door, and the car pulled away.

GLORY SAT DOWN ON THE PORCH STEPS. SHE THOUGHT, IF Jack had been here, he'd have felt that terrible shock of joy—no, worse than joy, peace—that floods in like blood pushing into a limb that has been starved of it, like wild rescue, painful and wonderful and humbling—humiliating as she remembered it, because she had been so helpless against it. But that was the fiancé. Della was Jack's wife, she said so herself, and it made all the difference. Della had looked at the world of his old life tenderly, all the particulars there to confirm themselves, proof of his truthfulness, which always did need proof. I used to live here, I wasn't always gone, I was usually closer to home than he thought I was. So Jack had said, and how could he have seemed so estranged to them? And how cruel it was that he loved the place anyway. His little boy touching that tree, just to touch it. The tree that sounded like the ocean. Dear Lord in heaven, she could never change anything. How could she know what he had sanctified to that child's mind with his stories, sad stories that had made them laugh. I used to wish I lived here, he said. That I could just walk in the door like the rest of you did.

And they would not walk in the door. They had to hurry, to escape the dangers of nightfall. The boy was with them, and his father would not want them to take chances. She knew it would have answered a longing of Jack's if he could even imagine that their spirits had passed through that strange old house. Just the thought of it might bring him back, and the place would seem changed, to him and to her. As if all that saving and keeping their father had done was providence indeed, and new love would transform all the old love and make its relics wonderful.

Della had met Jack on a rainy afternoon. He was just out of prison, and he was wearing the suit—almost new, he said—he had bought with the money that was supposed to have brought him home for his mother's funeral. The suit he sold because it made him look like a minister. And he had come by an umbrella somehow. Just the terror of his release into the world, certain he had lost his family for good and all this time, would have made him wry and incandescent, and so would the inadvertent respectability of a dark suit and a working umbrella. And there before him was a lady in need of assistance. She had said, "Thank you, Reverend." Such mild eyes, such a gentle voice. He had forgotten that, the pleasure of being spoken to kindly. Finally he told her he was not a man of the cloth. So began a long instruction in whatever he could trust her to forgive.

She has forgiven so much, he said. You can have no idea. And how would she forgive this, that she felt she had to come into Gilead as if it were a foreign and a hostile country? Did anyone know otherwise? Worn, modest, countrified Gilead, Gilead of the sunflowers. She carried herself with the tense poise of a woman who felt she was being watched, wondered about. Jack could hardly bring himself to dream she would come here, and there was reason enough to doubt, though he could not stop himself from dreaming of it, either. They had the boy with them, Jack would be frightened for the boy, so they had to be back to Missouri before it was dark. They had a place to stay in Missouri.

She thought, Maybe this Robert will come back someday. Young men are rarely cautious. What of Jack will there be in him? And I will be almost old. I will see him standing in the road by the oak tree, and I will know him by his tall man's slouch, the hands on the hips. I will invite him onto the porch and he will reply with something civil and Southern, "Yes, ma'am, I might could," or whatever it is they say. And he will be very kind to me. He is Jack's son, and Southerners are especially polite to older women. He will be curious about the place, though his curiosity will not override his good manners. He will talk to me a little while, too shy to tell me why he has come, and then he will thank me and leave, walking backward a few steps, thinking, Yes, the barn is still there, yes, the lilacs, even the pot of petunias. This was my father's house. And I will think, He is young. He cannot know that my whole life has come down to this moment.

That he has answered his father's prayers.

The Lord is wonderful.